He was l

"James, it's all right," ~~she said~~, taking his hand in hers and pressing it to her cheek.

"Is it truly?" he asked, caressing her face.

"Yes," she said, kissing the tips of his fingers. When his hand left her lips and found the buttons at the front of her dress, she took a deep breath. Then she relaxed and let the shame that was trying to surface again be suffocated by the warm, sure hand that now covered one breast.

"You're sure, Lenora?" he asked again, already slipping her dress down over her shoulders with the other hand. "I don't want to take advantage of you," he added, stroking her naked flesh.

"What am I doing?" she thought. "Is this really myself, consenting to this?" But the question came from the rational part of her and was sublimely irrelevant as he lowered her, clinging, to the ground, and made her forget the dampness of the night. His breath coming in sharp rasps silenced all else in her ears as he bent his head and touched her lips with his.

Lenora began to writhe with pleasure, losing all thought of what was soon to happen. All she knew was this new existence, outside of time and reason, and this new urgency demanding to be quelled....

Other *Leisure Books* by Cassie Edwards:

ISLAND RAPTURE
EDEN'S PROMISE
WHEN PASSION CALLS
ROSES AFTER RAIN
TOUCH THE WILD WIND

The Savage Series:
SAVAGE SUNRISE
SAVAGE MISTS
SAVAGE PROMISE
SAVAGE PERSUASION

CASSIE EDWARDS

Secrets of my Heart

LEISURE BOOKS   **NEW YORK CITY**

Lovingly to my brother
Joe Decker,
sister-in-law
Ann,
nephew Brian and niece Aimee.

A LEISURE BOOK®

June 1993

Published by

Dorchester Publishing Co., Inc.
276 Fifth Avenue
New York, NY 10001

PART ONE

SAN FRANCISCO

The human heart is often the victim of the sensations of the moment; success intoxicates it to presumption, and disappointment dejects and terrifies it.
—VOLNEY

'Tis in my memory lock'd
And you yourself shall keep
The key to it.
— *Shakespeare*

Chapter One

July, 1873

Behind him were days and days of countless graves. James Calloway gave the reins another slap, chewing angrily on a piece of grass. He had not realized what a large part death played in the pioneer experience. "Damn cholera," he whispered. "Damn, damn cholera."

Since having separated himself from the wagon train, he had only to follow a trail of discarded furniture, broken down wagons, and fresh graves to know that he was headed in the right direction: to San Francisco, California, where his dreams were now leading him.

The ocean of yellow poppies flooding the fields and slopes on all sides of him was a welcome sight. There was a peacefulness in the way they rose and fell in gentle waves. Another welcome sight was the sparkle of water tumbling down the side of the mountain that stood nearby. He would make camp there before nightfall. Perhaps in the mountain stream, he would find his breakfast. After many days spent in search of water and game, now that he was finally anticipating the end of his journey, water, fish, and fowl had become abundant.

James suddenly brought the horses to a halt. There was something else ahead. Was it a mirage, or was that a woman—a beautiful woman—sitting on the ground beside an overturned wagon? He had not seen any signs of life for days. And now? To have happened along the same trail where this enchanting creature sat alone, in need of help?

He spat the sprig of grass from his mouth, lifted the reins, and clucked to the horses.

The shade from the overturned wagon gave some relief to Lenora Marie Adamson. But she couldn't push aside the fear that was fast consuming her, for nightfall would soon be settling around her in a dark shroud. And what would be seeking her out in the dark? Would it be some hungry animal, some stray tribe of curious Indians?

"Oh, Papa," she whispered. "What am I to do?"

Cholera had been the evil lurking on this trail for weeks now. And when her father had first shown signs of it, all other members of the wagon train had moved on ahead and eventually disappeared over the horizon. Lenora had left her father's fresh grave earlier in the day. How hard it had been to say farewell in such a manner.

A throaty moan, a ghastly gurgling noise, made Lenora cringe. She turned her head to look toward the one remaining ox. It lay on its side, foaming at the mouth. Its leg lay all twisted and swollen, and Lenora knew that it was broken.

She picked up the pearl-handled pistol from her lap, knowing what needed to be done. But she could not do it. She could not pull the trigger that would take the life, and thus the pain, away from this living thing. She remembered the great, empty sound of the shots when her Papa had had to shoot their cow and one other ox.

"The water's been scarce and poor, Daughter," her Papa had stressed. And when the ox and cow had taken sick, vomiting until they grew dehydrated, the inevitable had to be done.

"But, I just can't," Lenora whimpered, dropping the gun back onto her lap as though it had burned her. "I just can't."

She looked wearily around her. The poppies smelled of her Mama's garden back home in Springfield. But they were losing their lustrous gold, it seemed, as the sun was leaving them for the day. And even though the sun was making its descent toward the mountains, the heat of the day was still oppressive. Lenora pulled her straw bonnet from her head and began to fan herself with it, then unbuttoned the front of her bodice halfway to the waist.

As she fanned herself, she surveyed the disarray on either side of her. When the ox had stepped into what appeared to be a gopher hole, it had broken not only its leg, but also a wheel of Lenora's wagon. The wagon had lunged sideways, tossing Lenora and everything she owned off onto the ground.

"Oh, Papa. Your books," she whispered, dropping her hat to the ground to pick up a volume on which the leather binding was torn. On its inside cover, she traced the plain handwriting, the grayed ink that formed her Papa's name: Joshua Caine Adamson. Touching his written words was almost like touching him. For a moment she caressed the sun-warmed leather and closed her eyes.

Then another book drew her attention. She picked it up and opened it to find Abraham Lincoln's signature. How her Papa had treasured this law book after Lincoln had been elected president.

"Abe was the most unfailingly honest lawyer I ever had the honor to work with," her Papa had bragged. "And when I asked to borrow this book, he told me to keep it. Said he had got his learnings from it already and was glad to pass it on to one of his cohorts."

When Lincoln had been assassinated, it had taken the steam from her Papa's existence. "Fate struck Abe a fierce blow, Daughter," he had told her. "And it's high time for us to be movin' on, get away from the damn politickin'. Let's head west." The actual leaving had taken a few more years, and when the time had come, it meant leaving behind a small grave on a hillside: Lenora's Mama.

"She never was strong, Daughter," her Papa had said at the funeral. "But, damn it, I never thought malaria would be the way she'd go."

Lenora had been the only child born to Joshua and Sara Adamson because, Lenora knew, of her mother's frailty. Lenora could not remember ever meeting another woman who was as tiny and fragile as her Mama had been. Even a day's labor in her beloved flower garden would put her Mama to bed the following day.

But Lenora's Papa had made sure Lenora would not be like her Mama. In a sense, Lenora had become the son that her Papa would never see born to him. He had seen to it that Lenora worked splitting and cutting wood alongside him, as well as doing the rest of the chores, such as milking the cows and planting the garden that the Illinois spring always brought to glory.

"I had to see to it that you could fend for yourself, Daughter," her Papa had said. "Your Mama, it was too late for her long before we married. No way to change the fact that her parents treated her like a delicate flower that might blow away with the slightest wind. But no way I can let you be as fragile. You're going to be able to take care of yourself. You're not going to have to depend on a man's muscles. No, siree."

And, so cultivated, her independence had enabled Lenora to take over when her Papa had grown feverish and delirious. But now with an ailing ox, no cow, and a wheel that was broken, Lenora suddenly knew how her mother must have felt all those years. Lenora had never felt so helpless.

Placing the books back on the ground beside her, she picked the gun up and studied it. Was it her only means of survival now? Would she have to kill not only her ailing ox, but possibly an intruder in the night? She gulped back a growing lump in her throat, beginning to tremble in the heat.

And trembling so, she became aware of the soreness in her muscles, suddenly remembering her fall from the wagon with every part of her body. She slowly pushed up the sleeves of her cotton dress to rest above the elbows, flinching when her fingers made contact with the purplish yellow contusions now surfacing on her flesh. How ugly they were. And was she as marred elsewhere? It did seem that every way she moved her body produced an ache.

But then she stopped and held her breath in to listen. Was it—could it possibly be—an approaching wagon?

She listened more carefully, feeling hope rise inside her aching bones. Yes! It was the clattering of hoofs and the squeaking of wooden wheels, and they were growing closer.

Dropping the gun to the ground, she jumped up and peered into the distance. Through the fast falling dusk, she saw it: a covered wagon being pulled by two horses, one black and one white. And as the wagon drew closer, fear began to grip her again. The only occupant of this wagon that she could make out was a man. Was she to be confronted by a lone male, with only a small gun to defend herself? What if he forced himself upon her? No man had yet touched her, even kissed her.

Yet she knew that this man could be her only way of escape from the night that she had been dreading. And her Papa had taught her to be strong—to think like a man. Perhaps she could even act like a man and make this stranger feel no desire for her as a woman. Yes, that was what she'd do. She set her jaw firmly and waited for the wagon to pull up beside her.

James felt the pounding of his heart grow steadily as his wagon approached the young woman, who was now standing, waiting for his arrival. God! How long had it been since he had seen a young, vibrant female? The trail from Ohio had been a long, never-ending procession of clinging wives or sickly daughters.

But never had James encountered a woman as healthy looking—and as beautiful—as this. He could not help staring at her. Even though it was fast growing dark, he could see the redness of her hair, tied in a tight bun on her head. And how could he not notice how the breeze was molding her cotton frock to the curves of her body? His gaze locked itself on the bodice of her dress, which was almost unbuttoned to the waist. The well-developed bosom was almost inviting a kiss from his lips, making an ache rise in his loins.

"Damn it, James," he thought to himself. "Practice a little self-control, will you?" He had never forced himself on *any* woman, and certainly would not begin now, especially with a woman who was apparently in need of other services. "But, God. Alone?" Could she truly be alone, without . . . It had been so long.

Pulling the wagon to a halt beside her, he placed his rifle on the seat next to him and removed his sweat-stained hat, revealing tousled, tawny hair.

"Are you alone, Ma'am?" he asked, scratching his head and mussing his hair up even more. His gaze traveled over her, covered the entire scene, and finally lit upon the ailing ox.

Straightening her back, Lenora answered. "Yes, quite." She wanted to sound strong, but she had to wonder if he had heard the strain in her voice.

"What happened to the rest of your travelin' party?" he asked, looking at her again.

"It was only my Papa and myself," she answered, lowering her eyes. "I buried him this morning."

"Damn sorry."

"Thank you, Sir."

When he climbed from the wagon, turning his hat in circles between his fingers, Lenora felt her body tighten with fright, now fully realizing just how much larger than she he was. She knew that if he wished, he could rest his chin upon her head, just as her Papa had done laughingly so many times.

But the closer he drew to her, the less apprehensive she felt. There was a softness about his features, and the laugh wrinkles around his mouth and brown eyes were proof enough to her that he was a good-natured person.

"James Calloway, at your service, Ma'am," he said, extending a gloved hand, again unable to keep his eyes off the swell of her bosom.

"Lenora Marie Adamson to you, Sir," she said, accepting his hand in hers. She felt her cheeks flame as she saw that his eyes were looking not into her own, but much lower. She looked quickly downward and gasped.

"I simply forgot," she answered, pulling her hand away from his and turning her back to him. Her fingers trembled so, they could hardly work the buttons into their buttonholes.

What was the feeling this man's gaze had aroused in her? She had never felt it before. It could best be described as a tingle, originating somewhere near the base of her spine. This frightened her, since the strange tingling seemed to make her grow weak in the knees. She could not have this! She had to be strong. She had to fend for herself, as her Papa had taught her to do.

17

She turned around again, her green eyes flashing. "And can you help me, Sir?" she asked flatly, stooping to pick up her pistol. She would show him that she was armed— that would teach him to let his eyes wander over her body in such an upsetting fashion.

Seeing the gun made James chuckle silently. She probably didn't even know how to shoot it, he scoffed to himself. Most girls didn't. He dismissed this show of force, walked over to the ox, and stooped to touch it. Feeling its clammy coldness, he looked back in Lenora's direction. "We've first got to do somethin' about this animal," he said.

"We?" she asked, putting the gun back down on the ground. She hoped he wasn't going to ask *her* to do the killing.

"You do have a gun," he said, looking up at her with a half-smile playing on his lips. He had noticed how quickly she had discarded the gun when faced with the prospect of using it. And, damn! He wondered if she realized how beautiful she was. Her lips were sensuously full and looked inviting even now as they drew into a pout. But there was a sort of determination about the firmness of her set jaw, no matter how lovely.

"Yes," she said quietly. "So?"

"So, you can kill your own animal, can't you?" he teased.

She bit her lower lip. "Well, I . . . ," she stammered. She knew that she was not proving anything to him but that she *was* a woman—a woman who hated killing.

"Well? Can't you?"

"Darn it," she blurted, stomping her foot. "Don't you think I'd have already done it, if I could? Do you think I like seeing him lying there suffering?"

"Does that mean that you want me . . . ?" he asked, rising and placing his hat back on his head.

"Will you?" she asked softly, pleading with her eyes. Again she felt the strange tingling, as if something was awakening inside her, when her gaze lowered to his snug tan breeches and then moved upward to the loose plaid shirt opened at the throat. Not only was he tall; he was apparently quite strong, with large muscles rippling along his arms.

She was quickly realizing that in her Papa's struggles to make her strong like a man, he had forgotten one thing: that deep inside, born within her, were the instincts of a woman. It was a fact Lenora was being made increasingly aware of by this stranger's presence. Somehow, now, she felt as though she wanted to seem weak. How else could a man, this man, desire her?

Her eyes blinked nervously. Had she actually just thought such a thing? Why would she want this man to desire her? Shame washed over her like waves. She could not help being confused by the sudden irrationality of her feelings. Was it because this was the first man she had ever been completely alone with? Her Papa had not allowed it while he was alive.

James pulled a gun from his holster. "You'd best not watch, Ma'am," he said softly. "It can be an ugly sight, especially if you've had this animal for some time and are a bit fond of it."

"Yes, I am," she gulped, hurrying to the other side of the wagon. Lenora covered her ears with her hands and waited until the sound of a single gunshot made her heart jump. Unable to stop them, she let the tears come into her eyes. Losing the last ox was almost the same as cutting all ties with her past. Now, all she had left were her Papa's belongings and his dreams. Those dreams, she knew, would always be with her. She turned when she heard the rustle of the grass behind her.

"Ma'am?" James came back, replacing his gun in his holster.

"Yes?" she said, putting her hands to her eyes to wipe the mistiness away. She couldn't let him see her tears. What if he should decide to pull her into his arms to comfort her?

"We'd best be movin' on," he said, eyeing her warmly. "You do plan to travel with me, don't you?"

Lenora laughed awkwardly. "I'd appreciate it if you'd let me join you, Sir." The darkness of night was now around them in such density, she could no longer make out his wagon or horses. The thought of spending the night alone sent shivers through her.

"You're cold, Ma'am?" James asked, moving closer to her.

She stepped back. "A mite," she answered, not wanting him to know that her shaking was caused by fear, "but I'll get my shawl. That'll warm me."

"As you might guess, Ma'am, my wagon's quite full. I'm sure you understand that you'll have to leave most of your belongings here."

Something grabbed at Lenora's heart. She looked around her at her Papa's books, and at everything else that had meant "home" to her. The thought of having to leave all this behind had not entered her mind. That she'd actually have to abandon all her own and her Papa's personal belongings? But it only made sense. "Might I bring along a few small items?" she asked, looking wide-eyed into his dark eyes.

Her look melted his heart, but he tried to assume a gruff manner. He already knew that she had only to look at him with her wide, heavy-lashed eyes and she would be able to get her way, but he would not let her realize it. They had a couple of days of travel ahead of them. He had to remain the voice of authority.

"A *very* few," he grumbled, walking away from her to check on the horses.

"But what about my ox? Aren't you—we— going to bury it?" she asked, seeing the lifeless animal now peacefully at rest.

"We can't take the time to do that," he answered. "It's out of the question."

"I see," she said, lifting the full gathers of her dress up into her arms. She remembered all the other dead animals she had seen lying beside the trail, often with smaller animals devouring the carcasses, and the large hawks that would swoop down and fly away with talons filled. Again, she shuddered.

"Hurry along," James said. "It's been my habit to make camp before dark. Seems I've been delayed a bit this night."

Lenora's eyes widened. He was a moody cuss! Now she felt as though she were going to be in his way, whereas earlier he had appeared eager to have her companionship. "All right," she mumbled.

"And you'd best find your bedroll and whatever provisions you might have on hand for the remainder of the trip. We could use any sort of grub."

Lenora nodded her head and began sorting through her clothes, choosing a few things to stuff inside her travel bag. Out of the corner of her eye, she looked for James. When she could not make him out in the darkness, she felt a slow panic rising. She hurriedly chose the remaining items to take with her.

In the wreckage, she could not find any possessions of her Mama's and Papa's that were small enough. But of her own, she chose to take the diary she had written in faithfully for several years now. By taking the diary, she would also be taking fixed memories of both her Mama and Papa with her, to keep in her possession for the rest of her life.

She thrust the book along with all the clothing into her bag and pulled the strings shut.

Then, stumbling over the strewn articles, she found her bedroll and gathered up what few provisions she could find. She was glad when James came to her side to begin to assist her.

"I'll take these things on to the wagon while you finish roundin' up whatever else you're going to take with you," he said. He walked away from her, leaving her standing with only the travel bag tucked into the crook of her arm.

"Very well, Sir," she said. Her gaze settled on the two books that she had been looking at earlier. How nice it would be to take them along with her, but they would have to stay behind. Books were not only bulky, but heavy as well. And she only wanted to take what could be placed inside her own travel bag. She did not want to inconvenience this stranger to the point that he might decide against helping her.

She threw her knitted shawl around her shoulders and began to walk away, unhappy with her forced decision. Then she stopped to eye the gun that she had so carelessly left on the ground. This had been her Papa's gun, and now it was hers. Mightn't she someday find a need for it? No, there was no way she could leave it behind. She stooped to pick it up and thrust it inside her travel bag, hiding it among the clothes, then began to search through the darkness until she found the horses. Walking around them, she felt a relief of sorts when she found James standing, still patiently waiting for her.

"Sir?" she said, clearing her throat.

"Ready, I see," he said, eyeing all that she was carrying.

"Is this too much to take?"

"Aw, I guess not," he said. "Just throw your bag in the back. Then let's go search out the mountain stream that should be up ahead a ways, so we can make camp."

"Yes, Sir," Lenora said.

James laughed. "Please quit callin' me 'Sir.' My given name is James," he said. "Bein' called 'Sir' makes me feel like an old man. I'm only twenty-one. And you?"

"Sixteen, Sir—I mean James," she answered.

His eyes twinkled as she walked away from him. She looked a damn sight older than sixteen. She had surely been gifted at an early age with womanly assets. It would be difficult traveling with her without taking advantage of those assets. Yet he had no choice but to push such thoughts from his mind.

When she returned, he helped her up onto the seat, then arranged himself beside her. He slapped the horses with the reins and commanded them to move.

"How much further do you think it is to this mountain stream, James?" Lenora asked, pulling the shawl around her shoulders. The night air was just beginning to settle around everything in damp grays, and the absence of her straw hat was beginning to make a difference. She had left it lying on the ground along with the rest of the Adamson household valuables. She swallowed back a lump in her throat. No, she couldn't let him see her cry.

"Only a short distance," he said.

"How long is the rest of the trip?" she inquired further.

"To San Francisco? Maybe one day out, maybe two."

"I'm sure glad you happened along, James."

James chuckled to himself. "Yeah, me too. Me too."

They drove in silence a little farther, until the shadows of bluffs appeared above them. "Ah, just what I've been lookin' for," James said, pulling his horses to a halt. "We can make camp in that little cove over there—get out of the dampness and build a fire to keep the animals away. And if we look real close, we'll find ourselves that stream."

Lenora was helped down from the seat and stood shivering while James crawled up into the back of the wagon and began to toss blankets, bedrolls, and cooking utensils out onto the ground. She looked slowly around her, wishing this was a moonlit night instead of one of solid blackness.

James had been right about a stream being near. Lenora could hear the splashing of water and knew that it was coming from the mountainside and settling into a stream that had to be only footsteps away. She could smell the freshness of the water and a faint odor of fish.

"Handy with buildin' a fire?" James asked, stepping to Lenora's side.

25

"The best," she laughed. She began to gather dried twigs and soon had a fire going while James took his two horses in search of the stream.

"Over here," he shouted through the darkness. "Come and refresh yourself, Lenora."

Letting the sound of his voice be her guide, Lenora made her way through the dampness of the tall grass and sighed with relief when she came upon him standing at the edge of a shallow, rippling brook. When he extended his hand to her, Lenora hesitated for a moment, then smiled as she felt the softness of his glove on her arm, pulling her closer to him.

"Beautiful, isn't it?" he said quietly.

"Yes. Quite," she answered, feeling the pressure of his hand warming her flesh, making her forget the soreness of her bruises.

"Has it been a long journey for you, Lenora?" he asked her softly.

She was entranced by the moment—his touch, and his voice blending together had a soothing, massaging effect on her inner self. All her life, she had been accustomed to the loud, authoritative voice of her Papa. But this man's voice was like a song being sung to her, gentle and soft as a lullaby.

She sent a smile in his direction. "Quite long, James," she answered him. "My childhood was spent in Springfield, Illinois. And yours?"

"Athens, Ohio," he said. It was strange, but this was the first time on the journey that he had actually felt the need of companionship.

Was it the closeness of Lenora, and the sweet smell of her? But no, that was foolish. And he most certainly did not need a woman to get in his way. He quickly took his hand from Lenora's arm and began to pat and smooth the mane of his black mare. This horse had been good to him. Back home James could always depend on a full day's work from her. The horse was always ready for bucking more straw from the thresher. And now, on the trail, neither of his horses had failed him as it seemed so many other animals had failed others on the wagon train. Yep. Damn good horses.

Lenora had felt the abruptness with which he had released her arm. Had she said something wrong? She had only told him she was from Springfield, Illinois. And now, he was fooling with his horses as though she did not exist. She gathered the skirt of her dress up into her arms and went in a huff back to the campfire. She truly did not care whether he spoke to her anymore or not. They would soon part and he would go out of her life, but now it was important that he stay with her until they reached San Francisco. But suddenly her thoughts were troubled. What would she do when she did reach San Francisco? She had sorely depended on her Papa for their future there.

Trying to put all this from her mind, Lenora set about preparing their supper with the provisions James had laid out near the fire. It was apparent that he had planned for her to do the cooking. He was obviously a man who expected a woman to act like a woman which meant to be a cook and heaven knew what else. She tensed when she heard him returning with the horses.

"Smells mighty good," he said, tying the horses to a low branch of a tree.

She ignored him as he had only moments ago been guilty of having done to her. She set her jaw firmly, arranged her dress around her, and sat down on the ground as close to the fire as it was safe to do.

"I say, it smells mighty good," James repeated, settling down beside her and leaning over to pour himself a cup of coffee. Taking a sip, he eyed her, amused by her sudden game of silence. Even though she had the body of a woman, she had a way of behaving like an insolent child.

"Just how good can beans smell, Sir, after a steady diet of beans for weeks," she finally said, feeling almost ill at the thought of another such meal. How she craved a table setting of iris-trimmed china filled with steaming asparagus, fried chicken, and milk gravy on toast. Would she ever have such a meal again?

"Once in San Francisco, that will be taken care of," he said, offering her a filled plate. "There you can have all the fresh fruit, seafood, and steaks your little heart desires."

"Oh, please, James," she said wearily. "Don't even let's talk about it. My mouth waters at the thought."

He helped himself to a spoonful of the beans and washed it down with a swallow of coffee. Then he leaned back on one elbow, mesmerized by her beauty all over again, no matter how much he would rather not let it affect him.

God! She was even more beautiful by firelight. She had loosened her hair from its bun, and it was now spread across her shoulders in shadowy reds. And as he watched the way her bosom rose and fell with each breath taken, he could not control the renewed ache in his loins.

Emptying her plate of food, Lenora placed it on the ground before her. Even though she detested the mere mention of the word "beans," they had succeeded at filling her stomach once again. She leaned back on both arms, inhaling the fragrance of hot coffee and drinking in the night air. She closed her eyes, with sleep trying to possess her, and suddenly she had the feeling she was being watched.

She opened her eyes and self-consciously began to rearrange the folds of her dress beneath her. She blinked her eyes nervously, realizing that James was still watching her— even admiring her? At first his attention had offended her, then it had confused her, and now it flattered her. She had been wrong to snub him moments before. She *did* care that he talked to her, liked her. There was something about him that made her pulse race, no matter how much she hated herself for feeling this way. He was so very handsome. His dark eyes were accentuated by his weathered, tan face, and there was a boyishness about him as a sly smile played upon his lips. She returned his steady gaze, feeling suddenly very bold.

James swallowed hard, for he recognized a knowing look in her eyes. Was she also attracted to him? After all, she was only sixteen. She had probably never even been kissed, let alone— anything else. And he had to remind himself once again that he did not need a relationship that would complicate his plans. He pulled the gloves from his hands and slapped them together nervously.

"And might you want to tell me a little something about yourself?" he asked hoarsely, having the need of light conversation to divert his thoughts.

Lenora sat more upright and pulled her shawl around her. In a way, she had been enjoying this new game with James, but she was relieved that he had put an abrupt halt to it. She knew that such games could prove dangerous with the wrong man. Hadn't she read of such in the romantic novels that she had managed to hide from her Papa's eyes? She wet her lips with her tongue and flashed him another look, but only a friendly one.

"What would you like to know?" she asked, toying with the yellowed lace trimming on the skirt of her dress.

He thrust his gloves into his rear breeches pocket and stretched out lazily beside the fire.

He crossed his arms behind his head and leaned against them, watching some flashes of lightning in the distance. Then his gaze settled again on Lenora, who had just reached inside her travel bag and pulled a small book from it. Was it a diary?

"You said that you and your father were travelin' alone?" he observed. "Might I ask, where is your mother?"

Lenora laid the diary down beside her. She would write in it later, after James was asleep. She had many thoughts to enter for this day. "My mother died of malaria some years ago," she answered. It was easy enough to speak of it now; the emptiness had been filled by life itself. But, oh, Papa. It would take much more living to conquer the pain of his absence.

"And your father? You said that you buried him this mornin'. Was it cholera?"

Lenora's eyes widened. "Why, yes," she said, her words barely audible.

"Don't act so surprised that I guessed," James said. "I've witnessed too many deaths from cholera these past months."

"Oh, I see," she said, lowering her eyes, also remembering the graves.

"And what was your father's occupation while livin' in, did you say Springfield?"

"Yes. Springfield, Illinois," she said, remembering the picket fence encircling a small brick house. Papa had taken pride in the thickness of the ivy climbing its front walls. "Papa?" she quickly went on, swallowing hard. "He was

31

a lawyer. He actually worked with President Lincoln at one time."

"No kiddin'?" James blurted, rising to a sitting position.

"Papa was going to take up the same occupation once we'd reached San Francisco," she said sorrowfully.

"And now, what will you do, now that your father is no longer with you?"

Lenora's eyes wavered. "I'm not at all sure," she said. "And you? Why are you on this journey?"

James got another glimpse of lightning dancing on the horizon. He only hoped that, as had happened the past several nights, the storm would not materialize overhead but stay in the upper heights of the mountains. "Me?" he finally said. "Oh, I'm afraid you'll laugh when I tell you."

Lenora's eyes sparkled with expectation. She swung her hair over her shoulders and leaned forward more. "No, I won't. Please tell me," she urged, smiling.

He stretched his hands out before him. Lenora had never seen such long, lean fingers.

"See these hands?" he said, turning them palms up.

"Yes?" she said, wondering why there were no calluses. After several days on the journey, her Papa had been cursing the raw, swollen skin of his own fingers.

"These are the hands of a weaver," he said.

"Oh?"

"I learned the weaver's trade from my father," he continued. "And when I turned twenty-one, I still found myself workin' in the woolen mill where I had started as a boy."

"But why would this make me laugh? Being a weaver is a proud profession."

He lowered his eyes, half smiling. "What I was speakin' of was a dream of sorts that I had one day," he said quietly.

"A dream?" she persisted.

"Well, a sort of a dream," he answered, "or a vision. One day, while workin', I saw somethin' in my loom besides woolen threads."

Lenora's eyes widened even more. "What? What did you see?" she asked eagerly.

"Well, there was this map. I actually could see this map flashin' before my eyes. A map of the United States. And on it were thousands of people moving. They were in covered wagons, pushin' west, while I was stayin' home, weavin' like a woman."

"How fascinating," she said.

"So, as I had my team of horses, two powerful son-of-a-guns, I decided to just take off. Just like that."

"And now you're about to reach San Francisco. Isn't it exciting?"

James leaned back on one elbow and stared into the flames. He chuckled to himself, remembering. "I had this Uncle Abner, my father's youngest brother. Uncle Abner's adventures were what set me to dreamin' about my *own* adventures."

33

"What'd your Uncle Abner do?"

"He made a trip out West in the 1850's to investigate some minin' interests. But he never did do any minin'. He just wrote me stirrin' letters about Indian skirmishes. He even experienced a stagecoach holdup. And then there was his cowboy life, which he wrote of while in Montana."

"I can see how that would set a young boy's mind to wandering," Lenora commented, placing her diary on her lap. She was enjoying the conversation, but her weariness was fast making her realize how badly in need of sleep she was.

"But Uncle Abner never mentioned such a thing as cholera," James said darkly.

"I guess you and I are lucky to be alive," she said, reminded once again of her Papa.

"Yeah. I guess we're two strong cusses," he laughed. It was true that on this trip some of his skill as a weaver had probably been lost, but he had made up for it by building the strength in his arms and shoulders. And he had noticed Lenora silently admiring his newly acquired physique.

"Papa made sure I was strong enough before setting out on such a journey," Lenora said, blushing as she felt his gaze sweeping over her, assessing her again. The thrill was rushing through her body again as though his eyes had caressed her. She shook her head to clear her thoughts, then rose to go to her bedroll.

"Ready to call it a night?" he said.

"Yes, quite," she murmured, spreading the bedroll out next to the fire. She climbed into it and watched James arrange some more wood on the fire, then settle into his own bedroll.

"Sweet dreams," he said, then turned his back to Lenora and the fire. It was damn hard to say good night to such a tempting morsel so close by. Any other man would. . . . No, he could not dwell on such thoughts. He was a gentleman, not a brute. He forced his eyes closed and took a deep, trembling breath.

"Yes. You, too," she answered, puzzled by his brusqueness. She had half expected to have to fight him off, and now she was fighting only her own disappointment. She sighed deeply, torn between the relief she should have felt and the need she was feeling. Such things had never plagued her before. She set her jaw firmly. It was this James's fault. He had caused these feelings to surface in her. Would she ever be able to understand the reasons for them?

The sudden quiet was unnerving for her, but it did give her the opportunity to search her thoughts for entries she could make in her diary. Reaching inside her bodice, she pulled out a gold chain that she wore around her neck. She quietly opened a heart-shaped locket that hung from this chain and took out a small, flat key.

With two turns of the key, her diary pages were open and waiting. She took the small pencil from the book's side pouch and began to write beneath the flickering light of the fire. She had not meant to, but she had three pages filled before closing and locking it again. Then she was ready finally to give in to her drowsiness.

Snuggling down into the warmth of her blanket, she shut her eyes, but soon they flew open again. A jagged streak of lightning assaulted the sky. And then the thunder suddenly seemed to have invaded their camp.

Looking toward James, whose back was still turned to her, Lenora wondered if he was truly asleep. She listened to his breathing. It came in a slow, even rhythm. Even when another powerful clap of thunder echoed suddenly around the steep bluffs above their heads, he did not move.

She clutched the blanket. It was her first full night ever to be away from family. She did not like this feeling of being so alone. She realized now the only reason she had been able to get as far as she had while her Papa lay ill was that, even though he was ill, he was still with her, lying in the back of the wagon, only a heartbeat away. But now the loneliness tore at her heart.

An emptiness in the pit of her stomach made her sit upright. "James?" she whispered, feeling a strange racing of her heartbeat at the mention of his name.

"Huh?" he answered, turning to face her.

"I'm kind of afraid," she whispered, not wanting to tell him of the loneliness she was feeling. She did not want to tell him of her need to have arms around her, the need to be comforted. This would be a particularly female show of weakness.

"Of what?" he asked.

She glanced upward at another flash of lightning. The ground rumbled beneath her as the thunder quickly followed. "The storm?" she offered meekly.

James laughed. "It's no closer than it was two hours ago. It'll pass on by soon, you'll see."

"All right," she whispered.

But even though they no longer spoke, the flickering campfire seemed to draw them closer together as it played on both their faces, lighting up their eyes.

James felt the heat of the fire, the violent flashes of light, the resounding depths of thunder, as if he were creating them out of himself, as if their power were somehow manifested in the erection now growing inside his breeches. "Damn it, girl," he thought. "Turn those eyes from me before it's too late."

"I just can't go to sleep," she murmured, running her fingers through the thick flames of her hair in her restlessness. Her unease was real, but it was caused more by his staring at her in such a way than by the lightning or the thunder.

She could not understand why the palms of her hands were damp with perspiration in spite of the chill of the night. And what was this sensation of juicy ripeness, simultaneous with a feeling of great emptiness, between her thighs? She had felt it earlier as well, when he had looked at her.

"Would you want to sit by the fire a bit longer, Lenora?" James asked thickly. "Until you feel more like sleepin'?" he added quickly.

"Yes, let's do," she answered, feeling a trembling in her knees as she pushed herself from the confines of the bedroll. She went and sat down next to him, and when a loud clap of thunder broke the silence, she found herself reaching out for him. When he caught her up into his arms and pulled her body against his, she almost lost consciousness, but rather she passed into a completely new kind of consciousness. She had never been in a man's arms before. And, she thought weakly, shouldn't she be making an effort to free herself? But the thought existed in a different world from where she was now.

"Lenora?" he said, tilting her chin up with his forefinger.

"Yes?" she whispered, looking up into the dark eyes that clearly spoke his desire.

"I must kiss you," he said, watching her thick lashes lift like veils. He knew that she was hardly more than a child, but if she desired him as much as he did her, she was woman enough. And the glazed look of her smoky green eyes suggested that she did.

"If you must, you must," she answered, feeling an indescribable urgency, an impatience to have it happen, even though she knew that such a thing should not be. She should be feeling shame for flaunting herself so in front of a man who had been a complete stranger only a short time ago. All the teachings of her past life told her that. But with all the excitement of leaving the past and embarking on a new life, she wanted him to kiss her. She was ready to break the fetters of her girlhood and walk through the open doors of experience, though she was not sure how far.

She shivered with anticipation, and her heart hammered wildly as his lips lowered over hers. There was such a sweetness about those lips; presently she heard someone moaning—and then she realized it was herself.

"Oh, God Jesus," James whispered, pulling away from her. He knew that he should not go on with this. What if it were his sister, on the trail with a stranger? Wouldn't he then kill the man who would take advantage of such a situation?

"James, it's all right," she said, taking his hand in hers, cherishing the softness of his fingers as if they were his lips. They were like the petals of her Mama's summer roses. How she had loved holding those petals against her cheek as she now did this stranger's hand. It had been a moment of ecstasy, just as this was, and every bit as natural and right.

"Is it truly?" he asked, applying gentle pressure to her face with the hand she held there.

"Yes," she said, kissing the tips of his fingers. When his hand left her lips and found the buttons at the front of her dress, she took a deep breath. Then she relaxed and let the shame that was trying to surface again be suffocated by the warm, sure hand that now covered one breast.

"You're sure, Lenora?" he asked again, already slipping her dress down over her shoulders with the other hand. "I don't want to take advantage of you," he added, squeezing her hardened nipple between two fingers until he thought his heart would beat its way out of his chest.

"It is I taking advantage of you," she whispered, moving his free hand to her other breast. "What am I doing?" she thought. "Is this really myself—consenting to this?"

But the question came from the rational part of her and was sublimely irrelevant as he lowered her, clinging, to the ground and made her forget the dampness of the night. His breath coming in sharp rasps silenced all else in her ears as he bent his head down and took a nipple in his mouth. She began to writhe with pleasure, losing all thought of what was soon to happen. All she knew was this new existence, outside of time and reason, and this new urgency that demanded to be quelled.

"Oh, Lenora," he gasped, slowly pulling her dress and underthings down and away from her. "I must have you. My sweet Lenora, let me teach you how to love."

"Yes, yes," she sighed and then felt the first stirrings of excited fear when she realized that she was actually lying naked beneath the unabashed eyes of a man. The old Lenora, the thinking Lenora, knew that she should feel guilt, should put an end to what was happening. But the new Lenora had become one with the firelight that was dancing on his face. The guileless way his eyes were taking in her nakedness only made her joyfully immodest.

His hands traveled very slowly over her throat and breasts, causing her to tremble violently. She then closed her eyes as his fingers continued to trace a path downward, setting small fires all along the way, until they rested between her thighs. She stiffened, waiting for him to touch her there, but was surprised when she suddenly felt him draw away.

After a moment she opened her eyes, and then swallowed hard, for he had removed his shirt and was now unbuttoning the fly of his breeches. She gasped when she saw the stiff erection being uncovered. She had never seen a man naked before. She had always wondered how he—it—would look and now found that it only excited her more.

"Don't be frightened," he said, caressing himself in long strokes. "It will be pleasurable. And I'll be gentle, my sweet Lenora."

Her eyes couldn't leave the sight of him and the way his fingers were moving on himself. The more she watched, the more impassioned she became. Inside her was a woman who she hadn't known existed, and now that woman had stepped forward and assumed complete control. A stranger to herself, Lenora gazed without shame at the shameless behavior of this strange man who was now her only friend. And when he lowered his body down over hers, she found herself parting her thighs and arching her body upward to meet him.

"Slowly," he said, entering her. "Very slowly," he said again, caressing her shoulders, then kissing her breast as he made one strong thrust until he was inside her.

She gasped at the sudden sharp pain, but then felt her body relaxing as the pain slowly blended into a smooth plane of desire and pleasure. "Oh, James," she murmured, awaiting his every thrust with renewed appetite. She needed this, wanted this, just as much as she knew he did. She clung to him, kissing him feverishly all over the face and neck, and his hands never left her breasts.

Their bodies blended into one, melting against one another in a song of wetted flesh, building to a crescendo until spasms made Lenora's mind seem to lead her toward some deep, peaceful place. She could feel another Lenora moaning and writhing and clawing against flesh, but she knew that she, her *self*, was about to find perfect serenity, and then she found it. She did not want the sensation to end. But it did, and to her disappointment much too quickly.

James continued to work his body in and out, gasping, moaning, panting. She still clung to him, loving the feel of his flesh against hers. Soon she began to feel a stiffening of his body as he held her even more tightly, until spasms overtook him, but, just as with Lenora, they only lasted for a brief moment.

She began to run her fingers over the tautness of his shoulder muscles, then felt a quiver in his flesh as her hands crept down to move around his hips.

"I didn't know it would be so beautiful," she murmured, shuddering as he pulled away from her.

"Then I didn't hurt you?"

"How could you have hurt me, James?"

"Well, you were a virgin," he said, pulling his breeches up to hide his new limpness.

"Yes, I was," she said, rising, now ashamed of her nudity. She quickly pulled her dress up around her, thinking, "Now I'm a woman. Whatever that means." And after what they had shared together—did that mean they were in love? He had not forced himself upon her. They had entered into it together, with only a bond of true affection for one another. Only lovers could have shared what they had shared. Now would they marry, share a small house like her Mama and Papa had shared, and eventually have children? Did he truly love her? Would he look after her now, especially now that she was alone in the world? She turned toward him with eyes cast downward.

"God, Lenora!" James said, abruptly pulling her dress aside and turning her more toward the fire to scrutinize her body.

"What is it?" she asked, trying to overcome her sudden modesty.

"Those bruises on your arms and thighs. Did I do that to you?"

Lenora looked down and saw the brownish colored contusions on her thighs. They were the same as the ones she had discovered on her arms earlier in the evening. She felt a keen sense of relief. She did not know about the ways of love. She had thought because of his startled expression that perhaps he *had* damaged her in some way while they had been carried away, for she herself had become virtually senseless at the height of her passion. "Oh, those," she said. "When I was thrown from my wagon, I was tossed pretty hard against the ground."

He went to her and pulled her into his arms. She began to feel again the racing of the heart that his nearness had a way of causing in her, especially now, as his hands were searching over her body once again.

"I'm so glad it wasn't somethin' I did," he said. "I would never want to hurt you."

"Never," she said. "You could never do anything to hurt me. You love me, don't you?"

James released his hold and stepped back away from her with an astonished look in his eyes. "Love?" he repeated quietly.

Lenora pulled her dress over her head. "Yes. Only people in love do what we just did and have it be so beautiful. Isn't that right, James?" she asked. He had been so tender, so sweet, awakening her to loving him. He *had* to feel the same way about her. No man would be so gentle if not in love.

James began to massage his brow. God, she was an innocent, a naive child. He did not know how to react to this development. Now he *did* feel as though he had performed a kind of rape on this girl. How could he tell her that he was only led by his animal instincts, that he would have been ready to bed up with any female at this point in his journey?

"James?" she implored, drawing nearer to him, looking up at him with her wide, trusting eyes.

"Yes," he muttered, walking away from her. Damn. What was he to do? What else could he have said? If it had been under other circumstances, he would walk away from it. But now, he felt responsible for her. He walked out to the stream and stared down into it, glad that he could now see a reflection of the full moon rippling like many moons in the water.

"Looks as though you were right about the storm," Lenora said, coming to his side and taking one of his hands in hers.

"Appears so," he said, feeling the warmth of her hand on his. He glanced up at her. There was that trusting look in her eyes again. Damn, she was beautiful. Even now he could feel the same ache returning to his loins. Maybe she *was* different from other women. Maybe he *was* falling in love with her. But he couldn't. He just couldn't be saddled with her—not now.

"Looks like we'll have fish for breakfast," he laughed, trying to turn both their thoughts to other things.

"How do you know?"

"Don't you see them splashin' up out of the water? This stream's alive with fish. We'll have ourselves a fine breakfast before headin' on to San Francisco."

Lenora's fingers glided smoothly over his. She leaned to kiss one and then faced him, eyes wide with wonder. "James, how do you keep your hands so smooth, so callus free?"

"My gloves," he said. "I've never been without them on this trip. I only remove them in the evenings. Why?"

"My Papa's hands were so rough. Yours are so soft, I don't want to let go of them."

"I like to take care of my hands. It began long ago, when I started learnin' my craft."

"Oh, I see."

"And I have a question for you. I'd like to know whose picture you have in that locket around your neck," he said. He had felt it pressing against his chest when he had held her—as he'd like to do again, and keep her in his arms all night.

"It's no picture," she said, laughing. "I keep the key to my diary in it, so I won't lose it."

"Have you written in the diary today?"

"Yes, only a little while ago."

"That's nice," he said absently.

"I made mention of you in it, James," she said, teasing with her eyes.

46

"Oh, you did, did you?" he laughed awkwardly.

"Would you like to read it?" she asked, tracing his lips with her fingertips.

"No. Might be too embarrassin' for my eyes," he laughed, walking away from her.

She followed close behind. "James, I'm hungry," she said. She did feel famished, exhilarated. Yes, she knew she was in love. How lucky she was to have found him.

"I have some dried apples," he said, going to the wagon. "They might go down good this late at night."

He brought a covered can back with him and sat down beside the fire once again. "Here. Sit and share," he said.

She took a few apple slices and snuggled up close to James, sighing heavily. Only for one instant this evening had she thought of her Papa and what he would think of her if he knew how she had behaved. She had not been able to keep her female instincts from taking over once she had learned what it was to desire a man, and she was glad.

Her Papa had been wrong, keeping her from men while in Springfield. There was more to men than what their "muscles" could do for a woman. Yes, he'd been wrong.

Chapter Two

Listening to the slapping of the water against the San Francisco shoreline and the creak of ropes stretched from the moored steamers, James was certain that his appetite for adventure had not yet been fully fed.

He stood tall and tense, gazing wistfully at the throng of people that packed the deck of the *Empress*. He tipped his hat and listened. He heard the rumbling vibration of the engine beginning and knew the steamer was preparing for departure.

James turned his gaze back to settle on a notice posted on the side of a warehouse near where he stood. Though the notice was yellowed with age and curling at its corners, he could still read what had been luring people to a new city called Seattle.

Since arriving in San Francisco only hours earlier, James had heard several people make mention of this city carved out of a primeval forest, which one could reach after several days traveling north by steamer.

Squinting in the sun, he read the notice again, feeling his heartbeat quicken with each word. "Last chance! Last chance!" proclaimed the ad. "Hurry, before all choice lots are taken by early birds. Only a small down payment required on each piece of ground. First come, first served! Benefits go to the smart chap who comes on tomorrow's steamer!"

He turned to watch the chaotic waterfront scene and noticed that the steamer *Madrona* was now being loaded. He pulled his passage ticket from a shirt pocket and began slapping it nervously against his gloved hand. Somewhere among these wooden crates being carried aboard were his own personal belongings. And somewhere on the forward deck his two horses were settled in, ready to add more miles to their own adventures.

Guilt was the only thing detracting from James's excitement this late afternoon. He could not push Lenora from his mind as easily as he wished to. His plans had been to settle in San Francisco—until Lenora. Now he had to move on, as far away as possible, and leave her behind. He had to admit to himself that he had fallen in love with this girl with the wide, trusting eyes, but he was not ready for such a commitment as taking on a wife. He might never feel ready for that.

He began to make his way toward the steamer, looking nervously from side to side. Surely she would not notice him boarding. She would be watching for two horses, one black and one white, pulling a covered wagon. And he knew that he was disguised well enough among the many other men clamoring around him dressed in the same way. He felt invisible, and exhilarated, and at the same time perfectly miserable.

The sun was suddenly only knifelike streaks of gold cutting their way through the masts of moored seafaring vessels on the waterfront. Lenora began to pace back and forth along the shore, wondering what was taking James so long. He had left her standing alone hours ago, insisting that he had business to attend to and that he would soon return.

Had she been foolish to trust him? Had he, in truth, only been toying with her affections? Had he made love to her three nights in a row knowing that he would leave her once they had reached San Francisco?

Men continued to crowd around her everywhere in loud confusion, hurrying to and from the steamers, carrying, and even sometimes dragging, crates and sea bags. Also along this waterfront were many men who were only loitering. As they would slink past Lenora, she could sometimes smell a strong stench of alcohol and tobacco and she knew that the darker it became, the less safe she would be. No female could be safe in such undesirable surroundings, which she had been abandoned to become an unwilling part of.

Lenora blinked her eyes nervously. They burned from the strain of having watched so closely for James's covered wagon. She knew that only by his wagon would she recognize him amidst this horde of men dressed in street clothes similar to what he had worn.

The ache in Lenora's arms had grown steadily as she had had to support her travel bag first on one hip, then on the other. But she felt fortunate that James had thought to toss it her way before making his departure. At least she had her possessions, though few they were, to cling to.

A hopelessness surged through her as she waited, fully aware of the fact that she was without funds. She did not have money to buy even one meal to fill her empty, gnawing stomach. And where could she spend the night? She felt her cheeks burning, remembering the past three nights. Even now she could feel his lips exploring her body, making her long for him again in spite of herself. How he had awakened the woman in her! She had felt certain that what she felt for him was true love. And because of the gentle way in which he had treated her, she had thought he felt the same. She had even thought fate had thrown them together and that they would possibly share the rest of their lives.

But it was apparent now that James had *not* felt the same as she, for if he had, they would be together now. She would not be standing all alone, tasting the salt air on her lips. Instead, she would be tasting the sweetness of his kisses.

Clenching her fists in anger, she set her jaw firmly, knowing she had to push him from her mind. She would never see him again. She did not even want to see him again. He was a rogue, the type of man *no* woman could truly love. And she had herself to worry about now. Without money how could she even survive one night in this large city that it had taken her months to reach? She knew that having finally reached San Francisco should be an exciting accomplishment for her, but her only emotion was growing fear. She was alone, without her beloved Papa.

"Oh, Papa," she thought to herself, "what am I to do?"

A coldness ran through her as she remembered looking at her Papa's fresh grave and suddenly realizing that along with her Papa she had also buried the money belt that he had always worn beneath his shirt next to his skin. In her grief, she had not thought of anything but her Papa and how much she would miss him. And when she *had* remembered where the only money she would have to get by on lay, she could not bring herself to open the grave and retrieve it from her Papa's lifeless body.

With shoulders sagging and her soiled calico dress hanging limply from its gathered waist,

Lenora turned and began to walk away from the throngs of smelly men and the strong aroma of fish. She looked up and was amazed all over again at the way this city was built on such a steep hill. The houses rose above her on each side of the street in a colorful array, each house seeming to have been deliberately painted a different color by its occupants.

She walked up the hill a bit, then turned to venture down a street into what appeared to be the beginning of the commercial part of the city. She meandered down this long, wide street, where large warehouse buildings and trading markets stood with scores of gambling halls, saloons, and tiny shops intermingled among them.

The aroma of food being prepared in some unknown café made her stomach rumble fiercely, but all she could do was walk on, her gaze captured by the carriages and buggies weaving in and out on the crowded streets. When a loud clanging rang in her ears, Lenora gasped and stopped to watch a cable car clatter past her on its tracks. She had read of this new invention, but this was the first time she had actually witnessed such a grand thing. And the men on board looked to be so richly endowed, with their dark suits and hats—some even with gloved hands.

Lenora swallowed hard, unable to control an ache around her heart at the sight of those gloved hands. She couldn't help wondering where he was in this large city. Was it possible that she might catch a glimpse of him one day by sheer accident? But no, she could not want to see this man. She had to remember always the way in which he had deceived her. He had loved not Lenora, but only the pleasures she had let him take from her body.

The gaslights along the sidewalk began to twinkle in pale golds, reminding Lenora that night was upon her. She stiffened inside, seeing men loafing inside the darkened doorways of saloons and in the darkest part of alleys, and realized that she had to find some place of safety in which to hide herself.

The loud, boisterous shouts of men and the sounds of music blaring on all sides of her made her seek a different direction, and soon she found herself staring into a store window with a display of jewelry lined up on purple velvet that made the diamonds sparkle in lustrous colors of bluish purple casts.

Suddenly she looked up to discover that she herself was being studied, appraised like one of these jewels, by the pale, deep-set eyes of a man inside this establishment. Her eyes widened, having never seen a man with diamond studs in his earlobes before. When he beckoned with a flutter of the hand for her to come inside, Lenora peered into the darkness on each side of her, then quickly darted through the front door.

"Yes?" she stammered. She tried to hold herself erect, though she was weak from both hunger and mounting fear and though she knew the disarray her hair must be in and the limpness in which her once freshly starched dress now hung.

She watched this tall, very thin man walk gracefully toward her, dressed in a gray woolen suit and vest with lace rippling at his throat and wrists. His hands showed carefully manicured nails and a series of rings set with diamonds. His gray hair was sleeked down around his ears and forehead, and the prominent cheekbones moved up and down as he began to speak.

"And what, may I ask, is a young lady like yourself doing out on the streets alone at night?" he asked in a soft, breathy voice, walking around her and studying her as if amused. She was quite unkempt at present, but beneath the grime and filth was a well-kept lady. He was sure of it. And she looked fit and healthy enough too, with even a few possible muscles hidden beneath the sleeves of her dress. He placed his fingertips together before him as he stopped to await an answer.

"I'm not sure that's any of your affair, Sir," she answered, tilting her chin up and batting her lashes nervously. This man was the palest in color that she had ever seen, even paler than her Mama had been in her last days on this earth. It was as though he kept himself hidden from the sun—and from people? But his foreign accent was intriguing.

He pursed his lips together and cocked his head. "Hmm," he said, then added, "Are you in need of a place to live, madam?"

A sense of panic was rising inside Lenora, for she was wondering what this man could want of her. It was obvious, as she glanced quickly around her, that he was a man of means if he was the owner of such breathtaking possessions. There was row upon row of silver and gold ornaments, delicate china, and all manner of jewels and gems sparkling beneath their shields of glass.

"And what if I am?" she snapped, again setting her jaw firmly.

His eyes held a penetrating coolness as he continued to stand poised, watching her. "You appear to have just arrived in San Francisco from a long journey," he observed, pursing his lips again as he waited for her response.

"Why, yes, I have," she answered. She wondered if it was so obvious that she was not of the San Francisco breed. Would he laugh at her if she told him she was from Illinois? But surely not. Abraham Lincoln had been from Illinois, had he not?

"And you're obviously without a guardian?"

"Yes, Sir," she gulped, not knowing what else to say in answer to such an abrupt question.

"And no means by which to support yourself?"

"No, I do not have, Sir."

He walked away from her, leaving behind him a faint odor of cologne which Lenora had become aware of while standing next to him. She had never been around a man who wore cologne. And the earrings piercing each of his earlobes had continued to fascinate her.

"Where are your parents?" he asked abruptly, picking up a liquor glass and holding it to the light to inspect it for smudges made by inconsiderate customers. "Always looking, never buying," he thought angrily to himself. But now, with the possibility of having finally found an unattached female to take home with him, all such troubles could be brushed from his mind.

"My Mama died of malaria some years ago," she answered. "And my Papa died on our journey from Illinois."

"You traveled by wagon train?"

"Yes, Sir."

"And you *are* alone?"

Lenora studied his eyes. She felt she could read a person's inner soul by studying the eyes, and she did not see any evil lurking in these almost colorless eyes. But why all the questions? Should she even answer them? Should she not just turn and leave? But one glance through the window and she realized that she was too afraid to leave. At least this man was not reeking of alcoholic beverages. Surely he could be trusted. Maybe he only wished to help her in her present dilemma. "Yes, I'm alone," she finally answered, casting her eyes downward.

"I'm in need of a woman's services at my private dwelling," he said with a smile breaking through his cool expression. "Can you clean and cook?"

"Why, yes," she stammered. "Quite well."

"Would you like to go home with me this evening and become my chief maid and cook?" he asked, hoping she would not be aware of the slight tremble in his voice. He had been trying for much too long now to find a female who would stay with him. After only a few days, the ones he *had* managed to find would disappear and he would never hear from them again. Perhaps this young girl would be different. It was apparent that she had nowhere else to go.

"At your house?" she said. "Alone? You have no other family in your dwelling?" She did not feel that this could be proper. Wouldn't he be like James, using her for his own needs and then doing away with her in whatever fashion would suit him? Perhaps not. This man had not made any reference to a sexual relationship and had not looked at her in the same manner James had the very first time their eyes had met. Apparently this man was not sexually attracted to her—but who *would* be at this moment? Her dirty hair hung, separated, around her shoulders, and the dress she wore had been a part of her daily attire for days now. She curled her nose, even able to smell the unfamiliar odor of herself.

"I have a comfortable dwelling on Nob Hill," he said, beginning to drape white linen cloths over the glass-covered cases of his shop. "*Quite* comfortable, with a separate room for my maidservant. And, yes, I live alone." He swung around and faced her. "But I do entertain friends," he added. "Usually every night. I would expect to be left to my private entertaining. You would understand, wouldn't you?"

Lenora could feel a flush rising. He could only be speaking of women friends. He was apparently a bachelor, and bachelors of course needed the companionship of women. And his abruptness had made Lenora feel assured that he had no interest in her. He apparently already had a waiting line of women friends, possibly all hoping to marry such an affluent man who owned not only a home but a thriving business.

"Yes, I'd understand," she answered meekly, lowering her eyes again.

"Then you will accept the position?"

"I would appreciate the opportunity."

"My name is Francois Chantal," he said, extending a hand toward her.

"Lenora Marie Adamson to you, Sir," she said, accepting his handshake, surprised by its limpness.

"But please call me Francis," he laughed stiffly, pulling the hand away to smooth a nonexisting stray hair back into place.

"Francis?" she repeated. She would have thought he would prefer to be called "Mr. Chantal" or even a continuation of "Sirs". Wasn't Francis more often a woman's name? Why would he prefer it above the romantic French name of Francois?

"Let's keep our relationship informal. I want you to feel relaxed around me at all times," he said, covering the last showcase. He would not give her any reason to leave. He would be discreet in everything he did. He would prove to the townspeople that he was able to have female companionship, even if it meant only to have a woman hired on as a maidservant. Yes, he would show them. He locked the front door and turned the gaslight out, leaving them in darkness. "Does that bag you are carrying contain the only possessions you own?" he asked, guiding her into a back room where another gaslight flickered dimly.

"Yes, Sir—I mean Francis," she answered. She pulled her bag more tightly against her chest. "I had to leave all my family's personal belongings to rot on the trail."

"A pity, a pity," he said, extinguishing the last light. "Come. Follow me," he said, guiding her through a door. "My carriage is in back, and we should be at my dwelling shortly."

He helped her onto the seat, aware of the trembling in her fingers as their flesh made contact. He knew that she must be fearing what any female alone would be fearing at a time like this. And he wanted to assure her that she would never have reason to fear him in that way. But if he did try to explain, she would no doubt fear that unspeakable side of him even more.

He climbed up beside her, gave the reins a slap, and commanded the horses to move, directing them out onto the main thoroughfare, which was still active with people, horses, and carriages even at such a late hour.

As a cable car clattered past the carriage in which she rode, Lenora sat more upright, trying to look the lady that she in no way felt. She craved a warm bath and a plate of hot food. And wasn't it grand to have a night ahead of her in a bed and not on the ground?

Her heart began to race as she felt the anxiety building within her, finally able to see a glimmer of hope on her horizon. She had found a place of employment—without even having to look! And in San Francisco, not the drab, severe town of Springfield, where the long winter nights were only good for one thing—to freeze a person into an early grave—or the hot summers could leave a body panting for air even into the night.

But now Lenora was experiencing a new type of evening while driving, it seemed, straight up into the sky on this steep street to—Nob Hill, didn't Francis say?

Fog had hidden the city beneath it on the waterfront below them, and shreds of misty saltwater were in the air, putting a warm sort of chill into Lenora. She sighed heavily, smelling a strong scent of roses following her and the carriage, and somewhere in the distance a foghorn broke through the blanket of fog.

The clip-clop of the horses' hoofs and the rattle of the wheels against the cobblestones came to a halt as Francis guided the carriage onto a driveway and then into a garage, which stood behind a two-storied frame house.

Lenora looked up. A magnificent house that seemed to be all windows rose before her, its windows enclosed by rich moldings. "Just beautiful," she sighed. She could not tell if the house was cream colored or gray, for the fog seemed to have followed them uphill and now settled in layers of gray around everything that lay in its path.

"I thought you might approve," Francis said, helping her from the carriage. "Come inside and let me show you around. Then I will leave you to your bath and the amusements of your choice."

Lenora's brows tilted upward. What amusements could he be speaking of? Surely he was not including himself among them? No, he still had not looked at her in that way—the way most men did—and she felt safe to enter the house with him.

Once inside, Lenora crept along silently beside him, until several wall-hung gaslights were lighted to reveal a spacious room, with the most informal of furnishings, surrounding her. No rugs covered the gleaming wooden floors. Several high-backed chairs were grouped in front of a squatty, white brick fireplace, which at this time failed to offer the warm glow of a fire. Against one wall was a glass case, like those in the jewelry store, which held a collection of ornate music boxes. Looking around her, she noticed the long, wide windows of the room. They were without drapes, having instead an abundance of hanging plants arranged in front of and beside them.

"I hope you'll find the place to your liking," Francis said, placing his fingertips together in front of him as Lenora remembered him doing before, apparently as a habitual gesture.

"Oh, yes, quite lovely," she said. She turned her gaze again to notice the lustrous shine of matching dark red wine mahogany tables, placed on each side of a tan horsehair couch on the far side of the room and arranged to face bookshelves that were overflowing with leather-bound books. A creeping sadness made Lenora's eyes begin to burn, as she remembered her Papa's love for books. He had had to be fitted with an endless series of spectacles for using his eyes so unmercifully. Ah, how he would have loved to gaze upon these treasures.

"And now I'll show you the rooms you will use," Francis said.

Lenora wiped at the corner of her eyes with the back of a hand, then let her gaze settle on his buttocks and the way in which they swayed as he walked ahead of her. As she had noticed before, he walked as gracefully as a female—or perhaps *more* gracefully. And his walk was so light, his shoes made not a sound against the wooden floor.

"Here is the kitchen," he said, stepping aside to let Lenora enter. "Small, but adequate."

Lenora was again aware of the gnawing hunger inside her growling stomach as she detected a faint odor of fresh fruit and aging cheese. She went to the immaculate woodburning range and ran her fingers over its ornate front, noticing the copper cooking utensils arranged on its top burners.

"Nice," she said. "Very nice."

Francis opened one of the several doors that led from the kitchen. "And in here is a pantry that is supplied with anything you might need to prepare food for, I'd say, many days, maybe even weeks."

Lenora stepped inside the small room of shelves. Her eyes feasted upon row after row of provisions, all similar to those that her mother had kept in full supply in her own pantry back in Illinois.

"Illinois," she thought. It had become a part of her past now, as incredible as it seemed. And the homesickness was growing so strong inside her that it rivaled her hunger.

"The laundry room is through the far door," Francis continued the tour. "But now I'll show you to your room. You look as though this day has become a bit too much for you."

Lenora blinked her eyes nervously and swallowed hard. "Yes, it does seem that way," she answered. She was anxious to be left alone, even in a strange house, surrounded by strange furnishings, and beneath the same roof as this unfathomable stranger. She only hoped there was a bolt on her door, just in case he *did* have mischief on his mind.

"You can see the upstairs rooms tomorrow," he said, opening another door. "I will expect you to begin displaying your talents as my maidservant in the morning, when I will want a full breakfast before leaving for my shop."

"Yes, Francis," she said shyly. "I understand."

"Now, this is to be your room," he said. He lighted a gaslight on the wall opposite a bed that invited the touch of Lenora's fingers. She went to it and pressed downward, feeling the softness of a feather bed. She could hardly wait to rest her weary back deep in its softness. The headboard gleamed back at her in polished brass.

Then, turning, she found the whole of herself staring back from a pier glass set in the door of a wardrobe across from the bed. A deep intake of breath at the mere sight of herself seemed to be a clue to Francis, who chuckled amusedly.

"I almost forgot to mention that the bathing room opens off the kitchen next to the pantry," he said. "There you will find a sitting-tub and any type of perfumed bath oil you might desire." This was another extravagance; in Springfield she had taken her baths in the kitchen, and so had everyone she knew.

He opened the door, watching her, hoping that she would take advantage of the invitation, and soon. He had never before smelled a woman in such need of a bath. But he had to remember how long she must have been without that luxury. Had he not also traveled from such a distance when he had decided to leave that dreaded, unfriendly New York City? An old bitterness returned and made his brow furrow. While there, he had been treated as an outcast. But was it not beginning all over again here in this great city? The only thing that helped salvage his reputation was the fact that he held such a respectable position in this city as a successful businessman, although becoming one had also made it easier to meet his lovers.

"Francis, this is all so kind of you," Lenora said. She placed her travel bag on a pale blue velveteen chair next to a mahogany table. "You don't even know me, yet you take me in."

"I know the cruelties of a strange city, Lenora," he said.

At this moment, his deep-set eyes seemed to waver nervously as though he had experienced cruelties of some sort himself. "But surely not," Lenora thought. "He is so obviously rich." And couldn't money be a shield from cruelties—and even loneliness?

"I'm sure," she answered. She glanced toward the door, wishing that he would leave. It was she who now needed privacy; suddenly it seemed a blessing, not a curse, to be alone. And she had her diary. To read its entries was to relive the past, to revivify her Papa's love for her and all that they had shared. And there were also the few passages that she had written about James. Would she be able to read them without blushing, even in the presence of only herself?

"I shall leave you now, Lenora," Francis said. He had seen her look toward the door. He understood the gesture well enough, and he was also ready to retire for the evening. He had only to remember his argument with Anthony earlier in the afternoon for the ice to fill his veins and break his heart all over again. Yes, he needed sleep. Only in sleep could he forget the torment gnawing at his insides. "And please feel free to prepare yourself a bite to eat," he added, turning to face her once again. "You *do* look a bit famished, my dear."

"Yes, a bit of food would be nice," she said, adjusting the gathers of her skirt around her. She knew that she had lost weight these past several days. She could tell that his eyes had detected how loosely her bodice hung about her waist. After having grown used to James's gaze always settling on her bosom, it was a relief to have this man pay no particular attention to this part of her anatomy, though his lack of interest was a bit confusing to her. She had been told over and over again by James of her magnificence in that category.

"My time for arising is six A.M." Francis said. "You will please have my breakfast of corn gruel, stewed fruit and coffee ready by six-thirty?"

"Yes, Sir," she answered.

"Francis?" he corrected her, smiling.

"All right, Francis," Lenora laughed, beginning to relax.

"Good night to you then, Lenora."

"Thanks again, Francis."

"Thank *you*, Lenora," he said, pulling the door shut behind him. He stopped, closed his eyes, and leaned heavily against the door. This young woman seemed much nicer than all those who had preceded her. Perhaps if he explained his hidden desires to her, she would understand. God, it would be so wonderful, at least, to have another person share the empty spaces of this house.

He had grown so tired of the sneaking around and the one night stands. How happy it would have made him to have his lovers share the house with him. How utterly heavenly it would be! How he'd love to share every waking moment with. . . .

But he knew the consequences of such boldness and did not care for any more raised eyebrows in the community. He sighed heavily and walked toward the staircase that would lead him to his own private room. Maybe tonight sleep would come to him.

Lenora quickly bolted the door and slouched down onto the chair, almost too hungry and weak to go and draw her bathwater. She looked around the room once again. It was cheerful enough with its wallpaper of tiny rosebud design, but as in the rest of the house, there were no curtains or draperies at the lone window of the room. Only a pulled shade separated her from the view of the outdoors.

But the rest of the room held all that she would need to make her comfortable. She gladly acknowledged the presence of a rolltop desk, knowing that she would spend fruitful hours there entering her thoughts in her diary. And a small gas-fed heater had been installed near the bed, to insure her warmth when she desired it.

All in all, she knew that she was very fortunate to have stopped to gaze into the window of Francis's shop. Had she not, where might she be at this very moment? Possibly at the mercy of some drunken madman? She shuddered to let such a thought enter her mind.

Then she let her thoughts settle on this Francis Chantal. She had never in her life met anyone as strange as he. He was so feminine in speech and manner—nothing like her Papa or James.

Ah, James. Would she ever be able to erase him from her mind? She quickly rose, setting her jaw firmly, determination seizing her. Yes, she would forget him. Now, she had more important things on her mind. She had the warmth of a bath waiting for her, then something to fill the emptiness of her stomach. Then, tomorrow, she had much exploring to do.

Chapter Three

"Are you still feeling poorly, my dear?" Francis asked, sliding his chair back away from the breakfast table.

Lenora leaned against the sink, feeling another wave of nausea pass over her. It had been the same now for the past four weeks, always upon arising. She had even begun to expect it. "Yes, a bit," she answered. She wiped the nervous perspiration from the palms of her hands onto her lace-trimmed apron.

She did not understand this illness. She had been eating well enough. She had even gained back the weight that she had lost on the journey from Illinois. If she persisted in feeling so unwell, she knew that she would soon have to seek out the services of a doctor.

"You seem to have things in good order

around here," Francis said, rising. "Why don't you take the day off and entertain yourself with a bit of shopping? The fresh air could do you good. And while shopping, please pick out some fresh fruit for my guest and myself to have at hand this evening."

Lenora's brows tilted, for she had wondered about his guests. Not one female, other than herself, had to her knowledge entered his house since Lenora had begun to work there. And, having been told to remain in her quarters while he entertained, she had not become acquainted with any of his guests. But she had, on occasion, heard their voices, or laughter mixed into the conversation, and no female chatter had ever been heard. She had begun to be very curious about it.

"Yes, a little outing would be nice, thank you," she murmured. She eyed the jewelry that he wore this day. Each day he displayed a different assortment. Today, his earrings were tiny gold hoops, his only ring was a large square diamond, and his shell-pink silk shirt was graced by a pair of diamond cuff links of the same shape as the ring, but smaller in size.

"I'm having a very special guest tonight," he said, placing his fingertips together in front of him. "I will expect you to retire to your room earlier than usual."

Lenora lowered her eyes and toyed with a button on the front of her freshly starched gingham dress. "Who is this special guest?"

she asked, wondering what his reaction would be to such a bold question. Up to this point in their relationship, they had only spoken of his guests in impersonal tones. But Lenora had grown tired of being alone every evening. Her room was small, and even her diary could not occupy her forever. With so much solitary leisure time to fill, her thoughts invariably came to dwell on James.

He pursed his lips and eyed her questioningly. "Why do you ask?" he said. He had begun to feel secure in his relationship with Lenora. She had seemed to know her place from that very first evening. She had never pried, until now, and what bad timing. Anthony and he had finally been reconciled, and this would be the first time for many weeks that they would be sharing an evening together.

When Anthony had insisted on being made half owner of Francis's shop in order to insure his silence about their relationship, it had hurt Francis deeply. But now, Francis had decided to agree to anything if it meant being with Anthony. No other lover had been able to fulfill Francis's needs as Anthony had so skillfully done. Ah, and so young he was, only nineteen, yet so learned about life and how to get what he wanted from it.

The necessary papers had been drawn up and signed, and now, this would be their first day of full partnership, which included the sharing of their bodies later in the evening. Francis had insisted that this had to be a part of the agreement, and Anthony, with a pinch of Francis's buttocks, had agreed.

Lenora began to clear the dishes from the table, avoiding his eyes. She had never seen him so unnerved, and by such an innocent question. She cleared her throat nervously. "I'm beginning to experience claustrophobia in my small room alone each evening," she pouted. "Why can't I join you and your guest, only for a little while? I would be happy to serve you an extra-special meal—anything to get out of my room. Couldn't that please you, Francis?" she added, turning, pleading with her wide, green eyes. She could remember James's reaction to such a look. It had seemed that she and James would always melt into one another's arms shortly afterward. She did not want this from Francis, but only a greater sense of freedom while she was part of his household.

"Oh, but she *is* beautiful," Francis thought to himself. And what was this feeling her wide-eyed innocence was arousing in him? It had been so long ago that he had felt similar stirrings, when another young woman, Tabatha, had taken his heart. But she had used him only for her own personal vendetta—to make her previous lover jealous. Francis had vowed that no other female would ever again do such a thing to him. But now, could he truly be feeling something for Lenora, even as young as she was?

His eyes swept over the swell of her bosom, making his heart skip a few beats. Weren't her breasts even fuller than when they had first met, or had he not taken the time to notice before?

Then his heart was seized by thoughts of Anthony once again. Would Anthony even possibly be captured by the loveliness of Lenora? And Lenora and Anthony were so much closer to the same age.

No, Francis would not have it. He turned abruptly away from her, picked up a velvet frock coat, and draped it across his left arm. "My dear," he said coolly, "you know what is expected of you. It will be the same tonight as always. You must observe such rules in order to remain in my employment."

Clenching her fists tightly to her sides, she went to him. "Then it is you who may have to abide by your rules," she said with a set jaw. "I shall begin my search for a new position this very day." She tilted her chin up into the air and held her stance, waiting for his reply. She knew that she was taking a chance, having grown to love this house of windows. She had almost come to regard it as her own, being left to her duties all day and allowed to do them however and whenever she pleased. But the evenings had become almost intolerable, and she simply could not bear them any longer.

Francis ran the back of his hand across his forehead. "Damn her insolence," he thought. She was indeed a determined one, and he was glad that she was not using her eyes any longer to sway him. But her full, sensuous lips were even more beautiful curved into a pout. It *was* possible that he was beginning to have feelings for her. But how could that be? His heartbeats were marking off the time until he would embrace Anthony and have Anthony's lips awaken desire in him once again.

Still, he could not afford to lose Lenora, no matter what mixed feelings he was having. She had been good for him. She had made it possible for the community to think they could have been wrong about him. It was important to Francis that no one, except his secret lovers, be truly aware of that side of him. He did not like being treated as an outcast, like dirt beneath some people's feet. Oh, God, if people could only understand that he was not a monster. He was a man, with feelings.

His shoulders slouched forward. "All right, Lenora," he said. "I'm sorry to have been unfair. You may join me tonight in the parlor to listen to music, if you choose. But we won't be having a guest. Not this evening." He could not have Anthony to the house—not until he could manage it in a way that Lenora and Anthony would not meet. His instincts told him it was not a wise thing to let happen. Then his mouth grew dry, as he realized that he had just chosen Lenora's company over Anthony's. With a flush rising from his neck to his face, he began to walk toward the door.

"But, Francis," Lenora said, hurrying after him, "why?" The only answer she received was the banging of the door in her face.

She turned from the door, trembling. She went into the parlor and sat stiff-backed upon the couch, watching the sun's rays settle on the floor around her in streaks of gold. The dust motes floating through the air reminded her of her thoughts—muddled and confused. Why had Francis changed his mind about this evening's guest, when earlier he had acted so anxious for the evening—and this mysterious guest—to arrive? And how close had she come to being unemployed?

But she had only to remember now that look of need in his eyes when she had pleaded with him. Something grabbed at her heart as she realized that this was the first time she had ever received such a look from him. Did it mean that he might expect more from her now? Had she actually played right into his hands? Surely he had not planned it this way all along.

She rose and went to the front window to admire once again the view she had enjoyed so often this past month. Francis's house stood high enough on Nob Hill to enable her to look down upon the bay. How beautifully serene it was this early in the morning, with only three vessels moving along on the sun-gilded water. And the cry of the circling seagulls was ever present, except when the evening fog captured everything beneath it.

Lenora untied her apron and began to fold it carefully. "What if he does expect me to . . . ," she said aloud. Could she? She had only known one man in that way, and she had loved him.

But could she let Francis, who did not stir her insides to such marvelous feelings as she had experienced with James? No, she was certain she could not. If he tried, she would again have to tell him that she would seek employment elsewhere, no matter if it *did* mean moving from this beautiful house of windows.

But did she really have anything to fear? It was quite obvious that he was old enough to be her father.

With this thought in mind, she smiled, hurrying to complete her duties so she could take that walk in the fresh air. The nausea had subsided, as it magically seemed to do each day at this same time.

The waterfront always seemed to draw Lenora to it. She often wondered if it was because that was the last place she had seen James. She knew that many times she had been guilty of searching through the crowd for a possible glimpse of him, as she was doing today.

She hated herself for not being able to push him from her mind. It seemed that he had left an impression in her thoughts, like a leaf fossilized onto a stone. Would she ever be free of him? She felt like a weak person, someone her Papa would not be proud to call his daughter.

The sun had drifted behind a line of low-lying clouds, making the afternoon grow chilly and the air more pronounced in its usual dampness blowing in from the bay. Lenora pulled her shawl closer around her shoulders and moved away from the hustle and bustle of rude, pushy men.

When she reached Washington Avenue, she turned onto it. This particular part of San Francisco never ceased to amaze her. The cable cars and carriages seemed always to be fighting for space in the streets, as did the many men on horseback.

She looked quickly around her at the activity on the walkway. Most of the women shoppers were dressed in the same manner as Lenora, in full-skirted cotton dresses worn above many crinolines trimmed in delicate lace. Some wore bonnets tied beneath the chin in brightly colored satin bows, but Lenora did not. She preferred to feel the breeze from the bay lifting her hair to give it the fresh, clean smell of sea air.

The men strolling along this walk were attired in different garbs. Some were businessmen with stiff collars and round-brimmed hats, and some were dressed as she remembered James having been dressed, in cotton shirt, cowboy hat, and tightly fitted breeches.

She began to make her way along the crowded walks in front of the long, three-storied brick buildings, engrossed once again by the many sights that had a way of teasing her eye. She walked past a wooden, outdoor open stall where seafood was being prepared and offered to the passersby for only a few cents. Lenora inhaled deeply. The aroma had the power to entice her soul, even though fish was not her favorite food.

Another such stall displayed a kaleidoscope of fresh fruit. Lenora smiled to the vendor and chose for her own basket a smaller version of this multifarious collage of colors, textures, and scents: a cluster of early white grapes, some purple plums, wild raspberries, and ripe persimmons, a sweet pink grapefruit, a pomegranate, and a fragrant muskmelon. Then she cheerfully paid the vendor and set off again.

Settling the basket of fruit in the crook of her left arm, she stopped to admire a new stall that had been added along this walk. On the shelves lining the sides of it were many collections of butterflies pinned to boards. Lenora caught her breath. "Are they real?" she asked the young lady in charge.

"You like?" the girl asked, smiling widely, showing yellowed, crooked teeth.

Lenora looked more closely. The wings of each butterfly were marked out in patterns of golds and oranges, and the tips looked as though they were of sheer black lace. But when she saw how the pin had been thrust through the thickest part of each abdomen, her insides began to quiver with distaste. It was a cruel act, she thought. How could anyone do such a thing to a living creature, simply because it was beautiful? She shook her head emphatically, said, "No, I don't like," and walked away from the stall.

Gathering the fullness of her blue and white checked dress up into her arms, she stepped upon the curb, hurrying toward a crowd that had gathered a bit further on up the sidewalk in front of a dress shop. When she reached the gathering, she inched her way through it, and stood aghast at what she saw. It was the lone figure of a man who had painted his face white, having left exposed only his dark eyes, long, narrow nose, and lips. And what was he doing? It made no sense to Lenora. He was making faces and gesturing with his hands and hopping around occasionally. But why was he not speaking? Wouldn't it make more sense to the audience if he would explain what he was doing?

Lenora turned her gaze from the man when she heard whispering behind her. A young lady was saying something about this man being a—what was she saying—a mime? Lenora was about to ask this person who was whispering just what a mime was, when she caught sight of a gloved man.

Her heartbeat increased as she spotted the tousled sandy hair towering above the crowd, but she could not see his eyes or facial features. They were hidden by a lady's high-piled hairstyle.

"James?" Lenora whispered, suddenly feeling a compulsion to push her way toward this man. "James? Is it really you?" she said, her thoughts clouded by anxiety. She hated herself for being so eager to see him. Had he not deserted and lied to her? Yet she ached for his touch, and she would do anything now, it seemed, to be able to gaze upon him. There had been such a gentleness to his smile and the way in which he had caressed her.

Receiving frowns and uttered remarks of annoyance, Lenora made her way through the crowd. But when she reached the gloved man, it took only one glance upon this stranger's face to realize how foolish she had been.

Tears burned her cheeks, and a weakness came into her head, until all things around her became a swirling mass of staring faces. She could not stop her body from crumpling onto the sidewalk, and then she saw only total darkness.

When she awakened, she found herself stretched out on an uncomfortable horsehair couch. She rubbed her eyes to clear them, and then looked around her. She was in some type of office. A desk filled most of the room, and on the wall behind it were many framed documents. The aroma surrounding her was a mixture of medicine and stale cigar smoke.

A soreness of her flesh reminded her of what had happened. An embarrassed frustration surged through her. How could she have let such a thing occur? And where was she now? Who had rescued her after her discovery that it had not been James who had caused her such agitation? Was she in this stranger's dwelling now? She hoped not. How could she explain to him why one look upon his face had made her faint?

She tensed when she heard the squeaking of a door's hinges behind her. She leaned up on one elbow, experiencing further queasiness momentarily, then watched a short, squatty man enter. He wore a wrinkled black jacket over sagging brown serge trousers. It seemed to Lenora that his thick gray brows made up for the loss of hair on his head. When he looked at her, there was a sternness about his thin lips and dimly colored eyes.

"Feelin' better, are you, little Missus?" he inquired gruffly, reaching a hand toward her in a gesture for her to stand.

Lenora's eyes widened. She pushed herself from the couch and stood eyelevel with him. "Yes, Sir," she said, rearranging her hair. She was relieved to know she would not have to confront the stranger whom she had thought was James. She was not even sure if she could wander the streets of San Francisco again. What if the same thing should happen? She would not be able to stand such humiliation twice.

"Come over and sit beside my desk, eh, Missus . . . what is your name, now?"

"Lenora Marie Adamson," Lenora said. She settled down onto an overstuffed chair next to the desk as he slouched down onto a high-backed wooden chair behind the desk.

"And why would you faint, do you think?"

A flush rose to Lenora's face. "I'm not sure," she mumbled, then added, "And your name, Sir? I don't believe you mentioned it."

He threw his head back and laughed raucously. "I thought everybody knew Doc Rose," he said. "But I guess San Francisco's growin' faster than my name can spread."

"Oh. You're a doctor."

"Yes'm, little Missus. Ol' Doc Rose at your service," he answered. He leaned back into the chair and lighted a cigar.

"How did I get here?" Lenora said, looking around the room once again. She was glad to see her coin purse lying closed next to her shawl and basket of fruit. At least she had not lost any valuables through the mishap.

"Some gent called himself Raef Wescott," he answered, puffing eagerly on his cigar. "He's one of those seafarin' chaps from Seattle, came by ship for supplies to take back to that city."

"Oh, I see."

"Now, let's get to the main issue at hand, little Missus," he said, furrowing his brows. "Can you tell me if you've ever fainted before?"

"Not to my recollection."

"Did somethin' startle you, or have you been feelin' poorly of late?"

The flush began its slow ascent upward again. She lowered her eyes and clasped her hands tightly in her lap. She could not explain about James and the mistaken identity, but she could tell this doctor one truth out of two.

"Well, Sir," she began weakly. "For the past, let's say, four weeks, I've been nauseated quite a bit."

His brows shot upward. He took his cigar from his mouth and rested it on an ashtray. "Hmm, I see," he uttered. "And might'n these spells be, would you say," he stopped to cough into a cupped hand, "in the mornin'? Mainly upon first arisin'?"

Lenora's eyes widened. "Why, Doc Rose, that's *exactly* when I experience them. How could you know that?"

He laughed raucously again and stood up. "These things are quite familiar to me, little Missus," he replied. "And now, I'll need to examine you, to see for sure."

Lenora's insides tightened. "To see for sure? To see what?"

"First the examination, please; then the diagnosis. Come into the next room with me. My assistant will help you to undress."

Putting her hands to her throat, Lenora gasped. "Get undressed?" Only two people had seen her disrobed in her entire life: her mother and James. She just couldn't—this elderly man was a stranger.

"Routine," he laughed. "Just routine."

"But I can't."

"You must, little Missus."

"But Sir—Doc . . ."

"Little Missus, to see for sure if you're with child, I *must* examine you. Now will you get up off your little fanny and follow me?"

Lenora felt the blood rush from her face, and she felt faint all over again. "With child?" she gasped. "Me? Why, I can't be."

"All signs indicate it," he said, opening a door that led into a small examining room. "You and your husband might have somethin' to celebrate tonight."

"My husband . . ."

Doc Rose turned and eyed her questioningly. "There *is* a husband, ain't there?"

Casting her eyes downward, Lenora whispered faintly, "Yes, Sir." How could she not? Any woman having a child out of wedlock was classified as a whore.

"Well? Ain't you a comin'?"

Lenora pushed herself up from the chair, a leaden numbness rendering her almost too limp to move. But she managed to put one foot before the other, full of outrage and complete despair. "Oh, Papa, what am I to do?" she thought to herself. But she knew that her Papa would more than likely disown her if he were alive and knew.

Perhaps the doctor was wrong. Maybe the hours spent in James's arms had not resulted in a baby growing inside her. But she had to admit that she *had* been puzzling over the fact that she had not yet had her monthly, not since arriving in San Francisco. And since she had turned twelve she had never been even one day late having the "weeps," as her Mama had called it.

"Oh, James. Where *are* you?" she whispered to herself.

At this moment she did not know whether she hated him or loved him more. The feelings seemed to her to be lost in the growing wonder of a new life.

Chapter Four

The small flower girl tugging at Lenora's free hand was ignored as Lenora pushed her way through the throngs of people still milling around in the busy streets.

"A cluster of violets for the beautiful lady?" the girl pleaded again. "Only five cents. Please?"

"Could this be what my fatherless child will be doing in the future," Lenora thought to herself, "having to turn to begging?"

She jerked her hand free without looking back. She could not bring herself to look at this child whose voice held such sadness. And were she to stop to search through her coin purse for the five pennies, there was a chance she might not arrive home before Francis. She had to think out this new dilemma in which she had found herself.

Pulling the shawl more securely around her shoulders, she began the ascent up the hill that would take her away from this Doc Rose who had just informed her that from all indications she was with child. Her womb had already begun to soften, he'd said, and had enlarged somewhat.

Lenora began to bite her lower lip as tears swelled in her eyes, shame almost making her grow nauseous again. A child! At age seventeen, which she would be when the child was born. How could she possibly let anyone see her in such a condition, since she wasn't married? She would be an outcast from society, and the child would be labeled illegitimate and called a bastard.

She stopped abruptly at the side of the walk. Should she search the city until she found James? Surely somewhere among the row after row of houses on these hillsides she could find him. She could tell him that she was with child, *his* child. Surely he would not also abandon an unborn child?

But a sense of hopelessness gave her the answer. If he had deserted *her*, he would not hesitate to desert a woman carrying a child. She knew that no man liked being cornered— *made* to wed.

"No," she mumbled aloud. "That's not the answer."

She resumed the trip up the hill, again walking past long, brick buildings. But when she saw a group of men and women gaping at a notice posted on a side wall of one of these buildings, she stopped to see what the attraction was.

Holding her basket of fruit closer to her, Lenora leaned forward and read the ad: "Young women of San Francisco, you are in luck! Many needed for wedlock to lonely, unmarried gents in Seattle. Free passage by boat will take you to a desirable husband and way of life. Come one, come all! Signing up at Dancer's Landing every day."

Lenora's heart skipped several beats. Had she read this notice correctly? Had she actually been provided with an answer to her problem? If there were men looking for wives, then one of them could pose as the father of her child. But, surely it wouldn't work. No man would want a woman with child, no matter how lonely he might be.

Then her eyes brightened and her hands encircled her waistline, which was still trim. She could fool a man, certainly, and he could be made to think the child was *his*.

She listened carefully to the comments from the others who were reading the same notice:

"Seattle? What is this city, Seattle?" said a man in a brilliant green frock coat.

"A seaport much like our own San Francisco, I've heard," another said.

A buxom lady of around thirty years of age said, "I think I'll give it a try—no decent men left in *this* city."

"I'll take the free boat ride," a girl dressed

in a brightly flowered, low-necked dress said. "But once I'm there, I don't need no husband. I have my own ways of makin' a livin'."

The buxom lady giggled and walked away from the posted notice, hand in hand with the other girl.

Lenora smiled. She was not the only one full of scheming this late afternoon. But she had already decided against her own plot. What if the man who chose her was ugly, or cruel to her, and later to the child? No, there had to be another way.

With a heavy heart, she left the commercial part of San Francisco and began to make her way past the Victorian houses she was usually delighted to gaze upon, though not today. Her thoughts were now on Francis. He was such a prudish fellow, she *knew* he would order her from the house the minute he learned her secret. And didn't it look as though she would, after all, have to leave the house that she now stood across the street from, admiring it all over again?

The setting sun was reflected in the windows at the front of the house, and it looked as though a million candles were aglow inside the rooms. Wouldn't it be a romantic setting— a feast of fruit, wine, music, in one of those elegant rooms—by candlelight?

Something clutched at the pit of her stomach as she realized where her thoughts had just wandered.

She *would* be enjoying such a feast this very

night, with Francis. Of course, the fact that it *would* be in a very romantic setting had not occurred to her until now. Lenora's heart raced with her thoughts of Francis. Wasn't he an eligible bachelor, a man who could give both Lenora and her unborn child a name *and* the means by which to live quite comfortably in his house of many windows? Had he not gazed upon the swell of her breasts this very morning with lust in his deep-set eyes?

Her face flushed scarlet with such wicked plans. Francis was an elderly gentleman—maybe even in his late forties. Could he even still be capable of fathering a child? And could *she* be capable of seducing him, like some sort of harlot from a brothel?

Lifting the skirt of her dress above her ankles, Lenora rushed across the street and into the house. She *did* feel wicked, but she had not only herself to think of now but also a growing child inside her womb. If James could not be a father to that child, then she would do her utmost to entice Francis into being one. Yes, she decided, her only hope was in seducing him—and making him fall in love with her.

"Papa, forgive me," she whispered as she hurried to arrange some of the fruit in a bowl for a centerpiece on the table. "I have no other choice," she added, feeling shame, but also vaguely eager for the evening's arrival. She would wear the green satin dress that she had purchased with her first two weeks' earnings and make special efforts with her hair. And she would be sure her breasts were partially exposed for Francis to feast his eyes upon. She knew that this part of her anatomy was important to men. Hadn't James enjoyed touching, kissing, licking the softness of her ripe nipples until they had peaked to a stiff erectness?

A pulsating warmth spread through her inner thighs as she remembered how James had taken her to heights of ecstasy with his fingers and mouth. Maybe she could also enjoy such pleasure with Francis. Weren't all men capable of doing the same thing to a woman? It was true that Francis's presence had not aroused any pleasurable feelings or yearnings in her, but perhaps it would be different, if she chose to let it be.

The night had crept up on Lenora, leaving her to finish her chores in semidarkness. She hurried through the house igniting the gaslights, then with hammering pulse planned her seduction scene.

In the parlor she placed long, tapering candles around the room and rearranged several bouquets of pink roses and Queen Anne's lace that she had wisely chosen to bring in from the garden that morning. She stood back, hands clasped before her, admiring the room. The candles would reflect like magic wands in the large, wide windows of night.

She was glad that the house stood high above the street, for thus she could feel free to proceed with her plans. She did not need an audience on this night that was to be for only her and Francis. She looked down and patted her stomach lightly. "And for you, little one," she whispered, her eyes burning with tears of renewed shame and confusion.

The nights of love that had made this baby now seemed so long ago. And James? She had begun to think he had not truly existed, that he had been a figment of her imagination, to pass her lonely vigil on the trail. But, in a few short months, stirrings inside her womb would be proof enough of his having been with her.

"Oh, Papa," she blurted, tears stinging her eyes. "Why was I so foolish?" And was she being foolish this night, as well?

Chapter Five

The candles flickered, sending dancing shadows along the walls and over the ceiling. The night was warm, and the lazy summer sound of crickets drifted into the windows. Francis opened the glass case that displayed his collection of music boxes, brought forth a golden box inlaid with mother-of-pearl, wound it up, and set it down on the mahogany table.

Lenora sat stiff-backed, breathing deeply, wondering if she was attractive enough. When she had entered the room, with her many crinolines rustling beneath the satin dress, Francis had only briefly acknowledged her arrival, with a raised eyebrow in her direction.

The music reverberated throughout the room, rising and falling like waves on an ocean. Francis had told her that he had acquired this box, which contained the arias from his favorite opera, from a German customer who frequented his shop. Much was lacking, of course, but to a true opera lover even the sounds coming from this machine were welcome.

Lenora glanced down, seeing the deep cleavage of her bosom, then felt a blush rising when she felt his eyes also upon her.

"Ah, listen to that delightful melody," Francis said, putting his fingertips together in front of him.

Lenora was glad when he closed his eyes for a brief moment, appearing to be enraptured. This enabled her to relax a bit against the plump cushions of the couch. She was not sure if she could go through with this farce. He had still to lend her any encouragement at all.

"If only you could have heard it sung, as I was fortunate enough to do. Such magnificence I've never heard," Francis added, nodding his head in time with the music.

"What opera *is* this, Francis?" Lenora asked. Should she show some interest, maybe he would come and sit across from her. Only in this way, it seemed, could she get his full attention.

Francis secured the belt around his maroon silk smoking jacket, wondering why Lenora was dressed in such a seductive fashion. If he let himself, he knew that he might even desire to kiss her. But oh, how young she was, and he had sworn off women long ago. Once he had found that the touch of another man could excite him so, he had sought no other sources of pleasure. Had there only been more understanding from all who knew him, life would have been so much simpler for him. He cleared his throat and began to make his way toward Lenora. He would try not to notice the magnificence of her shining hair, her delicate throat, her ample bosom. Wouldn't he only be hurt if he let himself be captivated?

"The opera?" he finally answered. He settled into a high-backed chair and crossed his legs. "It's called 'Martha.' It's a grand romantic opera written by Friedrich von Flotow. It's French, but sung in English."

"Oh, I see," Lenora said, batting her lashes tentatively. But, no, it was too soon to use her eyes on him. She had to let him get more relaxed. She could tell by his expression that her appearance had puzzled him. He had only seen her in cotton dresses and aprons, with her hair bound up in back with a ribbon and allowed to hang loosely around her shoulders. She reached up to touch the smooth coil of hair at the base of her neck, with a few tendrils of curls left out to frame her face, and sighed inwardly. It had taken her far too long to work it into such perfection. Had she not arranged her Mama's chignon so often, Lenora would not even have had the skills to style her own for this special night.

"Would you like me to explain the opera to you?" he asked, fidgeting with the diamond stickpin that anchored his cravat.

"Please do, Francis," Lenora said. She leaned forward, wide-eyed and reached for a bon bon that he had surprisingly brought home with him this evening. Lenora had not been treated to such a delicacy since she had traveled from Springfield. She placed one into her mouth and ran her tongue across her lips, savoring every bit of its sweetness.

Francis's heartbeat quickened, watching the curling of Lenora's tongue. What pleasure she would be able to give to a man! His gaze swooped over her breasts once again. When she had leaned over, not much had been left for his imagination. A girl of sixteen? He scoffed. Surely she was much older and had told him a nontruth. A stirring of desire was rising beneath his snug trousers surprising even Francis. He put his hand to his mouth and coughed absently.

"The opera? Oh, yes, the opera," he stammered, recrossing his legs, hoping to conceal between them what had so magically risen. No female had managed to cause this since. . . .

"Let's see," he said, looking up toward the ceiling with fingertips together in front of him. The candles in the room? He also wondered why Lenora had gone to that trouble. "I think I remember the story well enough to relate it to you," he then began. "The scene is laid in England, during the reign of Queen Anne. Lady Harriette Durham, maid of honor to the queen, is bored with court life. She disguises herself as a peasant girl and seeks relaxation at the village fair. She takes along her maid Nancy and an elderly but devoted admirer, Sir Tristan Mickelford. Lionel and Plunkett, two young farmers who are foster brothers, come to the fair. They wish to hire someone to do their housework, and they ask Lady Harriette and Nancy to take service with them. Jokingly, the girls agree to go. They discover too late that they are actually bound to service for a year."

Francis paused to cough into his hand. "My dear, I am afraid my throat has gone dry. I believe sipping a glass of wine might be a suitable remedy for such a problem," he smiled. He rose, went to a small liquor cabinet, and chose a bottle containing a liquid of a rich, ruby color. "Claret," he pronounced. "My favorite. Made in my own country, France, in the region surrounding Bordeaux. May I offer you a glass, Lenora?"

Wanting to appear mature, she smiled and nodded. "Yes, Francis. That would please me." She watched him pour the wine into two long-stemmed, delicate glasses, strangely enjoying the evening thus far. Listening to Francis describe the opera in such minute detail reminded her of when she was a child, sitting by candlelight, listening to her Papa telling the many stories that he could so masterfully conjure. But she had to remember—this was not her Papa, and she was no longer a child. This was Francis—and she was *with* child. She swallowed hard, scooted to the edge of the couch, and sucked in her breath in an effort to display the largeness of her breasts and the smallness of her waist as Francis handed her the glass of wine. She gave him her most alluring smile, with a tilt of the head, and looked meaningfully into his eyes. "Thank you, Francis," she said, making sure her hand brushed against his.

"That's quite all right," he said absently, seeming to have lowered his voice a full octave. He raised a brow as he sat back down across from her. Had she done that purposely? God! When their hands touched he had felt such a burning desire for her. Could it be that she was actually *trying* to seduce him? But why? He had to be careful. He did not want to let a female cause him to lose his head again. And, what was Anthony doing at this very moment? Could he even be soliciting for himself another lover for this night? God! Surely not, Francis insisted to himself. It would absolutely shatter him if Anthony should stoop so low. Yet Anthony was so young, it was true, and had such driving, hidden needs.

"The opera, Francis," Lenora said, leaning back in the chair again. She held the glass before her as if it were a delicate bird, ready to take flight. "Please tell me more."

Francis took a deep draught of wine and let its tartness wet his throat. He had to push Anthony from his mind, and no matter how much he hated himself for it, he was enjoying the company of a beautiful woman for a change. He pursed his lips for a moment, then forced a strained smile. "The opera? Oh, yes," he said, "let's see. The two girls have found they are bound for a year to the service of these two farmers. Ah, yes. That's where I ended the tale, isn't it, my dear?"

"Yes, it is, Francis," Lenora said. "What happened then? I'm enjoying this so." Then she blushed, realizing she was sounding more like a child than a woman. She lowered her eyes and took a sip of wine.

"I'm glad you are, my dear," he said, laughing softly, having seen her blush. Such a child, yet not a child at all. "I shall continue, though it seems the music has come to an end. One day someone will invent a machine that will play music for hours upon hours." He placed his wine glass on a table near where he stood and strolled to the machine, all the while continuing to speak. "It seems that these young farmers lead the girls away to their farmhouse in spite of Sir Tristan's protests. They instruct 'Martha' and 'Julia,' as the girls are called, in their household duties. Shortly after midnight, Sir Tristan helps the girls to escape. Lionel becomes melancholy through the loss of his beloved Martha. Later the two brothers come upon the girls in a hunting party and soon learn that the whole affair was a jest."

Having rewound the music box, Francis went to the liquor cabinet and carried the bottle of wine back to where he sat. "More wine, my dear, before I reach the conclusion of the story?" he asked, leaning forward.

"No, Francis. I don't believe so," she answered. She reached her hands up to touch her cheeks. Her face felt inflamed after the one glassful. She had never before drunk any alcoholic beverage and was in wonder about the way she was feeling now. She could feel a tingling of sorts in her fingers and especially in the pit of her stomach. She wondered if Francis was also experiencing those feelings, and, if so, would another glass increase them, making him even easier to seduce? She replaced her hands on her lap and clasped them tightly together, watching him with eager, wide eyes. Shame had left her long ago, and she was filled with a strange inner excitement. Could it even be pleasurable to seduce a man who appeared to be in need of a woman?

Francis rearranged himself on his high-backed chair and sipped from the freshly filled wine glass. "And now, the finis of my story, my dear," he said, smiling more freely. He watched her intently as he continued to speak. "Through a ring he bears, Lionel is discovered to be the heir to the banished Count of Derby. Lady Harriette seeks a reconciliation with Lionel, but the wounded lover spurns her. She wins back his love by repeating the scene of the fair. The opera ends joyously with Lionel and 'Martha' and Plunkett and 'Julia' planning marriage. And that is the story, my dear."

Lenora rose, clapping her hands. "Bravo! So beautifully told, Francis," she beamed. She walked toward him rustling the skirt of her dress and the stiff crinolines noisily. "And quite romantic," she added softly, again gazing deep into his eyes. She was fast learning the ways in which to charm a man, and somehow it gave her a sense of power.

"You think so?" he asked weakly, taking another sip of wine.

"Yes, quite."

"How nice," he murmured, rising to place the music box back in its display case and choose another.

Lenora moved to his side. "This whole evening has been romantic, Francis," she whispered, lifting a finger to touch his lips. She felt so daring, so bold. But she *had* to do this—her whole future depended upon it.

Recoiling somewhat, Francis flashed her a look of utter disbelief. God, she was trying to seduce him! Was it because she had been alone for so long? Had he been wrong to confine her to her room each evening? Would it not be a kindness to her for him to give in to her wishes?

But *could* he climb into bed with a woman, after all these years? And hadn't all maid-servants before Lenora despised him, even deserted him without even giving notice? Why had Lenora become attracted to him? Was it his jewels? His house? But, no matter—he did want a taste of her lips, her breasts. The ache in his loins was such a welcome sensation—an ache that recently only Anthony had been able to stir, until he had discovered this young miracle standing beside him.

"Lenora?" he said, turning to face her.

"Yes, Francis?" she replied, batting her lashes and smiling, though she knew it to be quite wicked.

"Would you . . . ? Could I . . . ?" he stammered, reaching out a hand that brushed against the swell of her bosom and caught her under the arm. God, how he hated himself at this moment. He seemed to have forgotten even how to approach a female. But the one brief contact with her flesh had set him afire inside. He would have to have her, now. There would be no backing away.

"Could you what, Francis?" she asked. She reached up to run a hand over his slicked-down gray hair until it rested over the black velvet bow at the nape of his neck. She had to play the seductress to the hilt. She saw the pulsebeat quickening in his temples and knew that it was working. And what was this? She was also feeling a need pulsating inside her thighs. Could just any man do this to her now—now that she was aware of such feelings, since James had introduced her to them?

"Kiss you, my dear," he said. He circled his arms around her waist and pulled her against him. "God, how different," he thought, to have such breasts crushing against him instead of a bare-chested male. His mind was swirling with desire. He parted his lips and made contact, prying her lips open, to thrust his tongue inside her mouth, to capture, to entwine, to drink in the power of her womanhood like a healing potion and so restore his power as a man.

The silence of the music box broke the spell. Francis stepped back away from Lenora, trembling. "We must have music," he stammered, walking toward it.

The kiss had not been the same as Lenora remembered James's having been. She even wiped her lips with the back of her hand, hating the wetness his tongue had left behind. When he had thrust his tongue inside her mouth, she had at first been shocked by the sudden intrusion; then a keen revulsion had passed through her. The taste of his saliva still lingered, detracting from the excitement of the moment. But perhaps his next kiss would be different, would do to her what James's kisses had done. She would never forget the waves of pleasure that had come over her as James's lips had met hers.

She watched in silence as Francis began to make his way around the room, snuffing the life from the many candles. Her excitement was slowly changing to dread, for she knew what the darkness of the room would lead to. How would he approach her next? Would he take her on the couch, or would he guide her upstairs to the privacy of his room? She swallowed hard, waiting.

No words were spoken between them as he took her arm and led her from the parlor into her own room. In the dim lighting from a table lamp, he began to fumble with the tiny buttons at the back of her dress.

"Francis?" she said.

"Shhh," he said. "Please don't say anything."

"But, Francis," she said, suddenly realizing that she was no longer the seductress, that he was now going to seduce her.

"It's been so long," he whispered, reaching inside her bodice to capture her two breasts in his hands. Then he released his hold and slowly removed the dress from her shoulders, letting it drop to the floor. "And now your underthings," he said, beginning to remove his own clothing. "Please remove them, my dear," he added more firmly.

Lenora began to tremble, not liking this turn of events. She looked into his deep-set eyes and noticed that the black of his pupils almost erased the irises' pale grays. When his brows furrowed in a frown, she grew afraid and stepped out of her undergarments hastily. Wasn't this what she had wanted—to lure him into bed, in the hope that it would lead to wedlock? She shivered in the chill of the room as she stood completely naked before his devouring eyes. She circled her arms around her breasts, only to have them be removed again by him and placed at her sides as he dropped the last of his own clothing to the floor.

Her gaze lowered, and she discerned another difference between the two men—the only two she had ever seen in the nude. This man's member was short and lean, with only a trace of pubic hair around the shaft. Her eyes widened. How could Francis be capable of giving pleasure with such? Was this why he was not wed?

And though he was tall and lean, his flesh hung loosely from his shoulders and arms. His physique was not tight and muscular as James's had been. She stiffened inside as he came to her. She even recoiled at his touch as he inched her down across the bed. His breath sounded harsh as he lay down next to her and ever so gently began to explore her body, as though there had been no women before her.

The touch of her skin against his fingertips aroused in him further longings, but he wanted to prolong things, to enjoy this moment to the fullest. And he knew that fear was mounting inside himself; would he be able to make love to her in the normal way? Had he forgotten the art of it?

His hands traced her body as though he were planning to memorize it and capture it on canvas with paints, tracing its curves, outlining the fullness of her breasts and hips, her buttocks, and then the softest, deepest part of her, as his fingers entered her from below.

Lenora tightened from reflex, experiencing only revulsion from his continued probings. How fumbling, how clumsy he seemed. It was not the same as with James, but she had not to let her revulsion show. She needed a father for her child—why *not* Francis?

When he mounted her and entered her body, she could hardly feel the intrusion. She could only hear his grunts and moans as he began to work his body up and down over hers. She looked onto his face. It held a look almost of grotesqueness, as though he were experiencing anguish or pain, not a building pleasure as such ministerings with the opposite sex were supposed to arouse. Then, as suddenly as he had mounted her, he released himself from her and climbed from the bed.

"Lenora, you must help me," he said. He pulled her to an upright position on the edge of the bed.

"I must what?" she gasped, as he guided her head toward his throbbing member.

"God, Lenora," he groaned. "This is the only way I can get release. Please help me." He felt humiliated, disgraced. He now knew it was impossible to achieve fulfillment with a female in the normal way. There was only one method for him, and surely she could master it, as Anthony had. He shoved her head downward, feeling an ache in his loins so intense that he felt he might explode.

Lenora began to sob. What was he doing? Why was he putting her face so close to his . . .? No! She could not let him do this to her. It wasn't right! Only a mentally deranged person would expect her to put her mouth on such a part of his anatomy. She jerked free from his hold and shoved him away from her. She put her hands to her mouth and gasped when he fell across a chair and sprawled awkwardly across the floor.

"Oh, what have I done?" she thought desperately to herself.

In one swift movement, he scooped his clothes up into his arms and disappeared from the room, leaving Lenora to stare at the open door, not understanding what had happened. She hurried from the bed, went and bolted the door, and stood sobbing against it. Then she threw herself across the bed, knowing that she had been unsuccessful in securing a father for her child. Now what was she to do? Would he drive her from the house this very night, when he had composed himself?

She continued to weep, pounding her fists into the soft mattress, then grew silent when she heard the clatter of horses' hoofs and the squeaking of carriage wheels. Soon she realized that it was Francis's carriage, leaving the house.

Lenora rose and wrapped a robe about her nudity, then went to the window and pulled a corner of the shade back in time to see Francis sitting slouched over, lifting the reins to urge the horses onward.

"Where is he going, and in such a state?" she thought. Listening to the silence of the house, she wondered what his return would bring for her. Again tears began to wet her cheeks.

"Papa, oh, Papa," she sobbed. "What *am* I to do?"

Chapter Six

Having fallen into a fretful sleep, Lenora tossed and turned, seeing many different things in her dreams. It was as though she were reliving the past several months all over again. She was in the library of her home in Springfield listening to her Papa read her a story. . . . She was watching her Papa load the last of their personal belongings onto their wagon, experiencing the fear and excitement of the coming journey to California. . . . She was patting the dirt more firmly around her Papa's fresh grave . . . She was lying on the ground, experiencing a brief moment of bliss in James's arms. . . . And she was shoving the hideous Francis away from her.

She awakened with a start, hearing the familiar jingle of the bridle and clatter of iron wheels, and she knew that Francis had returned. How long had she been asleep? Was it moments or hours? Her hair had fallen from its careful design and lay in disarray around her face. She tensed, pulling the blanket up under her chin and eyeing the bolt that was in place on her door. In no way could he enter to approach her again with his twisted ways. She swallowed hard, feeling ill all over again, remembering her mouth so close to his. . . .

"No," she thought angrily. "I mustn't even think about it." Perhaps she should even flee, but where? It was quite dark and late. She had heard tales of women who walked the night streets of San Francisco, and she in no way wanted to be taken for one of them. No, she'd leave early in the morning, before Francis even awakened. But where would she go?

Lying still, she listened for approaching footsteps outside her door, but when none could be heard, she turned on her side, knowing she should rest. The next few nights might well be spent away from the softness of a bed. Tears trickled down her cheeks. She was going to have to leave this house of windows after all. And what about her baby?

She lifted her gown and placed her hand on her abdomen, wondering just how large the baby now was inside her womb. She knew nothing of having babies. Her Mama had never told her much about those things. When Lenora's monthly period had started, she had not even been forewarned. When the red spots had first appeared on her undergarments, she had thought she was dying from some rare disease. How relieved she had been when she was told this was a normal occurrence for a woman, and that she would "weep" in red down there once a month until she was much, much older.

But there had been no mention of babies and how they came into the world. And shouldn't she know, especially now that she would possibly be alone when the time came for her own to be born?

Her eyes widened as she remembered the many books lining the shelves in Francis's parlor. Might there be something among these that could give her a clue—perhaps a novel that described a wife having a child? Yes, that's what she would do: go into the parlor and search through the books for several novels to bring back to her room. She would thumb through them, and maybe doing so would not only help her with her questions, but also make drowsiness creep over her so she could eventually fall asleep again.

Quietly, she threw the blanket aside and arose, not slipping on any shoes. Being silent was of the utmost importance, and walking barefoot on the hardwood floors would be the quietest way to go. She only hoped that Francis had gone on to his room and was fast asleep. In no way did she want to be near him again. And was she not taking a chance on this happening? But she scoffed at herself, remembering how easy it had been to shove him away from her. It seemed that her muscles had come in handy after all. Francis had seemed to have none himself. She suddenly felt no fear and flipped the bolt aside.

A gaslight was flickering dimly on the hallway wall across from her room, as well as one that Lenora could see at the head of the staircase. She paused to listen, knowing that opposite the wall where the gaslight glowed was Francis's room. When no sound came, she began to tiptoe toward the parlor, then stopped suddenly when she heard the floor of the room above her squeak. And was that a soft moan she had heard? She stiffened and listened again. There was a rustling of feet and another sound, a groaning of sorts.

Lenora put her hands to her mouth. Was Francis ill? Did he need help? Her heart skipped a few beats and she stood still, not knowing what to do. Should she see if he needed assistance? He had at least been kind enough to bring her into his home when she had had nowhere else to go.

With no further thoughts of disgust or fear of Francis, Lenora rushed up the stairs. She stopped outside his door, noticing that it was already partially ajar. Another moan came from inside the room, making the hair stand on end at the nape of Lenora's neck. She suddenly recalled the familiarity of this moan. She had heard it when Francis had been riding above her, trying to achieve pleasure from her body.

One step closer to the opened door, and Lenora felt faint. She could now see inside the room, and what was being displayed before her eyes, beneath the dim gold flicker of the gaslights, was a man kneeling beside the bed. He was a dark, olive-skinned person with sleek, round muscles in his shoulders and buttocks. His hair hung in a dark, wiry mass around his shoulders. And he was completely nude.

Lenora was frozen to the spot, not believing what she was seeing. Francis was sitting on the edge of the bed, also naked, and what was this stranger, this dark man, doing?

She remembered what Francis had tried to get her to do and felt nausea rising. She knew that this was what the stranger was now doing for him. But why? It was sick.

Then her eyes widened in fear as this stranger momentarily pulled away from Francis and swung his head around to capture her standing there. But he did not speak; he continued to watch her with the darkest of eyes, smiling at her, revealing straight, white teeth that appeared even more white against the darkness of his skin.

Covering her mouth to keep a cry down inside her throat, Lenora turned and fled down the stairs to the safety of her room, locking the door behind her. She looked desperately around her. She had to get away, now! What if this stranger should tell Francis that she had seen them? This man was young and muscular, in no way, shape, or form anything like Francis. He could indeed force himself upon her, and she would be defenseless against him. And what if both decided to take advantage of her at the same time?

Nervous perspiration slid from her forehead as she hurried around the room, grabbing and shoving all that she could into her travel bag. Tears mingled with the perspiration. Her thoughts returned to Francis. He was sick, filthy sick, in a way that no one could help him.

She shuddered, remembering Francis's mouth on hers. Oh, how could she have been so blind? Why had she not realized earlier that he didn't desire women? If she had been living that long beneath any other man's roof, would he not have tried to take advantage of her earlier? She set her jaw firmly. She was fast learning the ways of life away from her Papa, and what a bleak lesson it was.

She chose the heaviest cotton dress in her possession to wear out into the fog-laden, damp night of San Francisco, and with a quick toss of her shawl around her shoulders she was ready to leave. She trembled inwardly as she slipped the bolt aside. Opening the door, she stepped cautiously out into the hallway, and finding no one waiting to seize her, she rushed through the kitchen, out the back door, and into the darkness of night, clutching once again a filled travel bag.

With one more backward glance at the house, she felt an emptiness at the pit of her stomach, then began her descent down the steep hill.

With her heart pumping nervously against her chest, she made her way, seeing shadows on all sides of her, not knowing if these were being made by some lurking evil or by a tree's limbs shimmering in the breeze above her.

The dampness seemed to cling to her like a thousand fingers groping, and each flickering streetlight was welcome, though only a haze was recognizable, with rainbows circling each one.

The low moan of a foghorn lifted from the bay, sounding very close. Lenora knew that somewhere below her was the waterfront and all the meanness that one might fear in the night. Tears stung the corners of her eyes, and she stood in the street not knowing where to go. The houses on all sides of her were bathed in total darkness. Where might she find refuge at such an hour?

Footsteps approaching her from behind made Lenora grip her travel bag more securely, feeling the comfort of her Papa's pearl-handled pistol inside it. Should she even take it out at this moment? Might she have to defend herself presently from some unknown attacker?

The footsteps grew close. Lenora hurried to stand beneath a streetlight. Surely no man would take advantage of her while in full view of the world. She stood trembling, hoping whoever it might be would pass her by and leave her be.

"What's this?" a deep, rumbling voice intoned. "A beautiful waif?"

Lenora moved to support her back against the lamppost, waiting for the stranger to make himself known to her. And when he did, she threw her hand to her throat, recognizing this man to be the one whom she had seen only the previous day—the man whom she had from a distance taken to be James. "You!" she gasped, seeing once again the sandy-colored, tousled hair and face scars.

"Well, I'll be a mule's ass. If it ain't the faintin' lady," he said, moving his face within an inch of hers. She caught a faint, manly smell of dried perspiration and chewing tobacco. "You ain't about to crumble at my feet again, are you, Ma'am?" he chuckled, spitting a rounded gob of brown at Lenora's feet.

Recoiling, she gripped the lamppost behind her with one hand. She did not like the mockery in his narrow, dark eyes. And was he mentally undressing her as his gaze covered every inch of her? She pulled the shawl around her in an effort to hide the heaving of her bosom. She could not let him know that she was afraid.

He ran his gloved hands through his hair, standing a bit stooped, partially disguising the six feet, five inches of his height. "So you're a quiet one, huh?" he observed, spitting again. "Those are the best kind." He chuckled again. She was perfect. He had to get her on board the *Madrona*. The men in Seattle would go wild over her. Look at those wide, scared eyes—and the size of those breasts.

"The best kind for what?" she finally said. She knew she had to carry on a conversation with this gentleman to show that she was a person capable of fending for herself. Then maybe he would be on his way. He did not really appear to be much of a threat to her. At least he was not trying to touch her. Looking was one thing—touching was another.

He pulled a pencil and tablet from his coat pocket. "See here?" he said, opening the tablet.

"See what?" she asked, tilting her head so that she could see. All she could make out was a list of what looked like women's names penciled on the pages in a row.

"This here is a list of unmarried women already on board a steamer, waitin' to be taken up north to Seattle, where men are a waitin' to marry up with them."

Lenora's heart began to race. She now remembered the posted sign that she had read this very evening. Hope began to rise inside her. "And what have *you* to do with all this, Sir?" she asked.

"I've been hired by these men to fetch the most beautiful women I could find. And you, if I may speak plainly, are the most beautiful I've yet to run across in San Francisco."

Lenora cast her eyes downward, knowing that a blush had colored her cheeks.

"You do look like you're a runnin' from somethin' or somebody," he said, thumping the pencil nervously against the tablet. "Maybe

119

we could be of service to one another. You could help me by addin' a bit of luster to my load of women, and I could help you by protectin' you from what you might be a runnin' from."

Glancing up the hill whence she had just come, she wondered if the dark-skinned man had told Francis about her spying on them? And if so, would she be safe?

Then she glanced downward at her abdomen. Had she not at first considered taking that boat ride to Seattle, to search out a father for her child? Her eyes shot upward. She set her jaw firmly. "My name's Lenora Marie Adamson," she said, releasing the lamppost and extending her right hand. "I'd love to go aboard with you."

"Raef Wescott at your service, Ma'am," he said, chuckling deeply. He spat sideways, then extended his left hand to clasp onto hers. The softness of the glove's leather brought tears to Lenora's eyes, for it so reminded her of James and the softness of his gloved handshake on their first meeting.

"Where is this boat?" Lenora asked, smoothing the skirt of her dress with her now freed hand. A new type of excitement was surging through her. She had read of many adventures on the sea, but had never thought it possible that she might become a sea traveler herself.

"Come with me to Dancer's Landing," he said, guiding her by the elbow down the steeply sloping street. "I was just on my way to board the ship. I thought I had reached my quota of women until I spied you; then I knew I could make room for one more."

"Please, Sir," she panted. "Your walk is much too brisk for me."

He laughed sardonically. "My apologies, Ma'am," he said, slowing his pace. "My long legs and these steep hills can get me goin' at a pretty damn fast clip."

She glanced sideways at him and smiled weakly. It seemed that again she was putting her trust in a man she did not know. But he seemed courteous enough and was dressed in a fashionable enough manner. His dark-colored jacket stretched snugly across wide shoulders, and his tan breeches clung to his thickly muscled legs. He wore no hat and carried no gun that she could see. His boots echoed through the night as they made their way down the cobblestone street.

If not for his pitted face, Lenora thought, he would be most handsome, with a long, straight nose and prominent cheekbones. Yet, there was mockery in his dark, narrow eyes whenever their gazes met.

"Not too much further now, Ma'am," he said, steering her around an occasional pile of horse dung.

The smell of salt air had suddenly become more prominent and the breeze more challenging, blowing Lenora's hair forward like a red banner around her face. In the darkened alleys, between the three-storied brick buildings, she could hear an occasional breaking of glass or hoarse cough, and she knew that somewhere lurking in that darkness was some homeless creature, taking refuge where he could find it.

A scream escaped from Lenora's throat when a rat raced in front of her and darted down another alley.

"Hey, Ma'am, nothin' to be afraid of," Raef said. "Ol' Raef's here. I'll protect you."

"I'm sure of it," Lenora said, sighing heavily.

The farther they walked, the more pronounced the sea noises became. Lenora could hear the creak of the timber of moored boats, the steady swooshing of the water constantly plying itself against the boats and shoreline, and an occasional foghorn, making shivers run down her spine. She did not believe anything else could sound so lonely as a foghorn. And she felt her own loneliness all the more, she knew, realizing that to leave San Francisco was also to leave James forever. If she had stayed, could she eventually have found him?

"Take a step up, Lenora," Raef said, helping her. "This is it. We're about to board the *Madrona*—best damn steamer that ever traveled from San Francisco to Seattle."

Lenora looked up and could make out only a small portion of this boat she was being led onto. She could just barely see the rounded smokestack looming up from the deck, next to the pilot house, but the darkness and the fog kept her eyes from seeing much more of what she could tell was a huge ship.

The floor squeaked beneath her feet as Lenora was guided on deck. She looked from side to side. Everywhere she looked, she could see people stretched out, sleeping on bunks that had been set up along the deck. Doubts assailed her. There seemed to be no room left. Where would *she* be made to sleep?

"Come this way," Raef said, steering her through the crowded deck.

"Where are we going?" she whispered.

"To my own quarters," he answered. "You'll be more comfortable there. As I told you, I had my quota of women already met before I found you."

Lenora began to stiffen. "You plan for me to stay in your quarters—with you?" she mumbled.

He laughed raucously. "No, my dear," he said. "I can work somethin' out with the captain. He and I have become the best of friends."

"But, I'd hate to take your facilities."

He stopped, pulling her to a halt also. "Take a look around you," he said, gesturing with his left hand. "Is this the way you want to spend your many days at sea?"

Lenora reassessed the situation. She got a strong odor of animals from somewhere on the crowded deck. The stench was so strong, it burned the insides of her nose. She lowered her eyes. "No. It doesn't appear to be too pleasant," she admitted, wondering what motive might be behind his singling her out from all those he had chosen to bring aboard. But she would deal with that problem if and when it became necessary.

Raef spat onto the deck. "Well, then come with me," he said.

"When will the vessel be leaving shore?"

"Daybreak."

"Oh, I see," she murmured. She wished that it could be sooner. What if Francis came looking for her? Would he think to search this steamer for her? No, she thought not. What had he to fear from *her*—unless it might be his worry of her telling what she saw. Could that not destroy his image in the city?

Raef opened a door leading into a small cabin next to another cabin that Lenora thought must be the captain's quarters. He stooped over and guided her inside after him. She stood in total darkness until he lighted a whale oil lamp that was attached to a roughly textured wall that appeared to have never been painted.

Looking around her Lenora saw one small, yellow-stained porthole, a bunk beneath it, a built-in bureau on the opposite wall, and a low, square table attached to the wall next to the door, with a chamber pot visible beneath it.

"It's not the San Francisco Ritz Hotel," he chuckled, "but it should make the trip more pleasant for you than for those out on the open deck."

Lenora placed her travel bag on the bunk, which did not appear to be very soft. But the ache in her thighs and lower back made her realize that any sort of bed was a welcome sight. It had already been a long night—a night full of anxieties and fear. She stretched her arms above her head and yawned.

"I see you're in need of some shut-eye," Raef said, swinging the door open. "I'll leave you now. The departin' whistle in the mornin' will be a warnin' that the steamer is leavin' shore." He laughed. "You won't miss it. It'll probably jerk you right out of your bunk."

"I sure do appreciate your help, Sir," Lenora said, afraid to move toward him. He still had a way of moving his gaze over her as he talked.

He stuck his head out the door and spat, then wiped some loose, brown-colored spittle from his mouth as he looked back in her direction. "Ain't nothin', Woman. Glad to be of service." He hated like hell to leave her. He knew that she could be capable of warming a body. Damn, he'd never seen such a healthy looking specimen of a woman. He was especially drawn to the color of her hair. Now, as the light flickered in shadowed reds across it, it shone with a sleek brilliance. He wondered if she had a temper to match—or a fiery way of making love. And he'd find out later, no doubt about that. The journey ahead offered days and nights filled with such opportunities. He gave her another quick appraisal, then leaned down and walked out onto the deck.

Glad finally to be alone, Lenora hurried to the door and shut it. She searched with trembling fingers for a lock but found none. There was not even a chair or loose piece of furniture to brace against it. She eyed the bunk. Would she feel safe to close her eyes? Would he enter and take advantage of her one of these long nights stretched out before her? She had not thought to ask how *many* nights, but what did it matter? Maybe at the end of the trip, in this city called Seattle, she would find a father for her unborn child.

Not bothering to undress, she moved her travel bag to the floor and stretched out on the bunk beneath a scratchy brown blanket that smelled of fish and mildew as the whole ship seemed to do. The smell combined with the rocking of the ship made her feel a bit queasy, but she pulled her diary from her bag nevertheless, needing to enter the latest secrets of her heart. Before she had even finished re-reading the previous entry, however, she fell asleep, dreaming sadly of James, knowing that surely now she would never see him again.

Chapter Seven

The swells of the ocean rose out of the west like shadowy ghosts, continually moving toward the ship, attacking it over and over again, causing it to plunge and roll perilously.

Lenora had spent the day confined to her quarters with her chamber pot close at hand. It had been the same the past several days and nights. The nausea had not left her except for brief hours of needed, forced sleep.

The tapping on the door of her small cabin made her grow tense. She knew it to be Raef; not one day had passed without his looking in on her. Even when he had brought her food, she had looked away from him, wishing he would leave her to her own miseries.

"Lenora?" she heard him say between persistent tappings. "Are you awake?"

Lenora pushed herself up from the bunk, swaying with the motion of the ship. She pressed her fingers into her temples, feeling the throbbing sensation beginning all over again. She shut her eyes and clenched her teeth.

"What is it?" she said, the words barely audible.

"Open up," Raef said. "A walk on deck might do you good. The wind is letting up and the waters will soon be calm. Fresh air might help to settle your stomach and clear your head."

Lenora turned to look out the porthole above her bunk but could only see a hazy, brownish green blur. She looked beneath the bunk and saw that the chamber pot was staying in place, so she deducted that the seas were calmer.

With trembling fingers, she tried to coil her hair up away from her face and hastily secure it with pins. She ran her tongue over her parched lips, then inched her way toward the door, opening it slowly.

"Yes?" she said, peering out.

Raef squared his shoulders and thrust his hands into the rear pockets of his tan breeches. "Like I said, might do you some good to leave your quarters—breathe some fresh air for a change," he said, giving her a fast wink, then spitting a mouthful of chewing tobacco sideways.

"You're very kind," Lenora said, smiling weakly. She still had not understood his reasons for having singled her out for such considerations, but oh, how glad she was that he had chosen to do so. One look at the clutter of the crowded deck, and she felt certain that she would never have been able to survive such a trip if she had had to live in such discomfort. And her child—how lucky for him, also. Yes, she had begun to refer to her baby with the masculine pronoun. He would be named after her father. Surely her father would have been proud in spite of himself.

"Step on out here," Raef said, offering her his arm.

"Oh, very well," Lenora said, laughing nervously. She clung to his arm weakly as they began to move through the hustle and bustle on the deck. She sighed deeply. It was good to be out of that crude cabin. Claustrophobia had begun to plague her there, as being confined evenings to her small room in Francis's house had done. Francis—she wondered what he had thought when he had discovered her absence.

A spray of sea water splashed onto her face, making her realize the sea was not so calm as she had thought it to be. Derelict coffeepots and pans rolled across the wet floor, but even so a group of women were frying fish on oil-burning stoves in the center of the main deck. The fresh air from the sea was quickly overpowered by the grease and the smell of raw and cooking salmon.

"Is this what we've been eating each evening?" she whispered to Raef, leaning toward him. Now she understood at least one reason for her nausea. She had not been able to tolerate seafood of any kind since becoming pregnant.

"Do you mean to tell me you didn't realize what I'd brought you?" he laughed. "You're a damn funny lady. First you faint the first day we meet, and on this trip all you do is puke up your guts. Now, to beat it all, you tell me you don't recognize fish when you taste it."

Lenora pulled her arm from his and set her jaw firmly. "How could anyone recognize *any* taste when it's saturated in pure lard," she snapped, walking past him. She studied the people around her, especially the women, wondering which of these many were also going to Seattle to seek a husband.

Some looked no older than she, though less hearty, with sad, large eyes watching her from where they sat crowded on the deck. Then there were those who were talking loudly, standing in groups, even using swear words as they watched her also, but with wicked, narrow eyes. Many had brightly painted faces and were attired in bright-colored, ruffled dresses with revealing necklines.

Lenora's own eyes widened when she recognized two faces in this crowd of women. They were the two women who had been standing behind her reading the poster the day Lenora had seen it. Even at that time they had been discussing this trip. Lenora tensed when the more buxom of the two stepped toward her with hands on hips.

"Whore," the woman hissed, thrusting her neck out like a hawk ready to attack. "Too good to live like us common folk, huh? Gave the fella what he wanted to get his comfy cabin, huh? Well, dearie, here's what us other girls think of *you*." She puckered up her lips and spat upon Lenora, then walked away laughing.

Horrified, Lenora rushed away from the women, gagging at the string of spittle hanging in loose shreds on her cotton dress. The ship lurched, throwing her against the railing. She caught the rail with one hand as sobs began to escape her throat. She had never been so humiliated, so ill-treated. To be spat upon? Why, Lenora would not even think of doing that to an insect, much less a human being. And in some ways worse, the implication that she and Raef. . . . However, though the thought sickened her, she realized that it must appear to be that way. And wouldn't he eventually? Was that why he had given her his cabin?

"Damn shrew," Raef growled as he stepped to her side. "I'll take care of that fat wench when we reach Seattle. No man'll ever want to touch 'er when I get through with 'er."

Lenora swallowed hard, looking up into his dark, narrow eyes. She could see a brutality in their depths and began to be afraid of him. He had only been nice to her, she felt, for some cruel reason of his own. "What do you mean?" she asked, wiping some damp locks of hair from her face. "What do you plan to do to her?"

He laughed hoarsely. "Whatever I do will be deserved," he said coolly. "Women should know their place, and that one seems never to have been taught. Leastways, not by the right man."

Another spray of sea water wet Lenora's arms and face. "But shouldn't you let the man who chooses to marry her worry about that?"

The scars of Raef's face deepened as he doubled over in a fit of laughter. "Marry?" he boomed. "Did you say marry?"

Lenora stiffened. "Yes. That *is* the reason we women are going to Seattle," she said, then felt prickles of fear riding up and down her spine. "It *is* the reason you've brought us aboard this ship, isn't it?"

Raef composed himself and spat some chewing tobacco over the rail and into the sea. He bent over and rested himself against the rail, looking into the water and not at Lenora. She was a smart one, all right. He had better be more careful. He did not need any more of her damn questions—there were too many legitimate people aboard this ship who would throw him overboard if they knew what he was about.

"Yeah, marriage," he murmured, glancing quickly in her direction. "What other reason could there be?" God, she was lovely, even unkempt as she had become on this trip. Her full, pouting lips could do him such a service! And they would, soon.

"For a moment there, I was wondering if you mightn't have something else in mind for us,

Sir," she said stiffly, tilting her chin up into the air and trying to act as though she had not seen that familiar lustful glint in his eyes. But he would not touch her. She would never allow it—even though he had been so kind to her. "Tell me more about Seattle," she said hurriedly, wanting to avert his thoughts.

Raef spat again and wiped his mouth with the back of his hand. "Some call it a paradise," he said, "and some call it hell."

Lenora swallowed hard. "And why would anyone call it hell?" She clung to the ship's rail, her eyes wide.

He moved closer to her side and spoke into the wind. "There's renegade Indians wanderin' the streets, all hours of the day and night," he snickered. "And wild dogs that'd tear the flesh right from your bones." It amused him to see the fear in her eyes. And when he reached Seattle, he would have the job of putting fear into *all* these women.

"Really?" Lenora gasped, putting a hand to her throat. "Then why do people want to go there? Just look at this ship. It's so crowded, and with Seattle as the only destination."

"It's a new city carved out of the primeval forest, with its feet dipping into the waters of Puget Sound. Many a man and woman are ready to try their luck in a new city. The women and married-up men go to find a new home, and some men go just for adventure, to make a quick fortune. There's been rumors of gold."

"The Indians are really not a threat, then?" She questioned further. "Nor are the wild dogs?"

"Not if'n you stay off the streets and keep your doors locked."

Lenora lowered her eyes and blinked nervously. "I wish I was back in Springfield," she murmured.

"Eh?" Raef said, spitting again.

"Springfield, Illinois. That's where I was born and raised."

"That right?" he said. "Knew a couple of fellas from Illinois once. One had been kicked out West by his ma and pa in hopes he might grow up a little. And the other, he went to Seattle to make a quick fortune and ended up bein' a remittance man."

"What's a remittance man?" Lenora asked, looking up into his eyes.

Raef laughed. "He lived on the monthly check received from folks back East."

"How lazy," Lenora said. "What about these men on board?" she asked, looking around her. The men sat in small clusters, gambling and smoking.

"Ah, some are hopin' to discover that gold I spoke of, like so many men did in California."

"And you?" Lenora asked, watching him closely.

"I've got my job, haulin' women such as yourself."

"You've done this before?"

"Hell, yes, many times."

"And a woman always finds a husband?"

Raef laughed sardonically. "Always," he said. "Always."

Lenora flinched as he slipped his arm around her waist.

"And you?" he said into her ear. "What kind of man heats your insides?"

Lenora tried to pull free of him. She knew that her face was becoming flushed. "What?" she gasped.

His left gloved hand brushed knowingly against her breasts. "What kind of man sets your heart a racin'? Maybe a man like me?"

Lenora turned to walk away without answering, but he stopped her by stepping in front of her, then wrapped both arms around her waist and jerked her to him roughly.

"Please take your hands off me," she said flatly, hoping to hide the tremor in her voice. She knew that if he chose to force himself on her, she was helpless. She did not know anyone on board to turn to for assistance.

"Now, you know you'd like to have a bit of fun. The trip's so borin' without some fun."

"I don't need *your* kind of fun," she hissed, struggling against his hold.

His lips lowered to hers, crushing them; then he eyed her amusedly. "Cain't say that didn't light your fire, can you?" he chuckled.

"Indeed I can." She wiped her lips with the back of her hand. "Let me go," she said, struggling to get free. She looked up into his ravaged face. "If you don't, I'll add a few scars to

135

your face," she added, trying her best to sound menacing.

He threw his head back and laughed boisterously. "You'd what?" he said, then eyed her more cynically. "It'd be fun watchin' you try," he added, tightening his hold.

Lenora looked quickly around her. She knew the other passengers must be watching them. Would they even think she was enjoying such flirtations? If so, she would change that quickly enough. She lifted a foot and brought the heel of her shoe down onto the toe of his, making him release her and lunge backward in pain.

"Now, *Sir*," she said in a huff. "Please keep your hands off me, do you hear?"

Her heart raced when she heard loud, boisterous guffaws bursting from the ship's crew, a cluster of gamblers, and the women. Lenora's face turned crimson as she realized they all *had* been watching. She lifted the skirt of her dress up into her arms and hurriedly made her way back to the cabin. Inside, she leaned heavily against the door, still hearing Raef's loud swearing behind her. *Now* what was she to do? She had learned to expect the worst from Raef.

"Open the door, Woman," Raef said suddenly from the other side of the closed door.

Lenora stood panting, looking wildly around her. There was nothing to defend herself with except. . . . Her gaze settled on her travel bag— her Papa's gun. Should she? Could she? But she had no chance to think any further about it. The door burst open, throwing her roughly across the room and onto the bunk. She lay there, stunned, sprawled like a fallen doll, as he slammed the door shut behind him.

"No woman gets away with that," he growled, removing a belt from his breeches. "*No* woman—not even you, beautiful as you are."

She shut her eyes as his hand reached up and then down, swinging the belt toward her in loud snaps. She flinched, waiting to feel the blow upon her body, but felt nothing but a slight breeze as it went past her. Then the belt was still for a moment, and she slowly opened her eyes, frightened even more now by the way Raef was laughing. It was an evil, menacing laugh. And he had undressed to his waist.

"No, Raef, please," she said, cowering against the wall behind her, but he was now unbuttoning his breeches and lowering them to lie in a heap on the floor around his feet.

"You should be punished, not made love to," he growled, now completely nude. "But I've waited too long already for the feel of that body against mine. I'm not goin' to mar it, even by givin' you a deserved whippin'."

"You can't do this," Lenora whispered, watching, with horror, his powerful, visibly aroused body moving closer to her. It had excited her to see James this way, but it only frightened her to see Raef. She knew that this would be rape. She in no way wanted to participate.

"We'll see what I can and can't do," he sneered, pulling her up to stand in front of him. When he crushed her body to his, she closed her eyes and turned her head away, not wanting his lips upon hers.

"Come on, you little wench," he snarled, forcing her head around.

She let out a soft scream when his lips met hers in a brutal fashion, making his teeth cut into her lower lip. She tried to fight against him as his fingers found the buttons of her dress and began to work with them.

"Please, *don't*," she insisted, finally able to free her lips.

"Want to be sent out on deck with the rest of the women? Is that what you want? And do you know, some of 'em haven't had one meal yet on this trip? Seems I've brought too many aboard this time. Want to go starvin' the rest of the trip? Huh?"

Guilt surged through Lenora as she remembered having been told earlier that he had reached his quota of women before finding her. Had *she* been the cause of some poor woman's going hungry? She cast her eyes down, feeling the burning tears trying to surface. She did feel shame, yet she did have her child to think about. She had to eat what she could manage to hold down, for her child. And, no, she did not think she would survive if he turned her away from this cabin. She let her limbs go limp, deciding to let him have his way with her. She had no other choice.

"Well, that's more like it," he said, managing to undress her completely.

Lenora felt her cheeks flaming as he stood back and admired her nudity. She knew that her breasts had already begun to fill out more because of her pregnancy, and she could feel the weight of them against her body. When his gloved left hand reached out to touch one, she flinched, letting out a soft gasp.

"Don't like my gloves, huh?" he said, stopping to remove them.

Lenora's eyes widened. His hands were mangled grotesquely—even more scarred than his face. But the rest of his body was smooth and taut.

He placed his hands before her eyes, forcing her to look more closely. "Ugly, huh?" he sneered. "Don't want me to touch you with 'em, huh?"

Lenora gulped hard and backed away from him. The smell of his perspiration and stale tobacco now penetrated the mildew odors in the room. She did not want to gag. She did not want to anger him further.

"My hands and face were burned, years ago, when I tried to rescue my Ma from her burnin' house," he said, backing off somewhat.

"Your mama?"

"She died, though," he said, his voice growing hard. "Some son-of-a-bitch was careless with a cigar in a room he was rentin' from my Ma. Burned the whole damn house down."

"I'm sorry," Lenora said quietly.

"That was a long time ago, Lenora," he said. "Since, I've learned to take care of myself. Was only ten when it happened."

"How horrible."

"But all these words are getting in the way of the subject at hand," he said, reaching to fondle her breasts with ungloved hands. "You don't mind my scars, now do you? My hands can excite you, if given a chance."

His hands cupped each breast and his thumbs pressed hard against the nipples. Then he forced her downward, onto the bunk.

Lenora closed her eyes and chewed on her lower lip, wanting to feel revulsion as she had done with Francis, but Raef's hands *were* exciting her. She didn't know if it was from the weakness of having not been well, or from the weakness of being a woman— a woman with the same needs as a man. She wanted to fight him, to move from his touch. Hadn't she wanted to claw him and add more scars to his face? But he seemed to have put her in a spell. Why was she so weak? All she could now feel was a building urgency inside her that she knew only one thing could quell.

"Beautiful Lenora," he said thickly as he lowered himself over her. "You do want me, don't you?" His hands moved along her body, not leaving any part of her untouched. His flesh was warm against hers and even somehow comforting.

"I feel your heartbeat," he said, now tracing her body with his lips. "You *are* enjoying this. You can't deny it."

When his mouth covered her breast, Lenora felt a sweeping warmth rush upward from her thighs, and she felt herself being supported like a swimmer on a surface of serene peacefulness. Though his hands were scarred, they traveled smoothly over her body and brought a sweet shudder to her flesh. Even now she leaned into them as they moved downward, synchronized it seemed, like feathers, tickling, arousing her, awakening a passion in her even more successfully than James had done. But her conscience was also awakening, and she felt a shame and self-loathing greater than any James had caused.

"I really mustn't let you, Raef," she said, pushing his body away. But a thousand heartbeats inside herself won over her brief moment of doubt when his lips fastened upon hers, quieting her pleas. She now knew that she was beyond saving. The building urgency inside her had taken control and was guiding her, even toward such a man as Raef.

"I've needed the taste of your lips from the very moment I saw you," he whispered, drawing away from her to rearrange his body over hers.

Lenora gasped with pleasure as she finally felt the hardness of him pulsating against her thighs. Without further doubts, she let his knee part her legs and felt a spinning in her head as he entered her fiercely.

His breathing began to come in short pants as he worked his body in and out of hers. She shut her eyes and arched her body upward, surrendering completely to him now, trembling as his fingers searched beneath her and began to dig into the fleshiness of her hips.

"Ride me, Woman," he groaned. "Make me soar."

She wrapped her arms and legs around his body and began to kiss his neck and in one breath spoke the word "James," as the most pleasurable of sensations washed like warm waves over her body, making her lose sight of who she was and whose body was now releasing torrents of liquid inside her. Only when Raef lay spent, breathing heavily next to her, did Lenora truly realize what she had let happen. She had let herself enjoy the touch—the manipulations—of a man for whom she should have felt only the strongest aversion. She turned her head away from him in disgust. How *could* she have? Sobs tore through her body.

"Hey! What's this?" Raef said, touching her gently on the shoulder. "Why the tears? You enjoyed it as much as I did. There's no reason to cry about somethin' that felt so good, now is there?"

"Please leave," Lenora sobbed. She pulled her body into a fetal position, covering her eyes with her fists.

"I will be back," he said, rising from the bunk. "Now that I've tasted you, I'm going to want more, much more."

Lenora's eyes opened widely, staring blankly at the wall. How many more days and nights would she have to endure of this journey? She knew that she would have to welcome him into her cabin. Shame made her feel ill, for she realized that she did not dread his further advances. In fact, she would welcome them. But wasn't she a—what the woman had called her, a whore— for feeling such lust for a man?

When he patted her familiarly on a hip, she trembled inwardly.

"Tonight, I plan to bunk with you, Lenora. No more nights in the captain's quarters for me," he said, then dressed and left her to lie alone listening to the crash of the water against the side of the ship and the rumble of the boilers below her.

"Papa, oh Papa, I just don't understand any of this," she cried, pulling the scratchy wool blanket over her to hide her defiled body.

PART TWO

SEATTLE

Chapter Eight

The monotony of the men singing "Three Blind Mice" over and over again drove Lenora from her cabin. She felt as though she might scream if she were to hear one more round of this song. The men had been singing this particular song for what seemed to her hours upon hours.

She stepped out onto the deck, her eyes searching out the culprits. Hadn't they anything better to do?

Her gaze settled on a group of bearded, dirty-clothed men squatting next to the captain's cabin, gambling. That was all they had been doing for days—singing and gambling. She clenched her fists, forcing herself not to yell in rage at them.

"Among the livin' again, I see," Raef said,

hurrying to her side. He was dressed differently this day, with a slouch hat covering his tawny hair, a heavy red flannel shirt, and loose gray serge trousers tucked into cowhide boots. Lenora even thought him to be handsome with the fresh growth of reddish brown beard hiding the scars on his face.

"You are feelin' better?" Raef inquired, leaning down to her so he would not have to shout above the sea noises and the singing of the men.

Putting her hand to her stomach, Lenora smiled weakly. "Yes, somewhat," she answered. The sudden onslaught of dysentery had begun to plague all aboard this ship and had not spared Lenora. Her cotton dress hung a bit more loosely around her waist, and her mouth still tasted of the bitters that had been administered by Doctor Preston, also on his way to this new city. The young doctor's excitement about the service he would perform for the community of Seattle had shown in the depths of his blue eyes.

Being so ill, Lenora had not shared his excitement. She had not even felt like trading words with him. She had not told him she was with child and in search of a husband for it. She was reluctant to confide in anyone for fear that the word might reach Raef's ears. Then he would surely cast her aside as one not fit to be given away for wedlock.

"Damn poor timin', is all I can say," Raef growled. He spat into the wind, spraying chewing tobacco in all directions. "I hadn't planned to sleep in the company of the captain these past nights, you know."

Lenora lowered her eyes, remembering their one time together. Shame rushed through her as she recalled how much she had enjoyed it in spite of herself. But the sudden new illness had put a stop to any further lovemaking, and she had been glad. She had not liked being put in a position where her weaknesses took over her mind. And she knew now that making love did not necessarily mean the man would marry her. James had taught her this cruel lesson.

She began to walk away from Raef, noticing some sudden commotion along the ship's rail.

"Land'll soon be in view, like a dewdrop on the horizon, Lenora," Raef said, resuming his vigil at her side and walking with her, step for step.

"Do you mean our trip is about to come to an end?" she said. She hurried to the rail and clung to it.

"Soon, very soon. And meantime, we can watch Seattle growing close. You'll see mountains that'll clean take your breath away. Just keep lookin' into the distance. Where you now see a foggy haze, you'll soon see the wonders of this northwest country."

"Oh, look," Lenora said, pointing across the water's surface, where dozens of porpoises were curving through the water in unison. "Aren't they beautiful?" she exclaimed. Then she spied a translucent jellyfish floating just below the surface.

"The closer we go inland, the more sealife you'll see. And with the water's bein' calm, you'll be able to enjoy it."

Anxiously, Lenora gripped the rail, watching the foggy haze swirling, then dividing, as the sun's rays began to stream through in yellow streamers to settle in glistening reflections in the water.

"Now watch closely," Raef commanded, pointing east.

"My goodness," Lenora gasped. "It *is* magnificent." Her eyes could not leave the great mountain. It rose in the east, with a white peak and streaks of blue-black ridges on its lower slopes. It was so splendid, she almost felt it was a mirage. Lenora thought it hauntingly beautiful, as clouds swirled around it like ghosts, restless and untamed.

"That's Mount Tacoma," Raef said, spitting across the rail. He gestured with his gloved left hand. "And to the west, Mount Olympus," he added.

Lenora's gaze went to the other mountain. It was less breathtaking, but also a wondrous sight rising very steeply out of the water. It was almost black with the firs and hemlocks that seemed to roll over its forested portions.

"It is lovely," she said, then turned again toward Mount Tacoma to admire the way its snow-clad summit rose into the thickening clouds. On her journey she had seen many mountains, but nothing could compare with the majestic serenity of this one. She shivered, thinking of the mountain's great age and how many civilizations of people must have gazed upon it. Had there been only Indians to witness this grandeur before the settling of Seattle?

A blur of rocks and bluffs suddenly appeared close, and Lenora's eyes widened when several seals bobbed up in the water before her, seeming to stare round-eyed back at her.

"Aren't they cute?" she squealed, having never seen such animals before. And as the ship passed these rocks, Lenora could make out giant starfish clinging to them.

Gulls constantly dipped down toward the ship, and even cranes could be seen flapping heavily into flight.

"This appears to be some sort of paradise," she sighed, erasing all fears of Indians and flesh-eating dogs from her mind. In Illinois she had never seen such breathtaking sights, nor even in California, and her heart raced with the anticipation of what else might lie before her ready to be seen and explored.

"And there she lies," Raef boomed, tilting his hat to scratch his forehead. "Seattle. Right straight ahead. The fog's liftin' has seemed to bring us here faster than I realized."

Lenora squinted her eyes. Yes, it was a city. Even though it was mid-August and usually sticky hot in Illinois, there was smoke swirling upward from the chimneys, mingling with the smoke of the steamers entering and leaving the harbor.

All aboard this ship grew silent as they watched Seattle coming into view. "It's much like San Francisco," Lenora said quietly to Raef. "The city clings to the sides of hills as steep as those in San Francisco. And look how these hills rise from the bay! You'd think everything would slide right down into the water."

Raef laughed hoarsely. "Mudslides have been known to be a problem. But I think there'll be no more of 'em, not since the streets were laid out and many buildings built. It's even lookin' good for the Northern Pacific Railroad to come through. Now, that'll make way for the population's growth."

The closer the ship came to docking, the more enraptured Lenora became. She inhaled deeply. The winds were not only sharp with saltwater, but sweet with the scent of red cedar. She looked anxiously up and down the shore, seeing a sawmill, a few wooden warehouses, and other unidentifiable buildings. "The waterfront isn't as busy as the one in San Francisco," she said, "and the houses aren't as colorful and nice."

"Nope, but what is lackin' in the town is made up for by the view, wouldn't you say?" he suggested, gesturing toward the mountain still in view in the distance.

Smiling, Lenora gazed again at the mountain and the blue-green mountainous shores. Seagulls and cranes still circling overhead seemed to be welcoming messengers from the paradise she was being carried to. "Yes, I imagine so," she said, but as the ship's engines began to slow, a creeping fear gripped Lenora. She would soon be introduced to a man whom she would be expected to marry. Could she really go through with it—could she marry a complete stranger? Could she ever find with him the closeness her Mama and Papa had shared?

"You'd best go to your cabin, Lenora," Raef said, turning to guide her by the elbow. "All hell'll soon break loose here when the ship docks—don't want you trampled."

"But what am I to do *there*?"

"Get your gear together and I'll fetch you soon."

"All right," she said, hurrying away from him. She rushed into the cabin, frowning, remembering her many days and nights confined to this small, smelly, unpleasant room. But she would soon be gone from it, and her only reminder of that time would be what she had written of it in her diary.

Hurrying, she reclasped her locket around her neck. After only one night at sea the salt in the air and the chain of her necklace had caused a reaction on her skin's surface. Even now, some traces of the red splotches remained around her neck.

As she packed her travel bag, she listened to the ship's noises, glad that they would soon be only a memory. Then she sat down on the bunk and waited, wondering if this meeting alone with Raef would end like the last one had. Her fingers trembled as she thought about it. She tried to busy them, working with her hair. She knew her hair was in need of being washed, but at least with it wound into a bun this fact was mostly hidden.

The clamoring of feet on deck had nearly ceased, making Lenora feel somehow lonely. Then the door swung open.

"Come along, Lenora," Raef said in a stern voice. His eyes were dark and narrow and spoke of business rather than pleasure.

"Are the rest of the women ready also?" she asked, rising and securing her travel bag in the crook of her left arm.

"All accounted for and waitin'."

Lenora walked out onto the deck and saw that everyone had gone except for about fifteen women. They all stood, quiet and wide-eyed, also clinging to their only personal belongings. Most appeared to be exhausted, doubtless having also suffered from dysentery.

Lenora's gaze darted from face to face, searching for the buxom lady who had spat upon her. But only this lady's friend who wore the brightly-flowered dress remained, standing with hands on hips, glaring back at Lenora.

"Raef, where is . . . ," Lenora began, but was stopped by Raef pushing her roughly amidst the others. Her heart began to pound; rough treatment was not what she had come to expect from him, after the gentle intimacy that had transpired between them. His eyes wavered when he glanced her way; then he spoke harshly.

"As you women know, we're ready to leave the ship to enter Seattle. Once on land, just follow along behind me. The men'll be waitin' for you in an establishment down by Kessler's Mill. It's not a long walk, but a pretty muddy one if'n you don't stay on the wooden planks that're laid down on the side of the road."

Again Lenora's eyes searched for the buxom lady, and she felt a warning of sorts in the back of her mind. Hadn't Raef said he would take care of her when they reached Seattle? What had he meant?

And, Lenora wondered, why was he acting as though he had never known *her*, after all they had shared on that intimate night together. So far her relationships with men had only left her with confusion. Would it always be this way for her? Her heart ached as she realized the probability.

Following along with the other women, Lenora was glad to be finally away from the ship. But Seattle was so unsettled—it appeared to be a city built only of wood. In one sweep of the eye, she could see rustic shacks that housed saloons, fish stores, a tannery, and a blacksmith shop, lining both sides of the street she and the other women were now being guided along.

And she soon ascertained that there was not as much activity on this waterfront as there was in San Francisco. Only a few men were hurrying to and from the three squat steamers moored nearby, and others were loafing in doorways. No women could be seen anywhere. It did seem to be a city in need of women.

The dampness in the air made Lenora shiver, but she could not secure her shawl to her shoulders. She had, instead, to lift the skirt of her dress, wanting to keep the mud away from its hem. She felt as though she might topple from the slanted boardwalk, the farther she walked. She tensed inside with such a thought, seeing the depths of the mud in which a team of oxen was trying to drag logs toward the mill that Lenora and the rest of the women were now approaching.

Lenora's brows furrowed as she looked around her. Though it had appeared from a distance to be a paradise, Seattle was anything but. She had grown used to seeing fancy carriages and streetcars in San Francisco. But only a few horses were plodding through these streets, and flies buzzed noisily around the open doors of the saloons.

Where the wooden planks sank more into the mud, slick brown bubbles oozed out from around the sides as the weight of the women pressed against them. A hand-painted sign on the large building before her drew Lenora's attention. "Kessler's Mill," she read. Then her gaze settled on the nearby building Raef had stopped in front of, waiting for the women to assemble. This building seemed to have been built on a fill of sawdust. Lenora choked on the smell: the sawdust, which lay all around in damp, brownish green masses, gave off an aroma like that of dead fish.

Lenora coughed and wiped her eyes, then studied this building more carefully. It was oblong and constructed of unpainted boards, and its windows overlooked the sound, in plain view of the ships entering the harbor. Men were moving to and from this establishment, some stopping to look at this group of women about to enter. Lenora searched the faces of these men, wondering if among them was the one she would marry.

Raef stepped aside. "Go on inside," he ordered above the loud music blaring from inside. "Sit down, and I'll instruct you further."

Lenora eyed him questioningly, watching for a hint of recognition, but he only looked away from her, spitting tobacco and tilting his hat back to return the gaze of the standing, gawking crowd of men.

Lenora shrugged and went inside after pausing momentarily to read the sign over the door. "The Illahee," she said softly, wondering if that was an Indian name and what it might mean.

She inched along with the rest of the women, peering through the smoke that circled in the air inside the large room they had just entered. She coughed and felt her eyes burning, wondering what kind of place this was, besides being apparently a saloon, and why Raef would bring a group of unwed women to such a place. No respectable woman would want to be seen here in the company of half-naked women, some of whom were standing beside gentlemen at a long bar and others swaying in a vulgar fashion in the middle of the large dance floor.

Then Lenora saw where the loud music was originating. There were three musicians at the far end of the room: a fiddler, a drummer, and an accordion player.

"Well, what do you think?" Raef suddenly boomed from behind Lenora. When she turned, she could see the mockery in his dark eyes, visible in spite of the dim lighting of the oil lamps that lined the walls on all sides. She flinched when he reached for her and heard his low, throaty laugh when he turned to the next woman and touched her familiarly on her heaving bosom.

"Where are the men who are supposed to become our husbands?" Lenora asked with a quavering voice. The only men present were the few standing at the bar, and they appeared to be lazy, drunken fools—not at all husband material. Lenora sensed something very wrong.

Raef tossed his hat from his head and laughed. "Husbands? What husbands?" he sneered.

Gasps arose from the women, except for several who had separated into a cluster and now resembled giggling flowers in their brightly colored, low-necked dresses. The others stood like wilting violets, waiting.

"What is this, Raef?" Lenora snapped, setting her jaw firmly. She could not let him see how afraid she had become. She had to remember the strong side of herself, even though she was with child. But when she looked squarely into his eyes, she swallowed hard, seeing again the cruelty in their depths. She now knew that he had only been nice to her for what he could get from her. How glad she was, now, that she had become ill with dysentery. It seemed as though, in that small way, the laugh was on him.

"All you women who were foolish enough to board the *Madrona* will go to work in this place," Raef sneered, gesturing with his left hand, then spitting onto the sawdust-covered floor.

"What do you mean—work?" Lenora asked. Her knees had gone weak, as well as her voice. Out of the corner of her eye she could see several of the other girls now clinging to one another.

"You're bought and paid for," Raef continued. "Some of you have already worked in such a— ah, would you say house—as this, and others ain't. Those who ain't'll learn fast." He went to the group of girls who were still giggling and flirting with Raef with their eyes. The only one of them who was not behaving so was the friend of the buxom lady who was still missing. She stood eyeing Raef darkly, with straight, narrow lips clamped together tightly.

Raef pulled one of these girls to him and tilted

her chin up with a gloved forefinger. "Seems I chose the wrong woman to bed down with in my cabin," he said. The girl's green eyes flashed up at him. Then she mashed her breasts against his chest as his lips brushed against hers.

Lenora looked frantically around her, thinking to escape. She considered the small group of girls who were still clinging to one another. Surely among them were others who would want to escape with Lenora. She did not want to be alone on these strange streets.

Raef suddenly appeared next to Lenora, as though he had read her thoughts. "There'll be none of you leavin' here. Like I said, you're bought and paid for, and I expect you to work it out."

One of the girls spoke. "Do you mean there are no men for wedlock as you advertised?"

Raef laughed boisterously. "Do you see any offerin' themselves to you?"

"But you said . . . ," another began, weeping noisily.

"In this life, you'll learn not to believe everything you're told. Take this as lesson number one."

"But, you're speaking of us as though we're slaves," another said.

"No kiddin'?" Raef laughed.

"Raef," Lenora said, as sharply as she could, for her courage had returned somewhat. "What is behind all this?"

He sat down and pulled the green-eyed girl down upon his lap. She clung to his neck possessively. Lenora's eyes widened when she saw this girl spread her legs so Raef's hand could reach up beneath the skirt of her dress.

"Like I said," he told Lenora, spitting sideways, "you're all to work here—even you, Beautiful. You were my best find on this trip to San Francisco. That's why I chose to see that nothin' happened to you on the trip. Bringin' you here will make me a heap of money. And you proved your worth in bed. Yep, you'll pull the customers in. They'll probably come from all over the country just to get a piece of that sweet little ass."

Lenora's face reddened, and her heart skipped a few beats. She now wished she *had* added scars to his face. "You can't hold us here against our will," she snapped. "You *won't* hold *me* here." She turned to leave, but stopped when she saw the door being blocked by a huge, dark-skinned Indian. She gulped hard and shrank away from him. He was at least six and one half feet tall, deep chested and broad shouldered and attired in deerskin pants, jacket, and moccasins. A blue feather was stuck into his long, single plait of glistening black hair.

Raef laughed. "Now, what was it you were saying, Lenora?"

"You're evil," she hissed. "You're the devil himself."

"No, I ain't evil. Just smart."

"I will run away the first chance I get," she said. "That Indian can't watch my every move. You'll see, I'll get away."

Raef eased the girl from his lap and went to the bar. He returned with a bottle of rye whiskey and a glass. "Anyone else who's thinkin' of escapin'? We have a special trap door waitin' for you out in the back room, once we've caught you."

"Trap door?" one other girl gasped.

"It'll drop ya right into the bay, where all the little fishies are a-waitin' to chew on ya."

Ice began to fill Lenora's veins. How could she ever have let him fool her—touch her? She put her hand to her throat, feeling quite ill. It all seemed so hopeless.

"And as for you, Lenora," he said. "I have another room for you and any other girl who's havin' a stubborn streak."

"Another room?" Lenora said weakly.

"With a lock on it. I'll leave you there a few days till you tame down a mite. And what other among you women feel the same as Lenora?"

A small, thin girl stepped forward. Her eyes were large and as dark as the hair that hung loosely around her shoulders. "What might it be, exactly, that you expect from us?" she asked, trembling outwardly.

"You *are* the innocent one, ain't you?" Raef answered, going to her. She flinched as his fingers explored the curves of her body. "All right, I'll explain it for you. First, you will dance with a fellow, and the fellow is expected to buy himself and you a drink after each dance. The bartender will substitute tea for whiskey in your glass but charge the fellow for whiskey. Then

162

when a man's tired of purely social intercourse, you will lead him down the hall to one of the rooms and show him what other kind of intercourse he can find here."

"Do you mean you'd expect us to . . . ?" the girl could not bring herself to finish.

"Show 'em your pussies?" Raef laughed. "Yep, and what they've been put on you for."

"Then I refuse also," the girl said stubbornly. "I only came here 'cause my Ma and Pa died on their way to California. I wanted to find a man to marry up with because I was alone. But I won't sell my body."

"Oh you won't, will you?" he mocked her. "Then make your choice between the trap door and the room with Lenora for a few days," Raef growled, bringing his face very close to hers with a menacing grin.

"No trap door, please," she pleaded.

"As you like, Ma'am," Raef said, sneering as he bowed from the waist. "Any more ready to complain?" he asked the group, walking in front of each girl and studying her closely. His answer was silence.

Lenora was watching closely the activity in the hallway at the far end of the room, next to where the musicians still sat, playing. The girls clinging to the men's arms were scantily attired in brightly colored costumes and had their faces painted to match. They did not appear to be uncomfortable in the role they were playing, and Lenora wondered if they had been forced into their jobs just as she and these women were being forced now. How, she wondered, could so many women be used in this one establishment? Were this many needed because something happened to some of them while here? And why weren't any of these men seeing what was happening to the newest group of women? Didn't they care about how the women came to be there?

Lenora felt an emptiness at the pit of her stomach as she continued to listen to Raef. She hated him. She only hoped that one day she could even the score with him. It would always be on her mind—some sort of vengeance.

"And now, my fair maidens, to your rooms to make yourselves presentable for the evenin's crowd of men," Raef said, banging his empty glass down on a table's battered surface. "Come along," he said, guiding them toward the long hallway. "But first, I must take care of Lenora and . . . what's the name, small one?" He swung the other young woman around to face him.

Her eyes lowered. "Tess," she murmured. "Tess Klein."

"Tess, my stubborn one, get to that room at the far end of the hall," Raef ordered, shoving Tess roughly ahead of him. "And you, too, Lenora."

Lenora straightened her back and followed, knowing that she had no choice but to obey. She was beginning to fear for her child. Even though she had found no father for "him," she still did not want to lose him. Having a child of her own meant never to be alone again.

"In there," Raef said, shoving first Tess and then Lenora into a dimly lighted room.

Lenora cringed when the door banged shut behind her, followed by the sound of the lock clicking into place.

"I'm so afraid," Tess said, sobbing.

Lenora placed her travel bag on a table beneath the one window in the room, then went to Tess and patted her on the shoulder. Then, when the girl collapsed into tears, Lenora pulled her into her arms.

"There, there," Lenora crooned. "It's going to be all right." She could feel the outline of bones beneath the loosely fitting cotton dress, and Lenora wondered if Tess was one of the women who had been deprived of food because of Lenora's presence on the ship. Hadn't Raef said as much?

"How can he get away with this?" Tess sobbed, resting her cheek on Lenora's shoulder.

"Most evil men get away with such things at first," Lenora said. "But in the end, they get theirs." She looked around her. The flooring was covered with loose sawdust, as were the outer room and hallway. The walls were of unpainted boards, and the ceiling slanted toward one end. The furniture consisted only of a double bed with a rusty iron headboard, a long, narrow table next to it, strewn with empty liquor bottles and cigarette butts, and another table beneath the window, on which

Lenora had placed her valise. The room reeked of stale cigarette smoke and impressed Lenora as an altogether unpleasant place.

Tess pulled away from Lenora and wiped wet strands of hair from around her mouth. "What can we do? I don't want to stay here. Can't we get away somehow?"

Tess's skin was stretched taut over her prominent cheekbones, which caused Lenora to feel more guilt for having accepted food whenever she could hold it down. She now wondered if Raef might even refuse them food while they were locked away here.

"Let's check the window," Lenora said, hurrying to it. She worked at making a circle in the grime to see through. When she peered out of it, she saw that the sun had been replaced by gray clouds weeping with rain. Then she looked down and noticed what lay just beyond the window. "Water," she gasped. "Only water. There's no land to jump down upon."

"Oh, no," Tess said, coming to her side.

"I believe we're trapped, Tess, unless you want to break the window and take our chances in the water."

"How deep do you think it is?" Tess asked, wringing her hands nervously in front of her. "Would it be over our heads?"

"You can't swim?"

"No. I never had the need to learn."

Lenora studied the water but could not tell its depth. All she could see was an occasional fish bobbing up and down. "We'd best forget it, then," she sighed. Then she eyed her travel bag. She had forgotten about her Papa's gun. But she knew that to shoot Raef would only be the beginning. Wouldn't she then have to shoot the Indian and whoever else might try to stop her? She just could not do it. She had not even been able to shoot her ailing ox—how could she possibly shoot a man?

She went and collapsed on the bed, releasing her hair from its tight bun. She had hoped that on this night she would be enjoying a bath and the luxury of washing her hair. But these small comforts had been indefinitely postponed—along with her badly needed marriage.

Tess crawled onto the bed beside her, kicking aside a dingy blanket. "I'm so hungry, and so tired," she murmured. She curled up and closed her eyes.

"Yes, I know," Lenora said. "I am, too." She stared toward the closed door, listening to the activity beyond it. The sounds of men's voices and laughter had grown louder. She felt the burning of her eyes and knew that finally she could cry. There was no man to see her. She could now be as weak as she pleased.

James Calloway rushed into the Illahee. He spotted a girl at the bar, went to her side, and shoved some money toward the bartender. "Hello, Beautiful. You can spare me any pretenses of sharin' that glass of tea with me this afternoon," he said, slipping his arm around her waist. "What's important is what happens in that little room you've been takin' me to each evening. I can't think of a better way to celebrate my good fortune."

"What good fortune, James?" the girl asked eagerly, clinging to his arm.

"I'll no longer be usin' my horses for haulin'," he said. "I've just bought myself a business of my own."

The girl sidled up closer to him, looking up with pleading in her eyes. "Then maybe you can take me away from this place, James?" she whispered, then glanced sheepishly from side to side to see if anyone could have heard.

James patted her on the rear. "Honey, it'll take a while to get the business goin', before I'll see much money to spend on a wife."

"But, James, you promised. . . ."

"I know, I know," he said. "I *will* take you away from this hellhole, and soon. Just be patient."

"But the other men—I hate them all," she said.

"Delia, please, don't ruin our time together," he said darkly.

"All right, James," she said, lowering her eyes.

"Second Avenue," he then said, beaming. "My own tailoring establishment on Second Avenue. It's not exactly the line of work I was trained for. But after decidin' weavin' was women's work, I settled on the next best thing: to sell clothes and make them fit the customer perfectly."

James began leading the girl down the narrow, semidark hallway, pausing to stare at a group of girls who were walking ahead of Delia and himself. One of these girls resembled Lenora. Was it the way she held herself so erect? Or was it the redness of her hair? But of course it couldn't be. What the hell would Lenora be doing in Seattle, and in a place like the Illahee?

"In this room, James," Delia said, opening a door. "Raef is going to be using the other ones for a while."

James paused, squinting, looking in the direction of the women once again. "Who the hell *are* those women?" he asked, scratching his head.

Delia tugged at him until he was in the room with her and the door was shut behind them. "Never you mind," she said hurriedly. "It's none of our affair. Truly it isn't." She loosened her hair to let it drape in golden sheets across her shoulders and began to lower her dress.

"God, you are beautiful," James said, lowering his mouth over a breast, forgetting everything now but these arms that he had grown so used to being in. Then he stood back and watched her blue eyes grow darker and take on a new depth, it seemed, as her fingers began to help him shed his clothes.

"Do it, Baby," he said thickly, pushing downward on her head, until her mouth began to work on him.

Chapter Nine

"Tess, wake up," Lenora whispered, leaning over the bed. Lenora knew that if she felt this weak from hunger, then Tess could be in serious trouble. Tess had admitted to Lenora that while on the ship Raef had seemed to purposely pass her by when feeding time came around. Tess had thought it to be because she had confided in Raef about her Pa having been a Baptist minister in Indiana. It had appeared after that that Raef had not wanted her to reach Seattle alive. He must have known that Tess would in no way cooperate with him in what he had planned for her. A Baptist minister's daughter would probably not be any good at working in a brothel—especially not Tess, with her gentle ways—and her strong will.

171

Lenora sat down beside Tess and began to shake her. "Tess, honey, you must get up and move around. Maybe Raef will bring some food. You must get up and get your muscles functioning."

"I can't, Lenora," Tess said, her words barely audible. "Please just leave me alone. I only want to sleep."

"Oh, Tess," Lenora said, choking on tears. Rising, she went to the window and stared out. It was still a gray, overcast day, as it had been the previous day. She pulled her shawl around her, but it could not stop the chills from wracking her body.

She moved closer to the window, wiped still more yellowish film from it, and leaned forward to look below. Her heart skipped a few beats when she saw rocks—*not* water as before. "Tess!" she shouted. "The water! It's no longer beneath the window. I never thought about it before, but the *tide*—that's what it is, the *tide*! It's at its lowest point. We can escape." She turned toward Tess, who still had not moved. Something grabbed at her heart. Was Tess strong enough to jump from the window to escape? She rushed to her side.

"Tess? Do you hear me? We must escape, *now*."

Tess pushed herself up on one elbow and stared, hollow-eyed, toward Lenora. "You go on, Lenora," she whispered. "I can't. I don't have the strength."

Lenora set her jaw firmly. "By God, you *do*.

You *must*. Come, come and stand by the window while I break it. I'll help you out first."

Tess inched herself to the edge of the bed, then leaned into Lenora's embrace as she was maneuvered upward. Lenora watched anxiously as Tess began to walk toward the window. True, it was a wobbly gait, but at least she was on her feet.

Determinedly, Lenora jerked her shawl from her shoulders. "We'll use this to muffle the sound of breaking glass," she said, giving Tess one side of the shawl and using her help to stretch it over the window glass. Then she removed the gun from her travel bag and hit against the shawl-covered window with its butt until no shreds of glass remained as a barrier to their escape.

"Now comes the difficult part, Tess," she said, replacing her gun in the bag. She tossed her shawl across the room, realizing that it could not ever be of use to her again. "You must climb through the window and jump to the ground."

Tess looked down at the many-sized rocks spread out below her. "But it's such a far way," she murmured.

"It's our only chance," Lenora insisted. "Come, now. Swing one leg over, then the other. Then jump and hope you'll land on your feet." She watched, only half breathing, as Tess did as she was told. And when Lenora looked down, she was relieved to see Tess now standing, wiping debris from her skirt.

Doubts quickly assailed Lenora. What about

her child? Could such a fall harm him? But she had no other choice. To *not* jump meant surely to lose the child and, worse, to lead the life Raef had chosen for her. She patted her stomach and whispered, "I'll be as careful as I can, Joshua."

Then, securing her travel bag in the crook of her left arm, Lenora climbed onto the window ledge and held her breath as she leaped. The jolt caused her ankles to give way, toppling her onto her side, but once the initial shock had worn off, she breathed more easily, knowing that she had succeeded at escaping from that small prison of a room and that cruel monster of a man.

"Lenora, are you all right?" Tess asked. She stooped down beside Lenora and touched her arm.

Laughing lightly, Lenora picked up her travel bag and stood up. She shook her hair from her eyes and slowly began to look around, assessing the next route of escape. "I'm wonderful," she answered. She did not feel any pain in her abdomen, so she felt fairly secure about her child. "Yes, I am indeed," she laughed. "And you?"

"Just a torn dress," Tess answered. "But it was ready to be used as a dust rag anyway."

"We've got to get away from here quickly," Lenora said, looking up and seeing all the windows that could expose her and Tess to many watchful eyes. Then she studied the possible routes of escape. The terrain on both sides of them was extremely rocky, and the water was continuously rolling back and forth onto the shore, lapping now at Lenora's feet.

Lenora looked behind her and upward. Trees were leaning out over the edge of the bluff toward the water, their trunks grown into the ground like wooden girders. Ferns and wild rose bushes skirted the trees, making a landcover of pinks and greens.

"We must either climb the bluff or work our way down the beach aways," Lenora said. "Which do you prefer, Tess?"

"If we go up to land here, might not Raef or his Indian friend see us?" Tess asked.

Lenora was watching Tess; she seemed to be struggling for each breath, and her color was ashen. "You're right," she answered. She did not think Tess could climb, anyway. Farther up the beach, perhaps, they would come to a pier or something closer to the ground to climb upon. "Come, Tess, let me help you along. We might have a fight on our hands, but I have my gun. I believe I could actually shoot anyone who might try to stop us."

Tess locked her arm through Lenora's, and they both began to stumble across the slippery rocks, watching, ever watching, for someone to swoop down upon them.

"Where shall we go, once we're away from here?" Tess wondered aloud, laboring more than ever for breath.

"Surely there will be someone to help us," Lenora said, gulping back her mounting fear of what might lie before them. She could feel

Cassie Edwards

a muddy ooze inside her shoes, and the fishy smell of the water kept her nostrils flaring. The only pleasant thing about this journey was the congregation of friendly seagulls that continually flew above them, eyeing them with dark, round eyes.

"I must stop and rest," Tess said suddenly, collapsing onto a strip of dry sand.

"All right," Lenora panted. "I must, also." She sat down beside Tess and studied what lay above and beside them. She could now only faintly hear the noise of the sawmill that they had left behind and could hear easily the creaking of the lines on moored ships that were within eye range just a bit farther down the beach.

Above Lenora and Tess, lining the cleared bluff, were the buildings Lenora had remembered seeing when she had left the *Madrona*. Then her gaze settled on a huge, white-painted house that she had not noticed before. Its many back windows overlooked the sound.

"See that house?" she said, pointing. "Anyone who lives in such a house cannot be all bad. Perhaps we should try to seek help there."

"It's so much further, Lenora," Tess complained, coughing into her hand.

"Not so far, if we want to save ourselves," Lenora said stubbornly. "Get up, Tess. We have to go there. What if Raef finds us missing? You know he'll come searching."

"Well, I'll try," Tess mumbled, then screamed shrilly, looking wide-eyed toward something covered in seaweed, lying near them at the water's edge.

Lenora's gaze followed, and then she felt ill when she also saw it—the dead, swollen body of the buxom woman who had spat upon her on the boat. "Oh, my God," she moaned, feeling her head spinning.

"It's her," Tess stammered.

"You knew her?" Lenora whispered, taking her eyes away, lowering them, and swallowing hard.

"Yes. Raef laughed and mocked her most of the trip, taunted her for being fat."

"Then why did he agree to take her aboard?"

"Her friend—the feisty, younger woman? Raef wanted her and couldn't have her unless this lady was also allowed to board."

"This is all so sick," Lenora said. "I so misjudged that man. At first, I thought he was kind. And now I see all this he's responsible for."

"What are we going to do?" Tess said, leaning against Lenora, trembling. "Shouldn't we remove her from the water?"

"She's too heavy for us," Lenora said darkly. "We have to save our energy to save ourselves. And the tide would only return her to the water in a short time unless we climbed the bank with her. We're going to forget we ever saw this, Tess," Lenora added, straightening her back. "We don't know the people in this city. If we complained publicly about Raef—and this body—we might be signing our own death warrants."

Tess began to cling to Lenora. "I'm so afraid," she sobbed.

"We must hurry along," Lenora said firmly. "We must get to that house before nightfall. Raef spoke to me of Indians and flesh-eating dogs. If he was telling the truth, at least while it's daylight we'd be able to see them coming. And if Raef himself caught up with us, we now know what he would do to *us*."

Lenora supported Tess, puffing and wheezing, until she spied a thick stand of giant evergreens rising out of a tangle of underbrush. They could be used as cover for their exit from the beach. They would be less noticeable climbing from the bluff there than behind a place of business. In the distance she could see clouds pulsing in from the Pacific and knew that rain was again on its way.

"Come, we must hurry," she urged Tess. "Hold on to my arm. We'll get away from the rocks and mud now. Just keep your faith."

She felt Tess's bony fingers digging into her flesh and began to climb upward one unsteady inch at a time. The sides of the bluff were slick with muddy slime, and jutting rocks wounded her legs and ankles. But she kept climbing until she reached a fern-thick slope.

"Here, grab onto some of these thick roots and pull yourself up," Lenora panted, feeling perspiration on her brow even though the chill seemed to reach clear to her bones.

"It's so hard," Tess wheezed. She stopped to wipe her nose, then clung to the thick tangle of roots, pulling upward until she lay exhausted on the bluff's edge.

Lenora stretched out beside her on some soft green moss and closed her eyes, breathing hard. She felt that the worst was over. Only a few feet remained, and then she would be knocking on the door of the grandest house that she had yet to see in Seattle.

"I don't think this nightmare will ever end," Tess sobbed. "Ever since Ma and Pa died on the trail, I have known only heartache."

"You said your Pa was a preacher?"

"Yes, Baptist, in Indiana. But he felt a calling to head west. On the trail he converted many lost souls who lay dying of cholera. Then he and Ma died of it themselves."

"That is very sad."

"And you, Lenora? What about your family?"

"My Mama died of malaria in Illinois before my Papa and I began our journey west. Then my Papa—he died of cholera also while on the trail."

"And now, what do you think will become of *us*?"

"We'll make it, you'll see. One day, we'll look back on this and laugh."

"I'd never laugh."

"I don't mean about losing our folks. I mean about us sitting here on this moss all bedraggled and ugly."

Tess smiled weakly, moving to an upright position. She began to run her fingers through her dark hair in an effort to remove the tangles.

"Yes, I see what you mean," she said.

Lenora sat up beside her, shaking her hair loosely around her face. "Would you believe my hair is normally a pretty red?" she said. "Look at it now. I can hardly wait to suds it out and get it to smelling good."

"And a good meal in our stomachs," Tess sighed, widening her dark eyes.

"Yes, yes," Lenora said eagerly, pushing herself up, then tugging on Tess. "What are we doing wasting time talking about it? Let's *do* something about it."

After a few steps Lenora was peering down a street that a wooden street sign proclaimed to be Front Street. There was more activity this day than when she had been here before. Men were scurrying in all directions, going in and out of ramshackle wooden buildings, and men on horseback were urging their horses to battle the deep mud of the road.

"What if Raef is among those men?" Tess whispered, clutching Lenora's hand.

"It's a chance we'll have to take," Lenora said, scanning the faces and not recognizing any. "Come on. It's only just a bit further—it has to be. Surely our judgment of distance isn't that poor."

Hurrying along, keeping her head ducked somewhat, Lenora finally spied a white picket fence that stood out from the rest of the street's poor, cheaply built establishments.

"There it is. I know the house must be set back aways from the street where we can't see it yet.

I know this fence has to belong to that house," she said, putting more energy behind her steady gait. And then she *did* see it: a white-painted house that stood two stories high, with a wide, stately porch reaching clear across the front. The house displayed three chimneys, each of which was puffing clouds of smoke into the fine mist of rain that had just begun to fall.

"Isn't it grand?" Tess sighed. "It looks like a place of refuge, all right. Let's hurry and knock on the door."

Neatly arranged wooden blocks led to the porch instead of the unsteady, warped planks that seemed to serve as the whole city's make-shift walks. And in bold print, painted in red on a sign above the door, Lenora read "Calder Hotel."

"Why, it's a hotel," Tess gasped. "What if Raef is there?"

"Ha. It looks too respectable for the likes of him."

"I hope you're right, Lenora."

"Do you have any money, Tess, to help pay for a room?"

"None whatever. Someone robbed me on the ship of everything I owned."

Lenora had wondered about her lack of a travel bag. "Well, I've come from San Francisco with a bit of cash, but I'm not sure how long it will last us." She slowly climbed the steps and with trembling fingers knocked on the door, afraid to go bursting into a house, even a hotel. She looked from side to side. No one was sitting in the two porch swings or the white rattan lounge chairs, but it was not a day for enjoying the out-of-doors. The rain had just begun to fall in torrents.

The door swung open fiercely. A woman of coarse and masculine build stood in the doorway with hands on hips, glaring beneath her furrowed brows. "Are you blind, or what?" she stormed. "Don't ya see that this is a hotel? Why bother a soul by knockin' on the door? A body's too busy to stand listenin' for knocks on a door."

Tess recoiled and began to cry. Lenora put her arm around her waist to comfort her, eyeing this crude lady darkly. "It's all right, Tess," she crooned.

"What the hell's wrong with *her*?" the lady shouted, opening the screen door to look at them more closely through gold-framed spectacles. She didn't like the looks of it. She didn't need a body dyin' in *her* hotel.

"She's weak and poorly," Lenora said, supporting Tess against herself, "and in need of some food. Do you have anything you might be able to spare us?"

The lady stepped out onto the porch, wiping her thick hands on an apron. Hair fell in gray strings out of a bun on top of her head, and her gums worked continuously, making her stubble-covered chin settle in deep creases. "You both look a mite shoddy," she said, studying them under a tilted, thick gray brow. "Where the hell you come from, anyway? Ain't seen such a sight in years."

Lenora set her jaw firmly, glowering. "Do you need to know our history just to feed us a meal? I have money to pay for the food. And we'd like a room, if you please."

Loud shouts reached them from the street. Lenora turned and saw two gentlemen standing beyond the fence, drinking from a flask they passed between them.

"Hey, Mother Damnable," one yelled again, spitting chewing tobacco onto the green, neatly trimmed yard.

Lenora's eyes widened when the lady flew into a rage and ran from the porch in the direction of the men. Then Lenora gasped as she watched the woman reach into her apron pocket and pull from it a handful of rocks, which she began to hurl at the mocking men.

"You get the Goddamn hell away from my property, you no-good scalawags," she shouted. "Unless you've got rent money, you'd better stay on the other side of my fence. I'll get my dogs after ya. Now get the hell out of here and go find some work. Make somethin' of yoreselves."

The men thumbed their noses before turning to move on, then laughed all the way up the street.

"Damned sons-of-bitches," the lady grumbled, huffing and puffing as she climbed the steps, holding the gray cotton skirt of her dress up to reveal black ankle shoes. "They pester the hell out of me all the time. Don't have nothin' better to do with their time than to pester a soul." She stood wiping her brow, again studying Lenora and Tess. "Now, as for the two of you," she growled. "Come on inside and sit by the stove. Then we'll take care of your ills." She had no choice but to help them. And she would even enjoy their company once they had had a decent bath. Men! That's all that surrounded her in this seaport town.

Lenora sighed with relief, then helped Tess through the door. Once inside, she found the hotel's interior to be as neat and grand as the outside. The large, comfortable lobby was filled with many overstuffed chairs and two matching brown horsehair sofas arranged before a roaring fire in the marble fireplace. The several tables in the room were of polished mahogany and held kerosene lamps. The wooden floor showed a trail of mud tracks leading to a long, narrow check-in desk, behind which stood a wall of cubbyholes.

"Here, come and sit by the fire, little one," the lady said to Tess, her voice having become more friendly.

"Her name is Tess. Tess Klein," Lenora said. "And I'm Lenora Adamson."

"Anna Calder to you," the lady said, extending a hand toward Lenora. "I'm the owner of this establishment, me and my absent husband Aaron. He's a whalin' captain, gone most of the time—leaves me in charge here."

Lenora accepted the gesture of friendship, but tilted a brow when she felt the coarseness of Anna's hand. It was more like a man's hand, not soft like her own.

"Now, I'll run and fetch some clam chowder for you girls," Anna said. "Jist sit you down by the fire and warm yore bones. Ol' Anna'll take care of you like you were my own." Then she would push them upstairs and get them into that tub of water! Whewie! How they smelled— like a skunk run over by a damn carriage!

Lenora felt her shoulders slouching, so relieved was she to have help with Tess. And seeing how Anna had treated the men on the street made Lenora feel safe with her. Anna appeared to be one who could very well take care of herself, and most likely anyone else whom she might take a liking to.

Lenora decided she would see to it that Anna would like her and Tess. Lenora and Tess needed the friendship of Anna, and Anna might need their friendship, too. Weren't the men taunting her? Lenora wondered how often that happened.

"Here, Tess," Lenora said, "stretch out on the sofa. The warmth from the fire will have you feeling better in no time. And did you hear? She's gone to get us some clam chowder." She guided Tess to the sofa, taking an afghan from a chair and rolling it into a ball for a pillow. "There, there," she crooned, smoothing Tess's hair back from her eyes. "You'll be all right. You'll see."

"But what if Raef should come in here and find us?"

"Don't you worry about Raef, Tess," Lenora said, sitting down on the floor in front of the couch and clinging to Tess's hand. "I think we're safe here. You're the one I'm worrying about."

Anna came back into the room. "This chowder'll give some warmth to yore innards," she said. She placed two steaming bowls of brown liquid on a table beside the couch.

"Tess? You do feel like sitting up to eat, don't you?" Lenora asked, seeing that Tess's eyes had closed. Fear began to grip Lenora as Tess continued to lie there unresponsive. "Tess? Wake up," she said, rising and shaking Tess gently.

"She seems a bit worse off'n I figured," Anna said, holding her spectacles on her nose as she bent down. With her free hand, she touched Tess's forehead. "Glory be. She's a burnin' up with a fever. This girl is damn sick."

"Oh, no," Lenora moaned. She began to bite her lower lip, feeling helpless all over again, as she had felt so often since her Papa had left her.

"There's a new doc in town," Anna said, hurrying away from Lenora. "He's upstairs now. Checked in here a couple of days ago. I'll go fetch him."

Lenora's stomach ached as the onion aroma beckoned to her from the steaming bowls of chowder. The smell was so pleasant, and she was so hungry, that she was sure her body must have lost its aversion to seafood. But she eyed Tess and again sat down on the floor in front of her. She knew that Tess was in much more urgent need of the nourishment than she was herself.

She picked up a bowl of the chowder and held it close to Tess's nose, hoping the smell of food might revive her a bit. Lenora knew how hungry Tess must be. Her heart skipped a beat when Tess blinked her eyes and stared glassy-eyed at the chowder.

"Tess, I'm going to try and get some of this down you," Lenora said determinedly, almost in tears because she was so thankful to see Tess awake. "Now, please don't choke on it." She lifted a spoonful to Tess's lips and slowly fed it to her, wanting to reach down and hug Tess for having swallowed it. "And another," Lenora said, this time searching for a chunk of clam or potato to add to the nourishment. "Take it easy, now," she whispered, feeding Tess, then recoiled when Tess began coughing. "Tess. Tess! Are you all right?" Lenora blurted.

"Yes, I'm fine," Tess said weakly, even laughing lightly.

Lenora continued to feed her, worrying about the redness of Tess's face. Lenora could not tell if she was flushed from the warmth of the chowder or because of the mounting fever.

The rising aroma made Lenora's own head spin from want of some of this nourishment, but Tess was uppermost in her mind now. She had to do what she could for her first.

The rustling of feet drew Lenora's attention to the stairs. "Why, it's you," Lenora stammered, rising. "Doctor Preston. Remember, on the ship?" She placed the chowder on the table and tried to rearrange her hair and the skirt of her dress as he walked toward her with a half-frown. He was as she remembered: dark-haired, tall, and slim, with a smooth, clean-shaven face and eyes as blue as the sky. He was dressed neatly, in dark trousers and shirt, and carried a black bag.

"I don't think I do remember," he said, studying her as he drew closer.

Lenora laughed nervously. "No, I doubt if you would," she said, remembering that when he had been doctoring her, she had kept her face hidden from him, knowing how bad she looked and smelled with such a case of dysentery.

"And what do we have here?" he said, stooping down in front of Tess. He opened his satchel and pulled a stethoscope from it.

"I got some chowder down her," Lenora said eagerly, clasping her hands nervously behind her.

"Good, good," Doc Preston said. He studied Tess's eyes, then listened to her chest.

Anna entered the room, speaking loudly. "Damn sick, ain't she, Doc?" She offered Lenora a cup of coffee. "Here, drink this down. You look like you're on your last legs too." Then Anna saw that one bowl of chowder had not yet been touched. She reached down and grabbed it and thrust it into Lenora's free hand. "Hell, girl, eat. Do you want to drop on the floor next to yore friend?"

Lenora's face reddened, and she lowered

her eyes. She walked to the other couch and placed her coffee on a table beside it. She then sat down and began to eat hungrily, all the while watching first Doc Preston, then Tess, then Anna. The warmth of the food worked through her, making her pulsebeat quicken. She had not ever tasted chowder before, but she would never forget it—its rich creaminess, its pungency, with bits of onion, potatoes, clam, and other seasonings to test her tongue. It was stimulating, strength giving.

"I believe we have a slight case of pneumonia here," Doc Preston said, rising. He rubbed his brow, frowning. "Where are you women staying?" he asked, turning to Lenora.

Her face flushed red again. "We're going to stay here, Sir," she said. Her gaze moved quickly to Anna. "You do have a room for us?"

"Yes, two, upstairs at the back of the house."

Doc Preston closed his satchel. "I have to ask," he said. "Where have you and this young woman been since the ship landed? You look as though you've been to hell and back."

Lenora cast her eyes down once again. She wanted to tell him about Raef and his evil ways, but did not yet trust anyone enough to do so. "No matter, Sir," she whispered. Then her gaze settled on Tess. "Is pneumonia serious? Might she die?" she asked, choking back a lump in her throat.

"If we can get her into a warm bed and begin treating her, she should recover," he answered.

He turned to face Anna. "Mrs. Calder, I'll carry her up to the room, if you'll have the bed prepared for her."

Anna smiled widely, revealing a chipped front tooth. She liked this young lad more and more each day. And wasn't it nice being called "Mrs. Calder" instead of the cursed nickname "Mother Damnable" that had been assigned to her by the riffraff of the town? "What a gentleman you are," she said, lifting the skirt of her dress to bustle away toward the stairs. "Mrs. Calder, he called me," she repeated to herself, cackling. "Come along, Lad, come along. She'll get the best treatment, I'm sure, if'n you'll be the one doctorin' her."

Doc Preston flashed Lenora a smile, even blushing somewhat. "Colorful person, isn't she?" he laughed. "Now, will you carry my bag, while I carry your friend?" he said to Lenora.

"Surely," she answered.

Tess opened her eyes weakly as she was lifted up into the doctor's arms. "Who are you?" she whispered, placing her arm limply around his neck.

"Doctor Preston," he said, "but Timothy to you, Ma'am," he added quietly.

"Tess," Lenora heard Tess say. "My name's Tess."

"How lovely," Timothy Preston said. "How perfectly lovely." Then he hurried her up the stairs.

Chapter Ten

The past two days had been filled with sleeping and eating—nothing else. This morning Lenora awakened feeling completely refreshed, for the first time since she had left her bed behind in Springfield.

Stretching, she crept from the bed and strolled to the window. She raised the shade and looked out. The day was like all the other days had been: gray and misty. Anna had laughed about this. "The durndest weather for keepin' floors clean, but a body grows used to it," she had said.

Lenora watched the rain clouds sailing past the great fir and hemlock forests and then lowered her eyes to watch the ships entering and leaving the harbor. Anna's husband Aaron had built this fine house for Anna here on the point, so she could get a good view of his whaling ship coming in from the sea.

Lenora would never forget her own trip by sea and was glad that she would never have to endure such an "adventure" again. Anna had told her that San Francisco, one thousand miles away by sea, was the only population center on the coast large enough to make much of a market for the products of Seattle's fisheries and forests. Lenora had not yet told Anna what other sort of trading was being done, which she had learned of the hard way thanks to the rogue Raef Wescott.

Chills went through Lenora, for she wondered if Raef had yet tried to find her and Tess. Lenora had felt safe here with Anna, despite Anna's tough exterior. And even Tess had begun to improve under the close observation of young Doc Timothy Preston.

Looking around her in the room in which she now stood, Lenora felt a sense of well-being. Anna had furnished each room to make a body want to spend another dollar for still another night in such pleasant surroundings. The great mahogany bedstead gleamed from a careful rubbing with lemon oil, and the mahogany tables, wardrobe, and bureau showed the same labor of love.

Arranged next to the one window in the room, two overstuffed chairs sat side by side, upholstered in white with a design of small red roses to match the wallpaper. Across the floor were braided scatter rugs of various bright colorings.

Lenora went to the full-length mirror that had been set into the door of the wardrobe and let her nightgown fall to the floor to study any changes in her body. She patted her stomach and stood sideways, not yet seeing any signs of the child, but her breasts appeared to have swollen a bit more, and as she touched them lightly with her fingertips, she watched the nipples harden to erectness.

"Yes, Joshua, you will be able to suckle freely from your mother's breasts," she whispered, enfolding both breasts in her hands, feeling the soft warmth of them. She felt a strange headiness with the thought of her child's tiny lips upon her body. She was anxious, yet afraid. Time was passing, and she still had not secured a father for her child. If she waited too long, any man would be able to see that she was with child.

A knock at the door startled her from her thoughts. "One moment, please," she said. She pulled her nightgown back up into place, then reached for a housecoat Anna had been kind enough to lend her. It hung like an emptied flour sack around her but served its purpose, and its heavy chenille had a way of holding her body warmth inside. She tied a belt around her waist, hurried barefoot to the door, and opened it.

"Thought you'd be wantin' some nourishment," Anna said, holding a covered tray of food. "Heard the floor creakin', so knew you'd be up."

Lenora opened the door wider and stepped aside. "You are so kind, Anna," she said. "Please do come in. I'm always hungry for anything you've prepared. You're not only an excellent housekeeper but also a marvelous cook."

"That's why my Aaron married me," she chuckled. "Certainly tweren't for my looks or way of talkin'. Now, darlin', if I had me your body, I'd not clean or cook another day. I'd go searchin' for more lovin' than my Aaron can keep me supplied in. Bein' married to a whalin' captain has its drawbacks. Absent most o' the time, ya know."

"I'm sure," Lenora said, almost shyly. But she was glad that Anna had spoken so freely of her married life. Maybe now would be the time to seek Anna's help with her own problem concerning men.

After Anna had placed the tray of food on the bureau, she went to the bed and began to straighten the bedding. "Mighty damn soft beds I offer, ain't they?" she said, working her gums, making the stubble on her chin more noticeable. She slapped at the pillows, then arranged them neatly in place, only to cover them with an embroidered bedspread.

"Yes, very nice," Lenora said, pacing the floor with lowered eyes. She ran her fingers through her hair, which was its normal lustrous red again and felt much thicker since it had felt the luxury of Anna's soap and lavender water. Lenora went to the food tray and poured herself a cup of coffee, then continued to pace as she sipped from it.

"Glory be, Lenora," Anna scolded, letting her spectacles slide to the tip of her nose to study Lenora more carefully. "Do you have ants in yore pants this mornin', or what? I ain't seen a soul so restless since my Aaron watched me deliver my poor dead baby daughter."

Lenora stopped, wide-eyed. "You had a baby and it was born dead?" she gasped.

"Yep. Many, many a year ago," Anna said, readjusting her spectacles. "It was a two-pound baby girl. The doc said I'd worked too hard. This was way before we had the kind o' money it took to build *this* place. I used to work the whalin' boat myself and kept a pretty little house at the same time. Guess I tugged and pulled on a whale one time too many, though."

"I'm so sorry," Lenora said, settling down on a chair. Would she also be put in a position where she would have to labor hard to make a living for herself and eventually lose her own child? It was true that her Papa had taught her to be strong, but was she strong enough to have a live, healthy baby born to her? She emptied her coffee cup and placed it on the table next to her. She wet her lips and clasped her hands together on her lap. "Anna, I need some more help from you, it seems," she said.

Anna settled down in a chair next to her, arranging the skirt of her dress above her black laced ankle shoes, spreading and stretching her legs out in front of her. She pulled a man's white handkerchief from her apron pocket and blew her nose into it. Then she wiped her nose fiercely and thrust the handkerchief back inside the pocket.

"If you mean about Tess and her stayin' here until she's well without havin' money to pay, forget askin'," Anna said. "Seems young Doc Preston has taken a likin' to your Tess. Says she's his responsibility from here on out. Might even be a marriage in the cards for those two young 'uns."

Lenora lowered her eyes, feeling a tinge of envy. It was *she* who needed to be wed more than Tess. Yet, she was glad, for Tess was also alone in the world. And Tess had already told her of Timothy's and her feelings for one another—love at first sight, it had seemed to be. "No, it's nothing to do with Tess," she said, winding the belt of the housecoat around her finger so tightly that the tip of her finger began to turn purplish blue. She quickly let it unwind. "It's about myself," she stated.

"Ol' Anna's here to help, Honey," she said, leaning forward and lifting her spectacles to study Lenora further. She knew the girl was full of troubles. But, hell, what woman ain't? "Don't care to help the Goddamned men around here, but sure as hell want to aid a female in distress. We must stick together, you know. Show the bastards we've got backbone and stamina."

Blinking her lashes nervously, Lenora continued. "Yes, I feel the same," she said. "But it seems no matter how I feel about men, I'm in need of one now, in a most desperate way."

"Whatcha speakin' of, Hon?"

"Anna, I'm with child," Lenora blurted, relieved to have finally told someone. This was the kind of secret that was a burden on the heart.

"Lawdy sakes," Anna gasped. She would not have expected this, not from this gentle looking lady who was still such a child herself. But it takes all kinds.

Lenora looked at her through misty eyes. "Yes, I am. And I'm needing a husband, real fast."

Anna leaned back into her chair and laughed hoarsely. "Hon, why'd you come to Seattle? Weren't there husband material where ya come from?"

"You mean the man who *is* the father?"

"Well, yes. Where the hell *is* the bastard?"

Lenora hung her head again. "I don't know," she said quietly. "And, you see, I had my reasons for coming to Seattle."

"Mind tellin' me what they were?"

Still afraid to mention Raef's name, Lenora felt an emptiness at the pit of her stomach. Anna had questioned her several times as to how she and Tess had come to be in such poor shape, but Lenora had just pleaded being too sleepy to talk about it. Now, Lenora thought it was time to tell. "Anna, it's kind of a long story," she began, and then she told all, watching Anna's expressions change from amazement to hatred.

"That Goddamned son-of-a-bitch Raef Wescott," Anna stormed, pushing herself up from the chair. "I'd suspicioned he was up to his ol' tricks. He was caught doin' this in the early sixties, when the only women here were Indians. The men didn't hanker after beddin' with an Indian wench every time they needed a woman. Them squaws didn't smell the best. Washed their hair in urine and such as that. So Raef got boatloads of white women and brung 'em here. But he was stopped. Damn, I didn't know he was at it again. Should've when I seen you. Sure should've."

Lenora rose from the chair, suddenly trembling. She went to Anna and grasped her arm. "He can't know I told. Then he'd know where to find me and Tess." She could not tell her about the body in the water. That would outrage Anna to the point of going directly to the sheriff, and Lenora was too afraid, if not for her child. . . . No, she could not let anything happen to Raef. Not yet, anyway.

"Hell, Hon. Don't you think I know that?" Anna said, patting Lenora's hand. "We'll wait until he's had proper time to forget about you and little Tess. Then we'll run him and his kind out of this country. Had my own run-in with that son-of-a-bitch a few years back. Set my dogs on him, I did. Tore the hell out of his face and hands, they did. Guess he won't mess with *me* anymore."

Lenora gasped. "Do you mean that's how he got those scars on his face and hands?"

Anna laughed hoarsely. "I 'spose he told you a sad tale about savin' his mother's life?"

"Well, yes," Lenora murmured.

"That figgers. Tells all the women that, to soften 'em up—before he takes 'em to his bed," Anna said. Then she tilted one eyebrow. "I guess he did *that* too, huh?" she asked, thinking, "Yep, he probably raped poor Lenora even while in San Francisco. Yep, he is probably the father, but Lenora would never fess up to such a man bein' a father to her child." She clenched her fists. "Damn that man. This time I'm gonna *really* teach him a lesson."

Lenora blushed crimson. She had not told Anna she and Raef had done *that*—only how cruel Raef was. Anna would not understand how she could let such a man touch her. Lenora didn't even understand herself. "No, Ma'am, he didn't," she said, hating to tell a nontruth. She had been taught differently. "But now I've still got myself a whopper of a problem," she said, wanting to change the subject from Raef. She went to the window to stare out. "I need to find my baby a father. I cannot allow him to be born a bastard." She caught sight of the wet shine of peeled logs as a lumber schooner made its way from the harbor. The blue-green water was shadowed by bluffs and trees. Why did such loveliness have to be accompanied by evil in the world, embodied by such people as Raef—and even James?

"I think I may have the right fella for you, Hon," Anna said, moving to stand beside Lenora.

Lenora swung around to face her, eyes wide. She saw the chipped tooth as Anna smiled almost mischievously. "You know of such a man?" Lenora asked weakly.

"Sure as hell do," she laughed. Yep, she knew the right man all right: Seymour. Of course, she'd have to tell him about the baby, but wouldn't knowing make his own inadequacies seem less important? Yep, he was the right man. He would anxiously agree to wed such a beauty.

"And the baby?"

"The man I'm speakin' of need never know."

"But who?"

Anna thrust her hands deep inside her apron pockets and stood closer to the window, staring out toward the sea. Lenora could imagine Anna standing, watching like this for hours at a time, wondering about and missing her Aaron. Even now there was a forlorn look in her eyes.

"He's a professor of Common English at the Territorial University, here in Seattle."

"A professor?" Lenora said. "Seattle has a university?"

"It's not as highfalutin as it sounds," Anna said, turning from the window. "Since there were no candidates here in Seattle for a university education, the university was started with the primary and grammar grades. One day there'll be a graduatin' class, and they'll start right off on a college education."

"Oh, I see," Lenora said. "And this professor—you say he needs a wife?"

"Ain't been much to choose from," Anna answered. "Mostly been the whores from down on the sawdust."

"Down on the sawdust?"

"The 'sawdust women,' they're called," Anna laughed. She removed her spectacles and began cleaning them with the tail of her apron. "That place where Raef had you hid away. The women that work there."

"Oh, I see," Lenora said again.

Anna replaced her spectacles, then began scrutinizing Lenora, touching her skin, then her hair. "Yep, I'm sure Seymour Harper'll want you for a wife. You speak like an educated woman—he'll like that—and sometimes you even act a bit shy. You blush, you know. Yep, he'll like that too, 'cause in a way he's a damn shy, introverted cuss himself."

"But, I'm with child. If he's a professor, won't he be smart enough to guess?"

"Like I said, he's shy. Don't know much 'bout women and babies. He's in his late thirties and ain't never wed. You sure as hell could tell him it was his'n, and he'd be proud as shit."

"He's that old?" Lenora said, feeling her hopes faltering. He was old enough to be her father. Somehow, it didn't seem right.

"Age ain't no problem, Honey," Anna said. "These days, age ain't no problem. A body takes what a body can get. Now, do you want to meet up with this Seymour or not?"

Lenora swallowed hard. "I'd appreciate it if you would arrange a meeting for us, Anna," she said, "the sooner the better. My baby grows more each day. It has to be a hasty marriage."

Anna moved her face close to Lenora's. "Honey, when Seymour sees you, he won't want to wait another day. He'll be too afraid some other bastard will get to you first. Now, you get into the pretty cotton frock I washed and ironed for ya, put yore hair high on yore head, and I'll have him fetched and in the parlor before you can blink an eye."

Lenora swung her arms around Anna's neck and hugged her tightly. "Anna, I love you," she said, near tears.

Anna acted as though she did not know where to put her own arms, then quite awkwardly hugged Lenora back. "If'n I'd a had my daughter to keep, I'd have wanted her to be like you," she said thickly, then stepped back and wiped tears from her own eyes with the tail of her apron.

"You feel that way, knowing I'm with child?" Lenora said quietly.

"Honey, I love screwin' around as much as the next person. Why would I look down my nose at ya for somethin' so natural as lovin' a man and the way he can make you feel," she said, then leaned closer to Lenora. "And between you and me, I've had a bit o' my own fun whilst Aaron has been gone." She laughed, and her strength and good humor seemed to fill the room.

"Oh, Anna," Lenora said, casting her eyes downward, feeling a blush rising.

Anna guffawed and slapped her own thigh loudly. "You see? You're blushin'! I drew another damn blush from ya. Yep, Seymour and you'll make it just fine. I'll go and fetch him for you now."

"I'll hurry and make myself presentable," Lenora said, already untying the belt from around her housecoat. She listened to Anna scurrying down the stairs and then heard the banging of the front door.

"I must hurry," Lenora said, quivering inside with the prospect of meeting a man who might soon be her husband. She had not asked Anna what he looked like. Would he be tall? Short? Dark? Light? Perhaps even handsome?

"Oh, Papa, I'm so scared," she whispered. "Let him be like you. Oh, let him be kind and gentle like you."

Chapter Eleven

Before Lenora even had the chance to miss her second 'monthly,' she was standing before a minister in Seattle's tiny white Methodist church. The fragrance of wild roses and magnolia blossoms scented the air of its interior, mingling with the warm scent of many candles and making Lenora's head a bit giddy. She swallowed back a lump in her throat and straightened her back, listening yet not listening, feeling like a princess in her new dress of palest green silk worn over many lacy petticoats. Its low bodice revealed her deep cleavage, and the dress dipped in tightly at the waist to show off her tiny waistline, even though she knew that she was swelling inside with child.

She glanced sideways through the thin, gauzy veil to see again the man who so eagerly had agreed to wed her. The balding of his head showed his age, but he wore a full, gray-streaked beard to make up for the loss of hair on his head. Only a straight line of lips was visible between mustache and beard, but his thick nose and soft green eyes were quite prominent.

This day, even though he was short in stature, he stood even more stooped than usual in a severe black suit. He glanced in her direction, catching her studying him. She saw him flush crimson and cast his eyes down, which in turn caused her to do the same. She swallowed hard and forced herself to listen.

"Do you, Seymour Harper, take Lenora Marie Adamson to be your lawful wedded wife?" the Reverend Daniel Pagley asked, standing before them in his black robe with gold-framed spectacles perched on his long, aristocratic nose.

"I do," Seymour stammered, clinging more tightly to Lenora's white-gloved right hand. He swallowed hard, trying to focus his thoughts elsewhere, or his penis would swell right here in front of everybody, soon to be followed by the wetness on his pants. His premature ejaculation had always plagued him. Only one look at a beautiful girl could cause him such embarrassment. While in Boston, he had suffered severely with this problem. When a beautiful female student would stay after class to ask him a question, it would *always* happen. And when he would rush from the room, to hide in the cloakroom, he had gotten the reputation of being a most timid man—

thank heavens. In Seattle, he had only male students.

And now, could he control himself until he got Lenora home and safely in bed?

Anna had been kind to think of him when this young thing had come to Anna with her dilemma. No one would ever know this secret about Lenora, as nobody would know that it was he who would kill Raef Wescott.

And dear, dear Anna. He would miss her and her comforting of him those many nights. She had understood his problem and had been patient with him. She had grown tired of the waterfront riffraff and had felt honored that a college professor would take her to bed. It was Anna who knew that his own weaknesses would make it desirable for him to marry Lenora, knowing that Lenora had weaknesses of her own.

He glanced sideways again at her. Even with such weaknesses, wasn't she so very different from the waterfront whores whom he had refused to touch? Lenora was a refined person, one who could share his love of books with him.

Reverend Pagley coughed into his cupped left hand, then turned his gaze upon Lenora. "And do you, Lenora Marie Adamson, take this man, Seymour Harper, to be your lawful wedded husband?" he asked portentously.

Lenora straightened her shoulders and lifted her chin. "I do," she said, feeling elated. She had done it! She had just made her child quite legitimate, no thanks to James Calloway. And no one but she would ever know that James had fathered this child. From this day forward, Joshua Caine Harper was hers and Seymour's—their son. Now she could hardly wait for the day he would be born. And wouldn't such a man as Seymour be so proud? He seemed so kind and gentle and . . . "yes, Papa, just like you," she thought.

"You may now kiss the bride, Seymour," Reverend Pagley said, closing his Bible with a sharp click.

Lenora turned to Seymour and lifted her veil, waiting. Since their meeting, he had yet to kiss her. She was anxious to see if his kiss would stir any feelings inside her. She so wanted to feel deeply for him. She so wanted to be the best wife possible. He had done her a service, and she wanted to return his kindness. Trembling, she felt his arm circle her waist and pull her to him. But all his movements were quite clumsy as his lips only brushed against hers, leaving her with an unfulfilled, puzzled feeling. As he stepped away from her, turning to shake hands with well-wishers, Lenora felt tears burning her eyes. Had she just married a man who could not stir her passion? Where was the blaze of hidden desires and anticipations that had been kindled by the mere thought of James's kisses, and even by that rogue Raef?

"Oh, Lenora, you're so pretty today," Tess said, rushing forward and suddenly embracing Lenora fully. Their cheeks met for a brief moment, then Tess again stood next to her young Doctor Timothy.

"Thank you, Tess," Lenora said, casting her eyes downward and blinking nervously.

"I'll be next in line," Timothy said, stepping up to Lenora to kiss her lightly on the cheek.

Lenora's eyes shot upward and her heart began to race. She went to Tess and clasped her hands. "Are you really going to be married?" she asked anxiously. "When?"

Tess's face was flushed pink from the excitement, which became her, taking away some of the pallor left by her recent illness. Her dark hair framed a face with a small, upturned nose, dark eyes, and tiny laugh lines around her full lips even though she was only sixteen. She also wore a dress of silk, but it hung loosely around her, for she had not yet begun to fill out her too thin frame.

"Next week, Lenora," she said, beaming.

"Oh, I'm so glad for you," Lenora said, giving her a fleeting kiss on the lips. She whispered into Tess's ear, "We can share our housewifely secrets."

"Yes, yes," Tess said, giggling.

Seymour stepped to Lenora's side, nodding a greeting to Tess and Timothy. "Come and meet some of my friends, Lenora," he said in his low-pitched voice. "Then we must rush home. Seems it's begun to mist once again. I'd like to beat the downpour. You're much too lovely to get wet. We really must hurry."

Lenora flashed a nervous grin toward Tess and Timothy, then locked her arm through Seymour's and followed close beside him, past the long row of thin, tapering candles, burning and dripping, and then past the several arrangements of ferns, roses, and magnolia blossoms.

"You've already met Reverend Pagley," Seymour said, slouching more to whisper into her ear. "He's also president of the board of trustees at the university. He is a go-getter, and a very good influence on our community."

Lenora was being guided toward a man who was quite distinguished looking, though his white hair settled around his shoulders and though he was clothed in a threadbare brown tweed suit. His forehead was prominent and his jaw squared and set. "A man of determination," Lenora thought. But as she drew closer to him she was less impressed, because he reeked of whiskey.

"Doc," Seymour said, coming up to face this expansive figure of a man, "I'd like you to meet my wife, Lenora." Seymour freed Lenora's hand so this stranger could take it, which he did, giving it a polite kiss. Seymour turned his gaze to Lenora, blushing somewhat. "Lenora, you are in the presence of one of Seattle's founders—our kind and respected citizen Doc Stanford."

Lenora's eyes widened. "Doc Stanford?" she whispered. She remembered young Doctor Preston speaking of Doc Stanford while on board the *Madrona*. He had spoken of him with the reverence of a worshipper speaking of God. But she also remembered being told that Doc Stanford was now an alcoholic.

Knowing this made Lenora's heart ache for the man. His eyes told her so much. Their pale grays spoke of hard work, disappointment, failure, and triumph as well. "I'm so glad to meet you," she added. "I've heard much about your greatness." She lowered her lashes to veil the exaggeration, for Timothy had not actually told her *that* much, but it pleased her now to see this man's reaction, the way it made his shoulders square themselves and his eyes show a bit of a twinkle.

"A woman after my own heart," he laughed, bowing, watching her intently. Something surged through Lenora—a feeling of sadness that they had not met before, when he was a much younger man. There was something about him. She felt somehow that they were of the same kind—persistent, eager. . . . Yes, she could have loved this man. She swallowed back a lump in her throat and cast her eyes down. She was not sure if it was best that their eyes should meet again. Was he feeling the same?

"And come, Lenora," Seymour said hurriedly, steering her away from what had become an awkward situation for her. "I'd like you to meet a very good friend of mine, David Dennison, and his wife Sara."

Lenora turned to face a man with graying hair and a kind face who stood beside a buxom lady attired in a soft cotton dress and stiffly starched sunbonnet, tied around a suntanned face that was shining like shoe leather.

"And, David and Sara, meet my wife, Lenora."

David's handshake was as firm as his facial features. "You've got yourself a good, smart man," he boomed in a voice that filled the church.

"If there's anything you need in the way of garden eatin's," Sara said, "just give me a holler. We managed to terrace off a plot on a hillside of our backyard. I fight the mud, but we manage to grow our own taters, turnips, and beans."

"That's mighty nice of you to offer, Ma'am," Lenora said softly.

Seymour circled Lenora's waist with his arm. "David here is trying to rid our community of the bawdyhouses, aren't you, David?"

Something grabbed at Lenora's heart. She scanned the room in search of Tess, wondering if Tess had yet told Timothy about Raef and the Illahee. Lenora could never tell Seymour. Were she and Tess really safe, even though they now had men to protect them? Seymour did not appear capable even of swatting a fly.

"And all the alcohol as well," David said sternly, turning his hat in his hands.

"And when he's not preaching against these, he's having children," Seymour laughed, then blushed. "The last count is eight, isn't it, David?" he said, leaning to peer into David's face. The minute he said it, he knew that he should not have spoken of such intimacies. Did he feel the pulsating—was it beginning? He dropped his arm from Lenora's waist and stepped back a bit, cupping his hands down in front of him, knowing that his face had to be quite red.

David sidled up next to Lenora. "If you and Seymour are going to catch up with Sara and me, you'd best hurry on home," he said, winking.

Lenora's face paled and her knees began to tremble. Her hand went to her stomach and rested on it, feeling a bit of guilt for this charade she was acting out.

David backed away from her, eyeing her quizzically. "I'm sorry if I offended you, Lenora," he said, tilting an eyebrow. "Truly, I'm sorry. I guess I was a bit out of line."

Lenora shook her head and straightened her back. "No. It is I who must apologize," she said, meekly. "I guess I've never been much of one for teasing. I know I must learn the art. I could be much happier, I'm sure."

"But, we must indeed hurry home," Seymour interrupted. "The roads, Lenora, the roads." He simply *had* to get away from the crowd. Lenora's nearness had a way of affecting him, even when she wasn't trying.

"Yes, I'm sure," she said. Her eyes moved around to the others who remained. She had so missed Anna's presence. But Anna said that she'd have gotten more attention than Lenora since Anna was known to never enter a house of worship. "Jist ain't my style," she had said, working with dough, making bread for the evening's meal. Lenora would miss Anna. Anna had become a substitute mother for her, even though Anna was not at all like Lenora's poor, departed Mama. Maybe that was why Lenora admired Anna so. Anna was a woman of substance and grit!

All rushed from the church behind Lenora and Seymour. Lenora looked around and smiled, then let Seymour aid her in boarding the carriage. She removed her veil and folded it on her lap, then threw her newly acquired shawl around her shoulders. She secured a flower-adorned straw hat atop her head and held onto it as the horses lurched forward. Lenora felt eyes on her and looked to see Doc Stanford standing, watching her departure. Her heart ached again as she moved away from him.

The mist made even the trees appear gray instead of green as Seymour clucked to his horses, urging them up a steep hill. Lenora tensed, feeling the strain of the carriage's wheels in the mud, as they passed row after row of unpainted wood houses. Even in this most prominent section of the city, no one seemed to know that paint could improve the appearance of a house. In San Francisco, on the other hand, she had seen *all* designs and colors.

To Lenora, the houses in Seattle were quite boring. She pulled her shawl more closely around her, shivering against the steady, wet mist.

"Does it always rain in Seattle?" she asked, frowning at the thought that the dampness was fast ruining her new dress. Seymour had told her that one of the first things she was to do after their marriage was to go shopping for a new wardrobe, but still—this was her wedding dress. It would always remain special to her.

"Most all the time," Seymour replied, slapping the horses with the reins. "But it never gets too cold, even in winter. Even at Christmas, you will be able to pick roses from the garden."

Resuming the hold on her hat with her right hand, Lenora clasped the seat with her left hand, feeling as though she might fall backward, the farther up the hilly road the carriage traveled. "But don't you get snow from the mountains?" she asked, recalling the greatness of Mount Tacoma. She would never grow tired of gazing upon it. This day, as so many days, it was hidden behind what appeared to be swirling smoke but was only the voracious clouds, too stingy to share the mountain with Seattleites.

"Very rarely," Seymour answered. "Very rarely."

A square, two-storied, cupola-topped building came into view on the uppermost part of Dennison Hill. "There's the university," Seymour added. "It's not much now, but there are plans drawn up for a magnificent campus."

Not having yet seen the house in which Seymour and she would be living, Lenora quickly glanced across from the university, knowing that among the three houses that sat there in a row, was the one she would now be able to call her own, a house where her—*their*—son would be born.

Barely breathing, she sat waiting for the carriage to level off onto the flat strip of land in front of these houses, then watched wide-eyed as Seymour guided the carriage into a narrow white gravel driveway. Of the three wood frame houses, only this one had a thin layer of white paint and a small porch across the front with a porch swing hanging from the roof.

"Very nice," she said, although it seemed quite small. Would there even be room for a growing child?

"It will do until our new house is completed," he said, securing the horses.

"New house?"

"On the other side of the campus. They're just now clearing the land. I gave the word to begin yesterday. It will have two stories, with four bedrooms on the upper floor and an immense library, adjoining parlor, and kitchen on the lower floor. Does that sound appropriate enough, Lenora?"

Lenora slid to the edge of the seat and let him help her down. She was at a loss for words. She had not expected to receive so much with her marriage vows. How lucky she was. And, oh, she must thank Anna, over and over again. "It sounds quite fabulous," she finally managed to say.

"I want to make you happy," he said, hurrying her along through the dampness. "I've waited a long time for such a bride. And now that I've found you, I'll put my wealth to good use."

"Wealth?" she whispered, putting her hand to her throat.

Seymour laughed shyly. "Not from being a professor," he said. "I inherited it from my grandfather, when I lived in Boston."

"Boston?" she gasped. "Why did you come here?"

His face reddened. "Adventure, like everyone else," he murmured, then helped her up the front steps. Before opening the door, he stopped and stared at her, smiling. "I do hope you'll be happy, Lenora," he said shyly. "I myself have been quite lonesome the biggest part of my life." He wanted to pull her into his arms now, but if he did, it would happen, and she would be shocked.

"I'm already happy, Seymour," she said, squeezing his hand. "And you're responsible for this happiness."

Fumbling, he opened the door and ushered her in, then hurried out to stable the horses while she had a look at the parlor. He had left kerosene lamps burning, and black smoke was rising from their chimneys. Lenora went over to adjust their flames. It was a modest, sparsely furnished room, but well suited to a bachelor's needs. She knew that she would soon busy her fingers embroidering lacy fineries to place upon the furniture, which consisted only of a horsehair couch and one overstuffed chair with a mahogany table between them, and a rolltop desk. At the far end of the room stood a woodburning stove, and along one whole wall were bookshelves filled with books, which made Lenora's heart begin to race. She had been longing to read again, and now she would have the opportunity.

"Come," said her husband, returning, "let me show you the kitchen. I went to the Seattle Exchange and stocked up on many items, to surprise you."

"Oh?" Lenora said, clasping her hands together eagerly. She now had a kitchen to call her own, just like her Mama had once had. Some of Lenora's fondest memories of home in Illinois were connected with evenings spent around the kitchen table, as her Papa worked on his law papers, her Mama snapped green beans or molded biscuits for the next day's meals, and Lenora worked at her "book learning." Maybe one day Joshua Caine Harper would carry around such memories of *his* mother and *her* kitchen.

She stepped into a most cheerful room. She could smell fresh paint and saw that someone, probably Seymour, had painted the lone kitchen cupboard a bright, sunshine yellow. On the shelves had been placed white, daisy-patterned plates, saucers, and coffee cups.

"Do you like it?" Seymour asked, watching her closely, desiring her so deeply. He stood stooped, fidgeting with a button on the front of his suit coat, wishing they could hurry past these preliminaries. He knew that he was lucky to have held out so long, for she was the most beautiful woman he had ever seen. And she was now his wife.

"Seymour, I don't like it," she exclaimed. "I simply *love* it." She moved around the room, touching everything. She even had an ice chest, something her Mama had never had. And the cook stove looked as though it had never been used.

"Here, in the pantry, you will find the items I bought for you," Seymour said, opening a door that led into a small, dark room. He picked up a kerosene lamp and held it just inside the doorway, enabling Lenora to gaze upon a generous supply of food products, gleaming copper cooking utensils, and other kitchen implements.

"Seymour," she gasped. "It seems you've thought of everything. Why, tomorrow morning, I shall begin. Does an apple pie sound all right to you?" Her gaze had settled on a barrel of red, shining apples.

"So you can cook?" he laughed, moving away from her.

"And if I couldn't?" she teased.

He placed the kerosene lamp back upon a small, round kitchen table and eyed her with half-downcast eyes. "It seems that really wouldn't matter, Lenora," he said.

Lenora smiled, remembered the room that had been left to look at last, and waited for him to make his move. But could he, even? He did appear to be so shy. Would he even show himself to her? A strange ache between her thighs began, as she thought of the two of them unclothed and in bed. Shame surged through her. Since James, she had let most wicked thoughts enter her mind. And she had even enjoyed Raef—doing *that* to her. She knew her face was suddenly crimson and turned her eyes from Seymour.

"Would you like to see the one bedroom in our house?" he finally stammered.

Lenora swallowed hard, still not looking his way. "Yes, I suppose so," she answered, trying to pretend to be as shy as he thought her to be.

"Come with me. This way," Seymour said, leading the way with a lamp. The bedroom was located right off the kitchen and had one window which was hidden from the outside by a dark green window shade.

In the room there was only a bed, wardrobe, and nightstand. No mirrors of any sort were present, and Lenora suddenly felt quite awkward standing beside this bed that had been neatly turned down.

Seymour placed the lamp on the nightstand, turned his back to Lenora, and began to undress. Recognizing this as his own quiet but straightforward way of initiating the marital act, she set about removing her own clothing. She began to tremble, wondering how it would be with such a shy person, then climbed beneath the blankets of the bed and waited.

When Seymour turned to face her in his full nudity, Lenora gasped. He was a small man, but his male organ was thick and quite long, and seemed ready to do its duty. Fear gripped Lenora. Would Seymour be too large for her? Wouldn't he rip her apart, entering her? Might not he even damage the child?

She tensed as he jerked the blankets aside and mounted her, making her scream out. In three jabs, he had finished with her.

Tears surfaced in Lenora's eyes as Seymour continued to lie upon her, limp and spent, breathing hard. She was stunned. Was this the way it was to be? Would it always hurt so, and would he never take time to give her pleasure? She tensed further when he leaned up and began to explore her body with his small, wrinkled hands.

"You screamed, Lenora," he said thickly. "I didn't mean to hurt you."

"That's all right, Seymour," she said, feeling his hand fondling her right breast. His caresses were beginning to arouse her. Now perhaps he would also give her pleasure.

"You are quite beautiful, my wife," he said, brushing his whiskers across the now erect nipple, making Lenora release a sigh. His tongue came forward and began to lick its way downward, stopping at her thighs. He looked up at her with eyes foggy with desire, then continued to explore with his tongue until Lenora gasped with shock at where he had now placed it. His hand moved upward to clasp her own. "Silence, Lenora," he said. "I would never do this with anyone else—only you, now that you're my wife."

"But, Seymour," she said, but he had already begun again, sending the most exquisite sensations through her. She held her legs apart more and closed her eyes, feeling that what he was doing was most wicked. But, at the same time, it felt wonderful, like the warmth of a bath caressing her deepest inner self.

The trembling was beginning inside her, the same as when James—and Raef—had been doing it the other way. She began to toss her head back and forth, moaning, but then stopped, when Seymour mounted her again and released his own desires inside her, again with only three jabs.

"You will be good for me, Lenora," he panted, then rose from the bed and left her lying there alone, shocked, unfulfilled, and wondering. She listened for his return, but she had seen him taking his clothes with him. She supposed that he had gotten what he wanted and was not concerned about her needs.

She began to sob quietly. She had never been so frustrated. What was she to do? Had she married a man who had feelings only for himself? She put her fingers where she ached deeply. It was true that he had hurt her there, but it seemed the most hurt was from the pent-up feelings of nonrelease pulsating inside her. She began to caress herself in an effort to soothe

the ache, then was shocked when the waves of warm pleasure were suddenly present again, thanks to her own manipulations.

She spread her legs and rubbed herself, feeling her heart pounding against her chest and perspiration dampening her brow. She had never known this to be possible. Her whole body became a mass of tremors, sending sparkles of golden reds through her brain, and she realized she had just made love to herself.

When her body returned to normal she turned onto her side and began to weep, overcome with shame for what she had just done. She did not hear Seymour enter and lie down behind her, this time fully clothed.

"I have hurt her," he thought, touching the softness of her hair. Anna had loved his largeness. She had always climaxed right along with him, even though he always came so quickly. But Lenora was different. He was not sure how he was going to please her. Even touching her now made his penis rise anew. . . .

Chapter Twelve

"What are your plans for today, Lenora?" Seymour asked, dabbing his lips with a napkin while sitting at the breakfast table. He liked to watch her move around the kitchen with her partially swollen stomach. It was the waddle of a duck, but much more discreet since she was constantly trying to hide in any way that she could the fact that her pregnancy was showing.

It amused him a bit, knowing when the baby truly was due. Did she really believe him to be so naive?

"Not much of anything, Seymour," she said, pushing a lock of hair back into the bun that rested upon her neck. "I suppose I'll finish my chores, then read or embroider."

"But Christmas is upon us. Wouldn't you like

to go shopping? You could ask Tess to go with you. Or Anna."

A strained look made the dark circles beneath her eyes more prominent. "No, I don't believe so," she said. "I really don't believe so." The last time she had been on Second Avenue, where the best shops were, she had caught sight of Raef, and she couldn't seem to return home fast enough. Only in her small home across from where Seymour taught did she still feel safe.

Seymour rose from the table, went to her, and awkwardly touched her cheek, feeling the never-ending desire for her rising again. "You must get out of this house more," he said, thrusting his hands deep inside his breeches pockets, working against his erectness lest she see it. But didn't she already know his needs quite well? And wasn't she always ready to assist in the satisfying of these needs? Even now, if he asked, she would move toward the bedroom. But he had other things to do this day besides taking a wife to bed, or even teaching a full day in the classroom. This evening he would do as he had been planning.

Lenora glanced away from him, embarrassed anew. She had seen what his hands were trying so hard to hide, and she was still in wonder as to how he had managed without a wife for so long. But didn't even she know now the art of pleasuring one's self? Surely he had done the same for himself, all those years.

She began to gather the dishes from the table. "Yes, I believe I do spend too much time alone," she finally answered. "But you know the condition of the streets and walks. What if I should slip? I don't want to take a chance on harming our baby."

"You are certain that's all it is?" he urged. He would feel more like a husband if she would confide in him. As it was, he felt as though she only tolerated him because of the child. He did not want to resent this child, but he would see to it that Lenora would have another—*their* child—as soon as proper time had passed.

"What else could it be?" she said, hand-pumping water into a wash pail.

"If you don't see fit to discuss the matter with me, then I really must be off," he said, removing his hands from his pockets. "And I'll be a bit late this evening. Start supper late."

She turned her eyes to him. "A meeting?" she asked.

"Yes. Yes," he stammered, "a meeting."

"Sara Dennison gave me several fresh vegetables from her garden, so I'll have a stew cooking. You needn't worry about the time."

"Very well," he said, then walked from the kitchen, stopping at his desk in the parlor. He felt a queasiness in his stomach as he opened the desk drawer, but he had made this decision and he was not going to back down. Raef Wescott was not going to continue being a threat to Lenora—or himself. Now that Lenora's condition was showing, Seymour had to be sure that no one would guess that he himself was not the one who had fathered this child. At present, three others besides himself had knowledge of this: Lenora, Anna, and Raef. Sometimes he wished that Anna had not told him about Raef's being the father. It was leading him to an act of utter contempt.

With trembling fingers Seymour pulled an oblong, closed case from the open drawer. He glanced quickly toward the kitchen to see if Lenora was still busy with her dishwashing, and when he could see her shadow against the wall, still washing and wiping, he lifted the lid of the case and stared down. Two dueling pistols lay before his eyes, resting in a bed of blue velvet. Only one was needed. He lifted it, feeling the weight of the cold steel against the flesh of his hand, then pulled his jacket back and thrust the gun inside his belt.

At nightfall, he would watch for Raef, lead him by gunpoint down behind Kessler's Mill, and dissipate this problem with one shot. With all the noise and goings on at the Illahee, no one would even hear the gunfire, and Seattle would be rid of a bit of its scum.

"You will *never* brag that Lenora's child is yours," Seymour whispered to himself as he headed out to the carriage.

Stooping, Lenora shoved a few more pieces of wood into the stove, then gathered a lower corner of her dress into her hands to guard against burns as she closed the stove door. She stood rubbing her hands together over the top of the stove, watching the moving shadows of night settling in shades of gray outside the parlor windows. Seymour had never been this late. And hadn't he acted strangely when she had questioned him about the meeting? She shrugged her shoulders. She had grown used to his strangeness, even though it had not made for a comfortable relationship between them. He was a man of few words and would spend most evenings at his desk, either marking school papers or writing in his journal. Lenora only wrote of her personal feelings in her own diary when Seymour was gone. She kept the key hidden from him in her locket, for if he should read of her true feelings for him, he would most surely divorce her.

Feeling a sadness for what life had handed her, Lenora arranged herself on the couch, turned up the flame in the kerosene lamp next to her, and resumed work on a piece of embroidery. She now had many delicate furniture scarfs sewn, but she was tucking them away in her nightstand drawer to use in the new house. And when she had this final piece completed, she was going to start knitting baby things. Up to this point, she had not wanted to draw any unnecessary attention to her pregnancy, realizing that she was most definitely looking five months pregnant, instead of the three that she wanted to pretend to be. But it was hard—oh, it was hard. She even waddled, already! What would she look like when she drew near to having Joshua Caine?

A sudden knock on the front door startled Lenora, making her needle slip to prick a finger quite severely. She looked down and saw the spreading blood on the linen fabric of her embroidery work. "Oh, no," she said, thrusting her throbbing finger into her mouth.

Another knock drew her to her feet. She placed the needlework on the sofa and continued to suck on her finger as she went to the door. She started to open it, then stopped. She had grown to be most cautious, always afraid of having Raef find her. She put her ear to the door, clutching the doorknob tightly. "Who is it?" she called, waiting tensely. Seymour never knocked, and they had not had many visitors.

"Mrs. Harper? It's Doc Stanford," the voice boomed.

Lenora's eyes widened and her hands went to her throat. She had not seen Doc Stanford since her wedding day, but she still remembered the magnetic pull of their gazes. She hurriedly opened the door and stepped aside to let him enter, while her heartbeats seemed to fill her body. "Doc Stanford?" she said. "Why have you come?" she asked, closing the door behind them. She could not believe that Doc Stanford was standing next to her in her house. She had thought and wondered about him often.

Doc Stanford's hair had been trimmed, and he was attired in a freshly ironed red plaid shirt and dark, loose-fitting breeches, but he twirled the same stained hat between his fingers. His pale eyes showed warmth, and his determination for life was still evident in the set of his jaw.

"I've dropped by to see Seymour," he said in his loud, authoritative voice. "Thought we'd have a talk about the problems of the Northern Pacific Railroad passin' Seattle by. He should know about such things, since he's from Boston."

Lenora straightened her back and tried to hold her stomach in, glad to be wearing a loose cotton dress that might hide her largeness. "Seymour is late this evening, Dr. Stanford," she said, not knowing where to place her hands. She was feeling quite self-conscious in this man's presence, for she found that being near him affected her intensely.

"Still at the university?"

"I imagine," she answered. "But if you'd like to wait, you're quite welcome to do so."

"I wouldn't be intrudin' on your evening?"

"Not in the least," Lenora assured him, perhaps a bit too eagerly. She fluttered her eyelashes, laughing lightly. "Won't you please sit down?" she urged. She watched the broadness of his shoulders fill the chair he chose to sit upon. She was glad to see him relax against its back, instead of being awkward in her presence as Seymour still was whenever they were forced to face one another. She settled down on the couch, arranging her dress neatly around her. She *did* wish she had chosen a more colorful dress, but this one did have a revealing neckline, which his eyes had already found. She blushed and picked up her embroidery work, having the need to busy her fingers.

"Marriage seems to suit you fine," Doc Stanford said, still eyeing her warmly.

"Oh, yes. I'm quite happy," she lied. She wondered if he could hear the strain in her voice. "And you? Do you have a wife, Sir?"

"Just call me Doc," he said, stretching his legs out and crossing them. "Doctor Charles Steven Stanford is the long, boring appellation, but I like to be called just Doc."

Lenora giggled, lowering her eyes. "All right, Doc," she said.

"Yes, I've got me a wife," Doc said, laughing hoarsely. "In fact, I've got me two."

Lenora glanced up, feeling a tugging at her heart. "You've got two?" she gasped.

Doc tossed his hat on the chair next to him and guffawed. "Now it ain't as bad as all that," he said. "I've divorced my wife Nancy, who I left back in Ohio. Met me my second one on the trail here. Married my Catrina as soon as I had divorced Nancy."

"Oh, I see," Lenora said, pricking her finger once again. "Darn it," she said, holding it before her, seeing a fresh trickle of blood.

Doc rose from the chair and went to sit beside her. "Here, let me see," he said. He took her finger, pulled a clean white handkerchief from his breeches pocket, and dabbed it gently against the finger. Then, surprising Lenora, he put the finger to his lips and kissed it. "Now. That should make it better," he laughed awkwardly, releasing it. "See how handy it is to have a doctor around the house?"

Lenora could not take her eyes from him. His lips had been so warm. "Yes, very nice," she murmured.

He continued to sit beside her, settling back against the couch. "May I call you Lenora?" he asked, taking her embroidery work up into his large hands and studying it.

"Yes, please do," she said quietly.

"Well, Lenora, where did you travel from to arrive in this paradise called Seattle?"

Lenora's heart skipped a few beats. It was very hard to explain how she had happened to arrive on these shores. "I came by steamer from San Francisco," she said softly.

"I won't ask the why's of the trip," he said, wisely. "But I will ask: do you like our city?"

She lowered her eyes and began to fidget with the gathers of her dress. "I haven't seen much of the city, Sir—I mean Doc," she stammered. "Seymour is much too busy to take me by carriage, and I don't want to go alone."

"I have missed seeing you around town."

Her gaze shot upward. "You have?"

"Sure have. A pretty girl like you would brighten our streets, don't you know?"

Lenora was not sure where this conversation was leading. She did know that he was a highly respected man in Seattle and definitely not known as a womanizer. And he was even older than Seymour. But he *did* make her heart race so. "Tell me about yourself, Doc," she said hurriedly, hating herself for blushing.

He handed her the embroidery work, reached inside a shirt pocket, and removed a half-smoked cigar. "Do you mind if I smoke?" he asked, gesturing with the cigar.

"No, not really."

"I've taken it up while trying to stay away from whiskey—replacing one vice with another, as it were," he said, chuckling and going to the stove to open it. He held a piece of kindling down in the flames, then touched its smoldering end to the cigar hanging from his lips. After a few deep puffs, he took it upon himself to add some more wood to the fire, then shut the door. "The townfolk still marvel at the absence of snow here in Seattle in December, but snow ain't the only thing that makes a body cold," he added, rubbing his hands briskly together. He continued to stand there, his thumbs stuck into the two front pockets of his trousers. "So you want to know more about this old fellow, huh?" he laughed.

"Yes, please. Seymour has talked so highly of you and what you've done for Seattle."

He smiled, curling his lips at the corners. His eyes no longer looked so pale to Lenora, and his wrinkles only made his appearance that much more distinguished, showing that he had lived life to the fullest. "As I told you, I come from Ohio. Was headed for California to pan for gold, but instead was sidetracked by cholera."

"Cholera?" Lenora gulped, remembering her

own misfortune of—was it only months ago?

"My being a doctor changed my plans mighty fast," he said. "Just plumb got doctored out, on the trail. 'Fore I knew it, I was on these shores instead of California."

"Were you disappointed?"

He pulled the cigar from his lips and flicked ashes into the coal bucket. "Disappointed? Never. I fell in love with the mountains and the forests. Let me tell you, before those forests began getting thinned by Seattleites, you could stand in the thickness of those trees and think it nightfall when in truth it'd be high noon."

"Really?" Lenora said, leaning forward.

"And the Indians, they were a fascination to me. They were of the Duwamish and Suquamish tribes. The squaws carried their babies around strapped to boards and pressed other boards against their foreheads to flatten them. In search of beauty, these Indians bound their children's heads somewhat as the Chinese bind the feet of the girls."

Lenora remembered the one Indian she had encountered at the Illahee, Raef's friend. Other than that, she had only seen them from afar. "Were the Indians friendly?" she asked.

"Generally. *I* liked 'em, even though most others didn't. You see, most saw the Indians as crude, pushy. Some Indians would just wander into the new settlers' cabins unannounced for a nanitch," he related, sitting down beside Lenora once again.

"What is a 'nanitch'?" she asked, slipping one

foot up beneath her, to sit upon it.

Doc Stanford laughed hoarsely. "Nanitch?" he said, eyeing her amusedly. "That's Indian for 'a look around.'"

"Do you mean they'd really just walk right in?"

"Been known to fill a cabin with many Indians at one time," he said. "Scared the hell out of the women settlers. And the Indians smelled strong with salmon oil and were sprightly with fleas, which didn't help matters none."

"What did the settlers do about this?"

"After a while the Indians left 'em alone—their curiosity wore thin. So the settlers didn't have to do anything about it."

"But you said you liked the Indians?"

"Oh, yes, and one especially: Chief Seattle. Now, he was a likable man. He had the look of a philosopher. We sure did get along fine. It was by my suggestion that Seattle was named after the chief."

"Where is he now?"

"With his ancestors. Died a few years back."

"Then Seattle never had any true Indian problems?"

"Now, I never said that. We had us an honest-to-goodness Indian war back in 1856, but it wasn't Chief Seattle's doings. His tribe always stayed loyal and friendly. No, the attack on Seattle was the work of probably two hundred local Indians called Puyallups. When they ran out of ammunition and got hungry, they just retreated into the woods and never returned."

Lenora was thoroughly enjoying this talk with Doc. It reminded her of the long hours she had spent listening to her Papa's yarns, many of them invented to make her laugh. "This all sounds very exciting," she said. "Please tell me more."

Frowning a bit, he pulled a gold watch from his pocket and studied it. "Seems Seymour's got lost," he mumbled.

Lenora's nose twitched, and suddenly she remembered the stew cooking on the stove. "Oh, my goodness," she exclaimed. "I plumb forgot." She rose from her chair and rushed into the kitchen. She grabbed a potholder, tipped back the lid on a large copper pot, and peered into it. Then she sighed with relief. Her stew had not cooked dry—the vegetables and beef still bubbled in their brown gravy. When she heard a rustling of feet behind her, she turned and found Doc standing very near, watching her with a look of devout seriousness.

"What is it?" she asked.

"That smells powerful good," he said, taking the cigar from his mouth, "but, Woman, you *look* even better. You're one damn beautiful woman. Does Seymour know how lucky he is?"

"Sir, you are embarrassing me," she said, turning to pick up a wooden spoon on the pretense that the stew needed stirring. She was finding herself in another puzzling predicament and did not know what to do about it. She was now a married woman with child, and he was also married, and known and respected by all.

Doc dropped his cigar into the ash bucket next to the stove and took Lenora by the hand, turning her to face him. "I'd sure like to hold you, Lenora," he said thickly. "Sure as hell would like that."

She felt her heartbeat quicken, making her feel almost suffocated by her own feelings. She cast her eyes down. "Doc, I wouldn't want to hurt Seymour. He's been good to me by providing for me," she stammered.

"I wouldn't want to hurt my Catrina either," he said. "She's been my pillar of strength these past years. And I don't make it a practice to go askin' to hold women in my arms. Only you. Only now."

"Oh, Doc," Lenora sighed. She dropped the spoon on the table, then leaned fully into his embrace, suddenly feeling as though she belonged there. "Hug me tightly. Oh, please do hold me tightly."

"I thought I saw a sadness in your eyes," he said, caressing her back. "Is there somethin' that needs tellin'? Is Seymour truly treatin' you right?"

Lenora could not tell him how she hated for Seymour to touch her. She could not tell him that Seymour's only thoughts of her were the sharing of her "bedly" duties—be it night, or the middle of the day if he had time between classes at the university. Yes, Seymour had everyone fooled. He was not the shy person he had led people to believe—he was twisted in his mind, and she felt helpless, utterly helpless. "He provides a home for me and my child to be," she finally blurted. She had told no one besides Anna and Seymour about the child. She tensed, waiting, then was alarmed when his large hand reached down and touched her abdomen, ever so softly.

He laughed quietly. "I was wonderin' when you'd mention you were with child," he said.

"You knew?"

"Having memorized each of your curves the first day I saw you? Hell, yes, I knew."

She pulled away from him and looked deeply into the pale gray eyes. "Does it matter to you?" she asked, biting her lower lip nervously.

"It makes you even more beautiful," he said, then gathered her to him and searched and captured her lips.

She laced her arms about his neck, wanting to cry from the tenderness being shown to her. Being a married woman was no longer of any concern to her. Her mind was capturing only the wonderful, incredible peacefulness that this man's kiss was creating inside her.

Then, suddenly, he had pulled away from her and was on the other side of the room with his back to her, head and shoulders bent. She put her hands to her mouth, still tasting him. "What is it?" she whispered.

"I apologize for taking advantage of your innocence in the absence of your husband," he said. "I've never done anything like this before. I don't know what the hell's wrong with me. It ain't even whiskey. Ain't touched the stuff for a couple of days now."

Lenora took the skirt of her dress into her hands and went to him. She touched him gently on the cheek. "Don't feel guilty about any of this," she said. "You see, I want it also."

His gaze shot upward. Lenora faltered, seeing that same tormented look she remembered seeing on their first meeting in the church. She now noticed, as she had not before, that his eyelids were heavy with the weakened muscles of age, and his wrinkles hung more loosely as he continued to study her. "You know I'm old enough to be even your grandfather," he said dryly.

"It doesn't matter," she whispered. She snuggled into his arms again, exhaling deeply. She closed her eyes, trembling, when once again his arms reached around her and held her against him.

"I feel a bit foolish," she whispered.

"And why would you?" he replied, burrowing his nose into the depths of her hair.

"I didn't even offer you a cup of coffee," she laughed. "Aren't I just terrible?"

"Yes, terrible," he said. Then she felt him grow tense.

"What is it?" she asked, stepping away from him.

"Didn't you hear the sound of a carriage?"

Her face reddened and she began straightening her dress, for she also heard the neighing of horses just outside the back window. "It's

Seymour. He's returned home," she said. She glanced around her, wondering if everything was in place, as Seymour was used to finding it. Would he be able to know somehow what she and Doc had just done? But she refused to feel guilty about it. Hadn't Doc comforted her in a way that could only be right? Even now, she wanted to return to his embrace. "Let's return to the parlor," she then said, quite calmly.

"That's a damn good idea," Doc chuckled, taking her by the elbow to walk beside her. Even this slight touch made Lenora grow breathless. She looked up at him and blinked her heavy lashes nervously, smiling weakly. He in turn squeezed her arm affectionately, then sat down opposite her, waiting.

Lenora resumed her embroidery work, having a need to look busy. She seemed to feel again the throbbing of the two fingers she had pricked this evening. Would she even prick another when Seymour came through the door?

"What's keepin' the man?" Doc finally said, rising to go to the window. He leaned to look out just as the door jerked open.

Looking upward, Lenora dropped her embroidery work on her lap. "Seymour," she gasped. "You look absolutely frightful. What's happened?"

Seymour glanced across the room and began fidgeting with the buttons of his jacket, feeling the need to secure them so Doc Stanford and

Lenora would not see the gun. He knew that he was a sight to see, having thrown up all down his front. After he shot Raef Wescott, he had grown violently ill. Even now, his knees were wobbling from the weakness.

"Hey, ol' man," Doc Stanford said, hurrying toward Seymour. "What the hell's happened to you? Are you all right?"

Seymour ducked his head and headed for the kitchen. "I can't talk now, Doc," he grunted. "I'll look you up tomorrow."

"But, if you're ill . . . ," Doc said, hurrying after him.

Seymour interrupted quite bluntly. "I'm not ill and I don't need your drunken hands on me either to see what *is* wrong with me," he said. "Now will you please excuse me?" He then disappeared into the kitchen.

"Well . . . I was just . . . ," Doc stammered, leaning down to grab his hat.

"Doc, I'm *so* sorry," Lenora said, rising to hurry to him. "Seymour isn't himself. He didn't mean it. I'm sure of it. Please don't be hurt by his words."

"It ain't at all like Seymour," Doc said, frowning. "You'd best go and see to your husband, Lenora."

"Yes, I guess I'd best," she said, casting her eyes down. Then she felt her pulse race anew when Doc's large hand touched the nape of her neck, sending tremors of warmth down her spine.

"Can we see each other again?" he whispered,

kneading more warmth into her skin.

She sighed deeply. "Yes," she whispered back. She then turned and watched him walk through the door, not stopping to look her way again. She was torn inside with emotion. Could this really have happened? Did she have such deep feelings for a man so much older than herself? Something grabbed at her heart—was Doc in a way a substitute father figure for her, now that she missed her Papa so much? But the familiar ache in the loins told her the answer—she knew that she wanted more than hugs from this man of distinction.

Loud gasping and wretching noises coming from the kitchen made Lenora face the reality of now and the enigma of her husband. She hurried into the kitchen and stood wide-eyed, watching Seymour hanging his head over the sink, so ill that he looked gray. She went to his side, reaching out to hold him, but was shoved roughly aside.

"But, Seymour, you're quite ill," she murmured. "Isn't there anything I can do for you?"

"Just get that food off the stove and away from my nose," he groaned. "The smell of food is only making me worse."

"But, Seymour, whatever is wrong with you?"

"Just do as I say," he moaned, upchucking again until his whole body spasmed over and over again.

The smell of his sickness made Lenora clutch at her own stomach. She knew that she would not be able to eat. With a potholder, she lifted the pot of stew, carried it onto the back porch, and sat it down on the floor. She inhaled deeply the fresh night air, letting her mind forget her ailing husband, wondering only about her next meeting with Doc. She now felt as though she had a reason to wake up the next day.

Chapter Thirteen

The warmth from the kitchen stove was welcomed this December morning. Lenora brought her chair up close to it and arranged a crock of fresh green beans on her lap. Sighing resolutely, she began to snap the beans into thirds, discarding the ends onto a newspaper spread out on the table. Sara Dennison had been so kind to Lenora. Each day, Sara had brought a different gift from her garden. But these would be the last for a while, Sara had said, for she'd had to rescue even these from the cold dampness of the Dennisons' cellar.

A flutter inside her womb made Lenora remember her child—and Doc Stanford's acceptance of the knowledge of it. But shouldn't they both have felt shame for embracing in such a manner, if for no other reason, because she was with child? Her usually set jaw slackened. Life continually confused her. If she was to wait until after the birth of her child to meet with Doc, might he even lose interest in her? It had already been two days since their one and only meeting.

She glanced quickly at the clock ticking away on the table. She had carried it with her from room to room this day, watching the hands move closer to the time Doc had said he would be at Anna's hotel. He had sent Lenora word by a messenger boy and had promised that their meeting would be discreet, that he and Anna were long-time friends, and that Anna would aid them in their rendezvous.

But several things were holding Lenora back: her husband, her child, and the fear of running into Raef. Since the time she had seen Raef while shopping, she had remained in her house like a prisoner. Would her imprisonment never end?

A light tapping on the front door drew her attention away from her thoughts. She had not heard a carriage; who might it be?

She placed the crock of beans on the table, jerked the red checked apron from around her waist, and rushed to the door. She held her breath, thinking it might be Doc coming for her, to assure their meeting.

Stopping, she checked with her fingers to see if the bun on her head was still in a tight circle, then inched the door open.

"Tess! Oh, Tess, it's you," she exclaimed, seeing Tess standing there in a brown woolen cape with her dark hair hidden beneath a fur hat. Lenora grabbed her hand and urged Tess inside.

"Timothy had a house call to make down the street aways," Tess said. "I asked him to bring me by here."

"I'm delighted that you did," Lenora sighed, closing the door. "I do get so lonesome." She was confused by the seriousness with which Tess was looking at her. Was Tess in some kind of trouble? Had Raef, perhaps, caused Tess some difficulty? Since her own marriage, Tess had been nothing but happy, as evidenced by the sparkle of her eyes and the pink of her cheeks, which had filled out now to a healthy fullness.

Tess pulled a folded newspaper from beneath her cape. "Have you read the *Puget Sound Daily* this morning?" she asked, running her fingers along the creased edge of the newspaper.

"My, but you do look serious, Tess," Lenora said. "Is it something in the paper that's troubling you so?"

"Then you haven't read it?"

"No, I haven't."

Tess handed the newspaper to Lenora, her dark eyes wide. "Read it, Lenora," she said. She untied the bow at her neck and let her cape fall from her shoulders into her arms, then removed the fur hat to reveal an intricate pile of dark hair.

Lenora went to the couch and sat down, fumbling with the newspaper. Tess sat down beside her, still watching her. "On the front page," Tess whispered.

After one glance at the headline, Lenora felt her knees grow weak. "Was it truly Raef that they found?" she gasped, reading the fine print once, and then again.

"They seem sure."

"It says he was shot—*and* had torn flesh . . . from a dog's attack?"

"By the footprints, it would have been several dogs, Lenora."

A feeling of nausea seized Lenora with the thought of this happening to another human being, yet, on the other hand, she could not help being relieved. He was—had been—such an evil man. "And it says they found his body lying in the mud behind Kessler's Mill," she said. "But it doesn't say when he was murdered."

"It hasn't been determined, but last night is when they found the body."

"I wonder who would . . . ?"

"I imagine many had reason," Tess said softly. She smoothed her dark blue broadcloth skirt with small, dainty fingers.

"We certainly did, didn't we, Tess?" Lenora asserted, refolding the newspaper.

"But dogs—isn't it sickening?" Tess murmured.

"I wonder if he was shot first, or if the dogs . . . ," Lenora was saying, but was interrupted by Tess.

"Please, Lenora," she said, almost gagging. "Let's not speak of it any further. It makes me quite sick to my stomach. I only wanted you to know this has happened. I know how you've stuck close to home because of your fear of Raef."

Lenora cast her eyes down. "You've got Timothy. He is always with you. Seymour, is, uh, too busy to take me out."

"Lenora, aren't you and Seymour happy?" Tess asked, taking one of Lenora's hands in hers and squeezing it.

Lenora could feel her face reddening. She and Tess had not spoken much of the personal sides of their marriages. Even now, out of the corner of her eyes, Lenora could see Tess studying the now most noticeable swell in Lenora's abdomen, but she had not asked about it. "What's happiness?" she asked. "Do you really know, Tess?" She shot her eyes upward, fluttering her eyelashes nervously toward Tess.

"I'm truly happy," Tess murmured, smiling weakly.

"And can you define the reason, Tess?"

"Why, Timothy is so kind. That's why."

"And is that the only reason, Tess? Isn't there more to a marriage than that?"

It was Tess's turn to display a blush on her cheeks. She also cast her eyes down. "Lenora, you know you're embarrassing me," she uttered.

"Then you do know what I'm speaking of," Lenora persisted, having the need to discuss Seymour's inadequacies with someone. She had wanted to confide in Anna, but her fear of Raef had kept her from venturing even there.

"You do mean the nightly responsibilities of a man?" Tess stammered, squirming noticeably beneath Lenora's steady gaze.

"Yes, that's what I'm speaking of," Lenora said. "Does Timothy . . . consider your feelings? Or are all husbands in such a rush, thinking of their own pleasure only?"

"Lenora," Tess gasped, putting a hand to her throat.

Lenora rose from the sofa, realizing she was not going to get an answer. She swung the skirt of her dress around and walked to the front window to look out toward the university. "You know I'm with child, don't you, Tess?" she said, wondering what Seymour was doing at this moment. He had been acting so strangely since coming home late that night from the meeting. He had not even approached her sexually since. He just came and went without speaking to her. And in bed, he went out of his way not to lie near her.

It was all quite puzzling to her. Had there been more to his illness that night than met the eye? Or had he suspected Doc's and her feelings for one another? Whatever the reason, she liked this new Seymour much better. She hadn't had to lie beneath him listening to him receiving pleasure from her body. Yes, this was much better. But oh, how she ached for Doc's touch. He had almost made her forget James.

"I had noticed," Tess answered.

"It's not Seymour's baby," Lenora blurted, stiffening, realizing that she would again be shocking Tess. But she had to tell her.

Tess rose and went to Lenora. "Oh, Lenora," she said softly. "It's not Raef's child, is it?"

Lenora swung around and faced Tess with flashing eyes. "And why would you suspect that, Tess?" she snapped. She had not expected this from Tess. She would have expected, more likely, a gasp of disgust.

Tess's gaze lowered. "Those nights on the ship—I knew Raef must have forced himself on you."

"I'm sure everyone on board knew," Lenora said pensively. She went to the stove, opened it, and began shoving wood inside, trying to busy herself to hide her mounting uneasiness for what she was about to tell Tess.

"Yes," Tess went on, "it was ship gossip, plus the fact that he even mentioned it that day at the Illahee, when he was gloating over us women who had just become his prisoners."

"The baby isn't Raef's," Lenora said, turning to face Tess again. Her eyes wavered, and she bit her lower lip, waiting. Would she lose her best friend because of her sudden honesty?

"Then, whose . . . ?"

"Tess, if we're to be best friends and Timothy is to be my doctor, you must know all of this."

"I think I understand, Lenora."

"Then please sit beside me and let me tell you, so you can explain it to Timothy before I go to him for my first checkup."

"I don't know, Lenora," Tess said shyly. "I'm not sure I can talk of such things with Timothy."

Lenora grabbed Tess by the hand, trembling. "But, you must help me," she pleaded. "Don't you see—I need you. I can never confide in Seymour. He's such a difficult person to talk to even about trivial things, let alone such a thing as this."

"Then, you and Seymour aren't happy?" Tess murmured. "Is he cruel to you?"

Lenora's eyes were cast down. "Not exactly," she whispered.

"Lenora, go ahead and tell me what you want me to know. I'll try to help in any way I can."

"Oh, thank you, Tess," Lenora said. "Thank you."

She sat down again on the sofa, and when Tess came and sat beside her she told all, knowing that she was indeed shocking this timid preacher's daughter. But she *had* to tell. She had to have an ally when Joshua Caine was born early. Might not Seymour even toss her and the baby out of the house to fend for themselves if he suspected?

"And there it is," Lenora said, clearing her throat nervously, "the whole story. Do you think Timothy will aid me in my necessary deceit of Seymour?"

"But how?"

"He can tell Seymour that the baby was born early when the time comes. Please try to talk Timothy into helping me out of this predicament I've found myself in. Could you try? Please?"

Tears welled up in Tess's eyes. She fluttered her lashes and let a tear drop from them. "Yes, I shall, Lenora," she said. "I'll see to it that Seymour truly believes the child is his."

Lenora cast her eyes down. "Do you think me shameful, Tess?" she whispered.

"I think you brave, Lenora."

Lenora swallowed hard and looked suddenly toward Tess. "Brave? Why?"

"Only men believe this is a man's world, Lenora," Tess murmured. "You're carrying the child of one of these men and holding your head high while doing so. And look how cleverly you've secured a husband for yourself. I admire you. I'd like to have more backbone myself."

"I didn't know you had such feelings," Lenora said. "I would have believed you would accept the notion of this being a man's world—as you accept your nightly duties to Timothy, and as I have also done—most hatedly—with Seymour."

"I still embarrass quite easily, Lenora, while speaking of such things," Tess said, rising. She went to a window to stare outward. "You see, my Papa preached of hell and fornication in the same breath and put pleasurable thoughts right from my mind." She turned to face Lenora again. "But, now, today, I'm finding it easier to speak with you of such matters."

"I'm glad, Tess," Lenora said. She went to Tess and pulled her gently into her arms. "You know, we women must stick together, and perhaps one day we will have our voices heard all over the country. We shan't remain timid and closed-mouthed. It is not a man's world, and we shall prove it."

"I do love Timothy," Tess said, "most sincerely. And I do enjoy . . . his touches. But I find it so hard to say."

Lenora pushed Tess away from her and held her at arm's length, looking firmly into her eyes. "It isn't a sin to enjoy a man," she said determinedly. "If I hadn't enjoyed James's touches, I would not be blessed with his child now. I so want this child. It was conceived in love."

"You don't love Seymour, then?"

Lenora jerked around, feeling a sinking at the pit of her stomach. "I hate him, Tess," she said. "I purely hate him."

"I'm so sorry, Lenora."

"But I will endure with him, for my child's sake." So often she was reminded of the strength her Papa had instilled in her. Now, it was necessary.

"You are brave, Lenora," Tess repeated.

"I'm a woman with child, and I shall remain proud of that fact."

The sound of a carriage pulling up in front of the house made Tess scramble to secure her cape around her shoulders and her hat atop her head. "Timothy has returned," she said. She went to Lenora and hugged her affectionately. "I'm so glad we had this talk. And now you can come to visit me since, well, since you no longer have to fear going out."

Lenora brushed her lips against Tess's cheek. "Yes, my dear, I know," she said, feeling a sudden peacefulness. "Now I can venture out and go anywhere I choose. And this I plan to do plenty of, from this day on."

"I must run along," Tess said, swinging the fullness of her cape around to open the door.

Lenora followed behind her and leaned out into the cool air to wave to Timothy. "You take care of yourself, Lenora," Tess shouted, as she climbed into the carriage.

"And you also," Lenora replied, then shut the door and rushed to stand by the stove, shivering. Her heart raced; she felt truly free for the first time since she had reached the shores of Seattle. She knew that she should show some remorse for another human being's violent death, but she could not. His death had meant her freedom, and she felt she could almost as easily have pulled the trigger and done away with him herself.

A shudder ran through her as she rushed into the kitchen. She eyed the partially snapped green beans, and then the clock, and knew Doc would be waiting. Now she could go to him. She could walk the streets of Seattle without worrying about being followed or watched, and so she would. Couldn't the crisp winter air add a luster to her cheeks? Her house was on Fifth and Union, and Anna's hotel was on First Street, not so far away. In fact, it would be an invigorating walk for a pregnant woman.

Looking down, she held the skirt of her dress away from her and quickly decided it would not do for this meeting. She was tired of looking like a dowdy housewife. She could perhaps squeeze into a much smarter outfit to please the eye of a special man. Among the few items she had purchased as Mrs. Seymour Harper was one such outfit.

She rushed into the bedroom, chose a white shirtwaist blouse and gathered black serge skirt, and hurried into them, even though the skirt's waistband cut into her thickened middle. She sucked in her breath and stood straighter, determined to wear this ensemble.

The lining of the skirt rustled as she swung around to pull her hooded black woolen cape around her shoulders. Then she rushed from the house, not caring that Seymour might happen to find her gone. Her sudden sense of freedom made her feel quite daring.

The gradual downward slope of the street made her walk at a much faster clip, but not too fast to experience, it seemed for the first time, the true atmosphere of Seattle life.

The cold temperatures had hardened the muddy streets to stiff, rutty peaks, and the carriages appeared near to toppling as they moved along beside her. But the plank sidewalks aided Lenora in her continuing flight, and she felt relieved that the muddy ooze she had always had to pull her skirts free of was now as hard as the street.

After passing through the residential area, Lenora slowed her pace to become a part of the commercial section of the city. With the Christmas season upon Seattle, more women were entering the wood frame shops, though few shops there were. Most had their narrow, glass-paned windows decorated with red and green crepe paper chains tacked from corner to corner. Among the more sumptuous arrangements in windows were an assortment of wooden carvings, a collection of fancy women's hats, and a display of diamonds and gold necklaces that reminded Lenora of Francis and San Francisco.

A sense of disbelief surged through her. It had only been a few short months since she had lived with Francis, but it seemed years ago. She could not comprehend how life could change so fast. While living in Illinois with her Mama and Papa, the years had seemed to drag by.

Lenora sighed heavily. Was that what growing to maturity meant—to see life pass one by at a much faster rate of speed?

When she reached Second Avenue, she stopped to stare down its full length. It was a street of dips, spurs and angles, hills and hollows, with the whole roadway tilted sharply upward upon the eastern side. But this street displayed the best establishments and business enterprises in Seattle, and to get to Calder Hotel, Lenora would have the pleasure of walking down it.

On her way she passed the home of Reverend Lawrence E. Boyle, where Lenora had been told the first village school had been held. And next to this was the city's first orchard, which in early spring bore the finest of apples, named Washington Red Delicious apples to represent this fine territory of Washington.

A few more steps took Lenora past the White Church, where she and Seymour had been wed. She turned her eyes quickly from it, not wanting to be reminded of the many nights spent with Seymour since that afternoon. She had been filled with such false hopes.

Before continuing on her way, though, Lenora stopped to wonder at the activity surrounding the North Pacific Gardens despite the penetrating chill in the air this day. Anna had told Lenora that Seattle had been proud to boast of this, the first "pleasure oasis" in this great northwest country. The music blared as dancers swung each other around, and at many tables couples sat leisurely exchanging Seattle gossip while sharing foaming steins of beer. Even today, just as the one other time Lenora had stopped to watch the happy faces, there were pens of wild animals placed in a row for people to stoop and inspect more closely.

Lenora set her jaw and tilted her chin up into the air. She did not believe in caging defenseless creatures. Didn't the eyes of this cornered gray wolf show its fear and torment? If Lenora could, she would gladly free the animal and allow it to run for the safety of the forest. But, knowing this was an impossibility, she went on her way, glad that at least *she* was now free—free of Raef and his evil ways—and glad that Doc was waiting for her.

She walked past a millinery store, a dressmaking emporium, a dentist's office, and other "shingled" establishments, but soon stopped again, this time to stare in wide-eyed disbelief at a pair of horses hitched to a post in front of a tailoring establishment. Her heart began to palpitate as she studied the horses. One was black—and one was white! She had seen such a pair of horses only one other time in her life—and they had belonged to James Calloway.

As though the child in her womb was aware of her thoughts, it moved, causing a heavy rumble, then lay still again. "No, it can't be James," she whispered, feeling her throat grow dry. Why would *he* be in Seattle? He had spoken only of settling in San Francisco.

Lenora pulled her hooded cape more securely around her and crept past the shop, afraid to peer through the window lest, if they were James's horses, he might recognize her and rush out to speak with her. Then might he not notice the swell of her stomach and wonder about the child?

But once she had safely passed the shop, she could not help turning to look once again toward the horses. The trembling of her knees and fingers told her that she had not yet completely lost her feelings for James. If seeing two unattended horses could leave her in such a state, what might she expect of herself if she should ever meet James face to face?

She choked back the tears, remembering how frantically she had at one time wanted to seek him out, how she had wanted him to recognize her child as his. But now, it could never be. She had vowed that he would never know—that this must be a secret of her heart. She now had a husband—even though the husband she had secured turned her blood to ice. And she had to remember how James had toyed with her affections, and had then disappeared into the crowded city of San Francisco.

But, still, now that she was aware of her hidden love and longing for her child's true father, as well as her duty to her husband who would be named the child's father, she realized how wrong she had been to have such intimate thoughts about Doc Stanford. She knew now that she was not free in any respect to go to him and give herself to him. She brushed the tears from her cheeks, hoping he would understand. He was so kind, so gentle. . . .

Wiping her eyes with the back of her hand, she rushed away from the tailoring shop, not wanting even to see the horses, let alone discover who might be their owner. No, she could not possibly want to see James, if indeed he was in

Seattle. She had her child to think about, only her child. . . .

Smoke spiraled up from the three chimneys of Calder's Hotel. Lenora tensed as she pushed the fence gate open and looked up, wondering which window of the many that lined the second floor Doc might be standing before. Was he watching her now? Had he even seen her hesitation in front of the tailoring shop? She felt a blush rising to her cheeks as she hurried into the hotel lobby. She stopped to get her breath, then saw Anna moving heavily toward her.

"Damnation, girl," Anna blurted. "What the hell kind of game are ya playin' with yore life?"

Lenora swung her cape away from her and draped it over her right arm. She gazed back into Anna's blazing eyes, trying to maintain control of herself and look innocent, up to this point. "I don't know what you are speaking of, Anna," she said, holding her gaze steady.

Anna leaned into Lenora's face, pushing her gold-framed spectacles further up on her nose. "Doc Stanford," she hissed. "What's you and Doc doin', meetin' here? T'ain't right. T'ain't right for his Catrina and yore Seymour."

"My Seymour?" Lenora snapped. "Anna, I could tell you enough about Seymour to make your eyes pop right out of your head. And as for my meeting Doc: we're not planning to break any commandments. We're going to talk—to discuss politics, that's all." Lenora's face flushed crimson again as she realized how easily a lie had formed upon her lips. But it was true she and Doc were not going to bed up with one another—although she still had to break the news to Doc.

"Damn place to discuss politics," Anna grumbled, gumming her lips. "In a hotel room? What if gossip got 'round? And what's this you're sayin' of Seymour? Ain't he a good husband, or whut? I heerd he's even buildin' ya a brand new home."

Lenora checked her hair with her fingers, eyeing the staircase. This was not the time to discuss Seymour with Anna. It was a subject that could fill at least an hour's time. "First, Anna," she said hurriedly, "Doc said you'd make sure our meeting would be kept secret. Secondly, no, Seymour is *not* a good husband. But I don't want to talk about it now."

Lenora was interrupted by the banging of the front door. She turned and saw what she thought to be one of the most beautiful women she had ever seen walk toward her and Anna. Her hair hung like golden silk around her bare shoulders, and the delicate features of her face were accentuated by wide blue eyes. Only a knitted shawl was draped loosely around her dress, not hiding the deep cleavage of a large bust that emphasized the tiniest of waists. Her dark blue satin dress rustled as she stepped up to Anna.

"Good morning, Anna," the girl said in a flippy fashion. "Nice day for walkin', wouldn't you say?"

"Harumph," Anna growled, furrowing her brows. "So walkin' is all you've been up to, is it, Delia?"

Delia smiled wickedly as she touched Anna on her stubbled chin. "Now, now, Anna, your fangs are a showin'."

"Get along with the likes of ya," Anna snapped, pulling away from Delia.

Delia laughed softly, then headed on up the staircase.

"If'n that James person didn't pay me so well to shack up his mistress, I'd boot that girl right out o' my establishment," Anna said with a jerk of her head.

Lenora's knees grew weak as she gave another glance upward, only to see the tail of the dress as it disappeared down the long, narrow hallway. She bit her lower lip nervously, then asked, "What did you say about a person named James?"

"James Calloway," Anna said. "A nice bright lad who's opened the new tailoring shop. Cain't see why he'd take this Delia from the Illahee to board her here, when he could get all she dishes out for much less if'n he'd left her there."

Lenora's head began to spin with the realization that James *was* in Seattle, and only a few footsteps away. She wanted to rush to him—throw herself into his arms. The urge was so strong, but, of course, she couldn't. No. She couldn't. . . .

"Damnation, girl," Anna said. "You're not goin' to go faintin' on me, are ya? What would make ya suddenly go white as a ghost? Is it yore

Cassie Edwards

child? Are ya in pain, or whut?"

Lenora could not hold the tears back any longer. "Pain? Oh, yes, I'm in pain," she whispered, but she could not tell Anna that the pain was in her heart, not her womb. She let Anna lead her to a chair in front of the fire and was glad to be assisted into it.

"I'll run and fetch Doc," Anna said, then rushed up the stairs before Lenora could stop her.

Lenora hung her head in her hands and let the tears fall freely. "Oh, Papa," she sobbed. "Why is life so cruel? What have I done to deserve all this confusion and unhappiness?" She had a sudden vision of this lovely blonde girl being embraced by James. Did he love her, or only what she could give him? Even though Delia was quite beautiful, she appeared to be so hard, so cold. Surely James could not truly love someone like that. And maybe he didn't— he had not yet wed her.

A rushing of footsteps brought Doc to his knees in front of Lenora. She looked around, glad to see that Anna had not followed, so she could speak freely with him. "Doc, oh, Doc," she whispered, letting him pull her up now into his arms. She would always remember the comfort of his embrace, and now she realized that what she felt was love for him, but not a sexual love. She had been wrong to confuse the two kinds of love one could feel for a man. This particular love was a deep affection, much like a daughter's love for her father.

"What's wrong, Lenora?" he asked, caressing the nape of her neck. "Is it the baby? Are you in pain?"

Lenora placed her cheek on his broad shoulder. "No, the baby is fine," she said. "But I have much to tell you. I can confide in you, can't I?"

"Yes, my sweet dear," he answered. "Always. Come, sit down beside me."

Lenora did so, then opened up and told of her relationship with James, Seymour, her newly discovered feelings for Doc, and how wrong she had been to confuse her feelings of love for him, when all she really wanted was the warmth of his embrace and the comfort of his understanding.

Doc laughed hoarsely and lighted a cigar. "You really don't mind if I smoke?" he asked, eyeing her with sincere affection. She was relieved not to see hurt in the depths of his pale eyes, but an amused look instead.

"No. Please do smoke if you wish," she answered. She placed her hands on her lap, unable to take her eyes off him. In a way, it was as though she were in the presence of her Papa. Why hadn't she discovered this earlier? Her sexual fantasies must have been attributable to the deprivation she had felt since her marriage to Seymour.

"Oh, why has it taken the knowledge of James's presence in Seattle to make me understand where my heart still lies?" she thought painfully.

"Funny how things have a way of workin' out," he said. He leaned heavily against the back of the sofa, next to Lenora.

"What do you mean, Doc?"

"I've done much thinkin' since our last encounter," he said and laughed quietly. "Damn, you do know how to kiss a gent."

Lenora cast her eyes down and felt a renewed blush. Yes, she also remembered their kiss—his lips had been so warm—but that part of their relationship *had* been wrong. "I don't know what to say, Doc," she mumbled.

"You flattered an old man. That's what you did," he said. He took her hand in his and rested it on his knee. "But we both know now that can't ever be again."

"Yes, I do know."

"I don't know what possessed me to do such a thing, Lenora."

"Nor do I," she murmured. "For my own part, that is."

"But I feel we do have somethin' special between us," he continued. "And you've just expressed feelin' the same."

"Yes, I do."

"So we can remain close friends."

Lenora looked up at him. "Extra close, don't you think?" she asked eagerly. She knew that they had many things to talk about—surely there was not anything wrong with just talking. And he could teach her so much about life. He was the most intelligent person, besides her Papa, that she had yet to meet.

He flicked ashes into the fire. "Yes, yes. Extra close," he laughed. Then his wrinkles deepened as a serious expression took his smile away. "But I do have me a problem comin' to town."

Lenora leaned forward. "What might that be?" she asked.

"My first wife, Nancy."

"Your first wife is coming to Seattle?"

"Seems my divorce with Nancy was not valid in Massachusetts, which means I'm still married to her."

"But—Catrina?"

"She's bein' damned understandin' of this situation I've found myself in. She's even willin' to let Nancy come and share our house with us until the mess is cleared up."

"You mean getting a proper divorce?"

"There's more to it than that," Doc answered. "Nancy still claims to own half of my acquisitions here in Seattle, since the divorce wasn't valid, and she's comin' out here to look after her property."

"How horrible," Lenora exclaimed.

Doc laughed hoarsely. "She'll get the shock of her life when she arrives."

"Why is that, Doc?"

"Nancy doesn't know how generous I've been to my neighbors."

"Generous?"

"Right off, from the first day I settled here in Seattle, I've given away my wealth to anyone who seemed to need it to establish a claim of his own. Even now, before Nancy can get her hands on it, I've handed over one of the few pieces of property that I still hold clear title to, to the St. John's Lodge of the Masons for a new cemetery. She'll have quite a fit when she finds out her trip is for nothin'."

Lenora smiled to herself, envisioning Doc as a young man, full of spirit and good charity, helping the poor. She eyed his tattered clothes and now understood the reason for them. "You are so kind. I'm sure she'll understand."

"I sent her a wire, but I guess she didn't get it."

"When's she due to arrive?"

"In about two months."

"Then we still have time to see one another—to talk—before you get busy with two wives?"

"Now that I've tasted your sweetness, do you think I could resist your company?"

"I'm so glad you feel that way," she said, then turned her head at the sound of footsteps as Anna entered the room. She was reading a newspaper and smiling broadly.

"Seen the news yet?" she said, cackling.

Lenora rose and stood closer to the fire, knowing what Anna was reading. Anna was obviously pleased, as Lenora had secretly been.

"About Raef Wescott?" Doc said, also rising. He took the newspaper and read it once again. "Hate to see such goings on here in Seattle. I wanted this city to be one a body could feel safe in. Damn it. This man must've really suffered. To be shot *and* mangled by dogs—I hate to think of such violence."

"As far as I can figure, it serves the bastard right," Anna spouted. She went to the fire and lifted a good-sized log onto it.

"But dogs, Anna," Lenora said, shivering.

Anna turned her head sideways to smile back at Lenora, and suddenly Lenora grew cold inside. Anna did not have to tell what was in her mind—somehow Lenora could read it in the depths of Anna's eyes. The dogs had been Anna's—the three savage Indian mongrels that Anna kept on hand for protection.

Chapter Fourteen

The funeral in progress was the largest Seattle had known. It was March 14, the year 1874. Kessler Pavilion, the big new frame building at the corner of Front and Cherry Streets, was filled to capacity while Doc Stanford's body lay in state.

Branches from dogwood trees were piled around the casket, their four-petaled white blossoms dotting the masses of green leaves. They formed a peaceful, serene setting, as though Doc were sleeping in the midst of the forest that he had fallen in love with upon his first arrival in Seattle.

The whole town, it seemed, had come to say good-bye, except for one most noticeably absent Seymour Harper, who still avoided crowds since his night behind the Illahee. Lenora stood back from the crowd, largely swollen with child, beside Tess and Timothy. Her face was streaked with tears. Was Doc truly gone? It had all happened so fast.

She would never forget how the town had gathered at Kessler's Wharf to watch Doc's first wife step from the steamer *Olympia*, and how proudly Doc had given an arm to each of his wives and walked ashore between the rows of spectators. The men of Seattle had actually taken off their hats to Doc and his wives, watching, more enviously than not, the only man in Seattle who managed to have two wives at one time live under the same roof with him.

Then, in too short a time, he was gone. He had died suddenly only a short time later, leaving behind two widows and another grieving young woman who no one had ever suspected Doc to be involved with—no one except Seymour, who had begun to follow Lenora and finally witnessed one of Lenora and Doc's secret meetings at the hotel.

Lenora sniffled and gave Tess's hand a squeeze, glad to have a close friend in whom she could confide. Lenora's life with Seymour had become one of strained silence, which was all right with Lenora. At least he had left her alone sexually, and now that the baby was almost due she could fill her days with thoughts of Joshua Caine Harper.

But, oh, how she would miss Doc. He had taught her so much about life and had even helped to remove, for a while at least, her thoughts of James—who even now stood only a few feet in front of her, with his arm draped possessively around Delia's waist.

Lenora's anguish over the loss of Doc helped erase the further pain of James's closeness. Her heart had no more room this day for jealousy of the golden-haired, slim vixen standing next to James attired in a daring, low-cut, silken dress.

Through her thin black veil, Lenora tried not to let herself absorb the way in which James stood there so tall and erect, dressed in a formal afternoon coat and tight-fitting breeches, and the way his tawny hair appeared more curly in the damp climate of this northwest country. The way he towered over Delia was almost majestic, and Lenora was glad not to be able to see his eyes, for if she did she knew that even Doc would be forgotten.

Final words were being spoken over the casket by a grieving fellow citizen. "Without Doc Stanford," he said, "Seattle will not be the same, for indeed, without him, Seattle might not have been."

Then Lenora cried into her handkerchief as the casket was closed and carried away to be placed on a carriage.

"Are you all right, Lenora?" Tess said, turning to her. She lifted her own veil, revealing wide, worried eyes. "Perhaps you should go on home, for the baby's sake. You know that Timothy said you might deliver early."

"No. I must go with you to the cemetery," Lenora said, wiping her tears under the veil. "I'm all right. Honestly, I am."

Timothy stepped to her other side. "If you'd take your doctor's advice, you'd head straight for home and go to bed," he said. "You're not looking too well. Funerals are a bit depressing for a woman eight months pregnant."

Suddenly Lenora's insides seemed to turn a flip as James brushed against her, and her heart stopped for a moment when their eyes met.

"Excuse me, Ma'am," he said, most politely, stopping to catch her by the arm and steady her. "I guess the crowd is pushin' a mite too much." Something jerked his mind to attention when he saw the greenness of the eyes partially hidden beneath the dark veil. Hurriedly, he studied the rest of the facial features, having recognized something there. Yet . . . the face was more puffy than Lenora's had been. Then his gaze shifted downward, and he saw the size of her stomach. No, it couldn't be Lenora. Still, he tried to see the color of her hair, but it was too well hidden beneath the draped, dark cloth.

"Coming, darlin'?" Delia said, impatiently jerking on his arm.

James stepped back away from Lenora with a half-smile playing on his lips. "Pardon my rudeness for starin' at you, Ma'am," he said, "but I thought you might be someone I once knew."

Lenora cast her eyes down, dying a slow death inside. He had not even recognized her.

Had their time together meant so little to him? She hated him now, even more. And she must not let her feelings of hate be confused with love ever again. She cleared her throat and looked at him. "That's perfectly all right, sir," she said icily. "Mistakes are made. Every day of one's life."

"Then you do forgive me, Mrs. . . . ?"

"James," Delia persisted, with anger flashing in her eyes.

"Mrs. Seymour Harper," Lenora said firmly, tilting her chin up into the air. At this moment she was most proud to be able to boast of her marital status. She was glad that James would not know that he was to be a father. He did not deserve to know. And he was still flaunting that whore Delia for all to see. No, Lenora would *never* tell James of his son. It would always remain the most important secret of her heart.

"I'm glad to make your acquaintance, Ma'am," he said, half bowing. "I know of your husband the professor." He still saw so much in her face. If not for its puffiness and the redness from tears, might it not be Lenora? His heart was thumping wildly as he still could remember her in his arms. He had never before or since felt the same about a woman. Ah, how he had hated deserting her in San Francisco. But he had had to do it. She had wanted—had even spoken of—marriage. "Might I ask your first name, Mrs. Harper?" he quickly blurted, wanting to hear her speak the name that had been spoken so often in his restless dreams.

Lenora's head began to swirl and she leaned into Timothy's embrace. She had suddenly seen the gleam of awareness in the depths of James's dark eyes. He had finally recognized her beneath the swollen cheeks. "Too much water in the system," Timothy had worried.

"Lenora, are you all right?" Timothy boomed, holding her arm.

Lenora's eyes shot open and watched the color drain from James's face.

"Lenora? Is it you?" James said in a strained whisper. His gaze worked over her once again, scrutinizing her pregnancy and wondering. "Why . . . how . . . ?" he gasped, reaching for her.

She withered away from him and spoke to Timothy. "Please take me to the carriage," she pleaded. "Hurry. Please take me from this place."

"But Lenora . . . ," James was saying, as she was led away from him.

Tess also helped Lenora up into the carriage. "Oh, how horrible for you, Lenora," she sighed. She knew of James, for Lenora had spoken of him—and his child.

"I'm taking you right home," Timothy said, climbing into the carriage next to Lenora.

"No, you mustn't," Lenora said. "I must accompany Doc to the cemetery as the rest of the town is doing. I must."

"I can see your paleness even through the veil, Lenora," Timothy argued.

Tess leaned around Lenora. "Timothy, Lenora has made her mind up. Now, please catch up with the funeral procession," she said softly.

"Yes, dear," Timothy answered, then slapped the reins and clucked to the horses.

"Doc's to be stored in the toolhouse," Lenora said solemnly, placing her doubled fists on her lap. "He put so many hopes into the new Masonic cemetery, and now he has to stay in the toolhouse in the old cemetery to wait for the new one to be cleared. It's too sad."

"It won't be for long," Tess comforted.

"One night alone in a toolshed is too long," Lenora said, weeping all over again.

The funeral procession continued to move along the narrow, muddy streets, past the clapboard houses on the hills, until the old cemetery was reached.

Lenora stared around her at the scores of black carriages lined up beneath towering firs and hemlocks. Off in the distance, Mount Tacoma sat in its ghostly splendor, with its white swirling mists trying to hide it from searching eyes.

"You won't be alone, Doc," Lenora thought. "The mountain that you loved will always be there, looking down upon you." She and Doc had sat at the hotel window and stared together, for hours it had seemed, at the mountain and the way it constantly changed its appearance as the sun's rays would dance and play on its snow-covered sides. "Just a piece of heaven, right here on our earth," he had said.

Lenora shivered in the damp, steady breeze. Wasn't it eerily silent on this hilltop, as the casket was being placed inside the toolhouse?

"I think we can leave now," Timothy said, then pulled on the reins to turn the carriage around.

Something clutched at Lenora's heart when she realized this was her last good-bye to Doc. Then this fact was lost from her thoughts when Timothy guided their carriage past another, which was being pulled by a black and a white horse.

Lenora swallowed hard as her eyes met James's for a brief moment. There was such a look of hurt wonder in his brown eyes. Lenora wanted to cry again, for Doc . . . for James . . . for her child . . . and for herself.

Chapter Fifteen

The house still smelled of fresh cedar and painted walls, even though Lenora had made it her home for one full year now. The sound of a carriage's wheels moving away from the house made Lenora awaken with a start. She peered across the room and gazed proudly upon the sleeping figure of one-year-old Joshua Caine, glad to see that his sleep had not been disturbed. The kerosene lamp had been turned low, as it was most nights, to enable her to see Joshua if he stirred in the night.

"He should be moved to his own room," Mama Galvez had scolded often enough in her thick Mexican accent. "Want him to be a Mama's boy? Shouldn't the papa be sharing the bedroom with you, 'Nora, instead of his son?"

But Lenora had ignored the admonitions of her maid-companion, and when Joshua would creep into her bed, as he had done most evenings since he had learned to toddle, Lenora would gladly let him cuddle up next to her bosom. He was all she had in this world of misunderstandings, and she would see to it that he would have all the love he sought from her.

The silence of the house made Lenora wonder where Seymour might be off to again this night. After his unsuccessful attempts at getting her to his own bedroom, he had begun to wander elsewhere for his pleasures in the night. Lenora had heard whispers of Anna and Seymour, but Lenora could not help laughing at the thought of the two of them together—Anna with her brusqueness and he with his forced shyness. No, the gossip had to be wrong. Yet, Seymour had spoken so disgustedly of the girls in brothels, she knew he most surely would not be seeking *their* services.

Sighing resolutely, Lenora settled herself once again beneath the softness of her blanket, remembering having seen James earlier in the day . . . James, whose eyes would grow dark with passion when she passed him on the street . . . James, whose face would show his pain when Lenora refused to acknowledge that he had tipped his hat and spoken to her . . . James, who had married that hussy Delia and had her now housed in a white-painted house on Queen Anne's hill.

Jealousy tore at Lenora's insides the more she thought of James and Delia intimately together. Lenora had not had her tormented desires fulfilled for much too long now, and she so hungered to give in to the pleadings James had sent by messenger boy—pleadings to meet with him, anywhere, anytime that she chose.

Feeling the ache in her breasts and loins, Lenora murmured softly, "Oh, James, how I yearn to say yes to your biddings. And how long can I say no? We pass each other on the streets much too often."

And there was Joshua to think of. In one of James's messages, he had asked about Joshua, and had even vaguely mentioned how little the boy resembled his father Seymour. Lenora bit her lower lip nervously. Did James suspect the truth?

A light tapping at the bedroom door made Lenora stiffen, but then she remembered hearing the carriage leave and knew that Seymour could not have returned so soon. Once he left each night, she could almost predict the number of hours he would be gone. He never returned swiftly.

Hurriedly she climbed from the bed, slipped into some houseshoes, and pulled a sheer silk robe around her shoulders. She went to the door and opened it slowly, not wanting to awaken Joshua. She was surprised to find Mama Galvez standing there in a chenille robe with heavy-lidded eyes. Mama Galvez's stiff black hair framed the dark tan of her face, and her black eyes wavered as she stood there, almost cowering. She knew that she should not disturb 'Nora, especially not to tell her of a strange man calling at such an ungodly hour of the night.

"What is it, Mama Galvez?" Lenora asked, shutting the door behind her.

"A gentleman caller, 'Nora," Mama Galvez whispered, glancing back toward the shadows of the staircase. "I told him you were in bed, but he just kind of laughed and asked me again to let him talk to you."

Lenora's heart thumped nervously as she fastened her robe around her, realizing it did not hide the swell of her bosom or the way her sheer nightie clung to her thin waist and curving hips. She glanced quickly toward the staircase, seeing only shadows from the flickering lamp that Mama Galvez had lit at the foot of the stairs. Then a much larger shadow moved within eye's range and Lenora's insides quivered, knowing that only James could cast such a shadow against the papered wall.

"His name?" she questioned. She ran her fingers through her hair, wishing that she had used a brush on its tangles before retiring this evening. She now knew that if it were James she would agree to see him. He had come at the right moment—when her thoughts had been so full of him and of her desire to have him near her. But here—in her own home, which was also Seymour's? How could James be so bold as to expect her to see him under such circumstances? A remembrance of her needing to hate him swept through her mind, but only briefly. At this moment, hate was the last thing on her mind.

" 'Nora, he wouldn't say," Mama Galvez answered, wringing her hands nervously before her.

Lenora wished Mama Galvez would not always be so humble. It embarrassed Lenora. She had tried to instill her own stubborn beliefs into Mama Galvez—one being that Mama Galvez was a woman of substance and so should hold her chin up and her back straight.

Lenora had joined Seattle's Women's Suffrage Association, even though she knew it to be the radical wing of the movement. Since Joshua's birth, she had attended all suffrage meetings but had not been elected to office. She had been held back a bit by her husband, who had no interest in politics or abstract economics.

Lenora had heard Mrs. Laura De Fora Gordon lecture in Kessler's Hall on "Our Great Political Problem: Women's Suffrage."

She had even been among those who crowded into the Methodist Church to cheer Susan B. Anthony, the national leader of the suffrage movement, and Abigail Scott Dunway, the Northwest's female literary figure.

These women, along with Lenora, wanted to reform the world. They had seen deserving and undeserving make their fortunes through blind luck and saw others as deserving and undeserving go broke. They dreamed of a society in which this could not happen.

Lenora resented the instability of Seattle's economy. But Mama Galvez continued to walk and stand with head bowed, as though someone had beaten her with a whip to make her into the cowering fool she now portrayed.

Lenora placed her arm around Mama Galvez's thick shoulders and hugged her. "It's all right, Mama Galvez," she said reassuringly. "I can take care of this. Please go on to your room."

Mama Galvez flashed a smile of white, straight teeth toward Lenora, then hunched over still more as she shuffled to her room at the far end of the hall. Seymour had not wanted this Mexican lady sleeping on the same floor as he, but Lenora had put her stubborn side forward and won her way, as she now did with almost anything she desired. She was fast learning the worth of being a woman in what most men still argued was a "man's world."

The shadow had moved away from the light, leaving Lenora to wonder. Had he grown tired of waiting? Had he left? This thought made her move more anxiously, and when she had reached the foot of the stairs, she stopped abruptly and drank in his presence. This was the first time they had been alone since the journey to California. Shouldn't she feel guilty?

"I had to see you, Lenora," James said almost awkwardly. Even in the dim light, he could see her heartbeat pulsating in her throat. As his gaze lowered, he was glad to see her liquid curves scarcely hidden beneath the silken fabric, and she smelled of all the wild flowers of Seattle, making his longing for her even more intense. He wanted to grab the lamp, hold it before her, and memorize all the details of her beauty.

She feasted and feasted her eyes upon him. He was dressed as he was always dressed now, with the best of tailoring, in a brown coat that hung open to reveal a brown waistcoat and tight, clinging breeches. He wore no hat, which she was glad of, because she ached to run her fingers through his golden curls. But he wore gloves, as he always seemed to, retaining the habit from his days as a weaver.

"But why, James?" she asked. "You know you are in another man's house, speaking with another man's wife."

James took a step forward, enabling the light of the lamp to play upon his face, showing the gentleness of his facial features and the growing desire in his dark eyes.

"You know where Seymour is at this moment," he scoffed, removing his gloves to slap them nervously together.

"Yes, I have an idea where," she said softly. She fluttered her eyelashes nervously at him as he continued to watch her.

"So it shouldn't matter that his wife is entertaining a man," he said, remembering the power she had always had on him when she chose to use her wide eyes.

"But you also have a wife," Lenora whispered. "A wife who was once used by many men," she thought. "How *could* you, James?"

"You gave me no choice, Lenora. I couldn't have you, and I needed a wife—so Delia was there."

"You didn't want me, James," she said firmly, remembering. She looked toward the staircase, also remembering Joshua.

"I was a fool."

"And now?"

"Now, always, I love you, Lenora."

Lenora felt a blush rising and turned her back to him, busying her fingers with a tassel hanging from a lampshade. He was again confusing her. Had he truly always loved her? But if he had. . . . She felt his hands on her arms and felt a giddiness in her head as he turned her to face him once again.

"Lenora, I must kiss you, or I shall die," he murmured, then pulled her roughly into his arms.

She wanted to fight him, to shout at him to leave her be, and not start this thing all over again. It was even more impossible for the two of them now than it had been in California. They had both been single then; now they were both married. And she even had a child, created by the union of their bodies. But his mouth stopped all her words, all her thoughts, leaving only soft messages of love that she had been longing for so long to receive.

"Lenora, Lenora," he whispered, then kissed her anew, reviving feelings inside her that had not surfaced since their last night together on the trail. When his tongue probed and made entrance inside her mouth, her senses reeled. Feeling only a melting warmth, she welcomed—encouraged—his hands to search through the silken fabric for her breasts, which ached even more now from need. She gasped when his fingers circled a nipple, kneading it through the silk until it was hard and stiff, and when his lips left her mouth to cover the breast, she could feel her breast crying for release from its confines so it could experience the full wet warmth of his mouth. Yet, she also had the need to stop what was happening—it was wrong. . . .

She reeled somewhat as she shoved against his chest. "James," she sighed drunkenly. "You mustn't. What if Seymour . . . ?"

He locked his hands around her wrists and guided one of her hands to the crotch of his trousers, where she felt the pulsating bulge that also seemed to be crying for release from the tight garment. "You know as well as I do that Seymour only recently left," he said hoarsely. "And you also know how long he will be gone."

Lenora's eyes widened. "If you know this, then you've been watching his movements," she gasped.

"So?"

"So you've also been watching mine?"

"Yes, my dear Lenora."

"And while doing this, what explanation have you given your wife?"

"She's accepted my absences. She knows I've taken up a love for gamblin'."

"Gambling?"

"She thinks for money," he chuckled. "She doesn't know that it's you I'm trying to win."

"James, why?"

"There's never been anyone to compare with your beauty," he said, tracing her facial features with his forefinger and sending chills down her spine. "First, there's your wide, trusting eyes," he said almost reverently. "Green, ah, as green as the deepest parts of the Atlantic. And then there's your nose—straight and aristocratic, like your stubborn streak." His lips searched hers. "And your lips—I wish they were mine to possess for the rest of our lives—so full, and even more beautiful when they curve down in a pout. And so soft, almost as soft as I remember a more private part of your body being."

"James," Lenora gasped, feeling another flush rising.

"Is it still as soft, since the child?" he persisted, letting his fingers touch her thigh.

Lenora stiffened inside, having the need never to let Joshua's name enter into a conversation between her and James. She did not want to be tricked into letting the truth slip from her lips.

"Lenora, let me see if you're still as soft and sweet as I remember."

Her heart was hammering once again with James's bold advances. His hands had managed to work their way up inside her nightgown and were now tracing a path upward to where she had grown wet from excitement. She wanted to pull away from him but instead found herself leaning into his hand and sighed deeply when he found the soft mound of her inner thigh and gently parted it to begin skillfully stroking her, then began searching deeper inside her. . . .

"But where?" she whispered, feeling the exquisite sensations flooding her, making her forget that she was so vulnerable. He increased the tempo of his thrusting fingers until she felt as though she were ready to reach her peak.

"Your room?" he suggested.

Again she became rigid. Joshua was in her room. "In our spare room," she quickly whispered. "It's not fully furnished yet, but there is a bed." She could not tell him that this spare bedroom had been meant for Joshua—but that she had not yet released him from her own room, for more reasons than one. As long as Joshua shared her room, Seymour would not enter in the middle of the night to force her to do her wifely duties—which had never included her own sexual releases, only those hasty, selfish releases of Seymour's.

"But we mustn't take long," she said, taking his hand. With the other, she lifted the kerosene lamp and led him upstairs, not believing that she was truly letting this happen. Had he not so cruelly deserted her before? Should she not still hate him? But she knew that love and hate could be considered two sides of the same coin, so alike were the two in emotional intensity. She knew that, where James was concerned, the coin was easily turned over. She turned her eyes to him and smiled almost shyly as she found that he had been watching her. The flickering of the light played in his eyes, making them suddenly turn gold to match his hair.

"Oh, James," Lenora whispered. "I've waited, so long."

James pulled her next to him and together they entered a room that smelled of emptiness and newness. The small red rose design of the wallpaper matched the red satin comforter on the four-poster mahogany bed.

Lenora looked heavy-lashed toward James, then lowered the flames in the lamp and placed it on the wooden floor next to the bed. When James pulled her down next to him, she laughed softly. "The bedspread, James," she said. "I must remove the bedspread."

"And then your garments," he teased, getting up to remove his own.

"After I pull the shades," she laughed. "Then we could spend the full night in here and no one would even know."

"Ah, you are a dreamer."

"Yes, I've learned to do plenty of that."

"So you have, also?"

"Dreams have been my life since you left me standing alone on that pier in San Francisco," she said, then wished she hadn't. Had she ruined the magic of the moment?

Only attired in breeches now, he went to Lenora and pulled her into his arms, burying his nose in the depths of her hair. "My darling Lenora," he murmured. "I had different dreams then—dreams that could be interpreted only as a fight for my future. I was afraid of having a woman around to get in the way of my dreams of success."

"Would I really have slowed you down?"

"No, now that I know of your stubbornness and strong will, I know that you could have aided in my pursuits. But I had only known you a few hours when you began talking of marriage. You had captured my heart, but I was afraid to let you capture my mind."

"I wish . . . ," Lenora said, then stopped, knowing that it was too late to do such a childish thing as wish.

James began to lower Lenora's gown. "Why are we wasting time talking?" he said, brushing a hand against her breasts as he watched the gown crumple to the floor around Lenora's ankles. "This is now. We're together. Let us savor this moment, Lenora." He scooped her up into his arms, carried her to the bed, and lowered her gently down upon it.

She was ready to let him teach her all over again what he had taught her that night beside the fire and stream. Her heart hammered, her fingers trembled, her lashes fluttered; she was like a bird—ready to take flight, to soar to the highest point of ecstasy.

When he finally did stretch out beside her, she swallowed hard and turned her body to meet his. She did not close her eyes when his lips covered hers. This was no dream, and she wanted to watch every minute of it as it happened. She saw his broad shoulders tightening as his arms circled around her. She felt the bristle of his chest hair rubbing against her bosom. His hands never kept still. They found the small of her back, the nape of her neck, the thickness of her hair, and the bones of her spine that led downward to the curve of her buttocks. Then she shivered as his fingers began to caress her love mound once again, until she found herself arching her body upward and moaning with the need to release her pent-up emotions.

"Please," she begged. "You must love me. Now."

Words were no longer needed. He kissed her even more gently as he penetrated into the innermost part of her, and then the years of dreams and waiting were blending into one night of blissful pleasure, as she rode with his every thrust. His moans of pleasure matched her own, and as if by magic their bodies tremored in unison, leaving them sated, yet clinging desperately to one another as though there would be no tomorrow.

"Oh, God Jesus, Lenora," James uttered breathlessly. "It's as perfect as I remembered it being with you. Your body is made for loving—

I only wish it were myself that could be the one to share this wonder with you."

"But that's quite impossible," she murmured. She turned her back to him, wondering if they would ever make love again. Shame and guilt had just begun to spoil this night that had been so lovely.

"No, it's not impossible," he said firmly, climbing over her, to face her. "We've waited two long years to be together again because I let my own stupidity separate us. We can't let the world separate us again."

Lenora's heart melted when she saw the pleading in his dark eyes. The smile wrinkles had suddenly deepened around his mouth and eyes. "Oh, James, I do love you so," she said, then threw herself into his arms again. "We must be together again, my dearest. But how?"

"Your house is well hidden in the forest," he said, trailing kisses from her forehead to the stiff erectness of her breasts. "When Seymour leaves, I can arrive. I can come by foot, as tonight, so no one will recognize my horses or carriage."

"But I feel so wicked—so shamefully wicked."

"Lenora, I believe it is the only way."

"But Mama Galvez?"

"She's your faithful companion and servant, is she not?"

"Yes."

"Then she will cooperate."

"James, I don't know."

"Is it your child you are afraid of?"

Lenora stiffened and pulled away from him. "My child?" she whispered, biting her lower lip.

"Are you afraid he might see me?"

"No," she stammered. "I never worried for one minute about that."

"Does Seymour have a good relationship with Joshua?"

Lenora sat upright, staring wide-eyed at James, with a sinking sensation at the pit of her stomach. "James, why do you ask?"

"I've studied Joshua on your excursions to town," he said hoarsely. "Strange as hell, Lenora, how he doesn't resemble Seymour at all. With his golden curls, he could pass as my own son."

Lenora jumped from the bed and pulled her gown over her head, breathing rapidly. Fire showed in her eyes as she turned to face James again. "You must leave," she said. She hated the tremor in her voice. She knew that he had also heard it. She set her jaw and lifted the lamp up from the floor. She turned the flame up and watched the black smoke swirl upward from its chimney.

"What the hell did I say?" James blurted. He climbed from the bed and hurriedly dressed.

"Nothing, really," Lenora lied. "It's just getting late, that's all. Seymour might arrive home at any moment now."

"Jesus, Lenora. You know that he's not been gone that long."

"But I still worry."

"All right, I'll leave," he said. "But when can I return?"

"Let me be the one to send word by messenger," she answered. Something inside her—a fear for her child, possibly—told her that there might not be another meeting. She had much to think about. Yes, she loved James, but she could not let him know Joshua was his child, or Joshua Caine would become a child torn between parents. No, she *had* to protect him, above all else.

"And you will? Soon?" he said, brushing his lips against her lashes.

"Yes, my love. I will. Soon," she lied again. "But come, now. I'll walk to the door with you."

Arm in arm, they strolled down the staircase, but each step seemed to take Lenora one more step away from James, for she knew the impossibility of letting this happen again.

"I love you, Lenora," James whispered. His fingers touched the chain around her neck. "And will you enter into your diary this evening . . . your love for me?"

Lenora had forgotten that he knew of her secret key. Her face reddened. "I always fill my diary with the secrets of my heart."

"Which include me?"

"Yes, James. Always."

The shadows from the lamp flickered like ghosts' shadows on the wall beside them, blending with their two synchronized shadows—two bodies in one, hands clasped as one, until the front door was open, letting in the smell of the forest and sea water. In the distance, an owl screeched and a foghorn echoed up from the bay.

"Until then, Lenora," James whispered and disappeared into the darkness of night.

Lenora sighed deeply as she secured the door, then crept silently upstairs and into her bed, feeling a deep, empty sadness for what she so wanted and what she could not have. When she felt a movement in the bed beside her, she turned and saw the dark, round eyes of Joshua Caine smiling up at her.

"Hello, sweetheart," she whispered, then let him cuddle up next to her and bury his nose between her breasts. "Oh, my little one," she sobbed and did not remove his tiny hand when it reached down inside her gown to cup a breast.

Chapter Sixteen

The aroma of boiled eggs and potatoes filled Lenora's spacious, well-equipped kitchen. Lenora tried to keep her mind on her preparations but found it almost impossible, still feeling the presence of James in her house. Had it truly happened, or had it been a pleasant figment of her imagination?

"I think everything is packed and ready to go," Tess said, removing her apron. She stared in wonder toward the still silent Lenora. There was a glow about Lenora this morning, but also a look of hidden torment in the depths of her green eyes. Tess went to Lenora and touched her flushed cheek. "Lenora, what's the matter? You know you can tell me. Don't I know most of your secrets, and you mine?"

Lenora reached up and patted Tess's hand. "This is one time I've got to solve my own problem," she said softly. She stepped away from Tess, removed her apron, and smoothed the folds of her dress. She went to the two large picnic baskets and sorted through the covered dishes, mentally calculating all that they had planned to take. "Yes, I believe we have everything," she said, then tucked a red-checked linen cloth atop each basket.

"I'm quite excited about what the town has decided to do," Tess said. She began to gather dirty dishes and placed them in a wash pail in the sink, then began to hand-pump water into a teakettle for heating.

"I am, also," Lenora beamed. She needed something to busy her mind—to keep it from straying to her hunger for James's kisses and touches. "But it is too bad the railroad chose Tacoma over Seattle for its terminus. Seattle was promised the railroad as early as the 1850's. The pioneers cut the trees and built their cabins and pushed the wilderness back away from them. They fought the Indians and fleas, and they've endured the damp and mud. They left friends, relatives, and comforts behind. Surely they've earned the right to tickets in this great railroad lottery."

"Yes, I know," Tess murmured. "I've heard it all, many times. Timothy was quite upset about it. He fears for his practice. If most of Seattle's population gives up and moves to Tacoma, what might we who want to remain do to keep ourselves in food and clothing?"

"There will always be a university," Lenora said stubbornly. "Tacoma doesn't boast of such a claim. And there will always be a need for a doctor. Doc Stanford kept busy enough, even when there were only a few cabins built on this land."

"The Northern Pacific Railroad is run by shrewd men," Tess grumbled.

"But today we will show them just what type of people they are dealing with. We are even more shrewd," Lenora giggled.

"And weren't the dedication ceremonies of the railroad at Tacoma quite a disaster?" Tess said, smiling almost wickedly. She lifted the whistling teakettle from the stove and poured it over the dishes, then hand-pumped some fresh, cooler well water also into the pail to make the dishwater touchable.

"Just leave the dishes for Mama Galvez," Lenora said. "She's giving Joshua his morning bath, and as soon as he's back down for a nap, she'll see to this clutter." She picked up a picnic basket, went to set it down by the front door, and watched Tess do the same with the other basket. "And, yes, I laughed until tears rolled from my eyes when Timothy told of the ceremonies in Tacoma," she said further. "It rained the whole day, and there was no money for a golden spike. And then when the workers who hadn't yet been paid found out that they weren't going to be? It was quite humorous when they blockaded the track with logs and threatened to remove a few bridges and hold them as security."

Tess handed Lenora her cape, then secured her own around her shoulders. "But, all laughing aside," Tess murmured, "the steel bands stretch to Tacoma, not to Seattle. And since the government has sworn off helping Seattle, Seattle must help herself."

"Yes. We shall prevail, if it means having to grade the road and lay the narrow-gauge tracks ourselves."

"I wish we women could wear breeches instead of dresses for the occasion," Tess murmured, hating to dirty a dress by the hard labor she and Lenora had agreed to do.

Lenora laughed. "I wonder what the people of the community would say if you showed up at Steele's Landing in a pair of Timothy's breeches, and I in some of Seymour's."

Tess's eyes widened. "Never," she gasped.

"It would be interesting," Lenora mused. "It would be interesting."

"Listen," Tess said, then hurriedly opened the front door.

"It's beginning," Lenora said. "Seattle's war with the railroad."

Lenora and Tess stepped onto the front porch and stood arm in arm, listening proudly. The steamer whistles sounded in unison with the whistle at Kessler's Mill, and the church bells of the two churches of Seattle clanged with pagan enthusiasm. Then, closer still, these sounds were answered by Seymour pulling the rope on the biggest bell yet—that of the Territorial University.

"Let's go," Tess said firmly. "Seattle has given notice, so let's go with the rest of the town and break ground for our *own* spur of the railroad."

Lenora and Tess lifted their picnic baskets onto Lenora's private carriage and started out to join the entire population of the town at Steele's Landing. They had agreed to lay the railroad line over the mountains with their own hands.

"Do you think it's really possible?" Tess said, clinging to the seat of the carriage as Lenora clucked to the horses, urging them forward through the deep ruts of mud.

"All we can do is try," Lenora said firmly.

"Seymour isn't going to help?"

"Seymour?" Lenora laughed sarcastically. "Seymour only thinks of Seymour."

"Timothy left earlier with a group of men," Tess said. "Harry Kessler and that group."

"Harry Kessler seems to have had a hand in every stage of Seattle's growth," Lenora said. "He's been mayor over and over again, and now he has a pier and pavilion named after him. Doc did as much, and I see nothing bearing his name."

"The Seattle Exchange will always remain Doc Stanford's."

"But his name isn't inscribed in it anywhere."

"Lenora, Harry Kessler used his money wisely. Doc didn't."

"Yes, I know," Lenora murmured. "And I'll wager that a hundred years from now, Harry Kessler will still have something named for him."

Lenora's eyes widened when she and Tess arrived at Steele's Landing. The whole town *had* arrived, and the men were already busying themselves with picks and shovels and wheelbarrows, grading the piece of road.

The women were preparing a large noon meal and serving cool drinks to the laborers.

"I still plan to help in the actual building of this road," Lenora said stubbornly. "I shall not stand aside only preparing food for the men. What better way to show the men that we women are more than the wearers of dainty aprons?"

"I also want to help," Tess said. She removed her cape and tied her dark hair up into a scarf, and Lenora did the same. They left their baskets lying among the many others; then each picked up a shovel and began to dig.

The ache in her back made Lenora pause to rest. She wiped her brow with the sleeve of her dress and looked around her, realizing that she and Tess had become fruit for gossip. The women stood in small, furtive clusters exchanging nods of disapproval, and the men continued to invent ways of taunting these two women who were acting so unfemale.

Lenora had tried not to look James's way, but had found it hard, for it seemed that only he and Timothy had not joined in on the jeering remarks from the other men. Once, when James had worked his way to her side, pushing a wheelbarrow full of heavy rocks, she had felt a keen weakness pass over her, as she had the very first time he had looked at her on the trail. Would he always have such powers over her? Was this what love did to a person?

But he had not spoken. He had continued pushing the wheelbarrow past her, but his eyes had betrayed the intensity of his desire for her.

"Lenora, I don't think I can manage another minute's labor," Tess panted, dropping to the ground beside Lenora.

Squatting near Tess, Lenora felt an emptiness at the pit of her stomach, seeing the little that had been accomplished even though much sweat had been spent this long day. Only once had the laborers stopped—to enjoy the picnic dinner served by the women and then to listen to a few speeches of encouragement. John Dennison, the father of the Fathers of Seattle, had made a fighting speech from a wagon. And Harry Kessler had made the shortest speech of them all. He had turned his massive face toward the crowd and had said, "Let's quit fooling around and get to work!"

"It is impossible," Lenora said. She felt the blisters on the palms of her hands and the ache in each muscle of her body. "I know now that this is an impossible venture."

Tess sighed heavily. "I feel as though I'm going to die from aching," she murmured.

"Surely the men must feel it also."

Lenora arranged the skirt of her dress beneath her and slumped also down onto the ground, watching as men began to draw back from the labor, one at a time. "Yes, I'm sure of it," she said. She searched the men until she found James once again. He was still hard at work, and Lenora wondered if even his gloves could protect his hands this day from the blisters and calluses.

"It *is* an impossible task, isn't it, Lenora?" Tess sighed.

"Yes, Tess, it is. At this rate, it would take centuries to get the tracks across the mountains. Seattle simply must decide to set her dreams in another direction."

Tess curled her nose and pulled at her dress beneath the arms. "I smell like a man, Lenora," she laughed.

"I welcome the smell," Lenora said. "It shows we've done something besides sit in the shade of the balsams like the rest of the women."

"Did you notice that Delia Calloway is not among the women today?"

Lenora's heart faltered. She bit her lower lip nervously as her eyes scanned the clusters of women. "No, I hadn't noticed," she said. But she did now, and she wondered why. Had James revealed the truth? But, why would he? Hadn't he succeeded at bedding Lenora without any promises of confronting Delia?

304

"I feel I should tell you something Timothy confided most sincerely to me," Tess said quietly. She glanced quickly around her, to be sure that no one was in listening range.

Lenora's eyes widened, and she felt an eagerness flowing through her veins. "What are you speaking of, Tess?" she prodded.

"Promise you won't tell?"

"Have I ever betrayed your confidences?"

"I'm betraying my husband's by telling you."

"Please. Whatever is it?"

"It's Delia."

"What about Delia?" Lenora gasped. She would die, she knew, if Delia was going to have James's child.

"She's quite ill," Tess blurted.

Something grabbed at Lenora's heart. She shook her head, hoping she'd heard wrong. Had James made love to her knowing his wife was seriously ill? "What do you mean—quite ill?" Lenora asked, feeling the strain by way of a dryness in her throat.

"She's struggling with consumption, I believe Timothy called it."

"Consumption?" Lenora gasped. "Might she even die?" Lenora herself wanted to die. James had come to her while his wife lay so ill. Suddenly Lenora felt like a whore—someone James would only seek out because his wife was too ill to perform her wifely duties. She hung her head in an effort to hide her tears.

"Yes. There is little hope," Tess answered. "She's fading quite rapidly, Timothy tells me."

Lenora jumped to her feet and began to run toward the forest. When she reached the towering balsams, she pushed her way through the tangle of brush, sobbing until her body ached even more. A crushing of twigs behind her made her turn with a start. When she saw James standing before her, she began to beat his chest until he grabbed her roughly by the wrists and stopped her.

"Damn it, Lenora, stop it," he said. "I saw you run in here and saw how distraught you were, and I had to follow. What the hell's the matter? Why are you looking at me as though you hate me? What have I done?"

"How could you, James?" she sobbed. She could feel the tears washing the sweat into her mouth. She tasted a mixture of salt and dust and knew she must be a sight to see now after her day's labor, but she no longer cared. James had betrayed her. Once again.

"How could I what?"

"Your wife. She's so ill. . . ."

"What the hell does that have to do with anything?"

"You're hard inside, James Calloway," Lenora stormed. "How could you make love to me last night, knowing your wife. . . ."

"She knows of my true feelings for you, Lenora," he said. "She's known all along."

"She's known?" Lenora whispered. "I suppose she even knows about last night?"

"I'm not that cruel."

"How cruel are you, then?"

306

"Is loving you a wrong thing?" he asked, pleading with the dark of his eyes. "Whether my wife be well or ill doesn't change my love for you. When I've held her in my arms, I've even whispered your name. I've loved you since the very first moment I laid eyes on you."

Lenora turned her back to him and lowered her head. "Oh, James," she sobbed further. She was torn between loyalties to herself and to a woman who was dying—even if it was a woman whom Lenora had never had any respect for.

"Please don't turn from me, Lenora," James said, trying to turn her face to him. But she stood rigid, unwilling to be swayed by his sweet words this time. She refused to feel dirty in her love for him.

"Please leave me alone, James," she said sternly. "Just leave me alone."

"You don't mean that, Lenora."

"Yes, I do. Now, please just go."

"I'll always love you, Lenora. Please remember that."

The words were like knives piercing her heart. She clutched at her bosom with clenched fists as she heard him walk away from her. She did not turn to watch him go, but she did whisper, "I'll always love you also, James. Always and forever."

Chapter Seventeen

Lenora and Tess had been right. Seattle's attempt to build a railroad with citizen labor was the impossible dream of a young city. Yet, in an indirect way, the plan had a certain kind of success. On the other side of the continent, people read about this town called Seattle where the people were working with their own hands to build a railroad over the mountains. Through that story many readers heard of Seattle for the first time. And the story sparked the interest of men as far away as New York who soon headed west to add to the fight for the railroad that had been denied these spirited citizens of Seattle.

But no amount of manpower seemed able to help Seattle obtain its dream of a railroad. Railroad monopolies were being publicly criticized, and Congress still in no way cooperated with the citizenry of Seattle, continually extending the time for the completion of the Northern Pacific Railroad into the future.

The years slipped by. It was 1883. Delia Calloway had been dead now for five years, and Lenora still evaded James and the notes he persisted in sending by messenger.

Lenora held firm in her fear of Joshua Caine's learning about his true parentage, so she had successfully been able to push aside her feelings for James. She had learned long ago the ways not to let a man interfere in her life and was now busying herself to secure the vote for women in the territory of Washington. She believed that if the women could receive a degree of voting power, they could help clean up this town which had become congested with newcomers. Among these newcomers were men who had been working on the railroad construction gangs in nearby Tacoma. These were tough men, mostly alone and with little sense of civic responsibility. They usually found rooms in the dives that had sprung up on First Avenue, a street which had come to be called Skid Row.

As more and more of these men arrived in Seattle, establishments thrived to cater to their tastes. Operators of bawdyhouses were not indicted by grand juries, and Sheriff Wyndham had a habit of looking the other way. Crimes of violence increased faster than the population because of the mixture of bandits, burglars, and strong-arm men, as well as pimps and gamblers.

*   *   *

The light from the library fireplace cast shadows on a serious-faced Joshua Caine as he sat slouched in a chair, reading before the fire. Lenora sat at her rolltop desk, working on a speech she was to deliver at the Seattle Women's Club later in the evening. But something drew her attention to her nine-year-old son. She lowered her gold-framed spectacles and watched the movement of her son's dark eyes as they traveled across the page of a youthful novel that Seymour had secured from the Territorial University library.

A lump came to Lenora's throat. God, he was James! Every inch of him spoke of his true father. The golden brown curls still aggravated Joshua, reappearing no matter how often he smoothed and fussed to make his hair straighter and more manly.

"Curls are for sissy girls, Mother," he had complained often enough. "Can't you just cut them off, or something?"

Lenora had laughed and asked, "Now, Joshua, which would you truly rather have— your curly hair, or your father's lack of hair?" Lenora's eyes would waver as she referred to Joshua's father being Seymour—but wasn't he, truly? Had Seymour not fed and clothed the boy? Had he not taken Joshua deep into the woods for target practice with Seymour's beloved dueling pistols, handed down by Seymour's grandfather?

Whenever Lenora would refer to Seymour's lack of hair, Joshua's good nature was always apparent in the laugh lines around his eyes and mouth, even at his young age.

Joshua's dark eyes quickly left the book and met Lenora's steady gaze. "Mother, what's the matter?" he asked, shutting his book. He rose and went to her, putting his arm about her neck.

Lenora replaced her spectacles on her nose and pretended to study her papers once again. "Nothing of importance, Joshua," she murmured.

"But you were watching me with that same look that I've seen so often," he persisted. He began caressing the nape of her neck with his fingers. "Can't you tell me what it is, Mother? Please?"

Lenora closed her eyes and enjoyed the massage. It was helping to erase her tensions of the day. But her old worry had begun to plague her. Hadn't Mama Galvez warned of such closeness between mother and son? Joshua would still creep into her bed and cuddle up next to her, even though he had moved to his own room long ago. She had begun to fear the wrong of letting this continue. But since Seymour and she had not performed as man and wife since before Joshua was born, she had accepted the warmth of her son lying in bed next to her.

She removed her spectacles once again and placed them on her desk, then brushed Joshua's hand aside as gently as she could. She went to the fire and stirred the embers with a poker. "Joshua, don't you have studying to do?" she asked thickly. "The Christmas vacation is now behind you. You musn't let your studies slide." She turned and saw the look in his eyes as he so obviously studied the swell of her bosom. She quickly lowered her own eyes, thinking she should most definitely begin to watch what she wore around the house. Her boy was turning all too quickly into a man. She self-consciously let her fingers go to her blouse and work the buttons more securely in place, realizing that she was blushing. She did not know why she had not noticed earlier that he was developing so quickly.

Out of the corner of her eye, she let her gaze capture the whole of him. He was quite tall for his age, with fine, broad shoulders and a strong, graceful carriage. He already looked older than his nine years; by the time he was thirteen, she knew, he would be a man—and a very striking one.

"My studying is completed for the evening, Mother," he said with a half smile playing on his lips. "But you've been too busy to notice."

"As I've been too busy to notice many things, Joshua Caine Harper," she thought, then went toward the staircase. "I must repair my coiffure before your father arrives home from school, Joshua," she said. "Please go and inform Mama Galvez that I wish to have dinner a bit early this evening. I have a meeting to attend."

Joshua followed her to the staircase in long, exact strides. "But, Mother, you shouldn't be on the streets after dark," he said as his face became all shadows. "You know the meanness that nightfall brings to Seattle's streets."

Lenora turned slowly and glared back at him, much more sternly than she had meant to. "Joshua," she said. "I have one husband to try and order me around, and one is quite enough. Will you please refrain from doing thusly in the future?"

Joshua's mouth gaped open in obvious disbelief. She rarely spoke to him in such a manner. What had he said to cause it now? He only wanted to look after her, protect her. He was not blind. Through the years, he had watched the coolness that passed between his mother and father. His mother needed attention, and Joshua was attempting to give it to her. "Yes, Mother. I understand," he uttered. "I'm sorry. I shan't do it again."

"Oh, damn," Lenora thought, then swung her skirt around and hurried up the stairs, almost breathless when she slammed the door behind her. She hated herself now for being so abrupt with her son, but she was finding it harder as each day passed to hide the wonder of him from her eyes. She had to do something about this. They were together too much. What Mama Galvez had said might come of this had not—Joshua was not a "Mama's boy." Instead, he was becoming a man and soon would have a man's needs. He should have someone talk to him about the ways of life and the needs of a man.

Frustration surged through Lenora as she released her hair from the tight confines of its bun. She knew that most fathers had the duty of speaking to their sons about these needs, but Seymour was *not* the one to speak to Joshua. Seymour needed such a talk himself, it seemed. No, if truth were known, James would have been the person to speak to Joshua. James, it seemed, knew the truth about such things. But James was in no position to speak with Joshua, even though he was Joshua's true father.

Lenora swung her hair loosely around her shoulders and strolled to the window to search through the fast-falling dusk for Seymour's arrival from his long day's duties at the Territorial University. She was neither eager nor reluctant to have him home for the evening. They had long ago adjusted to their life together—a life that consisted only of a silent understanding that both were free to do of their choosing. The words that passed between them consisted only of household business or forced conversation in front of Joshua to maintain the illusion that all was well between them. Lenora had often wondered if Joshua had seen through this ploy; he had always been such an intelligent child.

A movement below her in the thicket of the Douglas firs that surrounded the house grabbed Lenora's attention. She pulled the sheer curtain aside and peered down from the second story window, still unhappy with Seymour for not having cleared the land any more than he had, leaving the house almost swallowed by trees.

Another flash of clothing made Lenora's insides freeze. Even though it was nearly dusk, there was no mistaking who it was sneakily jumping from tree to tree in his deerskin pants and jacket, with the familiar blue feather thrust into his long, single plait of glistening black hair. It was the Indian Blue Feather, who had been at the Illahee with Raef that very first day she had been brought to Seattle. But what would he want, and why was he now crouching so? And, God, was that a knife, now drawn?

Seymour suddenly appeared on the gravel path, hunched over in his dark suit with his books tucked beneath an arm, quite unaware of this intruder on his property. He had always rejoiced that his house stood so close to the university—he had liked not having to fuss with horses and carriage each day.

Lenora fumbled with the window, trying to raise it. Desperation seized her, for she knew what was going to happen in a matter of seconds.

"Joshua! Joshua!" she screamed, unable to raise the window to warn Seymour. "Joshua, your father. . . ." Then she felt her knees grow weak and pains shoot through her own heart, as she saw the knife being plunged through her husband.

"Mother, what is it?" Joshua said, entering the room in a rush.

"Oh, my God," Lenora gasped, feeling nausea rising in her throat. She turned her head from the figure who was now sprawled, helpless, on the gravel path.

Joshua rushed to her and took her by the arm. "Mother? Tell me! What's happened?"

She put her hands to her face and began to weep. "It's your father," she said. "You must go and tell Mama Galvez. Tell her that your father's been stabbed, and that we need help."

Joshua released his hold and rushed to the window, then let out a gurgling from deep inside his lungs. "Oh, no. Father," he shouted. "No, it must not be."

Lenora tried to grab him as he ran past her. "No, Joshua!" she shouted. "The Indian may still be lurking. Just tell Mama Galvez. You mustn't go out there yourself. No! Please don't!" She knew that if she lost her son, she would lose her world—her sanity. He was all she had. She gathered her skirt up into her arms and rushed toward the staircase, then hurried down the stairs, but not quickly enough, for when she reached the bottom step, she saw the front door swing widely open.

"Mama Galvez! Mama Galvez," Lenora shouted, then rushed outside herself, watching for any movement that could mean Joshua was in danger. She would throw herself between the Indian and her son if the need arose! She would protect him to the end.

317

But all was quiet, except for the heartbreaking sobs of son for father. When Lenora reached the site, she found Joshua sitting on the ground with his father's head cradled on his lap. A choking inside her throat made Lenora stagger as she realized just how much her son had grown to love this man whom he had always thought to be his father. She sat down beside Joshua and joined tears with him, and remained that way until Mama Galvez had secured the sheriff and his deputy to take the body to the Seattle morgue.

The fire in the parlor fireplace could not erase the chill from Lenora's insides. She paced back and forth, hugging herself, as she told Sheriff Wyndham just how her husband had been murdered.

"You *know* it was that Injun Blue Feather?" he asked, spitting tobacco juice into the flames of the fireplace. "There are many Injuns roamin' the city."

Lenora set her jaw firmly. "I *know* this Indian. There's no mistaking who it was," she said stubbornly. "Now, are you going to take up precious time asking questions while he gets away?"

Sheriff Wyndham tilted his hat further back on his head and furrowed his thick, red brows. "You're pretty damn sure of your description," he growled. "How would it be you'd know so much 'bout this particular Injun?"

Lenora's eyes wavered. She glanced quickly toward Joshua whose dark eyes were bloodshot from the shock of the evening.

Joshua continued to watch her. She was his life now, all he had left, and to him she was the smartest female in Seattle. She seemed to know all answers to everything. But how *did* she know of this Indian?

"It's a long story," she murmured. "One I'd rather not get into right now." She squared her back and stopped pacing, then placed her hands on her hips. "Sheriff Wyndham, my husband was killed this evening and I was an eyewitness. What more proof do you need than my word? Aren't you going to do something about it? Now?"

Sheriff Wyndham placed his hands on each gun at his sides. "Hangin' an Injun might be askin' for trouble," he mumbled.

"I should think it would assure this city of *less* trouble if you enforced the law," Lenora said stubbornly.

"I will give the Injun a fair trial," he said.

"I would expect that," she answered. She knew that justice would prevail: she would see to it.

"We'll start searchin' right away," Sheriff Wyndham said, and walked toward the door.

"Can I go also?" Joshua said anxiously, breaking his long silence. "He was my father. I want to help find his murderer."

"No, Joshua," Lenora said, growing even colder inside with the thought of Joshua on a manhunt that in the end might lead to his own death. The Indian had been so swift with the knife. . . .

"No, Son," Sheriff Wyndham said. "This is no job for a boy. No, you stay here with your Ma."

Joshua's face reddened. "I am no longer a boy. I'm the man of this house now, and I demand to be let go."

The sheriff laughed hoarsely. "No way. No way," he said, then turned to face Lenora. "And you cain't think of any reason why this Injun would want Seymour dead?"

This question had been plaguing Lenora, but she had not found an answer. "No, Sir, no reason at all." Since Raef's death, she had not seen much of the Indian. . . . Her brows shot upward, as something clutched at her heart. Raef's death? Seymour had begun to act so differently around the same time Raef had been shot. Had Seymour been the one? But why had the Indian waited so long, if it *had* been Seymour?

"You know the Illahee burned to the ground last night, don't you, Mrs. Harper?" the sheriff said.

"Why, yes," she whispered.

"The Injun had been holin' up there since the Illahee was deserted for the newer establishment up the road."

"What's that got to do with Seymour?" she asked, putting her hands to her throat.

"Nuthin', I don't reckon," the sheriff said, shrugging. He turned and went outside, not saying anything else.

"Shut and lock the door, Joshua," Lenora said, then slouched down onto a chair, feeling completely drained of thoughts and feelings. True, she had not loved Seymour, but she was already feeling his absence.

Joshua did as he was told, then went to Lenora with eyes heavy from grief. "I'm going to my room, Mother," he said, then turned and rushed from her.

Lenora sat for a while longer, then followed. Her evening's meeting had been forgotten. Everything in her life had suddenly changed. When she walked past Joshua's room, she noticed that it was dark. Slowly she pushed the door open and went to stand beside his bed. He was already in his nightshirt, and she could tell that he was forcing his eyes closed because the lashes were quivering. "What a little boy you are tonight," she thought and pulled the blanket up more securely beneath his chin.

With tears rolling down her cheeks, Lenora hurried to her own room, changed into a night-gown, and climbed beneath her own blanket. Exhaustion made sleep arrive promptly, but it was short-lived. She felt the familiar warmth of a body climb in next to her and form his body up against her back.

She sighed deeply as Joshua's arms wrapped around her, and she even accepted the inno-cent gesture of those many years ago, when his hand cupped a breast. His deep sobs kept her from removing it. Her heart ached for him and the loss he must be feeling. She had felt the same when both her Mama and Papa had died.

She turned to face him and pulled him into her arms. "It'll be all right, son," she murmured. "It'll be all right." He childishly snuggled his nose between her breasts and soon fell into a peaceful slumber.

Chapter Eighteen

The ringing of the town's firebell always drew Seattle's men to action—if not for a fire, then for the purpose of forming a vigilante committee after the announcement of another murder on Seattle's streets.

On the cold, blustery night of January 12, 1883, the men gathered together to hear the news of mild, meek Seymour Harper's death, and when the news broke that it had been the Indian Blue Feather who was responsible for this despicable act, all hell broke loose.

A city-wide hunt for the killer proceeded, and shouts of a lynching echoed up and down the streets. The Indian had killed one of Seattle's most prominent citizens and would have to pay in the swiftest way possible to rid Seattle of one more stinking, lice-infested savage.

It did not take long for one of the searchers to find Blue Feather. When a moccasin-clad foot was seen protruding from a pile of hay on Kessler's Wharf, the haystack was surrounded, the foot seized, and Blue Feather pulled from his hiding place, frantically grasping a half-emptied bottle of cheap whiskey.

Immediately, the citizenry was eager to hang Blue Feather from the wharf without further formality, but Sheriff Wyndham drew his revolver and persuaded the posse that it would be better to wait until a proper trial was held. Seattle's reputation was at stake here. An illegal hanging would draw too much ugly attention, which Seattle certainly did not need any more of at this time.

Kessler's Pavilion was filled to capacity. It seemed the whole of Seattle had gathered to take part in the preliminary hearing to investigate the evidence against Blue Feather.

Attired in a matching black velvet cape, dress, and hat, Lenora sat straight-backed next to Tess, watching in silent fear the stirrings of the crowd. A look of hate and strained anxiety was present on most faces, and there were still many whispers of lynching.

Lenora wanted justice as much as the next person, but she wanted it to be done in the proper fashion. She feared for her Seattle. Too many tales of ugliness in the town had leaked out by way of newspapers to be read clear across the continent. She feared that such stories could eventually cause the demise of the town that she had grown to love.

Out of the corner of her eye, Lenora could see a crowd of armed men assembling at the rear of the hall. As usual, she scanned the faces for a glimpse of James but was glad this time not to see his face among these masks of hate—and shame rushed through her for even having thoughts of him, when her husband had just been murdered.

With racing pulse, she looked toward the front of the pavilion and saw only an unarmed, uncomfortable Roy Graham, Chief Justice of the Territorial Supreme Court, who had climbed out of bed to make sure the Indian got a fair hearing. A few deputies stood behind Judge Graham, who was sitting slumped over a desk, gray-haired and thin-boned, studying some papers scattered before his eyes.

When Justice of the Peace Samuel Corn entered the room from behind the desk where Judge Graham sat, followed by Sheriff Wyndham and more armed deputies accompanying the handcuffed Blue Feather into the room, utter chaos broke loose in the makeshift courtroom.

"Let's get 'im," the armed men shouted from the back of the hall, surging forward. As the deputies drew their revolvers, a door behind them opened and another group of men rushed from the rear and disarmed them. Lenora sat in wide-eyed disbelief as she watched someone throw a sheet over Judge Graham's head. Others seized Blue Feather and rushed from the building.

The room suddenly became filled with hysteria, with women screaming and men shouting and at the same time rushing to follow the armed men and Blue Feather.

Lenora sat, stunned. "Tess, what's happening to this town? I can't believe any of this is happening."

Tess clasped one of Lenora's hands tightly. "Lenora, Timothy tried to dissuade me from coming this morning. He feared this, or something like this, would happen. But when I told him I felt you needed me, he agreed. Now I'm glad I came."

Lenora rose. "Come, Tess. We must hurry. Maybe someone among the men will come to his senses," she said.

"Timothy refused to come," Tess said, breathlessly following. "He said that the ill needed him, and he refused to be a part of such goings on as this."

Outdoors, the cold, damp wind swirled Lenora's cape around her ankles, almost tripping her. She stopped to take a deep breath, facing Tess. "Timothy should be ashamed of himself for turning his eyes in the other direction," she said firmly. "It's men acting like Timothy who are in truth defeating Seattle. We need honest, upright citizens like Timothy to stand up against the riffraff. If more had done this, then Seymour might be alive today."

Tess cast her eyes downward, making Lenora wish she could retract her cutting words. Attired in her hooded brown woolen cape, Tess still appeared to be the lost child she was that day at the Illahee. Had it been so many years ago? And Tess, unable to bear any children of her own, was still petite but round-faced, with dark, innocent eyes that appeared to grow even larger when her feelings had been injured.

"I'm sorry, Tess," Lenora said, circling her arms around Tess's shoulders. Then her gaze was averted suddenly when she noticed where the mob had finally stopped—at the corner of Front Street and Second Avenue, where two men were securing a pair of railings between the forks of two maple trees, while another was tossing a rope over them, with a noose already formed on the end.

Lenora broke away from Tess and began to run through the plank-covered mud. "Stop! You must stop," she shouted, but her words could not be heard above the shouts of "Hang the savage! Hang the bastard!" But when Blue Feather began to chant loudly in his broken English, the crowd suddenly grew still to listen to what the Indian was saying.

"You hang me for killing the white man. The white man killed my friend Raef Wescott those long moons ago, and what punishment did you give him?" he shouted in a deep, guttural accent, making gasps and cries of "No" rise from the crowd.

"I will be hanged for punishing one you should have punished. And who burned my Illahee to the ground? The man you treated as a great white father. The white man whose soul will never rest in peace in the country of my buried ancestors. . . ."

"Lynch him! Shut up his lyin' mouth," an angry onlooker shouted, and that was all it took for the mob to finish what they had started. The noose was slipped over Blue Feather's head, and he was soon dangling in the breeze.

Lenora felt frozen to the spot, with panic rising up inside her, as Blue Feather's words slowly, but firmly, lodged in her brain. Her knees grew weak as Blue Feather's body continued to swing back and forth. Then she watched in utter terror as the frail Judge Graham pushed his way through the mob and ran to the Indian. He pulled out a pocket knife and slashed at the ropes, but the crowd surrounded Judge Graham and began to drag him away.

"We must get away from here," Tess said, grabbing Lenora by the arm. "We *must*, Lenora," she urged. "This is no place for us. We are defenseless—don't you realize that?"

"But . . . Judge Graham," Lenora gasped.

"We must think of ourselves," Tess urged further. "We are only two women against many men. Please come on."

Tears burned Lenora's eyes. This was all becoming a bit too much for her. First to lose her husband, then to hear such accusations against him, and now to see the town turn to such violence. Suddenly a determination seized her. "You are right, Tess," she said. "We are only women, but seeing this today makes me even more adamant about getting the vote for us women. I shall now fight with all my might to get the power to rid this town of its vermin. I must."

"Please hurry," Tess said, relieved that Lenora was finally running alongside her. She wondered if Lenora had even heard what Blue Feather had accused Seymour of doing. Why, Tess would never believe it of the quiet man she had grown to know. She knew that Seymour had had deep-rooted problems, but she would never believe him to be guilty of. . . .

"I'm so glad I brought my carriage today," Lenora said, panting wildly. She and Tess hurriedly climbed onto it, Lenora quickly slapping the reins against the horses and clucking to them. "I do believe the weakness in my knees from the shock of this morning would prevent me from climbing the steep hills." Lenora kept seeing Blue Feather as he had stood shouting the truth about Seymour—a truth Lenora had suspected, and now believed. But why had Seymour done it? He had not known about her and the Illahee—unless Anna had told him. Anna! That was who Seymour had always confided in and even went to, Lenora knew, for more than what conversation could do for him. During the last couple of years, Lenora's suspicions had been confirmed, for she had seen Seymour sneak from Anna's back door as

Lenora had happened along after attending a late night suffrage meeting.

At first, the thought of the two of them together had repelled Lenora. Then she had accepted it as a welcome opportunity for herself. If Seymour was getting his sexual yearnings relieved by Anna, then Lenora could relax in the comfort of her own bed at night.

But, again, she could not understand the why's of Seymour's reasonings: why Raef had been a threat to him—unless Seymour had thought Raef to be the true father of Joshua Caine! Would Seymour go so far, to protect his own name so that no one would know that he had wed a woman who was already with child?

A hate surged through Lenora—a sudden hate for Anna, who in a sense was responsible for this whole tragic mess—even Seymour's death. Anna most surely had told Seymour of the child, probably even before their marriage, and then what else had Anna's confused mind conjured up to tell Seymour?

"Lenora! Be careful," Tess shouted, gripping the edge of her seat. "The horses! You're guiding them off the planks!"

Lenora blinked her eyes, realizing that she had almost lost control. Her face flushed crimson as she realized her ugly thoughts had almost blinded her to what she was doing. "It's those darn planks they've put on the roads," she murmured. "I think I'd much rather tackle the mud than those crooked, warped boards."

"Would you like to stay at my house, Lenora, until Timothy arrives, so he can see you safely home?"

"I have nothing to fear, Tess. And there's Joshua—I need to be home with him."

"Neither one of you is safe in that house," Tess said stubbornly. "You see how easy it was for Blue Feather to hide and wait for Seymour. Who can tell who might be waiting to attack and . . . take advantage of you?"

"I know the dangers of the trees," Lenora said, guiding the carriage to a halt outside Tess's neatly painted white house. "I've already seen to it that a crew of men will begin to clear the land tomorrow."

"Timothy has been studying that piece of property," Tess said eagerly. "He might purchase a piece of the land adjoining yours and build us a new house there, to sit right beside yours."

Lenora's eyes widened. "Oh, Tess, that would be so nice," she sighed. At least she could say she had heard *one* pleasant piece of news today. She and Tess could then enjoy one another's company even more. "Do you really think he might?"

"I should know soon," Tess said, climbing down from the carriage. Her dark eyes were even darker with fear for Lenora's safety. "With Timothy so close, you'd never have to worry. Now, please be careful, Lenora. Please be very careful."

Lenora laughed nervously. "I will, Tess. I will," she said. "And you. You run on into your house and lock the door. Trees surrounding a house are not the only dangers, as you know."

Tess turned and ran up her front steps, waved a good-bye, then rushed inside her house.

Cautiously, Lenora looked all around her, noticing the silence of the streets. The grayness of the day added to the eeriness of it all. She shivered, then urged her horses. Once inside her own house, she threw her cape aside and slouched down on a sofa in front of the parlor fireplace, seeing it all once again in her mind: Blue Feather plunging the knife downward . . . Blue Feather shouting the truth about her husband.

The slamming of the kitchen door and the rushing of feet made Lenora bolt upright with a pounding heart. But when she saw that it was only Joshua, she let a deep sigh escape from her lips.

"Mother, what is happening in town?" he asked, sitting down beside her. "Is there a fire, or what? I just heard the fire bell ring over and over again."

Lenora stiffened. She had not heard the fire bell ring; her mind had been on other things. She rose and went to the front window and stared out, wondering what it meant. She knew that it could mean many things. "I truly don't know, Joshua," she said, wringing her hands.

"How did things go for you in town this morning, Mother?" Joshua had begged her to let him go with her, but she had told him it would be too ugly for his young eyes to see. And the language was expected to be too rough for "tender ears," as she had put it. Oh, how he hated being treated as a child. When would she realize that he was almost a man? He watched her as she turned to meet his gaze, marveling again at her beauty—the green of her eyes, the red of her hair, and the smooth, clear complexion that he loved to touch. How could his father have kept away from her bedroom at night? He would never understand it—never.

"Joshua, I might as well tell you right now what did happen in town," she began. She gathered up the fullness of her skirt and went to sit beside him again. She could not tell him *all* that had happened, and she worried about how she would manage to keep the complete truth from him. It would possibly destroy him to know that his father may have murdered a man and burned the Illahee. This even *she* found hard to believe. Surely the Indian had only guessed about it.

"What is it, Mother?" Joshua asked, taking one of her hands in his. He could feel her trembling. If anyone had hurt her, he would kill him. He would take one of his father's dueling pistols and kill him! He was all she had now, and he would protect her.

"There will be no trial, Joshua," Lenora said, watching him closely. She saw his eyes darken and recoiled as he sprang from the sofa. "Joshua, let me finish," she blurted, but he had already banged a doubled fist against the wall, making a portrait crash to the floor.

"No trial?" he shouted. "Do you mean that damned Indian will get off scot-free?"

Lenora pushed herself up, shocked at the temper he had just exhibited. She had not known Joshua was capable of such violence. "The Indian is dead," she quickly blurted.

Joshua turned to face her with features softening, again reminding Lenora so much of James. "Dead?" he repeated. "How? What happened?"

"A mob took law and order into their own hands."

"Do you mean they . . . ?"

"They hanged him," she said.

"Even without a trial?"

"Yes, Son. Quite illegally."

Joshua placed his hands in the pockets of his trousers and stared into the fire. He was confused. Most of the people he knew in this town were so kind—how could they do such a thing? Yet he felt a surge of excitement as he realized suddenly that he would have truthfully liked to join such a mob. He would have gladly placed the noose around Blue Feather's neck. Even now, he felt a sense of loss for not having been able to at least witness it.

"Joshua, are you all right?" Lenora asked, going to stand beside him. She was not sure what she saw in his eyes. As he was coming into manhood, she saw many things about him that frightened her in a way. She felt as though as each day passed she was losing a little bit more of him and the link that had always held them so closely together.

A pounding on the front door drew Lenora's attention away from her worries about her son.

"I'll see who it is, Mother," Joshua said quickly, rushing to the door.

Lenora missed Mama Galvez's automatic duties of answering the door since Mama Galvez had returned to her own family. It had been a shock when she had left so suddenly, and at such a time—after Seymour's death and funeral, when Lenora needed her most.

Lenora's heart raced now, as she wondered who might be at the door. Maybe it was Timothy, checking to see if she was all right after the ordeal she had just been through. It was sweet of Tess to urge him to do such a kindness. She rushed to the door, just as Joshua opened it. Something grabbed at Lenora's heart, and she could feel a light spinning of her head when she saw James studying this young man standing before him.

"Oh, God," Lenora thought, swallowing hard. How long had it been since James had seen Joshua? At this moment, it was as though he was seeing him for the first time; the puzzlement was evident in the depths of his dark eyes and the curve of his lips. Was it possible at this moment that he knew her secret: that Joshua was his own?

"Yes?" Joshua said dryly, standing tall and erect, looking for all the world like a smaller version of his father.

"Joshua Caine Harper?" James asked. He removed his hat and ran his fingers through his golden brown curls, gazing down at this other set of golden brown curls that so resembled his own. God! It was as though he was looking at a photograph of himself when he had been the same age. What did it all mean? Had his suspicions been accurate?

"Yes, I'm Joshua," Joshua answered without smiling.

"I'd like to see your mother, please," James said, now seeing Lenora coming toward him.

"Why would you want to see my mother?" Joshua snapped in a rude fashion. He was to be cautious and suspicious of everyone if he was to protect his mother. And what was there about this man? It was as though they had met before, but he could not remember where.

"It's all right, Joshua," Lenora said, coming to his side. She patted him on the cheek. "I'll take care of this. Just run along." She shot James an angry look, wondering why he would choose to come to her house so boldly, especially at an hour when Joshua would be home. She had never wanted them to meet face to face, for there were dangers in this happening. She could already feel the tension and wonder passing between the two of them.

"Are you sure, Mother?" Joshua asked, tilting her chin up with a forefinger. A tremor ran through Lenora. She remembered the many times James had made this same gesture. Out of the corner of her eye, she could see James watching.

"Yes, Son," she said thickly. "I know this man. It's perfectly all right to leave me with him. Now, run on and start your studies. I'm sure you have plenty."

"Yes, Mother. If you say so," he answered, then began to walk away, stopping to take one more look at James, who still puzzled him. He *had* met him, somewhere. He would have to think hard to remember where. He hurried on into the library and tried to focus his thoughts on his books, but strained to hear what was being said between this stranger and his mother.

"James, what do you want?" Lenora asked, not offering to invite him into the house.

"We need to talk," he said softly, very aware of the ears that were only a room away from where he stood.

"Not now," she said firmly. "Please leave. What do you think you're doing coming to my house in such a way? People will talk. Seymour has only been dead a short time now."

"Lenora, there is something I need to tell you. Something that happened in town."

"I already know of the hanging, James. I was there," she said.

"You were there?" he gasped.

"Yes. I was needed for the preliminaries. To testify against Blue Feather."

"And you left right after his lynching?"

"Yes. Tess and I grew afraid and rushed home."

"Then you don't know what else has transpired in town?"

Lenora suddenly remembered Joshua telling her of the fire bells. "Was there a fire? Joshua heard more fire bells," she said, shivering in the cold air seeping into the room and clutching at her bare arms.

"Lenora, I see that you are cold," he said sternly. "I'm going to come in so you won't take a chill. We can surely talk in the parlor?"

Lenora stepped aside and let him enter, glancing toward the library, hoping that Joshua would be lost in his studies now. And what should it matter if she did ask a gentleman caller into her house, anyway? Hadn't the town all gone mad? They would not even notice. Joshua would just have to understand that she did have more friends than Tess and Timothy, and she needed friends, now. "Come on in, James," she said. "You are right. We shall have privacy in the parlor." She shut the door behind her and walked in silence beside James until they were in the parlor, sitting in front of the fire. She felt giddy with love, not having been so close to James in much too long. "Now, what is it you have to tell me?" she said, smoothing the pleats of her dress, needing to busy her fingers. As always, she felt his closeness confusing her train of thought.

James sat stiffly erect, turning his hat between his fingers. "I fear for your safety more than anything, Lenora," he said. "It seems a lust for law and order—or for blood—has seized the citizenry of Seattle. Only a short while after lynching Blue Feather, someone rushed into my shop and told me that the mob had not stopped with the death of Blue Feather. It seems they went to City Hall and chopped down the door to the jail, overpowered the guards, and seized a man accused of having killed a policeman three months earlier. The mob lynched him, also."

Lenora's heart skipped a few beats. She threw her hands to her throat. "Oh, my God, James. No," she uttered.

James put his arms around her shoulders in an effort to comfort her—and prepare her—before telling her the rest.

She at first tensed when she felt the weight of his arm, then relaxed, knowing that she indeed needed to be comforted. It was only right that it should be James comforting her.

"That's not all, Lenora," he continued. "Soon after this lynching, Sheriff Wyndham dropped dead of a heart attack, probably brought on by the pressure of not being able to protect his prisoners."

"Sheriff Wyndham—dead?" she gasped.

"I did not attend either lynching," he continued. "I feared for my shop. I know the ways of mobs. I expected to have to defend my shop from looters. Usually, once a mob has been formed, it continues until not only deaths occur, but property is destroyed."

"Oh, Sheriff Wyndham. He was so nice," she uttered, feeling tears burning the corners of her eyes. She had thought she knew the people of Seattle—now she was not sure that she even wanted to remain and be a part of this town's growth. Hadn't growth brought only murder and tragedy?

"I had to come, to warn you of the danger and check on you," he said. "I'd like to stay here this evening, to make sure you and Joshua will be all right. You are without a man in the family, and I would like to serve as such."

Lenora quickly rose, with tension lines evident around her mouth and eyes. "James, you cannot do that," she murmured. "Joshua would not understand."

"It's about time that Joshua begins to understand a few damn things," James said, rising and going to her, to jerk her roughly around to face him. "And you know what I mean, don't you?"

Ice water seemed to fill her veins. What was he implying? "James, I think it's time for you to leave," she said, steeling herself against the hands on her shoulders. "My son and I are capable of taking care of ourselves."

"You are not capable," he argued, then swung around when Joshua entered the room. James stepped back from Lenora with eyes wide when he saw the gun in Joshua's raised hand.

"Joshua," Lenora gasped, feeling faint.

"You heard my mother," Joshua said darkly, motioning with the gun. "You leave this house, right now. If my mother doesn't want you here, you'd best get the hell out of this house."

James placed his hat on his head and began to inch his way toward the front door. He did not know what to expect. He did not know this boy well enough to know his temper, or what would even possess him to pull such a stunt as this. James flashed Lenora a look of confusion, then rushed out of the house.

Lenora went to Joshua, whose face had gone white. "Joshua, what on earth possessed you to do such a thing as that?" she said, easing the gun from Joshua's fingers. She hated touching it. Had it even been the one used to kill Raef? She placed it on a table, not wanting to think of Seymour in such an act of violence.

"I heard you arguing," he said, with wavering eyes. "I wanted to show you that I could take care of you, that's all."

"Come and sit beside me, Joshua," Lenora said, leading him to the sofa. Her mind was made up. She had just witnessed what the unrest in Seattle was doing to her son, and she would not have it. She would put a stop to it. Now. Her mind had been working constantly ever since James revealed this second lynching. She knew that she did not want Joshua to stay in this town any longer, for many reasons: she did not want him to hear of Seymour's murdering Raef Wescott, she did not want to have to worry about his being attacked and murdered on the streets, and, most importantly, she did not want James to reveal to Joshua his true parentage by a slip of the tongue, which Lenora now knew could happen.

She knew that James had guessed the truth, and why wouldn't he? He had only to look at Joshua to see himself. Then, he had only to count back to when Joshua Caine had been born to know that Joshua had been conceived earlier than her marriage to Seymour. But still, she hoped that she was wrong.

"What is it, Mother?" Joshua said, looking at her with the dark, innocent eyes of a child. "Are you angry with me? Should I not have done that?"

"No, you should not have done that," she said. "And, no, I'm not angry with you, either. That is not what I'd like to speak to you about." She did not quite know how to put it. She had always thought she could never be separated from Joshua, even for one night. But now she had no choice. She could not let Joshua stay in Seattle, even for one more day. She had heard talk of a boys' school in Portland. Other children had been sent there by the most prominent families in Seattle. But how would Joshua take the news? He would most surely argue about it, perhaps even refuse to go, but she knew what was best, and he *would* go. She was still the voice of authority, especially now that Seymour was no longer around to influence Joshua's thinking.

"Then, what is it, Mother? You look so serious."

"Joshua, I've made a decision—a very hard one to make, believe me, but a needed one," she began. "The reason James Calloway was here was to tell me of another lynching in town besides Blue Feather's."

Joshua's eyes widened and he slid forward to the edge of the couch, sitting erect. "Another lynching? Who?"

"The mob that killed Blue Feather went to City Hall and took a prisoner from his cell and lynched him. Then, later, Sheriff Wyndham died of a heart attack."

"Really?" Joshua said, stunned.

"And these are my reasons for sending you to a private school in Portland, away from the streets of Seattle, where you will be safe, at least until things simmer down a bit around here."

Joshua jumped to his feet with anger flashing in his eyes. "A private school? In Portland? Mother, surely I'm not hearing you right."

"You are hearing right," Lenora said, swallowing hard. She did not know what to expect. She could see her son's two fists doubled in anger.

"Do you really want to send me away from you?" he said in a strained voice, eyeing her darkly, but with a keen puzzlement making his eyes almost slant at the corners. "Didn't I just show you that I am capable of taking care of you as well as myself? And by showing

you that, didn't I show you that I am a man?
Perhaps more a man than my father ever was.
He never did treat you like a man should treat
his wife."

Lenora's face turned crimson. She did not
know how her son could think of such things
to say. His words were quite embarrassing and
confusing to her. What was he implying? And
wasn't this even more reason to separate the two
of them before things came to a point where she
would not know how to handle them? "Joshua,
you shouldn't speak in such a manner about
your dead father," she said sternly.

"I loved my father," he said quietly. "But I
love you even more, and I won't leave you.
Never."

Lenora rose and headed for the staircase.
"You will leave. You will go to Portland. I want
you to pack your bags now. I will put you on a
stagecoach tonight. Then I will wire ahead of
your arrival. Now, will you follow me, young
man, and do as you are told?"

"Never," he said stubbornly, standing his
ground.

Lenora turned and stared in defiance at him.
She set her jaw firmly and crossed her arms.
"If I have to go and fetch Timothy, I shall," she
said. "But if you know what's best for you, you
will do as you are told. If I have to bring someone else into my family problems, you will only
regret it, Joshua."

Joshua rushed toward her and pushed her
aside and fled up the stairs, skipping them two

at a time. "I shall leave," he shouted. "If that's what you want, I shall leave. And you will miss me. You will see. You will beg to have me back. Then I shall only return if I am damn good and ready!"

"Joshua, I will also wash out your mouth with soap if I hear another swear word come from your lips. Do you hear me?" She followed him, trembling. She even wished she could shed the tears that were pressing against her eyelids. She and Joshua had never had harsh words before, and now these words were tearing at the inner core of her. She would miss him, indeed. She could already feel his absence, as if he had already left her. But she had to do it. She had to see that he was safe from the dangers that lurked in the streets, and from the mouths of evil people, and even from James, who would forever be standing in wait, ready to reveal the truth.

Lenora went into Joshua's bedroom and watched him throwing clothes from his wardrobe. She swallowed hard and began to wonder what she *would* do without him around. She did feel truly afraid to live in the house alone, but what else could she do? She could not just up and leave all that she possessed to follow her son to Portland. She would have to endure the loneliness. She had no other choice. She went to his bed and began to fold the clothes neatly, wondering when the next stagecoach left for Portland.

Chapter Nineteen

When the results of the election of 1883 became known, Lenora was able to beam with joy. After many fiery speeches, she and other women like her had succeeded in their fight to secure for the women of Seattle the right to vote. And not only could they vote, they could also hold office and work on jury duty.

Even with these rights, the women's voices were not loud enough to rid the town of its vermin. But they did succeed in seeing that the bawdyhouses, low theatres, and saloons stayed south on what had once been called Front Street and now bore the name of First Avenue.

With the violent death of Anna Calder at the hands of a derelict from First Avenue, the town had seemed to sober and return to a semipeaceful existence, letting the new

Sheriff John McNeff run things in the manner in which he saw fit. The lynchings and vigilante committees had seemed to encourage more violence than they curtailed.

Lenora was saddened by Anna's death, even though for a while Lenora had refused to speak with her. And Lenora was shocked that such a thing could happen to Anna, with her fiery ways and her three savage dogs for protection. But it *had* happened, and it had brought a silence over the town.

The sun reflected in yellow streamers through the shop window, where Lenora stood inventorying her new dress line.

With Joshua still at the private school in Portland, and having won the right of suffrage, she had need of something extra to fill her days. The estate Seymour had left her had made it possible for her to do almost anything she chose, which led to a decision to open an exclusive shop of women's ready-to-wear on Second Avenue.

A shuffling of feet behind her made Lenora turn with a start. "Oh, James, it's you," she said. She took her spectacles from her nose and let them dangle loosely from a gold chain around her neck, not wanting James to see those darn things on her face. She felt as though she looked like a schoolmarm when she wore them, and most schoolmarms were anything but attractive to men. She placed her tablet and pencil on a chair, to begin rearranging dresses on their racks.

"You should never leave the rear door unlocked," James grumbled. He lit a cigar and took in this new dress emporium which had just opened next to his own tailoring shop. Oriental carpets covered the hardwood floors, and gilt and satin chairs were placed in the corners beneath brass wall fixtures inside which flickered gas flames. The new smell of fabric from the racks of dresses that lined each wall filled his nostrils.

"I feel safe enough," Lenora answered. "You know as well as I that Second Avenue is only visited by the most respectable citizenry." She ran her fingers over the parallel, diagonal lines of a blue serge traveling suit, knowing it would be a hot item this autumn, with the rumors of another railroad that would possibly make its terminus in Seattle. A Mr. Jim Hill had spoken of a Great Northern Railroad that would be even greater than the Northern Pacific Railroad that had treated Seattle so poorly. Yes, Lenora knew that many traveling suits were in order, to wear on the trains that would happily take the place of the uncomfortable, dusty stagecoaches. She only prayed that this time the gossip about the new railroad was not only gossip.

"Your shop is mighty fancy, Lenora," James said, still admiring her handiwork. There were several three-sided, full-length folding mirrors now reflecting dozens of Lenoras, which made James's heart ache with longing. Since the day he had been confronted by Joshua at gunpoint,

Lenora had refused even to share a cup of coffee with James. And the damnedest, most frustrating thing of all for James, was the fact that she was now single, as was he, and he knew that she loved him, as he loved her.

"I wanted it to be the best," she answered. "And since they've regraded the road and laid fresh planks, I even feel my carpets are justified, don't you?"

James laughed as he burrowed his box calf boots into the plush, intricate pattern beneath his feet. "I certainly hope so," he answered. He watched her move from rack to rack, reminded of the first time he had seen her—how healthy she had appeared to him after the sight of many undernourished women on the trail from Ohio. She still wore this healthy appearance with grace—especially this day, in a pale green silk dress, its low-cut bodice emphasizing her magnificent bosom. And with her waistline still so trim and neat, no one would be able to guess that she had a child aged twelve years. She wore her hair tied up with a ribbon in back to hang loosely around her shoulders, and the ever-present locket rested close to the deep cleavage he found so hard not to admire openly.

He had so often wished that he could secure the key from this locket and unlock her diary to read her written thoughts, her deepest secrets, which he knew must include himself. He chuckled to himself, also seeing the spectacles. He had seen the speed with which she had removed them.

Lenora continued to busy herself, keenly aware of his eyes upon her. He looked so handsome in the white, pure silk shirt worn with his brown afternoon coat and trousers. The gray at his temples made him appear more sophisticated, but also made her aware of the passing years—years they had not shared, even though he continually tried to persuade her that they should. But she still had Joshua to think about. Joshua was even more important to her than her fleshly desires, on which she felt her love for James was based. "I hear there's a new jewelry shop opening, up the street aways," she said, flushing under his still constant stare. She even pricked a finger with a pin, and a tiny bead of blood appeared.

James went to her, lifted the finger, and blotted it with his handkerchief. The warmth of her flesh made him forget for a moment that she always turned from him now whenever he approached her. He pulled her into his arms and searched for her lips, only to receive further bruises to his ego when she turned her head aside and jerked out of his hold.

"James, please," she uttered, moving away from him. She knew her heartbeats betrayed her. She knew that he had felt the speed with which her heart was thumping against her chest. But she must not let her feelings betray her sense of loyalty to her son. Joshua must never discover who his father was, because such knowledge would destroy Lenora's image in her son's eyes. He would realize that she had been a loose young girl at age sixteen, on the trail to San Francisco.

James crushed his cigar in an ashtray, then ran his fingers through his hair. "Lenora, what the hell's the matter with a kiss? An innocent kiss," he stammered. He was almost to the point of giving up. Seattle was no longer a city of men. There were many unattached, beautiful women seeking a respectable gentleman to wed, and he knew that he could pick and choose among them. He knew that even though his middle had broadened and his hair was thinner and graying, he had much to offer a woman. If Lenora continued this little game of hers, he would just search and wed another.

"James, I'm much too busy to be bothered," she said, wishing the dryness of her throat would leave her. Would he always have such a way of disturbing her insides? Even now, she could feel the ache in her loins. "I have my shop to prepare for its grand opening tomorrow. You should understand. You have your own shop to worry about."

"My shop is not my life," he grumbled.

"Nor will my shop be mine."

"Ah, yes. There is your son."

Lenora's eyes flashed. "Yes. There's my son," she said sternly. "Now will you please leave me be?"

Damn. He'd done it again. Always when he mentioned Joshua, she would instantly become enraged. One day, they *would* discuss this young man, but the time would have to be right. He'd have to be patient a bit longer where Joshua was concerned, but could he be where Lenora was concerned? "Lenora, this is Sunday," he said. "Why not pull the shades on your shop window and take a carriage ride with me into the woods? July is a perfect month for a picnic." He went to her and held her at arm's length. "How about it? A picnic beneath the trees, surrounded by wild rosebushes and scampering squirrels?"

Again Lenora turned from him, noticeably shaken by his persistence. "I plan to pull my shades soon," she said, "but I don't plan to spend the afternoon with you. I plan to go home and write a letter to Joshua. He depends on my letters. He writes that my letters are the only thing keeping him from taking the next stagecoach home."

"Joshua!" James stormed, turning to stomp away. Then he stopped and turned to face her once again, with fire in his dark eyes. "Lenora, there's more to life than what a son can give you. You'd best think about that. A son can't keep you warm at night. A son can't make love to you."

Lenora picked up a hand mirror and flung it toward James. "Get out of here, James Calloway," she screamed. "Get out of here with your foul mouth. And don't ever show your face in my shop again."

James stood looking at the broken glass at his feet for a few moments, then turned and stormed from the room, leaving Lenora feeling as shattered as the mirror she had just broken.

"How can you be so cruel to me, James?" she whispered, then rushed to the back door and bolted it, wishing that she did not have to worry so much about Joshua. She had only recently begun to wonder if any child was worth the heartache she was constantly feeling. If it were Joshua who had to be the considerate one, would he? Would he protect her thusly, disregarding his deep longings to be loved by a mate of his choice?

"Oh, I just don't know," Lenora said, hating the emptiness that James's departure always left inside her. She removed her spectacles from their chain and placed them inside a velvet-lined case. She no longer cared to work in her shop. She felt the need to put much distance between James and herself. She draped white cloths over her racks of clothes, pulled the candy-striped shade, and hurried outside, anxious to reach her home even though it was much too large for only one person to be comfortable in.

The sudden growth of the Chinese population was beginning to stir trouble in town and kept Lenora from bringing Joshua home. She feared a new threat of violence.

The Chinese population that had immigrated from Tacoma and other parts of the country after the Northern Pacific Railroad had been completed had at first been welcome in Seattle.

The Chinese were called "John," and the stories of John's prowess as a construction worker almost reached the status of folk legend. John could work twelve hours on a handful of rice; impassive John could handle blasting jobs that other men were too nervous to carry out; inscrutable John had the best poker face in a poker-loving nation. "Good ol' John," people had said.

Then, when jobs became scarce in Seattle, the hard-working, industrious Chinese who were willing to take any job, to accept any wage, became symbols of discontent to the unemployed.

Lenora felt the tension rising, seeing placards in the windows of businesses that read, "Go home, John," or "Go, John." And, realizing just how fast a mob could gather, Lenora saw to it that Joshua remained where he was safe, even though his house sat across from the Territorial University, which now had an impeccable reputation as an educational institution.

Maneuvering her carriage around a horsecar filled with Sunday spectators viewing the stylish turnout after church on this, the grandest street in Seattle, Lenora felt the deep pride that riding along this street had a way of instilling in her. There were now many two-storied mansions mingling with the fine businesses. Most were made of wood, but the city could also boast of two-, three-, and five-storied brick establishments.

A telegraph office sat on the corner of Cherry Street and Second Avenue, and the magnificent St. Charles Hotel stood next to it, featuring furniture of solid black walnut.

On many street corners, small square plots of land displayed colorful roses and statuesque trees, making this street the showplace of the town.

Lenora slowed her carriage to study the front window of the new jewelry store she had mentioned to James. It brought another jewelry store to mind. She had often wondered about Francis and what had become of him. After a period of time, her thoughts about him had softened. Hadn't he only to be pitied?

She gave the reins a slap, turned the carriage onto Union Street, and braced herself for the strain that the steepness of this street always created. She had always feared the possibility of a horse refusing to continue upward. Would the carriage then begin to roll backwards and carry her to her death in the waters of Puget Sound?

She lifted the reins and clucked to the horses, suddenly aware of a lone rider on a horse only a short distance behind her. Trying to be inconspicuous about it, she glanced back quickly to see who it was, but she could only see a massive figure with a wide-brimmed hat shading his face.

"Come on, damn it," she whispered to her two panting horses. They had worked up a muddy lather with the strain of climbing the hill. She sank back against the seat, still hearing the clattering of hoofs on the plank road behind her. She had to remember the many men on horseback who ventured up and down this street each day, but the fact that he lingered behind and had not attempted to pass her was added cause for alarm.

Her thoughts went to James. Hadn't she given him cause to follow her and confront her again, after the anger in which she had just spoken to him? But another glance backward gave proof enough that this was not James. James sat much straighter in the saddle, and he would have on gloves to protect his hands.

A keen sense of danger engulfed Lenora, prompting her to slap the reins more severely than she had ever done before. She knew that she had to get inside her house, to let its walls protect and comfort her. And when the clearing appeared suddenly on each side of her, she pulled the carriage up in front of her house, secured the reins to a hitching post, and rushed, panting, into her house.

Leaning heavily against her door, she tensed as she heard the horse's hoofs grow closer, then stop. She did not have to look. She knew that this stranger was at the foot of her porch steps, and she waited to hear the knocking on her door.

When the thuds began to fill the silence of the house, Lenora swallowed hard and felt her heartbeats synchronizing with the knocks on the door. She now wished that she had gone to Tess and Timothy's house instead of her own. But perhaps one of them might be watching and would see this man.

A man's voice broke through the silence. "Mrs. Harper?" the deep voice boomed from behind the door.

Lenora stiffened even more, trying to recognize the voice. "Yes?" she answered, planning to listen even more closely.

"I have news of Francois Chantal," the voice then said, and was it said in a pleading manner? Lenora felt her heart in her throat, wondering why anyone would want to speak with her about Francis. And how would this stranger even know . . . ?

She turned to place her ear closer to the door and clung to the doorknob. "What might you want to tell me about Francis?" she asked.

"He's dead," the man said simply. "I wish to discuss his will with you. Will you please open the door? My name is Anthony Lorenzo. I'm not someone to fear."

Lenora's eyebrows tilted upward. Francis dead? A will? She had a sudden feeling of remorse and opened the door, thinking surely this was a lawyer, even though it all made little sense. Francis had felt nothing for her, she was sure, except a possible loathing when he had found her gone. But, still, she *did* want to find out.

"Yes?" she said, then felt a warning shoot through her. There was something about this man—was it the dark eyes, the dark olive coloring of his skin, the coarse, shoulder-length black hair? He struck a note somewhere in the depths of her memory, but she simply could not place him.

The man took his hat off and half bowed to her. "May I step inside the coolness of your house, Ma'am?" he said. "The heat is quite penetrating today, wouldn't you say?"

It was at this moment that Lenora's attention was drawn to a tiny diamond earring in this man's right earlobe. This made her thoughts wander. She had only seen one other man wear an earring and that had been Francis. Was this Anthony more to Francis than his lawyer? And where were his papers—the will—that he had said he needed to discuss with her?

A coldness surged through her as she glanced first at Anthony and then at the opened door, with suspicions surging through her. She clutched the side of the door, ready to slam it shut, when Anthony stepped quickly into the house and took it upon himself to slam the door shut with a bang.

Lenora's eyes widened. "What are you doing?" she gasped. The feeling of lurking danger was now so intense, she was beginning to feel ill in her stomach. The depths of this man's eyes told her that he was not one to be trusted and that he had no doubt told her an untruth to get her to open the door.

Anthony strolled around the parlor, taking in its rich decor: the green velvet chairs, the best mahogany furniture, the windows draped also in velvet. He chuckled. "Done pretty good for yourself since you left Francis's house," he said. "Knew you would, though. Too pretty not to have the best handed to you."

Lenora stood, barely breathing, as she listened to the sound of his boots clicking against her hardwood floors. His black knee boots were highly polished, and tucked inside them were trousers of brown twill. His loose white silk shirt hung open at the throat, and its long sleeves were full. On his fingers he wore a variety of rings, mostly diamonds. But the evil showed in his face as he leered at her with straight, white teeth beneath thick lips.

"Who are you?" Lenora snapped, setting her jaw firmly. "What do you really want of me?" The mockery in his eyes brought to mind some other time, which Lenora's mind refused to recall.

Anthony moved closer to her and stood with his hands on his hips, emphasizing the broadness of his chest and shoulder muscles. She knew that she would be helpless if he should decide to take advantage of her, which she feared was the reason he had entered her house. She glanced quickly toward the door, wondering if escape was possible.

"Your memory fails you, huh?" he said, laughing raucously. "You don't remember your last night at Francis's house?"

Lenora gasped, suddenly remembering. She put her hands to her throat.

He continued to speak, all the while smirking. "You don't remember sneaking around to watch what I was doing with Francis?"

"Oh, God, no," Lenora whispered. "It *is* you. What are you doing here now? Why on earth would you bother me? You're a vile, sick person."

Anthony threw his head back and laughed. "So that's why you ran off?" he shouted. "You didn't like seeing two men together making . . . love." He spat out the last word in a fit of sarcastic laughter, but sobered quickly and began to move toward her. "I no longer have the needs of the likes of Francois Chantal," he growled. "As a matter of fact, I think now I'd like to try *you* on for size. When I saw you standing at the shop window, I knew it was the same once-young thing that fled from Francis's that night. You haven't changed that much, you know."

Lenora felt her knees weakening and knew that if she was going to escape, she had to do so at this moment or it would be too late. She turned and lunged for the door, but was stopped by the rough grasp of his hand on her wrist. She began to jerk and kick. "Let me go," she shouted. "Let me go. Let me be."

He pulled her into his arms and held her, even though her struggles were quite strong to be coming from only a woman. "Damn, you're a vixen," he said, then crushed her lips beneath his. When his tongue forced its way into her mouth, she clamped down with her teeth, determined that this man's mouth would not search hers. She remembered too vividly another time, when his mouth had been used otherwise.

He jerked away from her, howling. "Why, you Goddamned witch," he said, spitting blood into the air and wiping at his mouth. "Nobody does that to Anthony Lorenzo and gets away with it."

Lenora felt her neck snap when he slapped her across the face. The intensity of the blow knocked her to her knees. Then her eyes grew wide through tears as she watched him undo the front of his breeches.

"I'll show you what your mouth is good for," he sneered. He pulled a knife from his pocket and opened it. "And if you bite down *this* time, I'll slit your throat."

"Please," Lenora begged, growing limp. "Just leave. Why would you want to treat me in such a manner?"

"You know of my connection with Francis," he said dryly. "You're the only one in Seattle who would recognize me and be able to turn me in to the authorities."

"Why would I do that?"

"Because I am wanted for killing Francois."

Lenora recoiled. "You killed Francis?"

Anthony pulled his penis from its tight confines and began to caress it, making his eyes haze over with pleasure. "I inherited all his wealth, and now I've got my own jewelry store on Second Avenue, close to your shop."

"You?" she gasped.

"Yes, me," he gloated. "Now, Mrs. Harper, you will do the final service of your life. You will put your mouth where a mouth is intended to be placed."

A loud crashing at the door made Anthony freeze. Lenora quickly rose to her feet when James rushed into the room, disarmed Anthony, and had him knocked out cold in one mighty blow.

"Oh, James! Thank God," Lenora sobbed, then ran to him and fell into his arms.

"Who the hell is this?" James stormed, holding her close. "And how'd he happen to get in here? Are you as reckless about the doors here as you are at your shop?"

Lenora clung to James, not ever wanting to let go. His hands felt so strong, yet gentle, as he caressed her back and smoothed her hair. "He fooled me, James," she sobbed. But she felt safe now; James had rescued her. He actually loved her enough to watch over her and rescue her. Then she pulled away and eyed him questioningly. "But, James, how did you know?"

James brushed some loose strands of Lenora's hair back from her eyes. "I was on my way here to have a heart-to-heart talk with you, when I saw this son-of-a-bitch trailing you. I hung back a ways and watched, then lost sight of him. But, just for caution's sake, I checked around your house when I got here and found that bastard's horse hidden in some brush in the back."

"Oh, James, if you hadn't come along," Lenora sobbed again, then let his mouth cover hers, but only for an instant. A soft moan from Anthony quickly reminded her of the violence the man was capable of. She pulled away from James's arms, trembling.

"He killed Francis Chantal," she murmured.

"The man who hired you on as maid in San Francisco?"

"Yes," she murmured, "and he was going to kill me."

"That bastard's not goin' to kill another person," James said darkly, going to stand over Anthony with doubled-up fists.

Lenora eyed the knife that had been kicked aside. A chill passed through her as she remembered how close Anthony had held it to her throat. She hurriedly picked it up, carried it to her desk, and hid it beneath the rolltop.

"Now, you run on over and tell Timothy to beat it quick as hell to get Sheriff McNeff. Tell him I won't be responsible for what I'll do to this son-of-a-bitch if I'm left alone with him too long—'specially if he decides to wake all the way up."

Lenora smiled crookedly and rushed for the door. "Yes, James, I understand," she said. She left the house feeling exhilarated from the experience, even though through it all a violent death had been revealed to her.

* * *

Arm in arm, Lenora and James stood watching through the window as Sheriff McNeff and two of his deputies led Anthony Lorenzo away on horseback.

"Well, that's that," James drawled.

Lenora shuddered. "What a horrible man," she whispered.

"He won't be bothering you or anyone again."

"Poor Francis," Lenora sighed.

"Don't even think about it, Lenora."

Lenora looked up into the soft warmth of James's eyes. She fluttered her lashes as she spoke again. "Did you say that you were on your way to my house to have a talk?"

"Do you truly care to know the answer to that?"

"Yes, James, I do."

"I think our living apart is a lot of nonsense," he said, watching closely for her reaction. But he knew that the time was right. This episode with Anthony Lorenzo had made it right. The one favor that bastard may have done him was to put a scare into Lenora so that she might now want to have James around—for protection and, he hoped, more.

"Yes, James. I agree with you."

His mouth dropped open and his eyes widened. He had not expected her to be so easily convinced. He had expected *some* argument. "You do?" he stammered, grasping her shoulders. "You *do*?" he shouted, then pulled her into his arms and began to swing her around in a circle.

Laughing wildly, Lenora could feel the hammering of her heart and the spinning of her head. "James, whatever are you doing?" she shouted.

He stopped and held her to him, burying his nose in her hair. "Honey, you know how long I've wanted this," he said hoarsely.

Lenora reached up and began to run her fingers through his hair. Suddenly Joshua was second on her list of importance. Lenora had been alone for much too long. Why had she waited so long? She would simply have to see to it that Joshua and James did not run into each other. She always knew ahead of time when Joshua was to arrive home.

"James, I've been so foolish," she finally murmured.

"Does this mean you might be persuaded to marry me, Lenora?"

Lenora stiffened and pulled away from him. She cast her eyes down as she went to stand before the window. How could she tell him? Would he even understand?

"Lenora? Why do you hesitate?" he asked, going to her side.

She continued to stare out the window. "James, I can't marry you." She heard his deep intake of breath. She looked quickly into his eyes and took one of his hands in hers. "But you can stay here with me," she hurriedly added. "Live with me, if you'd like."

James's brows furrowed in a frown. "But, why not marriage? You're free . . . I'm free."

"Please don't ask me to explain," she pleaded. She did not want to have to speak Joshua's name.

James knew, without being told, that it was because of Joshua. He also knew not to confront her about it. He did not want to give her cause to back down on her request to have him stay with her. He would have to accept her now, however he could get her. Certainly, this arrangement would have its benefits. He pulled her into his arms again and hugged her tightly to him. "Hon, I'll take you any way I can," he said, "with or without marriage."

Lenora cuddled into his embrace. She loved the smell of him, the feel of his muscles, the gentleness of his voice. The aching in her loins made her aware that what she had been desiring was only footsteps away, up the stairs. "Then, would you like to test the softness of my bed now, James?" she whispered. She felt wicked. Very, very wicked.

He stepped back and held her at arm's length, his dark eyes dancing. "My, but you are a daring wench," he mused. "You're inviting me to your bed in broad daylight?"

Lenora laughed hoarsely. "My love, can you think of anything better to do on this July afternoon?"

James went to the window and stared out, clasping his hands together behind him. "Hmmm," he said, teasing. "A picnic? We could have that picnic that I suggested earlier."

"Oh, James," Lenora said, then welcomed him as he went to her, smiling. Leaning into his embrace, she let him guide her up the staircase, knowing that she was happier now than she had been in years. She looked up at him and saw that he looked as happy himself.

"I love you so much, James," she whispered. Strangely, it had taken Anthony Lorenzo to wake her up to what she needed in life.

Chapter Twenty

James was silent as he guided his carriage down a crowded Marion Avenue. Out of the corner of his eye, he studied Lenora. Her set jaw showed the tension she was feeling this night, as was most of the citizenry of Seattle, who were headed for a meeting at the Opera House. The Chinese had been chased from Tacoma and San Francisco, and now groups of unemployed Seattleites had succeeded in convincing most of the Chinese of this city to leave, warning of possible violence if they chose not to heed the advice.

This meeting at the Opera House was something of a victory celebration for the anti-Chinese. But citizens such as James and Lenora, who had felt pity for the Chinese, had also decided to attend, to try to make sure this expulsion was to be handled in a nonviolent way.

James turned his gaze back to his horses and clucked to them, remaining silent. He had more than the Chinese problem on his mind this night; he was also worried about Lenora. It had been two years now since their agreement to live together, and James had grown tired of the arrangement. He had not liked being sent from Lenora's house each time Joshua returned home. It had made James realize just how much more important Joshua was to Lenora than James himself was.

And wasn't Joshua an overgrown, spoiled brat who needed taking down a notch or two? It made James's insides boil to realize how utterly possessive Joshua was of his mother. It just wasn't normal. James had to reveal the truth to Joshua, and soon. The truth, he now knew, was that James was Joshua's father. It had been so hard to keep his knowing from Lenora. So often James had wanted to shout to Lenora that he *knew* Joshua was his son. And James knew that Joshua needed a father's guidance at this time.

Lenora gasped loudly as James pulled the carriage up in front of the Opera House. "James, I never expected this many people to attend the meeting," she said, putting a gloved hand to her cheek. It was November, and her dress and cape were of black velvet, as was her hat.

A crowd was pushing and shoving through the gaslighted entrance to the Opera House, and James now wondered if it was wise to be a part of such a gathering. He remembered so well how easily violence was sparked. But, in a way, he needed this excitement. Maybe it could make him forget his worries concerning Lenora and Joshua, for a while at least. He secured his horses to a hitching post and helped Lenora down from the carriage. "We shall only be observers this night," he said firmly. "Don't let your fiery temper get away from you. Just sit back and watch and listen. Seeing this huge turnout, I'm convinced there's not much else we can do at this stage of the game."

"Yes, James. I'm sure you're right," Lenora answered, then placed her arm through his and followed along beside him until they were inside the Opera House and moving down the thick green carpet. They searched and found seats under the magnificent, flickering gas chandelier that hung from the gilt-lined ceiling. Lenora had attended many operas in this beautiful building, but it never ceased to take her breath away. It was one of Seattle's most prized possessions—one of its five brick buildings. She only hoped that its graceful beauty would not be disturbed by the scene that would be acted out this night.

Her gaze traveled around her, making her gasp anew. Not only were the plush velvet seats filled with people, but also the aisles were filled with standing, noisy participants. There must be more than seven hundred people, surely the largest audience ever for the Opera House.

Silence came upon the crowd, and Lenora's gaze quickly settled on the stage. Mayor Kessler was introducing a speaker—a stocky man with a bloated, fish-eyed face—Judge Thadeus O'Rourke, who quickly stepped up onto the stage.

Scattered boos and hisses rippled through the crowd. Others busied themselves trying to hush the demonstrators. Lenora quickly looked at the faces around her. She did not like to see such tenseness and hostility being displayed by the women as well as the men. Then she looked straight ahead again, glad to feel James's hand close over hers.

Judge O'Rourke began in a soft voice. "False stories have been put into circulation inciting hostility against the Chinese," he said. Then his voice began to grow louder and anger showed in his bulgy eyes. "We are all agreed that the time has come when a new treaty should be made with China, restricting Chinese immigration to this country. But due to the lawless action of irresponsible persons from outside, the people of this city are called upon to decide whether this shall be brought about in a lawful and orderly manner or by defiantly trampling on the laws, treaties, and Constitution of our country."

There was a noticeable stirring of added unrest in the crowd as boos increased. Lenora glanced quickly into James's eyes and smiled weakly as he returned her gaze. She was glad to feel the increased pressure on her hand and then watched and listened further.

"Would you, the men and women of Seattle, even if you had the power, overthrow the law of the land and set up a mandate of brute force and violence in its stead?" Judge O'Rourke continued. "For the first time in the history of this territory, an attempt is being made to divide the community into two camps: laborers on one side and all other workers on the other. This attempt is a wicked, un-American thing. Any man who would now seek to divide us along Old-World lines is an enemy to all."

He coughed into a cupped hand and continued. "Speaking as an Irishman to the Irishmen in the crowd, I cannot believe it possible that any man of Irish birth could be so base, could be guilty of such black ingratitude, as to raise his hand in violence against the laws, the Constitution, or the treaties of this country. If the Irishman is true to his own nature, he will love justice, and his sympathies will go out in overflowing measures to the weak, the lowly, the despised and oppressed. He will not deprive any of God's creatures, not even the defenseless Chinaman, of the protection of that law which found the Irishman a serf and made him a free man. Those who come from other lands to live here must obey the laws and respect and honor the institutions of our country or go back where they came from."

The Opera House walls rocked with boos, and one of the men jumped from his seat and shouted into the crowd, "I hope the workingmen will be patient and listen to what

Judge O'Rourke has to say."

Judge O'Rourke walked to the edge of the stage, glaring. "I can assure you that I need no one to plead in my behalf with this audience," he snapped. "I recognize the insidious and unworthy appeal to workingmen for 'patience.' But to them I say that if there is anything certain in human history, it is that of all men the workingmen have the most vital interest in upholding the authority of the law. 'Where law ends, tyranny begins,' and where tyranny reigns, the workingman is a slave.

"By conducting ourselves as true Americans pursuing lawful measures for the redress of any grievance, real or imaginary, this little trouble that as a mirage of passion now looms so large will soon vanish like a bad dream and we shall all wonder what we were so wrought up about. I thank you for this patient hearing. I knew you would listen to me whether you agreed with me or not, even though I say things ever so distasteful to you."

The anti-Chinese were enraged. It was obvious that they felt they had been double-crossed by the speaker and his allies, and they jumped from their seats shouting their usual anti-Chinese slogans.

"We've got to get out of here," James said, pulling Lenora up from her own seat. "I sure as hell don't like the looks of things."

Lenora began to tremble, watching the disorder quickly taking hold all around her. "But it was such a nice speech," she said, panting, trying to keep pace with James's long strides.

"Probably the greatest speech ever made in the Puget Sound area," James shouted above the noise. "But there's nothin' as painful as truth and nothin' so infuriating as an unanswerable argument."

Lenora did not like the way she was being pushed and shoved by everyone else now exiting the building. She clung to James with one hand and her hat with the other. When she stepped outside onto the plank walk, she gasped audibly. Many torches were being lit, and a procession was beginning down the middle of the street. "James, what do you think is going to happen?" she asked as fear began to grip her, making a lump knot up in her throat.

"The damn idiots are goin' to take their anger out either on our shops or on the Chinese who haven't yet fled."

"How horrible," Lenora blurted. She feared for her dress emporium and James's tailoring shop, but she feared even more for the Chinese, who had never done anything against the Seattleites but had only helped them when their services had been welcomed.

Lenora had loved walking by the small Chinese community at the edge of town. Their lanterns draped across the streets had been so colorful, as well as their clothing and the ways in which they spoke. Yes, she was sad for these gentle, friendly people. The ones who had not yet fled had not wanted to lose the beloved possessions that they had labored so hard for.

They had hoped that some compromise could be reached, but Lenora now knew all hopes of a peaceful solution had just been shattered.

"We must get to the telegraph office and wire the Governor," James said, helping Lenora into the carriage. "We must inform him of what has happened here. We're going to need some troops here to preserve order, if it isn't already too late to send them."

Taking a side street that ran parallel to the clamor of the crowd, James urged his horses onward with a slap of the reins.

"James, I'm frightened," Lenora said, remembering another mob . . . a hanging. . . .

"As soon as we wire the Governor, we'll head for home," James answered.

Lenora clung to the seat, watching all around her, relieved that most of the confusion had been left behind.

Standing at the parlor window, Lenora accepted a glass of red wine from James. She took a sip and welcomed its bitter warmth as it trickled down the back of her throat. "It is awfully quiet out there, James," she whispered, still watching through the window. He went to her side and pulled her into his embrace.

"Yeah. That was some smart fella who anticipated the violence. Callin' the Governor earlier in the day was damn smart," he said, then laughed. "Surprised the hell outta me when I saw the troops headin' up Front Street."

"What will become of the Chinese?"

"They'll be made to leave, but in an orderly fashion."

"It's sad."

"But necessary."

"Do you really mean that, James?"

He tipped his glass and drained it of wine. "You saw the people tonight," he said, walking away from her. "Damn, they hate the Chinese more than they ever seemed to hate the Indians."

"Yes, I guess so," Lenora sighed. She placed her glass on a table, yawning. The evening had taken much out of her. She was ready to retire for the evening, even though the hour was not late. She began to unbutton the front of her dress, then felt the usual thrill when James proceeded to unbutton it for her. Her eyes became hazy from need, and she trembled as his mouth searched inside the bodice of her dress and found a breast his fingers had so expertly released from its prison of clothing.

"Your breast is as soft as the velvet of your dress, Lenora," he murmured. With his other hand, he pulled the dress from her shoulders and buried his face in the depths of her bosom.

"James," Lenora blurted, looking toward the unlocked door.

All evening James had been planning this moment. He would make tender love to her, then initiate a serious talk. To him, their personal problems seemed to be even more serious than the Chinese problem. Yes, he would confront her about marriage again, and then tell her of his feelings concerning Joshua. James was tired of the raised eyebrows in the community when he and Lenora would arrive on the scene. He had seen those eyebrows just hours before, when he and Lenora had entered the Opera House. A wedding was in order. James knew it; the town expected it; why didn't Lenora?

"To hell with the door, Lenora," he grumbled, then swooped her up into his arms and began to climb the stairs that led to the bedrooms.

"Oh, James," she sighed, loving it when he became so forceful. She could feel the muscles of his arms contracting with each step upward, and she could smell his manliness as she placed her cheek against the open throat of his shirt. The wine had helped to erase the earlier unpleasantness of the evening from her mind, and all she could think about was James's fingers and lips that would soon be taking her mind to a world of pleasure.

The newly installed gaslights flickered in the bedroom, making shadows play on Lenora's face as she let James continue to undress her. A small tinge of guilt plagued her. She felt a bit too lucky to have so much when she knew the poor Chinese community was being turned away from Seattle with nothing. It was an impossible situation, though. She had to forget about it. She had given her last speech about it. Her eyes had grown weaker from the long hours of study beneath the gaslights and kerosene lamps, and her throat had become strained from the many debates and speeches. Now the ships seemed to be the only answer—ships that would soon be filled with Chinese people.

"My darling," she sighed, throwing her head back with pleasure. James had kneeled down before her and was kissing her now in the place where it created the most pleasurable sensations. She had ceased to feel wicked long ago about this way of lovemaking. How could she feel wicked when the warmth of James's tongue was making her mind swirl in multicolors? Then she let him guide her backwards until she was stretched across the bed, watching as he quickly undressed himself. When he climbed atop her, she spread her legs and arched her body upward, ready for the deep plunge into her and needing quick release. But he continued to tease her with his tongue and fingers, making her writhe and groan, until with her hand she found the part of him she most craved and took it upon herself to place it deep inside her.

"You're a vixen, Lenora," he whispered, laughing softly. "My red-haired vixen." The fingers of his left hand worked with a breast, while the other hand searched behind her and began to squeeze a buttock.

The familiar floating in her head accompanied the spasms that were slowly beginning to take hold, but a loud gasp from the other side of the room made Lenora's earthly senses quickly return. She looked toward the open bedroom door and felt her heart stop when she saw Joshua standing there with open mouth and gaping eyes, taking in this scene to its last intimate detail.

"Joshua . . . ," Lenora gasped.

"Mother . . . ," Joshua gasped in return.

Lenora pushed James aside and hurriedly pulled up a sheet to cover herself, then watched, as though in a trance, as Joshua rushed across the room and pulled James from the bed.

"You filthy man," Joshua screamed as he began to beat at James's chest with doubled up fists. "You Goddamned son-of-a-bitch! You have no business being with my mother. Get out! Get out!"

With a deep pleading in his eyes, James sought for help from Lenora. Hell, he hadn't thought something like this could happen. Why the hell wasn't Joshua still in school? "Lenora?" he said, then felt a piercing ache in his heart as she turned her head away and closed her eyes to him.

Confusion was quickly replaced by seething anger. His eyes flashed angrily as he grabbed Joshua's wrists and held them in the air. "Now you listen here, young man," he stormed. Then he felt the softness of Lenora's fingers as they covered his mouth. He looked down at her. She looked so angelic, standing at his side now with the white sheet wrapped around her.

"Please, James. Just leave," she said tremulously. She fluttered her lashes at him, hoping this time it most definitely would work. Hadn't she used her eyes on him so many times before? This time it was so necessary that she have her way with him. He *had* to leave. The situation was a most awkward one. But what was she going to do once James *did* leave her and Joshua alone? It was strange how she was feeling at this moment—as though she had been unfaithful to her *son*.

James felt a sinking sensation at the pit of his stomach. Joshua was winning again. "Lenora, are you sure?" he asked thickly, wanting so badly to seize this opportunity to make the truth known. Yet a quick look into Joshua's eyes told James this was *not* the proper time. Now, would there *ever* be?

"Yes, James," Lenora whispered, casting her eyes downward.

"Okay, damn it," he grumbled. He gathered his clothes up into his arms and rushed from the room.

Joshua glared accusingly at Lenora for a brief, silent moment, then rushed from the room himself.

"Joshua!" Lenora called after him and wanted to follow, but her attire kept her from doing so. She felt a desperation rising inside herself. Had she now lost the loving respect of both Joshua and James?

Tears burned her eyes as she threw the sheet off, quickly chose a robe, and hurried out into the silence of the hallway. She looked from side to side, wondering which way to turn. Then she ceased breathing for a moment when she heard the rush of a horse's hoofs leaving her house. She put her hands to her throat and choked back a sob, uttering the word "James."

A noise coming from Joshua's room made her hurry in that direction. She had to make this wrong right, somehow. And why was Joshua home? He had not wired ahead, and it was too close to the Christmas holiday at school for him to make such a long trip because of a childish whim. She rushed into his room and stood aghast at what she found. Joshua was just beginning to pull the curtains from the windows after having already pulled the bedclothing from the bed and shredded it all to a mass of unusable rags that now lay scattered across the floor.

Lenora's pulse raced. "Joshua, what on earth have you done?" she uttered weakly. "What are you doing?" She could not move to go to him. His eyes had darkened into a steady glare in her direction.

"You've become a whore, Mother," he said flatly, stiffening his arms at his sides, "As you always manage to do when that man comes around."

"Joshua, you . . . you're . . . ," Lenora stammered, feeling a lightheadedness sweeping over her.

"Who the hell *is* that man, Mother?" Joshua continued. "What kind of power does he hold over you?"

Lenora found it suddenly very necessary to gain control of herself. This young man who was talking to her in such a way was her son. She should not . . . she *could* not allow such a show of disrespect. She went to him and slapped his face, though inside herself she could feel the impact of that blow, a million times over, against the heaviness of her heart. "You will *not* talk to your mother in such a manner," she said, setting her jaw firmly. She wanted to cry when Joshua's eyes suddenly became those of a little boy of two, instead of an accusing young man of thirteen. His shoulders slumped forward, and his facial features softened. Then he swung his arms around Lenora's neck and began to cry.

"I'm sorry, Mother," he sobbed, clinging.

Lenora wanted to cry also, but she held herself rigid. She could not take her eyes off the room, still alarmed at the destruction her son was capable of. But she had to brush all this from her thoughts—as well as her embarrassment for what he had just seen in her bedroom. She had a creeping feeling of uneasiness, still wondering what was behind this surprise visit of his. "Joshua," she said, pushing him away from her and holding him at arm's length. "Why are you home? Has something happened at school?"

Joshua's eyes wavered and his face became flushed. "I was expelled from school, Mother," he blurted.

Lenora released her hold on him and stepped back, studying him closely. "*Why* were you expelled?" She was afraid to receive his answer.

She was sure his temper had more than likely been the cause.

Joshua reached inside his jacket pocket and pulled out a sealed envelope. He hid his eyes from her with the turn of his head. "Here, Mother. This was written by Dean Campbell," he said. "I told him that I wouldn't give it to you, but he said that he would send a wire to make sure you *did* see it. You will receive the wire tomorrow."

Lenora's fingers trembled as she broke the seal on the envelope. She pulled out a piece of stationery and began to read, feeling more ill by the moment, until she had read it all. A lump appeared in her throat as she slowly replaced the note inside the envelope, wishing this was a moment that had not had to exist. Would she ever be able to forget the shock and shame this note had brought her?

"It can't be true, Joshua," she said. Could her son truly be capable of such a despicable act?

Joshua's face reddened, and his lips became a narrow, straight line. "It's quite true, Mother," he answered. It was easier for him to confess to now, after finding his mother in the same act—except what she was participating in had not been called rape.

"But . . . rape, Joshua?"

His eyes became two dark pools, and a muscle began to twitch in his cheek. "That part of what the Dean wrote is *not* true, Mother," he said, turning to walk to a window. He placed his hands behind him and clasped them tightly together.

Lenora could remember James standing in the same fashion, oh, so often. "But, he does write that you raped your English teacher," she murmured. She stared first at the envelope, then at Joshua, and went to him. "Joshua, I have to know the truth," she said in a strained voice. She jerked him around to face her. "Now, please, Joshua. You tell me exactly what transpired," she added. Her heart was shredding, it seemed, into little pieces. Did she know this son, who had such hidden, tormented desires?

"My teacher, Claire Beaumont, made advances toward me, many times," he began, glaring back at Lenora. "She's quite beautiful, Mother." He reached up and touched Lenora's hair, letting his fingers work through it. "She has the same hair coloring as you, and she's your age."

Lenora gasped and felt a dizziness trying to help her escape from this truth.

"Miss Beaumont invited me up into her room," Joshua continued, still watching Lenora, wanting to see her reaction, even a bit amused by it all as he saw her eyes wider than he had ever seen them before. "So I accepted," he continued. "When I got to her room, she kissed me and touched me—you know where—and the rest just happened. But if it was rape, it was *she* who raped *me*."

Lenora turned from Joshua and cast her eyes down. "Oh, God," she stammered. She buried her face in her hands and began to weep. "Why, oh why, would you do such a thing," she said. "And how did it come to be called rape, if she . . . ?"

"I do not understand the minds of women," Joshua said, going to his bed to sit down upon it. As he had never understood his mother. In his thoughts, he was accusing her of this misfortune of his. It was his mother who had caused him such inner turmoil. He had always had such desires for her, even as a small child. She should not have ever let him sleep with her or touch her breasts. It had only left him confused and aching for her. Then when this beautiful, red-haired teacher began to be so friendly with him, and even invited him to her room, he could not refuse her when she touched the part of him that had always seemed to constantly ache with longing. But why *had* she called it rape? She had enjoyed their time together as much as he; only afterwards had she begun to scream. "Claire—Miss Beaumont—began screaming once she had had her fun with me," he said flatly.

"Fun?" Lenora screamed. "You call what you were doing fun?"

Joshua rose and went to Lenora and stood tall and erect as he glared down into her eyes. "And you wouldn't call what you were doing with that man in our . . . your bedroom fun, Mother?" he asked accusingly.

Lenora bit her lower lip, then rushed from the room. What had she done in Joshua's upbringing to turn him into such a vile, unlikable, twisted person? Was it Seymour surfacing from within Joshua? Had Seymour in some way been able to influence Joshua, even though Seymour had not been Joshua's true father?

"Oh, God, I want to die," she sobbed to herself, then rushed into her room and threw herself across her bed. What was she to do? And what must James be thinking of her now?

Lenora tensed when she heard footsteps moving toward the bed. She tensed even more when she felt the warmth of Joshua's body behind and against her.

"Mother?" he whispered, touching her gently on the hand. "Mother, I'm sorry," he said.

Lenora did not move, but her heartbeats were vibrating all through her body. "Joshua, go to your own room," she said. "Leave me be."

Joshua's hand crept around and brushed against a heaving breast. "I love you, Mother," he persisted.

Lenora knocked his hand away, crawled to the other side of the bed, and jumped quickly from it. "Young man, you go to your own room. Now!" she snapped, placing her hands on her hips. "I've had enough for one night. We shall discuss this further in the morning."

Glaring, Joshua rose from the bed, still clad in tight tan breeches and lace-trimmed white shirt. "You will be sorry, Mother," he hissed. "I assure you, you will be sorry."

Lenora watched in confused silence as he rushed from the room, then once again threw herself across her bed and let her body be swallowed up with heartbreaking sobs. Why would tomorrow be any different? Even then, she would not know what to say or do.

Joshua paced his room, watching the clock. Surely his mother would now be asleep. He began to tiptoe toward Lenora's room. He had made up his mind. He would steal her diary key. He *would* see what deep secrets she had written about himself and even this James who would not leave his mother alone. It would be easy. He would open the locket that she always wore around her neck, remove the key, and read her diary. What satisfaction it would be for him to be able to know his mother's deepest desires and longings. He only wished that he had thought to do this long ago. Wouldn't it have been fun, reading her many secrets all these years?

But the risk of removing the key even once was frightening enough. What if she should discover him opening the locket? But even if she did, what punishment could she hand down? It seemed that she was not capable of punishing him. Didn't she love him too much to stoop to such medieval actions?

Joshua stood over his mother for a moment, watching her breasts moving ever so gently with each breath taken. The ache was there again in his loins, but he had other things on his mind this night. He spied the locket.

Yes, it would be easy enough. It lay loosely on the bed, away from her neck, making it even easier than Joshua had anticipated.

Quickly kneeling, he reached for the locket and opened it slowly until the key was in his hand. He smiled sardonically, then inched his way backwards until he was safely out in the hallway.

Then he hurried to his room. He sprawled across his bed and found his heart racing as he placed the key in the lock. He was glad that he had already secured the diary from the rolltop desk in the library. All he had to do now was open its pages and begin to read.

Since this was a five-year diary, it seemed that the entries began four years prior to the present date, on January 1, 1883. Joshua read slowly, turning page after page, then felt his heartbeats quicken when he found the date of his father's death. With tears in his eyes, Joshua read of Blue Feather, the hanging, and Blue Feather's accusations about Joshua's father. Something tore at Joshua's heart as he read on. "No, it just can't be," he mumbled, eagerly turning the pages to read further. His eyes blurred as he read his mother's words: "When Joshua threatened James with Seymour's dueling pistol, so many truths could have escaped from my mouth. Wasn't it son against father? Oh, how shall I manage to keep this secret forever and ever from my son?"

Joshua looked up from the page, feeling a numbness seize him. "Son against father?"

he whispered. "What does she mean?" His thoughts raced as he continued to thumb from page to page until a moan filled the empty spaces of his bedroom, and Joshua was suddenly aware that this sound was escaping from his own lips. He felt hate for his mother, for his dead so-called father, Seymour, and most of all for this James, who had abandoned the woman he had gotten with child.

Tears smeared the last pages in the diary as Joshua mumbled, "No," over and over again. His temples were pounding. His stomach ached. He suddenly felt as though he no longer belonged anywhere, to anyone. He had been betrayed by the only person he had ever truly loved.

"Mother, how could you?" he said between clenched teeth, thinking of escape. He had seen several ships moored at the waterfront. He *would* escape.

The morning light filtered through Lenora's blue satin draperies, awakening her. She bolted upright, suddenly remembering the events of the previous evening. She put her hand to her head and groaned. The tension had left her with a throbbing headache. Would this day bring a lessening of tension? She knew that a serious discussion with Joshua lay before her. He was in need of some strict disciplining, and it would begin *today*. He would have to realize that he was the child and she the parent—if it were not already too late.

The coldness of the room made her pull the robe she had neglected to remove the night before closer around her shoulders. Slowly she moved from the bed and slipped her feet into some slippers, dreading to confront Joshua. But she had to do it, and she would delay it no longer. It seemed that too much time had already elapsed.

Not bothering to brush her hair, she headed toward Joshua's bedroom. She noticed that the door was open, and when she got to it she stood frozen to the spot, terrified at what she found.

"Joshua?" she whispered. Her eyes continued to search, but she knew that he was gone. With pounding heart, she went to his bed and discerned what it was that lay on the bed, gaping open. "My diary," she gasped, her fingers going to the locket, too late, and finding the key gone. And now, a brief glance told her that the diary was missing some—many—pages.

"Oh, my Lord," she gasped. She picked the diary up and saw that most of the pages were torn from it. "Joshua, now you know," she whispered. She crumpled to the floor, and a sudden blackness came sweeping over her.

"Lenora, darling. Please wake up."

Lenora could hear a voice—James's voice—but it sounded as though it was coming from the depths of a well. She reached out her hand and was glad to feel another hand take it. "James?" she whispered.

"I'm here, Lenora."

He sounded much closer now. She clung to his hand. "Joshua? Have you seen Joshua?" she asked, remembering.

"No. We've searched the town, but found no sign of him."

The haziness left Lenora's eyes and she could see James looking down at her, and she suddenly knew that her head was resting on his lap. She smiled weakly and looked around her. "How did I get in the parlor?" she asked.

"I brought you here to be near the fire."

"How did you . . . ?"

"I worried all night, Lenora," he answered. "When morning finally came, I had to see you."

"You found me?"

"In Joshua's room. I saw what he had done."

"My diary?"

"Yes, your diary, and the other destruction."

Lenora felt the tearing of her heart once again and began to cry. "He knows, James," she sobbed.

"He should know," James said firmly.

"As you should have known also, James."

"I've known."

"I thought you did."

"How could I not? He is my double."

"How long have you known?"

"Years."

"And you never said a word?"

"I started to, many times. But you'd manage to shut me up."

"And now, James, what about Joshua? Where do you think he's gone?"

"He's had a very trying experience. We will just have to wait until he decides to come home."

Lenora nestled against James, feeling the deep loss of her son, but feeling at last the unqualified gain of her lover. "I do love you, James," she murmured.

"And I you," he said. He pulled her up into his arms and searched for her lips. "And we shall pull through this; we're together. And you'll see: our son will return." His heart swelled, so proud was he to be able finally to say those words to Lenora. But was it too late? The world had cruel ways of treating young men of Joshua's age, but James could not reveal his fears to Lenora.

"Yes, our son," Lenora said.

Chapter Twenty-One

"If only Joshua would come home, it would be a most perfect June," Lenora said to Tess as they both stood looking out of Lenora's dress emporium window. "Two years and not a word, Tess."

"But you now have James as your husband," Tess consoled her. "And if nothing else came from your son's angered departure, at least you have the satisfaction of knowing that James finally is able to speak to you openly of his son."

"Yes. The years of secrecy were very hard."

"And you still have your dress emporium to occupy your days."

Lenora laughed softly as she wiped a smudge from her window with her handkerchief. "Yes, I do have that," she answered, "but not with

James's blessing, I assure you."

"He still wants you to give up your career?"

"Yes. He'd like nothing better than to have me sit home and spend each day pricking my fingers with an embroidery needle."

Tess swung her arm around Lenora's waist, laughing with her. "My dear Lenora, I don't believe you were meant to be just a housewife."

Lenora drew her lips into a pout. "Nor a mother, wouldn't you say?"

Tess squeezed Lenora affectionately. "Now, you know that you were the best possible mother to Joshua Caine," she murmured. "He was just born with a wild streak in him, that's all."

Lenora cast her eyes down and began to fidget with the deep folds of her blue-flowered silk dress. "I'm sure it was because of the way he was conceived," she said softly.

Tess stepped away from Lenora, with her dark eyes wide. "Lenora," she scolded. "You know that isn't so."

"And not only was James intimate with me during that period of time, but also Francis, and Raef, and Seymour."

"Lenora!" Tess scolded. "You stop that kind of talk, now! You are a fine woman, and always have been. Your passions had nothing to do with Joshua and how he has chosen to behave."

"I wonder where he is," Lenora sighed. "I wonder if he is even alive. You know, this is the year 1889. So many evil things are happening in the world these days."

Tess gathered up the skirt of her lace-trimmed white piqué dress and moved closer to the window. "Look out there on Second Avenue," she murmured. "Does that look like a world of evil doings? Isn't it just a beautiful day? There hasn't even been any rain for a full week now. You know *that* is something to be thankful for. Even the mud has dried up on the roads."

Coming to stand next to Tess, Lenora did see what Tess meant. It was quite a peaceful setting to gaze upon. Two small children walked by, carrying baskets filled with red and black raspberries, and out on the plank street a farmer was driving a team of horses, hauling a wagonload of freshly harvested lettuce, peas, and rhubarb to market.

She looked up into the forested hills, where firs were fringed with new green and ferns were fast covering the dead grass of winter. Mount Tacoma was even quite visible this day, and its coat of white appeared to be changing to pale orange right before Lenora's eyes, as the noonday sun continued to reflect on it.

Seattle had become a peaceful community again after the Chinese question had been settled. The last of the Chinese had left aboard the ship *Elder*, with the Congress paying the Chinese government a sum of $276,619.15 as full indemnity for the losses and injuries to the Chinese subjects at the hands of the American people. It was "out of humane consideration and without reference to the question of liability" that this payment had been made. And

Washington had just become the forty-second state.

"You're right," Lenora said, smiling at her friend. "I shall push my worries aside and enjoy this beautiful day to its fullest."

On First Avenue, Patrick O'Sullivan was busy boiling glue on the stove in the basement of his paint store. He shuffled his swollen feet through the floor's wood shavings, ignoring the fact that the glue was beginning to boil over, too caught up in worries about his kidney ailment. He had only discovered the swelling beneath his eyes the previous week, and now his ankles and feet had become the most discomforting aspects of the progressing disease. He had an appointment with Doc Preston later in the afternoon. Maybe Doc could reassure him that he would soon recover.

Smelling something burning, Patrick turned with a start and saw the flames dancing around on the surface of his stove. Then he gasped with terror as the burning glue dripped in torched, massive gobs to the floor and quickly ignited the shavings.

As quickly as his legs would carry him, he rushed to a sink and filled a bucket with water, realizing just how fast his ramshackle wooden building could go up in flames, then rushed back to the spreading flames and threw the water onto the inferno, but only succeeded at washing the flames over to some turpentine.

*   *   *

"Do you smell smoke, Tess?" Lenora asked. She went to the front door of her dress emporium and opened it. "Oh, my God!" she exclaimed. "Come, Tess. Look!"

From the direction of First Avenue, a pillar of purplish smoke was spiraling into the sky, quickly changing the blue to a hazy darkness.

Tess rushed to Lenora's side. "I wonder what is burning," she said, then tensed as she heard the clanging of the bells from the town's two fire stations, followed by the shrieking of the steamwhistles from ships moored along the waterfront.

"Do you think a ship may have caught fire?" Lenora asked, beginning to doubt it as the smoke increased in intensity. No one boat's burning could create so much smoke.

"I don't know, Lenora."

Fear grabbed at Lenora's heart. "I certainly hope it isn't one of those flimsy wooden establishments on First Avenue," she said. "Do you realize what that could mean? You know our city is wooden. It could possibly *all* burn."

"Even your dress emporium and James's tailoring shop?"

"Yes, and possibly our homes," Lenora said, quickly looking around her, seeing the row after row of lacy summer fashion. She had chosen carefully again this season, and she could boast that the dresses she sold were worn by most women of Seattle. How terrifying to think of these lovely clothes going up in flames!

Then, hearing the clatter of many horses' hoofs, Lenora swung her head around just in time to see Second Avenue's hose cart from Engine Company One galloping by, followed close behind by Seattle's polished first steam fire engine, from Engine Company Two.

"I'm beginning to be frightened," Tess blurted. "Just look at the smoke. It's as though the whole waterfront is on fire now."

The steamwhistles of the mills sounded, and churchbells began to toll.

"What shall we do?" Lenora said, feeling a slow panic rising. "It's as though it's the end of the world."

"Let's run next door and see what James is doing," Tess shouted, reaching for Lenora's hand.

Once out on the plank sidewalk, Lenora felt her fear heightening. The roar of the flames sounded as though a tornado was headed her way, and the smoke burned her eyes and throat, making her cough. When she and Tess reached the doorway of James's shop, she panicked further, finding it shut and locked.

Lenora worked frantically with the knob, wondering where James could be. "Look through the window, Tess," she shouted. "Do you see James? Is there any sign of life in there?"

Tess leaned against the plate glass window and peered inward. "The lights are out, and no one is in there. No one," Tess answered. She went to Lenora. "He's probably with the volunteer firemen, don't you think?"

"I guess you're right," Lenora said, turning to watch the confusion of people bustling around her. What had only moments ago been a beautiful, peaceful summer day was now filled with rushing people, panic etched on their faces.

The streets were suddenly busy with carriages and wagons moving speedily away from First Avenue. Most of the wagons were filled with furniture and racks of clothing, obviously owned by merchants trying to save what they could.

Lenora grabbed a young boy by the arm and stopped him. "Tell me what's happened," she said.

The young boy's face was black from smoke. Even his hair and eyelashes showed rusty signs of singeing. He panted hard, looking up at Lenora with worried hazel eyes. "Patrick O'Sullivan's paint shop," he shouted, still laboring for breath. "The fire started there."

"What else can you tell me?" Lenora persisted, almost stumbling into the path of a speeding carriage as a crowd of passersby knocked up against her.

"Then it spread, and whiskey barrels exploded in a liquor store, and then the Crystal Palace Saloon and the Opera House caught fire and made more explosions. Calder Hotel was the last thing I saw a burnin' when I began running this way."

"That's an entire block," Tess gasped.

"And . . . Calder Hotel," Lenora said quietly.

"The water pressure ain't what it should be," the boy continued. "The water mains are too small, and there's only a trickle comin' from the nozzles of the fire hoses. A bucket brigade is wettin' down the roofs, but that ain't gonna stop this fire. The whole town's gonna go!"

"What shall we do, Lenora?" Tess yelled.

"They're placin' a heavy charge of dynamite under the Palace Restaurant," the boy said. "The Mayor ordered it, to form a fire gap—somethin' like that."

Lenora's hands flew to her throat. "James," she blurted. "James is in danger, I know it." She turned in the direction of the smoke, just as an explosion rocked the ground beneath her feet. Then she watched in terror as the fire engines retreated from First Avenue to Second Avenue, with some of the firemen running alongside.

Lenora began to run in their direction, but was stopped by Tess. "Lenora, no! You mustn't," she insisted. "We must leave and get to a higher elevation ourselves. Don't you see the pieces of flaming materials raining down from the sky? We're in danger here."

Lenora's mind was a mass of confusion. She began to bite her lower lip nervously, watching the gathering crowd, searching the faces for James and watching the flames race from building to building, having now reached Second Avenue. She picked up the skirt of her dress and began to weep. "My shop," she cried. "My beautiful, beautiful shop."

"Hurry, Lenora," Tess yelled. "Come, we must hurry!"

Lenora raced along beside Tess, up the steep incline of Union Street. Looking backward, she saw flames taking hold inside James's shop. "James, oh, James," she sobbed, then stopped, panting, on a grassy knoll.

Shots rang out below her, making Lenora's knees grow weak. "What could that be?" she shouted.

"That must be ammunition goin' off in Gordon's Hardware Company," shouted a man standing behind her. "And wait till the flames eat into the Seattle Hardware Store. They've got twenty tons of ammunition in there."

A fresh explosion rocked the ground, and the force of the blast sent boards from the walks and streets flying up into the air. A pall of smoke was now lying over the city, even more ominous than the thick fog Lenora remembered creeping in from the bay in San Francisco.

The roar of the fire and the continuing explosions, mingled with the clanging of the fire bells and churchbells, made Lenora feel the end of the world had most surely come. Her fingernails dug into her two doubled fists; she was worrying so about James. How could he or anyone who was not yet out of that flaming inferno possibly escape? Even the wharves leading to the ships were all ablaze now.

"Let's sit and rest, Lenora," Tess encouraged, touching Lenora ever so gently on the arm. She knew that Lenora was fretting over James, just as Tess was fearing for Timothy's safety. A doctor's place was among the injured.

Lenora slouched down onto the ground beside Tess. "Yes, let's," she said, watching clusters of people who had formed a human conveyor chain, passing goods upward to safety. Lenora knew that she should help, but this was one time that her spirit was too low. And wasn't it useless now? The planking of the streets was even going up in flames now, rippling along like waves of an ocean turned yellow.

Black figures of men left the fire and stood watching the city that had been built in wood never fearing what might happen—what had just happened. They had only to wait now, knowing that the fire would be stopped on the west by Elliott Bay and hoping that the now arriving Tacoma Fire Department and the men who still persisted with buckets on ropes could stop it on all other sides. Many shanties had been torn down and dumped into the bay and sidewalks and street planking pulled up and thrown after them.

"It's all lost, Tess," Lenora said, trembling, "my dreams, and all of Seattle's, in only a short time. This is all so unreal."

Weeping women and children clung to each other on the hillside with Lenora and Tess, making Lenora's heart ache even more. She watched the crowd build, with added furniture and clothing being piled all around. Some had been lucky enough to save some of their possessions, but Lenora had sat watching her own shop burn to the ground.

Most of these people were less fortunate than she. Their small shacks along the waterfront had burned first, leaving them without a place to live or food to eat. These were the ones with the emptiest look in their eyes. Only a few yards from Lenora sat a woman with scorched hair and blackened face, openly nursing her child while another infant clung to her arm with tears rolling down its cheek.

This touched Lenora so, she suddenly felt a keen sense of responsibility to help these people. She knew that her large home had been empty and quiet for too long, and it did appear that the fire was not going to reach that far. Couldn't she invite a good portion of these people to stay there until new dwellings could be built for them? And as for those she could not place in her home, she could see to it that they would find refuge at the Territorial University.

Tears filled her eyes again, however, as her worries about James were renewed. There still had been no sign of him anywhere. But she had to keep her faith—she had to believe that his civic duties had kept him from seeking her out. She had to keep telling herself that he was all right.

"Do you feel it?" Tess suddenly said.

Lenora wiped her eyes with the sleeve of her dress. She turned her eyes to the sky and uttered a deep sigh of relief. "Yes," she whispered. "I feel it. It's rain." She jumped up from the ground and put her hands in front of her to catch the fresh drops in her hands. "My God, it *is* rain," she shouted. How often had she cursed the ever-present rain of Seattle, but now, oh, how it was welcomed.

All around her, she could hear the murmuring and rising laughter of the crowd, marveling over the timing of the rainfall.

"And the wind," Tess shouted, holding onto the skirt of her dress. "It has changed direction. The flames will not reach any further. The rest of Seattle will be saved!"

The rain began to fall in torrents, making a strained hush fall over the crowd, most of whom stood trembling from the shock of the moment.

"We must help these people, Tess," Lenora said. "I'm directing as many as I can to my home, and those who cannot find a corner to sleep in there can go to the Territorial University. I have a key to its main hall, since James is a member of the board."

"And I shall reserve my house for the injured," Tess said, eager to help and glad to see the familiar dancing in Lenora's eyes. The defeated and uncaring Lenora of only moments ago was not the Lenora that Tess had always known.

"Come, we must hurry," Lenora said, rushing through the wet grass. "We must make sure the children do not get chilled. They are Seattle's future."

The morning sun crept through the parlor windows, slanting awkwardly, it seemed, across exhausted, sleeping figures. Lenora and James stood arm in arm, both still smelling of smoke, but relieved to be together after the gutting of the city the previous day.

"Even though sixty city blocks burned, we are so lucky there were no deaths or serious injuries, Lenora," James said. "Timothy and Tess were kind to take the injured into their home since the small hospital on Second Avenue burned."

"And the people from Tacoma," Lenora sighed. "Can you believe so many have already arrived with provisions?"

James pulled Lenora close to him, whispering. "You're damn lucky that relief committee is settin' up tents with cooks and cookstoves to fix for the crowd," he mused. "Can you imagine yourself feedin' this many folks?"

"I was a bit worried about that, James," Lenora giggled. "And there are already tents springing up with signs showing the business they represent."

"This town won't be beaten," James said

stubbornly. "And when we rebuild, it will be all masonry. There aren't to be even temporary wooden shacks. The tents will remain until the permanent buildings are built."

"Are you going to rebuild, James?"

"Damn right I am. And, you, Lenora?"

Lenora laughed lightly. "Damn right I am," she said.

Chapter Twenty-Two

Almost overnight the town changed into a city of stone and brick, and Seattle also had its dream of a railroad come true. The Great Northern Railroad entered Seattle in 1893.

And on August 31, 1896, another of Seattle's dreams was to come true—Seattle was to become the gateway to the Orient. With the years' passing, the Asiatics had come to be looked on not as a menace, but as a symbol of the wealth of the Far East, and Seattle wanted some of that wealth.

Lenora clung to James's arm, watching with wide eyes as the steamship *Miiki Maru*, of Japan's Nippon Yuson Kaisha Line, steamed into Elliott Bay. The air was filled with excitement as tens of thousands of Seattleites lined the waterfront to cheer the steamship onward. No one wanted to miss seeing this, the first steamer to cross the Pacific on a regularly scheduled voyage with cargo and passengers.

"Isn't this exciting, James?" Lenora beamed. She was dressed for the occasion in a stiffly starched white cotton frock trimmed with green openwork embroidery, with its low-cut bodice emphasizing her still magnificent bosom. The breeze continued to whip at the long skirt of her dress, revealing dozens of petticoats trimmed in lace. Only a few strands of gray sparkling through her red, flowing, shoulder-length hair showed that she had almost reached the age of forty.

James leaned down closer to Lenora and tried to speak above the clanging of the churchbells and fire bells and the several bands that had just begun to play. "The future for Seattle is pretty rosy," he shouted, nervously tapping his ivory-topped walking stick on the sidewalk in front of him.

Lenora's heart pounded with pride as she looked up at him. His graceful aging so became him. Attired in his navy blue pinstriped worsted wool suit, he was even more handsome than he had been in his twenties. She giggled inwardly as she looked up at the balding of his head. He tried so hard to hide this fact by combing his hair back over the thinning crown, but found it impossible because of the still-stubborn curls, especially in the ever-present dampness of Seattle's winds. And as for the deep wrinkles around his eyes and mouth, Lenora knew that she was responsible for some of them—because these were his laugh lines, and in her presence he did much laughing and teasing.

Loud shouts and hurrahs caused Lenora to look in front of her again, just in time to see passengers leaving the docked ship. She sighed deeply. The Japanese were dressed in colorful outfits of what appeared to be the finest silks. Then something clutched at Lenora's heart, making her grab onto James and grip his arm tightly. There was something about this very well-dressed American who was now walking ashore. If only he would turn Lenora's way, so she could see his face.

As he continued to mingle with the crowd, Lenora could only catch glimpses of his golden curls. Then, when a clearing was made and Lenora caught sight of the full figure of him, she let go of James's arm and began to run, now seeing two of these golden curled gentlemen as the tears blurred her vision.

"Joshua! Joshua Caine," she yelled, stumbling against passersby, then tripping on her own petticoats, until she found herself toppling, to be stopped by his strong, muscled arms.

"Mother? Oh, Mother, it *is* you!" Joshua shouted, then pulled Lenora up into his arms and embraced her strongly. When he kissed her fully on the lips, he felt her clinging to him. She did not want to let him go, for fear he would disappear and never return home again.

"Joshua, are you really here?" Lenora cried, looking up into the face of a young man of twenty-two—a young man who was a younger James. "Where have you been, son? Why wouldn't you let me know that you were all right? Don't you know how worried I've been?"

Joshua stepped back from Lenora, eyeing her warmly. "Mother, I'm sorry for not having contacted you," he said, lighting a cigar to busy his hands. He was keenly aware of just how beautiful his mother still was. Damn, how he had missed her. But it had been better for the both of them that he had stayed away. He had found the ways of the Japanese quite satisfying and had been able to forget his longings for his mother. But now, would it start all over again? No, he would not give it the chance. His plans were to move on, immediately.

When James stepped to Lenora's side, Joshua knew that this was the time to make the proper gestures if not for himself, for his mother. He had already seen the wedding ring on his mother's finger and knew the answer to a question he need not ask. His face became all shadows as he extended a right hand forward. "Hello, Father," he said, smiling awkwardly.

Tears came to James's eyes as he extended his gloved right hand. "Hello, Son," he stammered, then held on tightly and pulled Joshua into his arms. He choked back a sob and clung to his son. "It's so good to have you home, Son," he added.

Lenora turned her eyes away and wiped them. It had taken twenty-two full years for father and son to actually meet as father and son, and she felt that her heart might burst with emotion if she looked upon this scene of mutual admiration for another second.

"I'm sorry I've been such an ass, Father," Joshua blurted.

"Like father, like son," James laughed, stepping back to Lenora's side.

Lenora wiped her eyes again and feasted them on her son. He wore a tan suit and white silk shirt, and he had *her* set jaw—the only resemblance between mother and son. "Let's move away from the crowd," she said, "so we can talk."

"Can we go home, Mother?" Joshua asked, tossing his half-smoked cigar aside.

"Home? Yes, let's go home," Lenora beamed. "Do you have any possessions to get from the ship?"

"No, only what I have on my back. I travel light."

"Let's go to the carriage, then," Lenora said, arranging herself between her two men.

In the parlor, Lenora poured coffee and handed cups to Joshua and James. She then sat down opposite them both, feeling an intense contentment. It had been a long wait, but now she had both her husband and her son with her. And how eagerly Joshua was talking to James, as though he had been starving for the

413

companionship of a father.

"And you say you boarded the *Elder* the night you left?" James was saying.

"I felt I had no other choice," Joshua said, casting his eyes down. "You see, I had had two shocks in one night—first seeing you and Mother in bed, then reading of my true identity in her diary. I felt as though I was an intruder, that I didn't belong."

"Joshua, I never meant for you to feel that way," Lenora murmured, feeling the corners of her eyes burning with tears.

"I know, Mother," he answered. "But I was a confused young man. Now I am a learned gentleman," he grinned. "I believe I understand the why's of the past."

James leaned forward and placed his elbows on his knees. "Tell us where you've been, Son," he said. "How in hell did you happen to be aboard the *Miiki Maru* today?"

"I've been in Japan," Joshua answered. "The *Elder* carried me to China, but I later took a ship to Japan. I'd read so much about it and wanted the experience."

"So that's where you've been—in Japan?" Lenora said, leaning forward. All of this was much too exciting. Her son was home, son and father were united, and she found that her son had been living in the Orient. Only storybook characters went to—actually lived in—the Orient.

"Yes, I've lived with a family named Kiyo-sama. They were very kind to me— even offered me their daughter to wed. But when I heard of this voyage to Seattle, I had to return home."

"We're so glad you did, Son," James said, pouring himself another cup of coffee.

Joshua rose, went to the window, and stared out. He hated having to leave after having just arrived, but his dreams were moving him onward. "I can't stay," he said, clasping his hands together behind him.

Lenora's heart skipped a few beats. She rose, went to Joshua, and turned him to face her. "What do you mean, you can't stay? Where are you going?"

Joshua's eyes wavered. "Haven't you heard of the gold that's being found in the Yukon?" he said. "Mother, I only came through Seattle to see you and Father and then to move on. I'm going to the Yukon, to seek my fortune."

James went to Joshua's side. "There are many opportunities opening up in Seattle," he pleaded, "every day. You can get rich from the gold rush indirectly. There is a great influx of people settling in Seattle because of its closeness to the Yukon. You could cash in on this—here in Seattle. I'd give you ready cash to start your business. You could pay me back and *still* become rich. Think about it, Son. Think about it."

"And there are tales of people disappearing in the Yukon every day," Lenora argued, near tears. "You could be among them. Please, Joshua. Don't leave us again."

Joshua circled his right arm around James's

neck and his left arm around Lenora's waist and pulled them up next to him, smiling. "I *must* go," he said. "Mother, Father, we're now a family," he stated matter-of-factly. "Do you think I'd let myself get lost in the Yukon when I've just found my family for the first time?"

Dear Reader:

I hope that you have enjoyed reading *Secrets of My Heart*. I also have an Indian series with Leisure Books called the *Savage* series, in which my endeavor is to write about every major Indian tribe in America. I hope you will look for these books in your favorite bookstore. The *Savage* series books are filled with much adventure and passion.

I would love to hear from you all. For my latest newsletter, send a legal-size envelope to:

Cassie Edwards
Route #3 Box 60
Mattoon, IL 61938

Warmly,

Cassie Edwards

Cassie Edwards